BEYOND CIRCUMSTANCES

Out of the Darkness

By Gloria Joynt-Lang

Everlasting
FIERY SEAS

FIERY SEAS PUBLISHING
Visit our website at www.fieryseaspublishing.com

For Lori a dear friend. Wishing you all the best. Hope your next 2 yrs go by fast (at least at work)
Gloria Joynt-Lang

This book is a work of fiction. Names, characters, places, and incidents either are products of the author's imagination or are used fictitiously. Any resemblance to actual persons, living or dead, events, or locales is entirely coincidental.

Beyond Circumstances

Copyright © 2018, Gloria Joynt-Lang

Cover Art by Kaitlyn Morris

Editing by Vicki McGough

Interior Design by Misty Williams

ISBN-13: 978-1-946143-53-2

Library of Congress Control Number: 2018948513

All rights reserved.

No part of this publication may be used or reproduced in any manner whatsoever without written permission, except in the case of brief quotations embodied in critical articles and reviews. Requests for permission should be addressed to Fiery Seas Publishing.

Printed in the United States of America

First Edition:

10 9 8 7 6 5 4 3 2 1

Dedication

For Johnnie – my friend, my love, my everything.

Acknowledgements

This book would not exist if it were not for Misty Williams and her incredible team at Fiery Seas Publishing. Thank you for the opportunity to tell Zak and Lexie's story. Much gratitude to Vicki McGough for all the hours you spent editing my work. It was an absolute pleasure to have worked with you. Wishing you nothing but success in your future. To Kaitlyn Morris for the covert art. It was love at first sight when I saw this design.

I am so grateful to Francoise Joynt and Caroline Popilchak. You have been looking after me even before I learnt to crawl. You have taught me so many valuable lessons, including books are to be read and not eaten, and have repeatedly shown me that pigs can fly. I would not be who I am today without your support and wicked sense of humor. Thank you for not only being my beta readers but for being my sisters, my mentors, and my friends.

To my parents, Marguerite and Mervyn for being positive role models. Throughout their lives, they opened up their heart and home to those of different beliefs, cultures, and backgrounds. Loving me unconditionally and always having faith that I would land on my feet, was one of the many gifts they bestowed upon me. Unfortunately, they are no longer with us, but their memory and what they taught me is infinite.

To my numerous friends and family members, I am grateful for your support and love. A special thanks to my beautiful mother-in-law Angie Lang-Thirsk. I cherish your kindness and prayers, and I hope you enjoy this book. To Jarrett, John Jr, Patrick, Melissa, Peyton, and Jack, I would love to promise you better home cooked meals, but who am I kidding. Although I love you guys, I'm far more comfortable in front of a laptop than a stove. To Muriel Van Parys for your enthusiasm. You are an inspiration in so many ways and I formally apologize for hurting Mr. Potato Head when we were kids.

Lastly, to my wonderful husband and final beta reader, Johnnie. Your wonderful feedback, suggestions, and ideas have been invaluable. Letting me into your darkened world of PTSD, has hopefully made me a better writer, and more importantly, a better partner. I've made some questionable decisions in my life, tobogganing down a grassy hill in a cardboard box comes to mind, but thank God I made the best decision of my life when I married you. Love you to Pluto and back.

BEYOND CIRCUMSTANCES

By Gloria Joynt-Lang

PART ONE

Chapter One

Wrapping his hands around the Glock, Zak locked on to his target. Most men would have gotten closer, but as a sharpshooter, he knew he would have no problem from where he stood. Besides, he wanted to be as far away as possible from the splattering blood. The vile stench that came from death would be enough to hurl him over the edge.

Closing his eyes, he eased back on the trigger. The shot echoed through the air, causing his ears to throb. When the throbbing stopped, the all too familiar eerie stillness swept in. It was over, yet he knew it had just begun.

The shot was spot on. They always were. There was no need to open his eyes to confirm. He should have walked away, but regrettably, didn't. He saw the blood oozing out, and his even breaths vanished. He began to gasp. Tilting his head toward the open sky, Zak began to shake. Eventually, the slow rhythm of the quivering turned to rapid trembling. If only he could gain control. Experience told him it wasn't going to happen. He slid down against the splintered fence post, sinking into the deep snow, grateful he was able to reach the ground before his legs collapsed underneath him.

When his extremities turned numb from the wet snow, he stood up. His body reconnected with his mind, urging him to seek shelter before hypothermia set in. Unsure how long this bout had lasted, he trekked across the field toward his house. As he climbed up the squeaky porch steps, he felt a vibration. At first, he thought the panic attack had returned, but hearing a low hum, he realized it was the phone in his jacket. He grumbled when he saw the number. Not a great time, but then again it never was when she called.

"Hi, Safia," he said, trying to keep his voice even and pleasant. He doubted she had any significant news for him. Just another one of her check-ins, making sure he was all right.

"What's wrong?"

"I'm fine," he lied. He figured his labored breathing had triggered her suspicion. "Just got back from a jog."

Two lies in a matter of seconds. Not unusual for a man skilled at deception, but nevertheless he felt guilt-ridden. Hopefully, they would be convincing. No good would come of telling the truth. Disclosing to Safia that he had just returned from shooting an injured deer would clearly signal that he wasn't okay. He didn't want her travelling over eight hundred miles to console him. And what exactly could she do? Hold his hand and tell him it was going to be okay, when clearly it wouldn't? And she wouldn't come alone. She would bring *him*. The man he considered his best friend. There was a time when he had enjoyed hanging out with Omeir, but not now. He would pester him to talk. To try and fix something that wasn't fixable, and probably never would be.

Lying was the only option. At least over the phone. It wasn't the first time he had lied to her, or to Omeir. He had done it more times than he cared to admit, but it was self-preservation back then. He'd had to get out of New York.

"I appreciate the call, Safia, but I should go. I'm standing outside on the porch, dripping sweat. It's rather chilly. Tell Omeir I said hi and don't worry, I'm fine." He was going to add "talk to you later," but stopped himself from spitting out the casual phrase. He didn't want to encourage her calls.

Hours later, he still couldn't shake the image of the deer. The poor animal had gotten its legs tangled in the fence. It was woven wire, topped with a single barbed wire strand. The animal had been bleeding profusely. Perhaps if he had arrived ahead of the coyotes, he might have been able to save the fellow. But seeing the ripped-open carcass and blood-soaked fur, he'd known he was too late. There had only been one humane thing to do – end the animal's suffering.

It was a horrible way to start the day. Even after a long hot shower, Zak remained anxious, nerve endings frantically pulsating through his body. He would stay away from the north end of his property for several days before going back. By then, hungry animals would have devoured the carcass so he wouldn't have to revisit the bloodshed. It felt cowardly, but he didn't see the point of hauling a dead deer and burying it, only for wild animals to dig it up later. Sure, he would do that for a dog, but a deer, no matter how soulful its eyes had been, belonged to Mother Nature.

His dog Abby was doing her best to get him to relax, but it wasn't so simple this time. The breathing exercises he had been told would help were useless, and so too were the gentle nudges from Abby. Looking out the front door, he could see the snow starting to swirl. The windchill would make the cold even more unbearable than it had been earlier. A sane person would resign themselves to staying indoors, but Zak wasn't feeling sane. He knew he had to do something physical to erase the images, not only of today, but also the ones from two years ago that were even more vivid and disturbing. Grabbing his winter parka, he headed out into the cold.

* * * *

The tires spun, but it wasn't doing any good. Easing off the accelerator, Dr. Lexie Draden feared she had likely just made the problem worse. She could feel the car sinking deeper into the snow. Putting on the hazard lights, she pushed against the blustery winds, opening the door. The sting of the crystalized snow pinged across her exposed face. She was desperate to see what she was up against. She couldn't solve the problem without first assessing it. It was what analytical people like her did. The biting winds stung her cheeks, causing her ears to tingle. She was quick, careful not to waste any time, for fear the numbness to her extremities would be permanent. Yup, she was definitely stuck. She hurried back inside the sedan, cursing as the door blasted shut against her hip.

When she'd left Chicago that morning, there had been winds, but certainly nothing like now. Although her official move was two weeks away, she had packed a carload of possessions, planning to drop them off at her new home before heading back to the city. Misjudging the shoulder of the road due to the whiteout conditions, she was now stranded.

She admonished herself for another poor decision. Her life was slowly becoming a stream of wrong turns and bad choices. Nevertheless, she couldn't turn back now. No, literally she could not turn back. She was firmly stuck.

She reached into her purse to grab her phone. Hopefully tow trucks operated on Saturdays in this rural area.

Crap. The phone was dead. She had meant to charge it, but then forgot. *Just calm down,* she told herself. *Maybe there's a charger in the glove box.* Frantically, she searched. *Damn.*

At least she had a full tank of gas. She could avoid freezing to death for several hours.

Hours? God no. She couldn't imagine being stuck in the vehicle for even several more minutes.

Maybe someone would come along. Yes, she was in the countryside, but it wasn't some remote mountain village in Peru. She was only about an hour and a half from Chicago, and although it wasn't a highway, it was a paved road. She thought back to how many cars she had passed on the way to town. She cursed, unable to recall any.

She tilted her head back and closed her eyes. No, she wasn't going to cry. Not because she was strong, but because tears weren't going to get her car to move back onto the road. She opened her eyes and looked around. It was so hard to see with all the snow swirling around. It was what meteorologists referred to as a ground blizzard. There wasn't snow falling from the sky. Rather the white stuff was violently twisting up from the ground. The sixty-mile-per-hour winds were creating havoc on visibility. If only the wind could slow down for a second.

Then it happened. There were a few seconds where the wind paused, and Lexie was able to catch a glimpse.

"A driveway," she exclaimed. She did a quick fist pump in the air. The gravel clearing was only a few yards away. The driveway would lead to a house. She would walk up the snow-covered road and ask to use a phone.

Oh, but what if it was a long driveway, or what if no one was home? Or maybe it was just an entrance to some wheat field with no house or residents.

She slammed her hands on the steering wheel in frustration, making the horn blare.

No, no. Don't you dare cry.

She stared into the distance as she racked her brain for options. None came to her. Finally, she pulled the hood on her jacket over her head. She would take her chances and trek down the lane. If it looked like it was too far, she would simply return to her car.

She was about to open the door when she saw the outline of someone approaching. Relief washed over her. However, it quickly turned to fright when she saw an ax-wielding, masked man coming toward her.

Oh, my God. I'm going to die.

Quickly, she locked her door. If he was intent on killing her, she wasn't going to make it easy for him. No, he would have to smash the window and pry her clenched hands off the steering wheel. She would make damn sure he exerted energy while dragging her away. Bludgeoning her to death would be work.

With no other options coming to mind, she did the only thing she could think to do: pray. She prayed that even through all her mistakes, her life mattered, that she was salvageable.

She hadn't had a prayer answered in so long that it astounded her when the man threw the ax off to the side.

"Thank you, thank you," she said, looking upward to a God she was ambivalent about.

"Put the car in reverse." The voice was deep, even stern, and it shook her back to the now.

He wasn't there to kill her; he was going to get her unstuck.

She focused on his *balaclava*-covered face and put her car into reverse. With his massive body, he pushed against the hood of the car. It moved slightly.

"Okay, now put it in drive and give it a bit of gas, but not too much," he said.

She did as she was told. The car moved ahead a couple of feet.

"Now, in reverse again and give it some gas until I tell you to stop."

She put the car in reverse, and again he pushed the car back. This time, she was able to keep going, steering her Toyota back up onto the road.

He didn't yell at her to stop, he simply held up his hand.

Lexie was free. She smiled, the first in a long time. She opened the passenger window a couple of inches to speak. He glared at her with intense dark eyes from behind the black knitted face covering. He stepped back a few feet, hesitant to come close to her.

"Thanks. I didn't think I would get out without a tow truck," she shouted, hoping it was loud enough to reach him through the howling wind.

He nodded, not saying a word. Or maybe he did say something under the ski mask, but with the wind whipping, who knew.

"Can I give you a ride back to…?" She stopped. She wasn't sure where he had come from, and she wasn't entirely sure she should let him into her car.

The man responded by pointing down the driveway, shaking his head no. As she watched, mesmerized by the imposing figure in front of her, he turned around and walked away. After a few steps, he bent down, retrieved the ax, and continued his steady pace.

Lexie waited until the outline of his body became invisible through the snow. She slowly drove away, distancing herself from the masked man who had rescued her.

* * * *

Zak was out chopping firewood in the blizzard, not because he needed more to warm his house, but because he needed a distraction. Something to prevent the flashbacks from taking over the gains he had made in the last couple of years. Killing the deer earlier today had set off an explosion inside of him. His role in death, animal or human, triggered helplessness and darkened shame. It was all too consuming, and he needed a diversion from it. The physicality of splitting logs helped to do just that.

The winds were horrible, biting into his flesh, so he had gone inside, grabbed the *balaclava* and returned to the task. When he heard the car horn, he knew he should go check it out. Normally he would have taken his dog, but Abby had endured enough of nature's harshness and was finally enjoying the comforts of a warm house. Besides, he had a concealed gun and an ax, should he need it.

When he saw the woman, he knew exactly who she was, but she had no idea who he was, other than some crazed masked-man carrying an ax. He hadn't meant to terrify her, and of course he didn't normally go around wearing a ski mask, but it was downright freezing. He dropped the ax as soon as he saw the fear in her eyes, but he wasn't going to freeze his face for her. Yes, it was cold, and admittedly, he could have survived a few minutes without being covered, yet he didn't do it. He didn't want to scare her, but he didn't want to stand there chitchatting either. Leaving himself wrapped in the face mask would make her realize he wasn't a man who would invite her in for coffee. Yes, she was pretty, and having her sit in his house sipping a warm beverage held a certain appeal. Any man with a pulse would notice her piercing indigo eyes and luscious, long, dark hair, peeking out of the hood of her coat. The pleasant smile that came across her face when she realized she was free from the embankment was a hell of a lot better than a thank you. Nevertheless, he hadn't gone to the end of the driveway to rescue a damsel in distress with a beautiful smile, and frankly, from what he'd read about her, she wasn't the damsel type.

He'd gone to ease his own mind, so he would know there was no threat. Or if there was one, to swiftly deal with it.

Okay, he could have handled it better. He could have removed the ski mask, spoken like a normal man, and even smiled when she thanked him. Well... he *had* smiled. He was in a surly mood when he'd headed toward the sound of the honking car horn, but somehow the corners of his mouth moved reflexively when she smiled to thank him. Of course, the woman had no way of knowing. The tiny mouth opening on his ski mask made it impossible. Now he risked her talking about the nutjob who lived a few miles from her new residence. It was a small community, and undoubtedly, she would find out who he was. Maybe not anytime soon, but within a few weeks she would end up running into him again. Sure, he wouldn't have his face concealed, but by then she would have made conclusions about his strange behavior and would avoid him. However, that wasn't as much a concern as the rumors that might arise. He had finally been accepted in the community, not necessarily well-liked or welcomed, but at least he was left in peace.

Maybe he was overthinking it. Maybe she made the connection with the blistering cold and wearing a face mask. Maybe it wasn't odd or creepy. Then he remembered the sheer panic in her eyes when he moved toward her with the ax in hand. *Damn, Zak, you're an idiot.*

* * * *

Lexie sat in front of the crackling fire, soaking in the warmth of the embers, relieved to have gotten out of the ditch. A masked superhero is how she'd decided to view the man she had encountered today. Masked ax-wielding psychopath didn't seem fitting. He had done her a favor. If he hadn't come along... well, she didn't want to think what her fate would have been. It was peculiar how he'd stayed behind the mask, not even muttering a word after she thanked him. Overall, what did it matter if he lacked social grace? She had been able to get to her new home and out of the cold thanks to his kindness. Okay, maybe not kindness, given she couldn't be sure of his motive. More like thanks to his brute strength. That she could be sure off. Even though he'd been bundled up, it had been easy to tell that he was an imposing man underneath all those layers.

Catching a glimpse of a large mouse scampering across the foyer, Lexie realized she had more important things to do than contemplate the motives of a masked stranger. She reached over to her phone, adding a note to call an exterminator in the morning. God, she hoped it had been a fat mouse and not some rat. She wasn't sure if she could tell the difference, as she had never encountered the furry critters in her Chicago condo.

She stood up and walked over to the large living room window of the nineteenth-century home. The window had frosted over near the edges and a slow steady draft emerged, causing her to shiver. Despite the unpleasant chill, Lexie didn't back away as the scenery outside provided her with a diversion. The swirling snow had left the red cedar trees covered in white sparkles that glistened in the emerging darkness. Living in the historic house wasn't going to be easy. It was too spacious for a woman living alone. The two-story red brick home was definitely larger than what she needed. She had considered passing on it, but when she realized the location, she had changed her mind. It was near her work, a mere fifteen-minute drive to town, yet secluded from others. She wasn't ready to have neighbors. Neighbors who would lean over a fence and chat, who would ask her questions about her personal life. Questions she didn't want to answer.

Chapter Two

Damn that Abby. She had taken off after the coyotes yet again. Hoping she would run to his side, Zak yelled her name. She could definitely handle herself with the coyotes, but Zak knew there were wolves out there and it wouldn't necessarily be a sure thing for Abby with a larger beast. Then there were the coywolves, a cross between the eastern wolf and the western coyote. At nearly one hundred pounds, Abby might have a fighting chance with one of them, but he feared it would be a bloody battle. The last thing he needed was for her to get all mangled up and come back bleeding. The incident with the deer a few weeks back had clearly put him on notice that he couldn't handle blood anymore.

Taking a deep breath, he called her name once more in a deep, firm voice. As he had hoped, Abby came scampering back to him. Zak shook his head, giving her a big grin when she planted herself at his feet, anticipating a token of appreciation for answering his call. He took comfort knowing she was loyal to him, being there when he needed her.

Two years ago, when he had fled New York City for small-town Baxley, he knew a life of isolation would raise suspicions. He just wanted to blend in with his environment, to be anonymous, and getting Abby was part of a calculated plan to make himself appear less of a threat.

He needed a guard dog that didn't look fierce. A canine which would come across as non-threatening yet adorable. One who would lessen unease toward him. A perceptive and protective dog, one who would not only alert him, but who would attack if needed.

He passed on the traditional power breeds. A Rottweiler or a Bullmastiff would cause more apprehension with the townsfolk. He was aloof to the locals, but he was aiming for socially awkward rather than menacing. After doing research on various breeds, it came down to either a Standard Poodle or a Komondor. He readily decided against the poodle, as he couldn't shake the images of the elegant breed walking down a fashion runway in Paris. He just wasn't a poodle kind of man.

Therefore, he went for the Komondor, a large Hungarian breed known primarily as a guardian of livestock. With its white corded coat, the dog looked friendly enough, but the breed could be counted on to guard and alert if needed. He was hoping it wasn't going to be needed, but he had to be prepared. He was aware of how some people viewed him due to his Middle Eastern ancestry and didn't want to add fuel to any speculation. Zak simply wanted to hide out, or least enjoy some anonymity for once. He knew he would not be able to just blend into the small community of Baxley, but maybe, just maybe, he wouldn't be targeted by those who were so quick to judge. But if they judged him to be dangerous, they weren't wrong, for if warranted, he could be, even lethal.

How long he would stay in Baxley, he didn't know. He hadn't had a true life for a long time, so if he had to pack up in the middle of the night to escape those who might be tracking him down, he would. And he wasn't even sure anyone was going to track him down. The longer it had been since the incident in New York, the more likely his true identity had not been detected. There was, however, no guarantee this was the case and it was still quite possible that one day, someone would come for him. It would mean trouble if they did, and he wanted to insure he had the best chance of getting out alive. Yes, he grasped how messed up and even paranoid his life had become, but after having a bullet penetrate his chest, he had to be vigilant.

* * * *

There were only a handful of vehicles on the road as Lexie eased around the dips and curves on the way to the clinic. This peaceful drive was in stark contrast to driving in Chicago, with its clogged freeways filled with anxious drivers, trying to control their seething frustration.

A simple fifteen-mile drive taking less than fifteen minutes, and, she was in Baxley. The same distance in Chicago would have taken three times as long. Although it might take some time to get use to her new environment, she certainly savored these morning commutes. She knew not all the drives in the area would be stress free. She'd experienced what the roads could be like in a blizzard, but today the roads were dry.

Baxley was a small town with no more than a thousand residents. It was picturesque with its well-preserved historical buildings and tree-lined streets. It didn't draw in the tourists that the nearby larger communities did, but it was just as storybook pretty, only with a more laid-back appeal.

With only a scattering of pedestrians in sight, it was obvious there was not much happening. This was certainly typical as there wasn't much happening on any other morning either. A few businesses had already opened for the day, including Colton's, the town's quaint little diner. It served home-style soups and gourmet sandwiches, and was also known for its mouth-watering baked goods and pies.

Since Lexie had plenty of time to get to the clinic, she decided to make a quick stop at the diner. Colton's occupied a red brick building on the corner of Main Street and the secondary highway coming into town, an excellent location. It didn't have much in the way of competition in Baxley, but there were a couple other little eateries, a greasy burger joint and a pizza place attached to the town's only bar. Colton's was Baxley's true gem.

"Good morning, Dr. Draden. The usual?" asked Emily as she stood behind the counter. A senior at Baxley High School, she worked part time as a server at Colton's. Wearing minimal make-up with her long blonde hair tied back into a simple ponytail, she was the type of girl who was prettier than she realized.

"Yes, a large coffee with double cream." Although unnecessary, Lexie felt compelled to specify her order. It struck her as odd that within a couple of weeks, Emily was able to recall how she liked her coffee.

Back in Chicago, it would have taken several months for a barista to remember, and only if they anticipated a generous tip.

Pouring the coffee into a disposable cup, Emily gave Lexie a genuine smile. "Here you go Dr. Draden. Just to let you know, we have whole-wheat banana-nut muffins. Cicily made them this morning."

Cicily was the owner of Colton's and one of numerous patients who had come with Lexie's newly acquired medical practice, although she hadn't yet attended to her. Cicily had named her diner after her deceased son. Lexie didn't know exactly how Colton had died but it sounded like it had shaken up the entire community.

At first Lexie was going to say no to the muffins, but she thought of Margo, the clinic's medical receptionist. She figured it might be a good gesture to bring in muffins since she had been rather abrupt with the poor woman yesterday. Margo had simply asked about Lexie's family. It was Margo's way of getting to know her. Lexie had realized it as soon as she had instinctively yet abruptly changed the topic to how Margo had the charts organized. It wasn't a criticism of the way she did the organizing it was simply a way to divert from the sensitive topic of Lexie's family. The death of her niece, Hailie, and the fall-out afterward, was too painfully raw for Lexie to talk about. Sure, it was the reason she left Chicago, but it wasn't something she wanted to confess to Margo, or anyone else in Baxley.

"They look great, Emily. I'll take a dozen." Besides Margo, the morning patients might also enjoy a snack.

With her box of muffins in tow, Lexie left Colton's with still plenty of time to get to the office. She hoped to be able to smooth things over with her receptionist, who was an integral part of the practice.

* * * *

When Lexie pulled up to the clinic, she noticed Margo standing near the doorway. She appeared to be talking to someone, although the large bush by the entrance prevented her from seeing who it was. The elderly receptionist's hands were frantically moving. Lexie drove around the back of the building and parked. Seeing that Margo wasn't inside the building, she knew the backdoor would be locked. She would have to go through the front entrance and disturb whatever conversation was going on. She grabbed the box of muffins from the passenger seat and leaned back to grab her coffee. She was about to slam the door with her hip, when she heard Margo's voice elevate. It was wrong to eavesdrop, but she couldn't help it when she heard her name being mentioned.

"You know… Dr. Draden's a top surgeon… who came from a major trauma center… in Chicago," Margo sputtered to the person behind the bushes.

"Yeah, well, I don't need surgery. I just need an annual check-up and I can get that in Lands Crossing," said a male voice. Lands Crossing was a neighboring community. Although it had three times the population as Baxley, it wasn't a large town by any means. Baxley was just that small.

"Oscar Morrison, I'm surprised at you," Margo bellowed.

"Surprised by what?"

"Well, it's a changing world, and I thought with those twin granddaughters of yours, Ashley and…"

"Ashley and Deeandra," he finished for her.

"Yes. Well, I was just thinking Ashley and Deeandra, they're in college now and soon they'll be starting careers. Probably working with men, men who might not see them as equals. Backward men who might not want to give them a chance simply because they're women. Oscar, I really thought you would be the type of man, the type of grandfather who'd support women, whether they be recent graduates working in corporate America, or an experienced doctor working in a small-town clinic."

"Damn it Margo, that's not what this is about."

"Well, if that's not it, why would you drive thirty minutes to Lands Crossing to see a doctor when you've been going here for well over thirty years?"

"She's a she…" The words he stammered out weren't helping his argument. Lexie didn't like what she was hearing, but she couldn't help but feel sorry for the man since she had a sense that Margo was just winding up.

"Oscar, shame on you for being sexist!" Yep, Lexie was right. Margo was just getting started. A part of her wanted to rescue the man, but a larger part wanted to hear how Margo was going to handle this.

"You know I respected Dr. Thornton as a great doctor, but Dr. Draden…" Margo went on. "Well, she's more skilled than he was. Dr. Thornton showed me the woman's credentials. She's unbelievable. She's more than qualified, and in fact, she's wasting her talent working at the clinic. I don't know why she chose to come here, and I don't know if she'll tire of our sleepy little town, but right now she is here. This town, this clinic, and Dr. Thornton's patients are fortunate to have her. Moreover, if we don't embrace her, she'll see no need to stay; she'll pack up and go back to the city. You know how hard it is to get a doctor to come to a small town? To get a good doctor, let alone a great one to come here?"

From her vantage point, Lexie could see the icy glare coming off Margo's eyes. She seemed to be daring him to defy her. Lexie readied herself for more stumbling words from the man.

"Fine, I'll give her a chance, but I'm not some chauvinist. It's just… well, she's pretty, and an old man like me gets embarrassed when he has to be examined and touched by a pretty, young woman."

Shit. Lexie wasn't expecting that. She cocked her head as if a simple sideways motion would make their words louder to her ears.

"I just wished she looked different, like older, like…"

"Like me?" Margo asked. Lexie loved the wide grin that came over her employee's face.

"Look, I said I'll give her a chance, so no further discussion." The man was clearly flustered and embarrassed just talking about the matter.

"Thanks, Oscar, and just one more favor."

"What?" His limited patience was all but drained.

"Talk to your coffee buddies, too. I know they listen to you. And if you want, I can be there when you guys drop your pants, to kill any thrill you may accidently get when the pretty doctor is examining you."

"Sheesh, Margo." Oscar shook his head and walked away, leaving Margo, as well as an eavesdropping Lexie, giggling.

* * * *

"Morning, Dr. Draden. The coffee is freshly brewed." Margo's voice was soft and friendly as Lexie walked through the door a few seconds later.

Margo was a perfectionist at the clinic. She was organized, responsive to the patients and quick to respond to emergencies. Yet there was one area she didn't excel in: making coffee. Tasteless was not the word to describe it, for Lexie would have welcomed tasteless. No, Margo's coffee was bitter mud. A nasty shock to the palate, leaving a repulsive taste, lasting hours. By the end of her first week, Lexie had tried making it herself, but Margo had quickly shooed her away with a scolding. Making coffee was clearly Margo's domain.

"Thanks, but I grabbed a cup on the way, as well as some freshly baked muffins. I thought you and the morning patients might enjoy them."

She handed the box to Margo, who smiled.

"Ahhh, from Colton's." She reached into the box and grabbed one of the muffins, taking a generous bite.

As Margo ate, Lexie cleared her throat, "I'd like to talk to you about yesterday."

"No need to, Dr. Draden. I realized I shouldn't be asking personal questions. It's clear you are grieving, whether it be of a person or a way of life, or both. God knows, I know about grieving."

Lexie had heard Margo had lost her husband many years ago, however, she didn't know the details.

Margo smiled as she continued, "It's perfectly fine you aren't ready to talk about your life. You don't need to talk to me or anyone else in this town, until you want to. Now, I only ask you not let me eat these wonderful muffins by myself."

She pushed the box of baked goods toward her boss.

Lexie grabbed a muffin. "Thank you, Margo." She meant for more than just the muffin.

* * * *

After filling Abby's food bowl, Zak sat down with his laptop to do some work. He needed to make a living, so he could pay for the necessities of life. The housing market was rather reasonable in the country, and he had used part of his savings to purchase the little blue, wood-panelled house. He wasn't pressured into taking a high-paying job, but he had to work. He still received remuneration from his past employer in New York, but he had committed those monies to others. He needed to work not only for financial reasons, but to occupy his time, to fill the spaces of his life with something other than painful memories.

Fortunately, he was able to find that work as a translator. He was fluent in a number of languages and could easily do translations in several of them, including French, Arabic, Kurdish, Berber, and Persian. The people in Baxley were naturally curious about what he did as an occupation. When asked, he told them he was a French translator who worked from home. It wasn't a lie, but of course it wasn't all he did.

He felt uneasy conversing with the locals, but it wasn't practical to cut himself off completely from others. He had to go into town and interact with people for a variety of day-to-day matters. He had to shop for groceries, get supplies at the hardware store, and occasionally take Abby to the veterinarian. But he would sometimes go to the larger neighboring towns or even into Chicago for more personal matters. And he would never go to the doctor's office in Baxley if he was ill.

Last year, he began to get sharp pains in his chest. Seeking treatment from old Dr. Thornton wasn't an option, not with the scarring of a bullet hole he didn't want to explain. So he had driven into Chicago and to a clinic there. In Chicago, the doctors weren't shocked to see a man with a bullet wound. The wound was well over a year old then. In large urban centers, if it wasn't fresh and bleeding, the doctors normally didn't care, and if they did, it was easier to lie about it. However, in Baxley, word might get out about the stranger who had been shot. The wound rarely bothered him physically, but emotionally it was always a reminder of the life he had chosen. A life he was afraid he could never shake.

* * * *

Checking the wall clock for the third time within fifteen minutes, Lexie was relieved that it was finally noon. With the last patient cancelling, and no further patients scheduled for another ninety minutes, she decided she would get away from the office. She had rarely gone out for lunch while in Chicago, and when she did, it had been on weekends with her sister Claudia and her kids.

She missed Claudia, who had been her best friend as well as her older sister. They were twelve years apart, and although age differences sometimes prevented siblings from being close, this was not the case with them. Claudia had been a wonderful older sister to Lexie, taking on a protective role when their father died. It was Claudia who'd encouraged Lexie to go to med school and become a surgeon. And it was Claudia who had toasted champagne with her when she'd became a resident surgeon at the trauma center.

Lexie had been the maid of honor at Claudia's wedding to Ted. She had celebrated Claudia's pregnancies. And it was Lexie who held baby Liam, and, ten years later, little Hailie. Beautiful Hailie, born premature. So tiny and fragile, having to stay in the neonatal unit for weeks.

But there had been dark days ahead for the sisters: the phone call from a tearful Claudia, when Ted had cheated with a young intern at his law firm; the text message that Hailie had an appointment with a specialist; and eventually, Hailie's devastating diagnosis of Alexander disease, a rare and fatal disorder affecting the nervous system. Lexie had still been in medical school when they found out and had spent countless hours researching the disease only to find out there was no cure and Hailie's life expectancy would be short. Claudia had refused to accept that one day she would bury her child. Even while witnessing Hailie's deterioration, she'd refused to let go of hope. But it had been taken from her the evening Hailie died.

Thinking about those days was self-destructive. It always put Lexie into a funk, taking her days to recover. Although she was well-educated in the workings of the human brain, she was powerless from preventing her mind from succumbing to the negativity associated with her niece's death.

"Hi, Dr. Draden. How's your day going?"

It was Jason, the young guy who delivered medical supplies. Inadvertently, he had interrupted Lexie's solemn thoughts as she ventured into the clinic's reception area.

"Great," she lied. "Would you like a muffin?" There were still two sitting in the box from that morning.

"No, thanks. I'm heading to Colton's to pick up some lunch on my way out of town."

Of course he was going to stop off at Colton's. She had overheard Tabitha, who was one of her morning patients, talking about some guy named Jason who liked her friend Emily. The Emily from Colton's. Lexie was able to fill in the blanks. It was amazing how easy it was to figure things out in a small town.

Lexie quickly signed for the delivery and wished Jason a good day. As he was leaving, Margo stepped through the door, returning from her lunch break. The elderly woman's eyes twinkled and she nodded at Jason as he exited.

"I see the supplies got here. Just in time; I was worried we might be in a bind."

Lexie stifled a laugh, knowing that Jason's delivery could have waited another week. They were not even close to being in a bind. There was half a storeroom full of medical supplies. It was simply Margo's personality to be well-prepared in case an emergency happened. What kind of emergency could happen in Baxley, Lexie struggled to envision. A multiple-car accident perhaps, but nothing like a gang shooting, which had kept her on her toes in Chicago. She had seen enough pulverized flesh and damaged organs from guns. Thank God for small sleepy towns like Baxley.

Chapter Three

Zak climbed into his truck. It would be a short trip to Baxley, and as usual, Abby would come along. People in Baxley responded better when Abby was with him. The dog had canine charisma and she made him less tense around the locals. They loved to talk and in the last six months had become comfortable in asking Zak for help. It all started when old Oscar Morrison had seen him with the latest smartphone. Oscar had assumed Zak was a tech-savvy guy who could help him and his cronies with their phones and tablets, an assumption, which was truer than Zak had hoped they would ever find out. He knew more than how to change a ring tone or utilize the privacy settings. He could hack into their phones and computer systems with ease, having learned a lot of this from Omeir, the true master. Since coming to Baxley, there had been no need to hack and therefore he didn't. But he'd taken the time to assist the residents, since it was a good way to keep up-to-date on any new happenings.

Besides keeping tabs on the natives, Zak also kept vigilant regarding any newcomers to Baxley. It was something he needed to do to ensure his own safety. Although he hoped he hadn't been compromised in New York, it would be naïve of him to think he would be safe in Baxley or any other place. So far it had been easy for Zak to keep track of strangers. It was a town with little movement. In the last three months, only four people had moved in. Three belonged to the same family, moving to be near their aging family matriarch. The fourth new resident was, by far, the more interesting one. He had known about her as soon as she'd acquired Dr. Thornton's practice a few months back.

Dr. Alexandra Draden, or Lexie, as she preferred to be called. A twenty-nine-year-old trauma surgeon from Chicago. After purchasing Baxley's only medical practice, she set about renting this enormous historic home not too far from where Zak's little blue house was. She probably wanted the seclusion, but certainly for different reasons than his. According to the file he had on Dr. Draden, she was alone. No husband. No romantic attachments. A single woman living in the countryside. This puzzled Zak. He wasn't suspicious of who she was. She checked out. He was puzzled because she was quite attractive, as he'd found out last month when she'd gotten her car stuck near his driveway. Beautiful and smart women were, in his experience, either taken or too high-maintenance. She didn't appear to be the latter from what research there was on her. Her career in Chicago had kept her busy. He knew she hadn't left her city life in Chicago due to some heart-rending break-up. That was good, as clearly no man should break the heart of this woman.

She did, however, leave Chicago for personal reasons and he knew those were linked to her niece's death. He felt empathy for her. The doctor's life had elements of tragedy so severe that it had led her to seek solace in a place as foreign to her as it was to him. Their lives were so similar in some ways, but also so radically different. The differences reminded him how unwise it would be to get close to anyone, let alone someone like her, a woman who devoted her life to healing others as opposed to what he had done. If that wasn't enough for him to keep his distance, then the ridiculous way he'd reacted to her during the storm should be. He was thinking of her way too often. Sure, it wasn't in a creepy, constant, infatuated way, only in the occasional moments of boredom. Unfortunately, living in Baxley provided a lot of boredom.

The distracting thoughts rambling through his head made him drive past his destination. When he reached the end of Main Street, he realized his error. Making a quick U-turn, he headed back toward the town administration office.

He had received a photo radar ticket in the mail yesterday. A situation that had happened a couple of weeks ago, where once again he'd gotten distracted. He had been thinking about what had happened in New York and didn't realize he had entered the town limits, where the speed limit dropped drastically. Now he started to wonder if he had done this again, but this time his thoughts were about Dr. Lexie Draden, a pleasant distraction, worth the cost of a speeding ticket.

Paying any traffic infractions right away was a must for Zak. He'd been trained to not leave any loose ends, and even an outstanding speeding ticket was a bad habit fitting into that category. He had been to the town administration office a few times before, to pay Abby's annual dog license and to get a permit to build a shed in his yard. The office was operated by Kristina McQuay, an attractive blonde about Zak's age. She always flirted shamelessly with him, even though she was married to the local sheriff.

As soon as Zak walked in the door, Kristina's eyes lit up and she smiled broadly. She quickly rose from a nearby desk and leaned over the counter to greet him.

"Good morning, Zak. So great to see your handsome face. What can I do for you today?" Even the way the words spilled out from her painted red lips was suggestive.

"Bonjour, Mademoiselle Kristina," he greeted.

Rightly, she was a *Madame* and not a *Mademoiselle*, but because the French language has no equivalent to Ms., he used the French term for Miss. He had learned from experience, younger American women tended to dislike *Madame* as it seemed old and staid, and Kristina was anything but.

"I see you added some highlights to your hair. It adds a nice shimmer to those golden locks of yours." The compliment rolled smoothly off his tongue.

"Thanks darling, I was afraid it might be too much." She leaned across the counter, exposing a considerable amount of cleavage in her too-tight V-neck sweater. "Emmett didn't even notice," she murmured.

Sheriff Emmett McQuay was an irritable man who spent more time scowling than realizing how lucky he was to have a pretty blonde wife. He clearly didn't like being the sheriff of a small town. An impressive, burly man, who most of the locals seemed to like as their number one cop, he had little patience with those who didn't follow the law, even minor infractions. Admittedly, he did keep things orderly in the town.

He was a bit shorter than Zak but there was no doubt he was an imposing figure, and, until Zak had showed up in Baxley, likely the toughest guy in town. Zak stayed clear of him, but not due to any intimidation. It took far more than the likes of Emmett McQuay to intimidate him. No, Zak stayed clear of the sheriff, because he didn't want him tracking his every move. The sheriff didn't trust him, but at least he left him alone. And as long as Zak didn't do anything to justify him acting, even something as stupid as wielding an ax while donning a *balaclava*, he could stay off the sheriff's radar.

He needed to let go of the ax incident. Obviously, Dr. Draden had. No one in town had mentioned the incident and there had been no visit from the sheriff. If there were any rumors circulating around, he would find out soon enough. Kristina would be the one who would know.

Fortunately, getting information out of her was effortless. The sheriff's wife liked Zak, even though at times he wished she would like him a little less. He wasn't attracted to Kristina, although she was certainly easy on the eyes. He found her a little too overtly sexual, a ridiculous notion to most of the men in Baxley. The local men loved Kristina and her flirtatious ways. They were, however, smart enough to keep their eyes from straying her way. After all, her husband carried a gun. To Zak, she came across like an insecure teenage girl, starving for some boy to notice her. He felt sorry for her and often wondered how such a gregarious woman ended up with such a grump of a man.

In addition to her fondness for flirting, Kristina was a terrible gossip. Being cold and aloof to her flirtations might annoy or even anger her. An angry woman with a propensity for gossiping was something to be avoided. So for his peace of mind, he was always friendly toward her, and when no one else was around, he would indulge in a little flirtation. It got him what he wanted.

"Well, I think your new hair color is perfect. You look like an angel," Zak reassured her.

With a blatant giggle, she softly said, "Thanks, Zak, so kind of you."

Now that he had made her feel good, he could get on to business. He pulled out the ticket from his jacket and set it down on the counter.

"Unfortunately, I got this speeding ticket." He then placed the exact amount of money beside it.

She took the cash and processed the outstanding fine. While she was handing him the confirmation receipt, she leaned in toward him.

"I know I would get in trouble if the mayor knew I was telling you, but I know I can trust you." Zak nodded, and she continued. "He told Emmett to set up another photo radar by Tim Dalton's place."

"Tim Dalton?" Zak asked curiously. He knew she would spill more.

"Yeah, Mr. Dalton's one of the town's wealthy residents. He's an ornery old geezer, but he does contribute rather generously to several local projects, including the restoration of the town's library."

She leaned in even closer. Surprisingly, she smelled good. A floral perfume with a hint of vanilla. It was alluring, yet subtle, unlike her cleavage, which was only inches away from him.

"Old Man Dalton's pissed about those teens with their loud trucks roaring by his place. He just wants to re-establish a peaceful haven for those hummingbirds he loves to enjoy on his front porch. He figures the kids will learn to slow down after getting a hundred-dollar fine."

"He's probably right. I learned my lesson after this ticket, and I don't have to worry about my dad taking my wheels away."

She started laughing and he faked a wide, charm-induced grin.

"*Merci, mon chéri,*" Zak said, thanking her for the information on the radar trap. With a quick wink, he turned and walked away, knowing her eyes would be glued to his backside.

He had a few more tasks to complete in Baxley, including a quick stop at the veterinarian's to pick up food for Abby. As a hundred-pound canine, she went through a large bag of food in no time. He could definitely relate to this. As a solid man, twice the size of Abby, he went through his fair share of groceries. After finishing at the vet's, he headed to the local food mart.

Unfortunately, it wasn't the ten-minute shopping trip he had hoped it would be. No, it was just his luck to run into a couple of chatty and perturbed locals. So there he stood in the dairy aisle, nodding in agreement to the ridiculous notion that Baxley needed more policing resources. Law enforcement officers to catch those "lowlife hoodlums" who sprayed peace signs and happy faces all over the water tower. At least there was no gossip about an ax-wielding lunatic roaming the country side. Thirty minutes later, after pretending to care about a defaced water tower, as if it was a crime against humanity, he emerged with a growling stomach. Heading back home would now have to wait. An impatient appetite needed appeasing.

The best option for lunch was Colton's. However, the owner, Cicily McQuay, who was also Sheriff McQuay's mother, had an obvious disdain for Zak. He recalled the first time he stopped into Colton's and met the woman. He'd introduced himself as a newcomer who just moved to the Baxley area. She had offered no smile, no welcome to the community, nothing but a scowl on her face. When he had inquired about the house special, she'd abruptly told him they had sold out. She'd given no offer of any other lunch suggestions. Instead, she had stood there looking directly at him as if daring him to respond in a way that would displease her. He'd kept a smile on his face, ordered a roast beef sandwich to go, and promptly left.

He sensed what she was all about, but he gave her the benefit of the doubt that day. If there were more eateries in Baxley, he might not have returned. But there wasn't much choice and besides, the food was really good, a mountainous heap of tender roast beef between freshly baked multi-grain bread. It was mouth-watering. A week later, he'd strode back into Colton's. Taking a seat in a booth near the front counter, he'd pretended to peruse the menu. Within a few minutes Cicily had noticed him. While glancing his way, she had told young Emily, one of her employees, "You can't trust *those* guys." Although the statement had confused naïve Emily, Zak had known exactly what Cicily meant. Getting upset hadn't been worth his effort, and besides, he couldn't risk drawing attention to himself.

If there was any plus side to Cicily's bigotry, it was Emily's response. After Cicily repeated her offensive comment, Emily finally clued into the insinuation. The girl was so embarrassed by her boss that she started treating Zak to the occasional free pastry when Cicily wasn't looking. It wasn't pity that got him the pastry it was compassion, so Zak accepted. Besides, those croissants and eclairs were damn good.

Emily was a good kid she had empathy for the plight of others. He could see why Jason, the kid who delivered medical supplies, was so infatuated with her. She was the type of girl who had no idea how brilliant and remarkable she was, sort of like Dr. Draden.

Damn, why did his thoughts have to go to Dr. Draden?

"Hi, Mr. Tifour, how's it going today?" Emily's words interrupted.

Tifour was an alias he used when he altered his identity. He did have family roots in the name Tifour; it was the maiden name of his maternal great-grandmother. He hated lying, so when he could he tried to impart some truth.

"Doing great, Emily. So did you hear back from Northwestern University?" Last month when he came in to grab some lunch, she asked him if he would look over her college application for any spelling or grammar errors.

"No, not yet. I probably won't for another few weeks."

"Well, I hope it all works out. I heard they have a great general science program there. So, what's the special today?"

"It's a roasted chicken sandwich with split pea soup. We have fresh oatmeal cookies, too."

"Well, the sandwich sounds great. I'll skip the soup but add a coffee and an oatmeal cookie. And to go, please." He didn't have to add the last part, Emily knew he seldom ate at the diner. The less he had to deal with Cicily the better.

* * * *

"Hey, Margo, I'm off to the diner to get a latte. Do you want one?"

Lexie knew that Margo was initially hurt that she didn't drink her brewed coffee. However, two weeks into avoiding drinking the coffee, her receptionist was now used to it. And once Lexie encouraged her to try the latte, she too was hooked.

"Yeah, that would be great dear. Thanks so much."

"I won't be long."

"Take your time. The next appointment isn't for an hour, and it's Mrs. Whitney, who always arrives late. Have a nice break, enjoy eating at the diner."

Margo saw the hesitancy in Lexie's face. "Go, take your time. If a major epidemic breaks out in Baxley, I'll come running for you," Margo joked.

"You know me, Margo. it's a habit I developed to eat on the go."

"Yes, I know, dear, but maybe it's time for some new habits."

Lexie knew Margo was right and silently vowed to start making some changes. Perhaps even a small change would help in transitioning to this life, a life she wasn't crazy about having, but one which was unfortunately her only option.

It was a short walk to the diner, but the crispness of the winter air kept her moving at a decent pace. Baxley was a pretty town, full of old brick buildings that weathered well for their age. A few were even a century old. She heard a rumor the town council was reluctant to approve any new construction, and especially not on Main Street. Lexie wasn't opposed to progress, but it was nice to know people cared about their town and preserving its past.

Reaching Colton's, she placed her hand on the diner's front door, wondering what wonderful smells would greet her. Cinnamon and rosemary were her all-time favorites. Before she could tug the door open, it rapidly swung open, catching her off guard. To steady herself from falling backward, she leaned forward, colliding with the startled man in front of her. Steamy liquid shot up in the air, landing on the man as a paper cup bounced onto the sidewalk. She could see the splashed beverage all over his right hand and down the front of his grey woolen coat. A low hiss emanated from the man.

"Oh, my God," she gasped. "I'm so sorry. Are you okay?"

The man looked directly into her eyes. He paused before answering, "All good here. I should pay more attention while going through the door. Sorry for startling you."

Without thinking, she grabbed his right elbow. "That's a nasty burn on your hand. Come inside."

"Seriously, I'm fine." Although he spoke words of reassurance, he didn't try to free himself from her hold.

Instantly, Lexie went into doctor mode, ignoring his weak protest as she controlled him by his arm back into the diner. Glancing around, she found what she was looking for. In no time, she had hustled him into the women's restroom. For a brief moment, it appeared as though he was going to object, then he shut his mouth, allowing her to take control. Gently taking his hand, she placed it under the sink taps, running cool water over the burn. After a few minutes of cool water flowing over his hand, she turned off the taps.

"Follow me," she demanded. And as if she didn't trust him to follow orders, she took his elbow, guiding him to the counter. "Emily, I need a large bowl of cold water."

Emily glanced down at the peculiar sight of Lexie holding Zak's arm, obviously confused about what was going on. "Yes, of course. Is everything okay?"

"I just had a little mishap with a coffee. It's really nothing," Zak clarified.

Emily looked down at his hand, where the burn had faded to pink. "I'll get it right away, Dr. Draden," she said, and her eyes filled with unnecessary panic.

Once Emily returned, Lexie took the bowl from her, guiding Zak to a vacant booth in the back. Calmly taking his hand, she placed it in the bowl of cold water. She looked up and saw the amused smile on his face. She reddened, realizing she hadn't introduced herself. This poor man probably thought she was some crazed woman, dragging him into the ladies' restroom. Like an elderly aunt, mollycoddling a child.

"I'm Lexie Draden," she said sheepishly. "The town's new doctor. I took over from Dr. Thornton when he retired."

"So that explains the wonderful care I'm getting." He reached out with his non-affected hand, introducing himself with a handshake. "I'm Zak Tifour, and I'm afraid we've already met."

"Pardon?"

"About two weeks ago."

She gave him a puzzled look.

"During the blizzard," he reluctantly tried to clarify.

"Oh, my God, you're the masked man who rescued me." There was disbelief in her voice.

"Yup, that was me. Sorry about the face mask, I didn't mean to scare you."

"Oh, that's okay. It was such a bitterly cold day. I could have used one, too." She didn't want to tell him the truth, her fear that he was going to chop her up into tiny pieces and bury her, only to have some wild animal dig up her bones in the spring.

"I was out chopping wood that day, so that's why I had the ax. Just in case you were wondering about that, too," he added.

"Indeed," she said, as though any sane person would chop wood in a freaking blizzard.

"I really should have left the ax by the house, but when I heard the car horn, I just headed out to see what was going on." His voice was apologetic.

"Well, I'm certainly glad you did. I wasn't sure how I was going to get out. My phone was dead and I didn't have the charger with me. And it doesn't seem like there's much traffic on that road." She forced herself to stop talking when she realized she was blathering on. Why would he care to hear about her phone? Maybe the annoyed guy with the mask wouldn't, but this guy… well, he seemed friendly and attentive. How could the same man make such opposite impressions?

"So now that I'm obviously not going to lose this hand, can I use it to buy you lunch?"

She didn't even hear him. She was distracted, recalling the man from that stormy day. When he'd appeared from the blizzard, he'd been bulky from all the layers he wore. He'd emerged like the Abominable

Snowman who was suddenly awakened by an intruder. And his dark, intense glare had revealed he was not too pleased by the intrusion. Even when she'd thanked him, he'd remained an awkward distance away from her car. It had appeared deliberate, like he hadn't trusted her, or perhaps himself. But the man sitting in front of her was different. With his jacket off, she saw a more solidly muscular physique. He was tall, maybe about six feet two, with wide shoulders and an expansive chest. Gone was the image of the almost cartoonish oversized brute of a man. He was still a solid force, but in a gentle way.

She discreetly inhaled his subtle yet pleasing aftershave, while she tried to sort the contrasting images she had of him. Yes, she saw the same dark brown eyes. The intensity was still there but there was a sultry warmth to them now. He had a beautiful, subtle smile that shone against his darker complexion. She was amazed how calm his voice was throughout the whole ordeal today. If it hadn't been for the slight wince he'd expelled when the coffee had come in contact with his hand, she would have thought he hadn't felt any pain. And he was definitely a patient man for he let her drag him around without saying a word, even when she took him into the ladies' room. It contrasted with the annoyance and detachment he'd radiated when he'd found her at the edge of his driveway.

She had been so pre-occupied with administering to the first-degree burn, that she didn't notice the rest of him. If he hadn't admitted to being the ax-wielding man, she would not have realized that they had met before. Now she was taking him all in, and there was a lot to take in. There was more to notice about this man beyond his flushed red knuckles she had just treated. There was his hair, short and strikingly glossy, an almost black hue to it. He appeared to be of Middle-Eastern descent, although she gathered he was born or raised in the United States for he spoke without an accent. He was clean-shaven with a strong jawline and a face that didn't warrant being covered in a woolen mask no matter how cold it was.

She now realized she must have been staring at him for too long as he cocked his head to get her attention.

"How about it then, do you have time?" he asked.

"Um, sorry, what was that?"

"Time for lunch," he chuckled. "A thank you for the great medical care."

And before she could think of an excuse, she answered, "Sure, but I'll get it. After all, you did rescue me."

He laughed lightheartedly. "Maybe next time, Dr. Lexie, but this time, I've got it."

* * * *

Maybe it was going to be okay. Lexie hadn't run screaming when she'd found out Zak was the ax-wielding masked man. She didn't mention how odd his behavior had been, or at least she pretended it was reasonable to keep a *balaclava* on while meeting someone for the first time. She even used the term 'rescued' instead of 'scared-to-death' to describe their first encounter. She treated him like some masked superhero. But no amount of pushing cars out of a ditch could ever make him a hero. That was not who he was, but he wasn't an ax-wielding psychopath either. So if the pretty Dr. Lexie was willing to overlook his unfavorable first impression, then he would have to stop admonishing himself. The corners of his mouth started to lift, but then he realized what he had done.

Having lunch with her and even flirting about a next time? It's careless. It's stupid.

He knew it was exactly what he was trained to avoid. But once she grabbed his hand, he no longer felt the burn, but something pleasurable. Her touch was gentle and warm. She was so sure of herself and determined in treating what was only a slight first-degree burn. Not only did she amaze him, but he was also amazed at himself. His reaction to her signified progress. He had been startled when they'd collided, but he hadn't overreacted. He'd remained calm. Although the burn had hurt, it was more discomfort than pain. Honestly, if she had not been so determined, and so alluring with those dark blue eyes, he would have been more insistent that he didn't need treatment. But how could anyone say no to being healed by her? And you'd have to be a fool to say no to anything else she would offer.

Damn, what's wrong with me? Focus, Zak. Stop being such a fool. Stop thinking she'd offer your sorry ass anything other than medical attention. She was just doing her job. That's what doctors do, even the nice pretty ones.

He tried to focus on the road as he drove out of Baxley, but his mind kept going back to Dr. Lexie. It was the best day he'd had in a long time. He convinced himself it was okay to indulge in a harmless fantasy where he was a regular guy, who had just met a nice girl at a diner.

When they'd sat down at the diner, he'd known it would be obvious to Lexie he wasn't originally from Baxley, and like most people he encountered, she would be interested in his origins. He hadn't wanted to lie to her, at least not more than necessary. So he'd told her some truths, mixed up with some untruths. He'd told her he had moved to Baxley from New York City. This was the truth. He'd told her he worked at home doing translations. This, too, was true. He'd disclosed being a first-generation American whose immigrant parents met while on student visas to the United States. Not only had he briefly mentioned his Algerian mother, but he'd also trusted her to know that his father came from Iraq. Again, these were all truths.

But he had lied to her. He'd known he would, and although he didn't like doing it, it was what he had to do, what he had been trained to do. So when she'd asked him why he'd left New York, he lied and told her how he wanted to get away from the pollution, the traffic, and how he desired a tranquil environment in order to focus on some major translation projects. He'd initially felt some guilt about lying to her, but this had dissipated when she'd lied to him about why she'd left Chicago, saying she had gotten tired of the crazy work hours and wanted to spend more time with patients. He knew the truth was related to her niece's death, but he also understood she wasn't ready to talk about it, and especially not with a stranger.

* * * *

Once she left the diner, Lexie realized she had forgotten Margo's latte. Preoccupied lunching with an attractive and fascinating man, she'd forgot the specialty drink. She was reluctant to go back to Colton's, but at least Zak had left, and maybe Emily wouldn't notice how scattered she was.

When she got back to Colton's, she was relieved to notice Emily was not there. Although she admittedly was a bit flustered, she didn't want to be seen as such. She was, after all, a mature professional, not some teenager who just met some dreamy boy on summer vacation. But she did have to admit he was dreamy.

Shaking her from her thoughts was the customer in front of her.

"Excuse me," the man said as he tried to step around a distracted Lexie.

Cicily, the owner of Colton's, was behind the counter. She had been at the diner earlier, but had been in the backroom and Lexie had only caught a glimpse of her then.

"Hello, Dr. Draden, what can I get for you?" Her tone sounded a little harsh to Lexie, but with Cicily it was hard to tell.

"Please, call me Lexie." She preferred to be called Lexie when she wasn't at work. She wasn't much for formalities and she loathed the idea of being put on a pedestal like a lot of the townsfolk did with Dr. Thornton.

"Sure, Dr. Lexie." The way Cicily said *Dr. Lexie* struck the young physician as odd. She was usually called Lexie or Dr. Draden since her arrival in Baxley. In fact, today was the first time she was called Dr. Lexie. It was Zak who had used the term. He made it sound sweet, like a term of endearment. Now, when Cicily said it, it seemed a little condescending, even mean-spirited. Maybe she was just imagining it; after all, Cicily tended to speak with a corrosive tone.

Realizing Cicily was still waiting to hear her order, she stammered out, "I'll... have a... vanilla latte, please."

Lexie hung around the counter, while Cicily was making the latte. When the latte was finished, Cicily was slow to hand it over. "Be careful, Dr. Lexie. You don't want to get burned," she cautioned. Her words were drawn out and intense, leaving Lexie to wonder if the woman was referring to the hot coffee.

Lexie offered a hesitant thanks as she walked away.

It was ten minutes past the hour when Lexie got back to the clinic. She handed the latte to Margo and before Margo could ask how her lunch was, Mrs. Whitney walked through the door. The appointment took longer than anticipated. The people of Baxley loved to tell stories and telling them to a new arrival, such as Lexie, was pure delight.

The chart Lexie held in her hand described her patient as a seventy-five-year-old woman suffering from arthritis. Amelia Whitney, however, was more than joint pain and stiffness, and was determined to ensure the doctor knew this. The white-haired woman eagerly shared her personal history, drifting into conversation about how she ended up in Baxley.

"Came here over fifty-five years ago with my husband, Mr. Joseph Edison Whitney. A fine man. Handsome as hell, too. He was a third-generation Presbyterian minister from a nearby community."

Lexie nodded as Amelia relayed the story of Joseph Whitney, a man of humble means. He had met and fallen in love with young Amelia, the only daughter of a wealthy district court judge from Massachusetts. When they'd wed, Mr. Whitney had brought his young bride back to Illinois, deciding to settle in picturesque Baxley. Unfortunately, their ideal life hadn't last long as the Reverend drowned in a boating accident. Amelia had only been in her early thirties.

"When Joseph passed, my family begged me to return to Massachusetts. My mother had plans to introduce me back into high society, rich people who wasted money and didn't know the value of a dollar. My mother even had some widowed doctor lined up to court me. Now don't get me wrong, dear, I have nothing against doctors. But I had experienced the love of my life with Joseph. I knew no other man would compare. Joseph had been my heart and Baxley my home. Mother was none too pleased with me staying here, but Father understood."

And understood he did, leaving a sizable inheritance to Amelia. She continued to live by humble means as a way to honor her deceased husband, and invested wisely with the monies from her inheritance. Admittedly she was wealthy, but accumulating more and more money held no appeal, so she set up a variety of trust funds, donating generously to a variety causes, including several local ones.

Amelia had made an appointment so she could get a revision to her existing prescription. It would have taken less than five minutes for Lexie to review and scribble a new dosage, but conversation ensued which had nothing to do with the woman's health issues. Amelia spent a considerable amount of time chatting about fund raising for the Historical Society. By the end of the conversation, Lexie had handed over a check, donating a hundred dollars to help Baxley hold onto the past. It was ironic donating to save the past, when Lexie wished she could erase hers.

Chapter Four

Diverting from the usual drive, Zak headed out to the south part of Deer Creek, a shallow creek running past his property, with its true appeal miles away at this particular spot. Parking his vehicle at the crest of the hill overlooking the panoramic valley, he marvelled at the beauty before him. Sure, the tourists flocked to more picturesque views near Lands Crossing, but this one suited him. It was an expansive territory, with only a scattering of trees. There were no hidden areas, no confined spaces closing him in. The changing seasons would provide different colors, modifying the landscape, but overall it remained predictable. Maybe it would be too boring for some, but he preferred predictable. Predictable was safe.

Clambering out of his truck, he drew in a deep breath. Clean, fresh air. It was frosty but it didn't matter. The frigid air, no matter how cold it became, never squeezed his lungs as tight as city smog. Abby, who had exited the vehicle, stood awaiting his command. As soon as he gave it, she sprinted off, liberated from the confines of a long morning spent looking through a windshield. Although he never absorbed the freedom like Abby did, just standing on this spot settled him. He needed this feeling.

Driving back from the stop-over at Deer Creek, he noticed the rental car. It was a newer model subcompact parked, without occupants, at the entrance to his property. To the locals, a little car on the backroads in the dead of winter would have been most odd, but not to Zak. He was well-acquainted with a man whose calling card was diminutive cars. He still needed to be cautious, since the driver or occupants might not have come of their own free will. He reached into his truck's console, grabbing his Glock as he drove up to the house. Placing his right hand, with a firm grip on the pistol inside his jacket pocket, he slowly emerged from the vehicle. Abby followed obediently at his side, heading straight to the house, ignoring the fattened squirrel skittering by. Slowly, the front door creaked open as two individuals casually wandered out onto the porch. Zak's shoulders sank in relief – his former colleagues, Safia and Omeir. A quick hand signal released Abby from guard duty.

"*Salaam*," they greeted each other before heading into the house.

Omeir was the first to speak once they settled around the kitchen table. "Hope you don't mind we let ourselves in. It's a little too cold to stand outside and I didn't want to go slushing back to the car."

"No problem. You could have parked in the driveway."

"Safia has no faith in my driving abilities. She said I would get the car stuck if I came all the way up the driveway."

Safia shook her head, and now that Omeir had a reaction, he couldn't resist teasing her. "And being the gentleman I am, I gave in to the lady's wishes. I wouldn't want her to worry about getting out and having to push the car."

Zak knew full well Omeir would be the one pushing the car if it got stuck. He was always teasing Safia, and it was clear to Zak why. Omeir had seriously been crushing on their attractive female comrade since he'd first laid eyes on her.

"But at least we know I would be able to push the car out. You," she gave Omeir a quick glance, "we're not so sure of, and especially not in those shoes."

Zak looked down and took stock of Omeir's now-drenched canvas athletic shoes. Refocusing, he responded to Omeir's break-in apology.

He looked at the lock to see if there was any damage, but there was none. "Great work with the lock. I can't even notice any tampering with it."

"Well, that Safia's fine work," Omeir remarked. "You know she is the best." Safia smiled at Omeir for the compliment.

One of Safia's specialties was breaking into and out of places. Omeir was the technological expert and a deadly hacker. They had been a great team back in New York.

Safia was widely diverse in her skills. Besides being brilliant at getting into highly secured areas, she was also an expert in Krav Maga, the deadly Israeli martial art. She was not only extremely athletic and fit, she was also incredibly attractive, a trait which both Zak and Omeir had readily noticed when they first met her. A relationship with Safia was never a consideration for Zak. Intimacy would complicate what they were hired to do. However, Omeir couldn't help himself, and although it was possible Safia was aware of Omeir's infatuation with her, she kept him in the friend zone.

Zak knew their visit was more than just social. The routine phone calls were their way of checking up on him. Although he lied to them on occasion, he was able to fool them into believing he was better, and for the most part he was. He had a few relapses, but nothing he wasn't able to handle. But now they were here, and he knew what their visit meant. Their purpose was to convince him to return. He dreaded this conversation, but it was inevitable and frankly he was surprised it hadn't happened sooner. After serving them coffee, he decided to get a dialogue going about their visit.

"So I'm guessing you guys are here because you're fighting and need me to mediate, or maybe you've stopped tiffing and that scares you. It would scare me, too," he joked.

Safia let out a small laugh, which surprised both Zak and Omeir, especially since it was accompanied by some redness in her cheeks. After a slight pause, she recomposed herself.

"Zak, it's good to see you. But we didn't come out here just to have coffee. It's been quite some time, and we need you back. There's quite the situation happening in New York. It needs to be resolved."

Safia noticed his eyes widening. "It won't be like last time," she said, trying to reassure him. "We have different protocols now. We all learned from that terrible experience."

Zak pushed back from the table to stand. Peering down at them, he spoke. "I'm not ready. I know what affected me affected all of us, but I can't go back as though nothing happened." He was pleased he was able to keep his tone even. "Yes, I'm good at what I do, but I'm sure there are others just as good."

Omeir, who had been silent regarding the issue, got up and leaned against the kitchen sink across from where his friend stood. "Zak, you know there are only a handful of guys out there who can do what you do. Even if we could utilize one of them, it's unlikely they know the intricacies. Besides, the contacts made it clear they want to deal only with you. It would take anyone else at least six months to get the contacts to acknowledge them and another six months before a meeting gets set up. There's no time for that."

Grabbing a small envelope from her purse, Safia handed it over to Zak. "Think it over. Just don't take too long, Zak. We can only stall this for another month."

Reluctantly, he took the envelope, peering inside to where there was a flash drive.

"I'll review it, but I'm still having the nightmares. Even if I wanted to, I'm not sure if I could. I came here to start over. This isn't just some break for me." His voice had trembled this time, making both Safia and Omeir take notice. The confident Zak they knew was gone.

To ease the tension, Omeir awkwardly transitioned to an unrelated matter. "Hey, Zak, what size feet do you have?"

"Twelve, why?"

"Great, me, too."

"Are you asking me for shoes?"

"Yeah, and socks, too. I'm soaking in these."

"Fine, I'll give you boots. You'll need them to push that ridiculous car if it gets stuck. Why didn't you get an SUV, city slicker?"

"Told him to," Safia piped in.

"Yup, you'd think he'd listen. Same Omeir, isn't he?" They were now talking amongst themselves, ignoring Omeir as he swished about in his waterlogged shoes.

"I didn't realize the shoes came with a lecture?" Omeir said with a tinge of annoyance in his voice.

"They don't, buddy, but the socks sure do."

It was good to joke. He didn't miss New York, but he did miss his friends.

* * * *

After Safia and Omeir left, Zak sat at the kitchen table and stared at the flash drive. He wasn't astonished that the tiny piece of metal could contain such an abundance of information. No, what astonished him was how such a tiny object could so profoundly influence his life. He knew if it wasn't today, a day would come where he would have to look at what was on this flash drive. He used to believe undesirable tasks were like removing an adhesive bandage: do it quickly and immediately, so the pain wouldn't linger. But this was more like a sticky open wound, where flesh would rip open when the bandage was torn off. Running his hands over his head, he stuck the USB into his laptop.

Examining the documents on the flash drive made Zak ill. Envisioning what the future would be like if he didn't get involved led to nausea and pressure in his chest. It didn't matter if he closed his eyes or not, the images were there. It had burned into his mind and he couldn't undo it, no matter how hard he tried. It was happening to him, and like the many times before, he couldn't control it. Tiny beads of sweat formed on his forehead. Feeling the first drop trickling down, he instinctively got up and paced. He needed to get away, but it was futile, for anywhere he went, the sensations would follow him. Collapsing back onto the kitchen chair in defeat, he felt the nudge. Abby had trotted over, pushing her nose against his thigh. He leaned down, unwittingly petting the dog. After several minutes, the pounding in his chest slowed down and his breathing became less erratic.

There was no cure, the doctors in New York had told him, but he was grateful to have Abby at his side. It wasn't immediate, and it didn't always work, but the canine's presence usually lessened the symptoms. A full-blown panic attack had been prevented, all because Abby connected with Zak in a way most people weren't able to.

Hunching his shoulders forward, he glanced back at the illustration on the laptop screen. He knew exactly what he was looking at. He felt it with stinging clarity, but for some bizarre reason he needed to see it again. Fight or flight sensations started radiating through him. But no matter how disturbing it was, he kept going back to the same question. Could he really forget what he had seen and abandon his colleagues? Safia and Omeir had known when they gave him the flash drive that flight would not be an easy option for him, or at least they were counting on it.

He continued stroking Abby, turning to look into her dark eyes. She didn't have the answer to his dilemma, but she was urging him to do something. He wasn't ready to run from the situation, but at least he could go for a run. Head out onto the back roads in an effort to clear his head. Hiding the flash drive with the other items in the floorboards under his bed, he quickly changed into his running gear and reached for his shoulder holster and gun. He was used to running armed during training, and although he preferred not to, it was necessary given how vulnerable he was should he be tracked. The contact's desire to deal with him, and only him, provided some reassurance. After all, if they wanted to strike a deal with him, they probably weren't interested in killing him, or not yet anyway.

Chapter Five

Lexie hadn't slept through the night. She had awoken from a bad dream just after one in the morning and had been unable to get back to sleep. She hated that it happened; she couldn't even remember any details, other than seeing Hailie's lifeless body.

She wanted the contempt she had for herself for failing Hailie to vanish, but it wasn't that simple. The most she could hope for was to occupy her time better. If she kept busy, maybe she would think less of what had happened and the dreams would go away.

Volunteering with the Historical Society in Baxley might be the distraction she needed. It may not be anything exciting, but perhaps she could use her researching skills. As a surgeon, she spent a lot of time researching newly approved medications and procedures. She wanted to ease into the community and she figured assisting with research wouldn't require her to interact with too many people. She saw it as a nice manageable transition.

After going through her usual routine of stopping by Colton's for coffee, she headed to the clinic, where Margo had the place smelling antiseptically clean.

"Morning, Margo." Lexie's voice was almost cherry.

"Morning, Dr. Draden. Looks like you might have some special cream in that coffee you're carrying."

She laughed, knowing that she was perky as a girl scout selling cookies. "Well, I can assure you it's just a medium roasted Arabica coffee. I got to thinking about something you said yesterday."

"And what was that, my dear?"

"About developing new habits."

"Hmm... so what new habit will you be picking up?"

"I thought I would call Mrs. Whitney and see if she could use a new volunteer with the Historical Society."

"Well, I guess it's a start."

The disappointment in Margo's voice made Lexie feel like her girl scout cookies had melted. It now dawned on her that Margo was probably looking for something a bit more drastic than volunteering with a bunch of elderly women in preserving old buildings. But Lexie didn't do crazy and impulsive… well, other than moving to Baxley.

Before she could rethink her choice, Margo handed her a yellow sticky note. "Here's Amelia's phone number. You should call her right away."

The call to Amelia Whitney caused confusion and panic in the elderly lady. To Amelia, a doctor calling first thing in the morning meant bad news. So she was relieved to hear it wasn't her health that prompted the call, and then almost giddy to hear the young doctor wanted to help the Historical Society.

"I know exactly where you can start," she told Lexie.

* * * *

The nice thing about working from home is setting your own schedule – and of course, no obnoxious co-workers. Zak had never worked a nine-to-five job. The closest he'd come to a structured life would have been the years he spent as an undergrad, studying in Paris. Even when he was working on his doctorate, back in the United States, he worked erratic hours. Since coming to Baxley, he kept an irregular schedule. It wasn't necessary; rather, it was habit. Besides, he didn't have a social life, so weekends held no meaning. In fact, he usually forgot when the weekend rolled around. However, today his phone vibrated with a reminder it was Saturday, the last Saturday of the month. The day Baxley held their indoor winter market.

Although he preferred solitude, Zak made an effort to attend the market. It was a chance to buy fresh food and casually mingle with others. It provided a safe way to engage. To eradicate being viewed as a nefarious loner. He would spend time talking to the older men as they congregated near the vendors selling freshly brewed coffee. They were generally a friendly group. Many were challenged by the ever-changing technological world. By using just basic skills, Zak assisted them with their mobile devices, and smart TVs. His willingness to help popularized him amongst the men of Baxley, or rather with the older men. Elderly women were also appreciative of his assistance in navigating social media to share recipes and keep up with their grandchildren's lives.

Then there were the younger women, near in age to him. Ones who obviously took a liking to him, but not for his techie skills, and who required careful handling. Encouraging this group would only cause problems with the testosterone-charged younger men in Baxley. For a man wanting to be left alone, problems of this kind were not only counter-productive, they were also dangerous. Zak knew that physical altercations over some guy's girl would result in him, the brown-skinned outsider, being the villain. It was enough knowing trouble might one day show up without courting it. So he smiled at the ladies when they smiled at him, but ensured he also let them know he was in a hurry when they tried to chat him up. "Gotta get back to work. Have a deadline due today," he'd tell them.

Becoming friends with anyone in Baxley would only risk people knowing too much about him. Zak was friendly, but not one's friend. Social detachment had been his life for many years. Any prior friends he had from college were dropped after his recruitment. It was part of the deal. He had no choice but to agree to this condition. His only friends now were Safia and Omeir, and although he explicitly trusted them, what they wanted worried him.

Just out of the shower, he grabbed a pair of worn jeans along with a long sleeved thermal shirt from the closet. He always strived to get to the market early, even if he had to wait for the doors to open. The fresh produce selection was best and crowds sparse during the early hours. He had a problem with crowds, and although Baxley and the surrounding rural area weren't populous, the idea of too many people in a cramped area made him nervous.

Browsing the market on Saturday morning was a way of leading a normal life. He needed a semblance of normalcy to his life, even though it was a life of lies. So today, he would savor the coffee and perhaps even the conversations with the locals. The people of Baxley were generally honest and hard-working individuals. Sure, there were a few who were narrow-minded and xenophobic, but Zak had dealt with people like that before. Most of them weren't essentially bad, they just looked at the world with a narrow view, didn't see beyond their own fears.

It was just before nine when Zak pulled into the parking lot adjacent to the market. The event was in the town's sports arena and the doors were opening. As he stepped inside the arena, the aroma of freshly baked goods gave him comfort. The blend of apple pies, cinnamon buns, and oatmeal cookies permeated the air. The simple culinary bouquet was soothing to the senses, providing him with a sense of peacefulness no therapy ever had.

Zak, who was both hungry and in need of a good cup of coffee, headed straight to the Colton's booth. The town's diner shut down on the last Saturday of the month, so it could participate in the winter market. It was a great way to showcase any test recipes as well as make a few dollars at the popular event.

Unfortunately, Cicily was operating the booth. She saw him approaching and instinctively her brows crinkled as a scowl crept over her face. He was aware that her dislike of him centered on her ill-conceived notion that he was a dark-skinned foreigner, and thus a natural enemy of her deceased son, who had died serving in Iraq. This was ridiculous in so many ways. Zak was an American, born in the United States. And even if he wasn't, why should it matter? How could this woman have such bitterness for a person she didn't even know? But as he wondered this, he realized that he had contempt for himself. It wasn't for the person he was born as, but rather for who he had become – a liar, with the blood of others on his hands.

As usual, he greeted Cicily pleasantly. After all, there was no point in poking the angry bear.

"Morning, Cicily. Glad to see the Colton's booth here." It wasn't a lie since he was glad to see the booth, just not Mrs. McCranky.

"What'll it be?"

"Large coffee, please. What do you have for muffins today?"

She pointed to the handwritten chalk menu off to the side, and because he wasn't fast enough for her liking, she said, "Raspberry, oat bran, poppy seed."

A few other customers had lined up behind him, so she was careful not to be overtly rude, however her impatient tone communicated her intent. He hastily decided on raspberry. Handing over a five-dollar bill, he gladly forfeited the two-dollar change in order to break away from her.

* * * *

Lexie was somewhat disheartened to find out that Amelia didn't need a historical researcher rather she wanted someone to man the booth at Baxley's indoor market. Amelia had intended to do it, but her godchild recently had a baby who was getting baptized in Springfield this weekend. Amelia had convinced Lexie that manning the booth would be both fun and easy.

"It's only for the morning and you'll get to meet the nice townsfolk," she had told Lexie.

Amelia had persuaded Harry Stitsman, with a jar of her rose petal jelly, to take the afternoon shift. Harry was a long-time Historical Society member, who would do almost anything for Amelia. Bestowing him with the jam let them both pretend he was motivated by food alone.

Amelia believed Lexie's status as the town's doctor would help in collecting donations and selling raffle tickets at the booth. "If it worked for Dr. Thornton, it will certainly work even better for you my dear," she said. "I know the men around here, and they can't say no to a pretty face."

Lexie doubted this, but she had nothing planned for Saturday. Besides, she had vowed to get more actively involved in her new life. Even if that life was in a small town where she wasn't sure she fit in.

Given her nature, Lexie arrived early. Taking a mere five minutes to set up the booth, she picked up one of the pamphlets on the Historical

Society of Baxley. Reading this took even less time. The smell of the freshly baked pastries and breads near the entrance, had begun to lure people in from the cold.

As she was getting ready to settle into a boring morning, an elderly lady came hurrying up to the vacant booth beside her. Lexie had to look twice, for the short round woman was carrying something peculiar. Yep, it was indeed a dead owl. Well, it wasn't exactly roadkill, more like some taxidermy display, but it was definitely bizarre, an idiosyncrasy that Lexie was unlikely to encounter living in Chicago.

Seeing the frizzy white-haired lady struggling with a purse, a large cardboard box, and the dead critter, Lexie set down the pamphlet.

"Here, let me give you a hand," she offered. Before she knew it, she was holding the dead owl.

"Oh, dear, please be careful with the *Asio flammeus*. Unfortunately, its head isn't sturdy," the woman said.

Ass e oh what? It kind of sounded a little obscene, but Lexie didn't ask while she was intent on setting the stuffed bird on the bare table. She wondered how she could destroy an already dead animal, but wasn't about to find out. She heaved a sigh of relief as she set it down, still intact.

"*Asio flammeus* is the scientific term," the peculiar lady said, as if reading Lexie's mind. "Most people just know it as the short-eared owl."

Or just an owl.

"I'm Willow Defaux, Chair of the Bird Watching Society of Baxley."

"Lexie Draden. I'm helping out with the Historical Society today."

"Ah yes, Amelia's group. Right, she had the baptism this weekend. Too bad. I really wanted to finish telling her what I found out about the northern cardinals in the area."

And before Lexie could say anything more, she was hearing all about the mating habits of the northern cardinal, more information than she really cared to know. But mundane details were part of small-town living, and fifteen minutes later, Lexie was weirdly drawn to Willow's enthusiasm. Willow was so involved in telling her about the local birds, she didn't get around to questioning Lexie about what had brought her to Baxley. For this she was grateful. Hearing non-stop about a species of birds was a small sacrifice for her own privacy.

In addition to handing out pamphlets to any interested citizens, Lexie's only other task was to sell raffle tickets and accept donations. The raffle tickets were for a quilt that she had draped across the table. The quilt was an intricate design in the tasteful combination of light blue and ivory, something you would see in a *Cottage Lifestyle Magazine*. Lexie was unfamiliar with the quilting world, but it was obvious that hours went into the making of this beauty. For the Historical Society's sake, she hoped she would be able to sell a fair amount of raffle tickets. Amelia had told her Mrs. Hannah Woodgrave had made the quilt. Hannah held a drop-in quilting bee for the local quilters. According to Amelia, more gossiping than quilting occurred at these gatherings.

Willow had now transitioned to chickadees, and Lexie, for no logical reason, was intrigued to find out chickadees were infamous for killing bats. A scattering of the market crowd was slowly making their way toward their booths, shifting Willow's focus to rearranging the dead owl. How Willow thought she could make it look more appealing baffled Lexie, but she had to admit Willow had a way of making bird watching exciting. Maybe not as exciting as climbing Mount Everest, or swimming in shark infested waters, but definitely more fun than joining a quilting bee.

Fifteen minutes after the doors first opened, she had a visitor to the booth. Not surprisingly, it was an elderly lady. Lexie was beginning to think that Baxley was the Florida of the North. The woman introduced herself as Bernice and eagerly shared that she was a member in fine standing with the local quilting bee.

Fine standing? So exactly what would one have to do within the quilting bee not to be in fine standing? Make your squares the wrong size, choose the wrong color, or God forbid use hundred percent polyester when cotton was required?

Lexie would probably never know. After the copious amounts of birding information she received earlier, she wasn't ready to plunge into the quilting-bee world.

Picking up one of the ends of the quilt, Bernice moved it toward her face. The end corners of her mouth turned downward as she peered down her nose. "Well, this is different," she snarked. "Who crafted it?"

"Hannah Woodgrave was kind enough to donate the lovely piece."

Bernice muttered. Her words were unclear, but her tone was indignant. Lexie deduced quilting was as competitive as gymnastics at the Olympics. Bernice wasn't interested in donating to the society, or in buying a raffle ticket. She probably would view it as a grave travesty to win a competitor's quilt. Slowly, Bernice wandered over to Willow's dead owl where she appeared to be just as terse.

Thankfully, the next half hour brought generous locals. Mainly they bought raffle tickets, with a few donating small sums of money. A man in his late thirties, with pressed jeans and a starchy collared shirt, was interested in making a larger donation. He seemed to enjoy opening his wallet, happy to display his wads of cash to Lexie, as he handed over a crisp hundred-dollar bill. He introduced himself as Tom Harring, owner of Harring's Service Station off Elm Street. He wasn't a bad-looking man, with dark blond hair and piercing blue eyes, but his air of arrogance distracted from his looks. He leaned in too close as he offered his oil change services at a discount rate. When he leaned back, he shifted his gaze downward, making Lexie uncomfortable and annoyed. Averting his attention away from her breasts, she handed him a pamphlet, relieved when he finally moved along.

An influx of more elderly people came by, but this time they were older men. Casually chatting, they purchased raffle tickets as their wives inspected the jams and baked goods near the entrance. For the most part, they were polite, even if they harmlessly tried to flirt with Lexie like Amelia had predicted. Not one of them stared at her the way Tom Harring had.

When there was a lull in the crowds, Willow eagerly shared more bird facts. The hummingbird and its eating habits became the new focal point. Lexie didn't dislike birds; however, it was not something she knew much about. Besides, Willow was talking non-stop, leaving Lexie with little chance to respond, other than a quick nod.

Through her peripheral vision, Lexie could see someone approaching the booth. Time to attend to raffle business, leaving the suspense of the ruby-throated hummingbird for later. Turning away from Willow, she was delighted to see it was Zak, the undeniably handsome man she had torched. Well, perhaps torched was too strong of a word. It had been more of a first-degree burn to the hand, and hardly the mark she wanted to leave on the man. As he approached her table, she tried to busy her hands by straightening pamphlets. When she looked up, she noticed the warmth in his chocolate-brown eyes and his dazzling smile. A smile that made her both nervous and excited.

"Hello, Dr. Lexie." Again, with a formality which wasn't a formality and sounded oh so nice.

She noticed he had two cloth shopping bags in his large, strong hands. Those hands she'd had the pleasure of holding only a few days earlier. It wasn't how she actually wanted to hold hands with him; however, her innate clumsiness did have its benefits.

"Oh, hi, Zak. How's the shopping going?"

"Good, they have some great items here. Did you get a chance to visit the other booths?"

"No, not yet, but I'm only here till noon. I'll take a look around then. Anything you would recommend?"

"Fresh multi-grain bread and great raspberry jam. Both are at the booths near the entrance. The homemade cappuccino ice cream is my primary reason for getting here early. It tends to sell out quickly. The fresh lamb is great if you like a lean meat. If lamb isn't your thing, then there's this booth selling precooked vegan dishes. Some great choices there."

"Um, lamb sounds interesting," Lexie replied.

"As a kid, I often had lamb. My mother made some great lamb dishes, which I've tried to copy with some success."

"I've never cooked lamb myself. I've eaten it and liked it, just not sure how to cook it."

"Well, how about I cook you some and bring it by the clinic this week?"

Lexie felt embarrassed; she wasn't hinting at him making her lamb. At least he didn't tell her to come by his place tonight for a luscious leg of lamb. That would have been more the style of that guy Tom Harring, owner of Baxley's service station. He was more than eager to take a look under her hood.

"That's kind of you to offer." And before she could stop herself, she heard herself say, "I would like that."

Before leaving the booth, Zak bought twenty dollars' worth of raffle tickets for a quilt Lexie was sure he didn't care to win. However, it did get her thinking about what his bedroom linens looked like. A thought she found hard to get out of her head.

* * * *

When Lexie gave Zak a pen to print his name on the raffle tickets, her hand brushed his. It was a quick touch, but he was struck by how smooth her hand was, like a cross between luxurious silk and the warmth of velvet. It hadn't been the first time he'd felt her touch, but there was no scorching coffee in the mix this time. He savored the moment, even though it was all too brief. Her constant smile not only ignited him, but it gave him hope. Hope that she was as interested in him, as he was in her.

Snap out of it! She's doing volunteer work. Giving back to her community – being polite because you bought some raffle tickets.

He tried to scold himself for reading more into it, but he had great instincts and those instincts were telling him the attraction wasn't just one-sided. It wasn't the smoothest of conversations. It was mainly about cooking a young sheep. Most women would find it weird, but he could tell Dr. Lexie wasn't like most women. Besides, conversing about food ended well. He now had another opportunity to see her. It wasn't a date, but that was okay. He shouldn't be dating. He had other priorities and didn't need distractions. However, he had inadvertently set up getting together with her again. Now he would have to cook a lamb dish and bring it to her place of work. Yes, it was a strange way to continue to see an attractive woman, but he had never planned to start anything with her and now he was uncharacteristically fumbling.

He liked her. What was there not to like? She was beautiful and intelligent. Her profession as a doctor probably led some to believe she was a caregiver. Zak didn't know her well enough to confirm this, but he could tell there was so much more to her than the label. It would be easy to obtain more information. But once he had actually met Lexie, the only additional information he would obtain was what she wanted to give him. He'd actually destroyed the Dr. Draden folder. The only reason he'd had any info on her was to protect himself. He needed to ensure no one moving into the area was searching for him. Gathering intelligence on Lexie, like the other newcomers, was the only way to do that.

* * * *

Lexie awoke on Monday morning eager to get back to work. Mondays tended to be a bit busier than other days of the week. Concerned parents with active children, who had incurred minor injuries over the weekend, would show up along with the regular scheduled patients. Lexie liked the hustling of a busy day. It was a nice contrast to the all-too quiet times. However, work wasn't for at least an hour, and this morning she was meeting with Amelia Whitney. Mrs. Whitney had invited her for an early breakfast at Colton's. Lexie readily accepted, she was looking forward to telling her about the sold-out raffle tickets.

Only a couple of tables were occupied when she arrived at the diner, however, a small line had formed at the counter. Emily was busy filling the takeout orders, while Doreen, a middle-aged woman and full-time Colton's employee, was seating customers. Lexie could see the shadow of Cicily in the kitchen. By now, she was used to the routine at Colton's. Soon Cicily would finish up in the kitchen and transition to serving customers alongside Doreen, while Emily hurried off to school. It was a well-established small business. There was no doubt the success was due to Cicily's incredible baking, and simple yet delicious culinary creations. What Cicily lacked in customer service, Emily and Doreen more than made up for.

Lexie was glancing around the café when she heard her name being called. It was Amelia Whitney, seated in a booth opposite the entrance. Lexie waved to Mrs. Whitney as she walked over to the booth.

"Morning, Mrs. Whitney. Hope you had a good time at the baptism."

Mrs. Whitney leapt up and gave her a big hug, catching her off guard.

"I can't thank you enough," she squealed.

Jolted by the embrace, it slowly registered with Lexie that the woman had already heard about the raffle sales. "Well, the beautiful quilt Mrs. Woodgrave made was certainly desired."

"My dear, from what I heard from Willow Defaux, the object of desire was the lady selling the raffle tickets."

Lexie blushed as she sat down. "I'm just glad it turned out so well. I must admit I was a bit hesitant when you asked me, but I enjoyed it. If you need help with the Historical Society again, just let me know."

"Well, I'm glad to hear. I was afraid Willow might have scared you away with her bird stories. I'm a birder myself, so I appreciate Willow and the wealth of information she has, but I know she can be a bit much. And dear, you must stop calling me Mrs. Whitney; that's my mother-in-law who's been in the ground for thirty years. It's Amelia to my friends."

She smiled and nodded.

"Another coffee, Dr. Lexie?" It was Cicily carrying the carafe of coffee. Her voice was pleasant and courteous this time.

"Please." She lifted her empty cup for Cicily to fill.

"I hope you enjoyed the market the other day," Cicily said.

"Yes, it was great, and it gave me a chance to meet some nice people."

"Yes, *the locals* are so nice." Oddly, it seemed Cicily had stressed the word *locals*. Before Lexie could respond, Cicily continued, "I noticed Tom Harring stopped by your booth. He's such a lovely man. A very *honest, single* man who would be a very good catch for some lucky lady." This time she was certain Cicily had over-emphasized both *honest* and *single*.

Amelia quickly piped in, "Well, I'm sure there's quite a few decent single men living in the area, whether they've been here forever or whether they came from somewhere else."

"Depends on where you came from," Cicily quipped back. "Not everyone belongs."

Amelia ignored Cicily when she continued to speak. "As you know, I'm really not a local. I came from Boston. Of course, that was a lifetime ago, but I remember how Baxley and the dear townsfolk embraced me. People were amazing back then. All they cared about was that you were a good person, didn't matter where you were from." Amelia gave Cicily a forced smile.

Cicily finished pouring the coffee and promptly left. It annoyed Lexie that Cicily was trying to push that sleazoid Tom Harring on her, but what disturbed her even more was Cicily's blatant loathing of Zak. She had seen bigotry amongst her colleagues in Chicago, but usually it dissipated once people got to know each other. To her understanding, he had been in the community for two years now. She had witnessed him being polite to others, never seeing him be contentious. Her own interactions with Zak had been positive. Yeah, the first encounter may not have been great, but he had helped her, and apologized profusely for scaring her. He seemed to be a decent man. Sure, there was something elusive about him, but the same could be said about her.

* * * *

The cerebral pressure was starting to build, but Zak continued to ignore it. It would eventually develop into a full-blown headache caused by anxiety and fatigue, but there was little he could do to prevent it. He needed to finish reviewing all the documents Safia and Omeir had delivered to him. Time was running out. He needed to make a decision.

It had always been his way to ensure he looked at all options. He was strategic by nature, and the training he received only enhanced this. It was clear the situation was getting dangerous again and he had to do something. Safia and Omeir were good at what they did; after all, they were trained by some of the best. They knew Zak's participation was crucial and therefore made their visit. They were pressuring him, and although he wanted to be angry about it, he knew he would do the same if the situation was reversed. *Damn, they were right.*

His time hiding would come to an end. He would re-emerge into the dark and desolate world he despised. His physical wounds had healed. That alone was considered just short of a miracle. However, the visual images and the screams of dying men still haunted him. The images shattering his life would never go away completely. The best he could hope for was to experience moments of joy. But those were always fleeting.

A few hours later, and with his head now throbbing, he could feel the anxiety starting to build. The impending panic attack would not shock him. He felt it coming when he pushed himself to continue reviewing the documents, and even though he'd predicted what would happen, it didn't make it any less alarming.

He knew what would occur before it happened. Abby would be at his side. When she first trotted over, she went unnoticed. Zak was too lost in the whirlwind of emotions to react. Eventually, thanks to Abby's persistent nudging, he had no choice but to reach out. When a hundred-pound canine tries to become a lap dog, it's impossible to ignore.

He gently pushed her front paws off his lap while he scratched her behind the ears, "Hey, I'll be fine girl."

He wasn't convincing Abby, he didn't even believe the words himself. She refused to leave his side and finally, he got up and did what he normally did in this situation. He got changed, taking Abby with him for a long run.

Although it was a winter day, and the temperatures were still quite frigid, both Zak and Abby were accustomed to the frosty air. When he felt anxious, any sort of distraction, even the bitter cold wind could help. He started running on the pavement, turning onto a gravel road fifteen minutes later. The roads had recently been plowed, making it easier for him and Abby to stay dry, unlike his last run. A Komondor coat, when long, would easily mat and stay wet for hours. To minimize the wet-mop look, he kept Abby's coat trimmed. She would still get soaked from the snow and slush, but at least she wouldn't be a cluster of mud.

He ran for half an hour before the edginess dissipated. He continued for another ten minutes before turning around and heading back. Returning to the treed property where his house sat, Zak noticed a mid-size silver SUV parked in the gravel driveway. The vehicle seemed somewhat familiar, but he couldn't place it. Besides, a silver SUV was as common as an elm tree. When he reached the vehicle, he looked inside. It was clean and empty. No used coffee cup, no loose change, not even a layer of dust on the console. It was totally immaculate. Any urge to open the driver's door vanished. The vehicle might be rigged. Paranoia? Perhaps, but paranoia had saved his life a few times. Knowing Abby's instinct to bark and call attention to the potential intruder, he signaled for the dog to be quiet. With her quietly by his side, he crept toward the front porch. Reaching the steps, he noticed the front door ajar. Whoever the intruder was, they had gone into his house. A house he had locked. Zak reached for his Glock from the shoulder holster he had under his running jacket. He carefully motioned for Abby to stay by the front steps as he quietly pushed open the door. Slowly, and softly as a man his size could manage, he walked forward, careful not to make the floorboards creak. Rounding the corner of the hallway, he saw the silhouette in the dimly lit kitchen. He steadily drew the pistol upward, aiming it at the back of the intruder.

"Don't move. I've got no problem fracturing your skull with a bullet," he said, his voice as steady as steel.

Moving closer, he noticed the intruder, who was now trembling, stood less than five feet tall. The notion that it was some local teen, trying to steal his laptop for drug money, jumped into his mind. Some stupid pubescent kid who had no idea who Zak was, and what he was capable of.

Slowly the intruder spoke.

"Please don't, I'm... I'm so sorry. Please don't shoot me." And then the uncontrollable sobs followed.

He knew that voice, although he had never heard her so vulnerable. It was the receptionist from the medical clinic in Baxley, the lady from whom he bought his house. *Why the hell had she broken into his home?*

"Margo? What are you doing?" His voice was gruff, but calm.

"I... I..." She trembled with fear, unable to release any more words.

"How did you get into my house? What are you doing here?" His questions demanding, yet his composure appeared unruffled.

"I... I dropped by to give you a spare set of keys I found when cleaning out my basement, and..." Her voice shook uncontrollably.

"And then what? You decided to use the key and snoop around?" This time he sounded annoyed.

"No, it wasn't like that. I... I got cold and came inside to wait." She continued to gasp as her tiny body shook frantically.

"Wait? Wait for what?"

"I'm waiting for Dan."

The woman was so flustered she wasn't making any sense. Aiming a gun at her only made her more rattled.

Maybe she wasn't a threat, and this was all some bizarre mistake. He dropped the gun down by his side and moved around to face Margo. He saw the tears streaming down her face – the utter fear in her eyes. Pulling back one of the wooden kitchen chairs, he slowly motioned for her to sit down. She hesitated before easing herself down into the chair. Grabbing another chair, he sat down next to her.

"Look, I'm just trying to understand. Who's Dan, and why are you waiting for him to come to my house?" He dropped the harsh tone, though he was far from letting his guard down.

No longer looking down the barrel of a gun, Margo was able to control the sobbing. Letting out the breath she had been holding in, she responded, "Dan Sebastien from Harring's Service Station. He's coming to tow my vehicle." She glanced at the gun being held by Zak's side, and then continued, "I dropped by to give you a spare key I found. I forgot I even had it until I was cleaning out my basement on the weekend. Since you weren't home, I decided to leave and call you later about the key. When I went to start my vehicle, it wouldn't turn over. I called Harring's and they said Dan was out by Johnson's Creek and wouldn't get here for a couple of hours. I stayed in my SUV for a bit, but it was getting too cold. My toes and hands were getting numb. So I used the key to get inside your place. I figured I'd keep warm until Dan arrived. I just didn't know what to do. Most of the folks around here would be fine with me waiting inside their home. I swear I wasn't going to steal anything."

He certainly wasn't concerned about Margo being a thief. He could read people well, and he could tell the woman was genuinely sorry about entering his home. Margo, like most people from Baxley, was unaccustomed to having a gun pointed at her. As she looked down at the kitchen table, Zak followed her eyes. A piece of paper rested on the table. He squinted as he read the handwritten note.

Hi Zak,

I found a spare key for your place when I was cleaning out my basement. When I came to drop it off, my vehicle broke down. Hope you don't mind, I used the key to get out of the cold while I waited for the tow truck.

Margo

After reading the note, he knew she was telling the truth. Shame clouded over him. This was, after all, an older woman, probably in her sixties. She was terrified, fearing for her life because of him.

Due to the unbearable regret gnawing at his gut, he briefly attempted to rationalize that he hadn't had a choice. After all, he didn't know it was her, or what the intruder's motive was. But when he thought of the situation from her perspective, he knew culpability was his.

Finally accepting the blame, he transitioned to mentally kicking himself for not changing the locks when he bought the place. It would have prevented this from happening. But he also realized it might have resulted in poor Margo being found frostbitten in his driveway. That was certainly not something he would have wanted either.

The oppressive silence permeated the air, neither wanting to speak, Margo trying to quell her nerves and Zak still processing what he had done to the poor woman.

Zak spoke, "I'm so sorry, Margo. I didn't mean to scare you. I would never harm you. I just saw someone who had gotten into my locked home." He reached out, taking her hand to console her. When she didn't pull away, he wondered if she actually believed his sincerity or if she was afraid to unsettle him further.

Margo tilted her head upward, giving him an intense glare.

"Zak, who are you?"

"What do you mean?" he asked apprehensively as he removed his hand from hers.

"I may be a little old lady from a small hick town, but I know something isn't right. You were amazingly calm, like some sort of professional. If you were just a homeowner who came upon an intruder, you would have been different. You would have reacted different."

He was going to make some light-hearted joke about watching too many mystery shows, but she arched her brow and glanced at the weapon. "I'm not a gun expert, but your gun, the way you handled it, it says something. So, Zak, who exactly are you?"

Zak knew she had him. If he didn't tell her something, she would go to someone else about him, someone like Sheriff McQuay. That's the last thing he wanted. He was taking a risk, the biggest risk he had taken in a while, but there was no other choice. He had to tell her the truth.

"My name is Zak, it's short for Zakariya. But my last name isn't Tifour, it's Ahmadi. I'm going to show you something, and I hope I can trust you not to share this with anyone."

He left the kitchen, praying she wouldn't run off in fear. The idea of chasing her down, triggering a heart attack in the poor woman, flashed in his mind. When he returned a few moments later, he was relieved to find her still at his kitchen table. He handed her a small leather folder. Cautiously, Margo open the folder and saw the official looking badge and photo of Zak. It was a badge from the New York City Police Department.

"You're a police officer?" she asked. She appeared both confused and relieved. He imagined she was thankful he wasn't some crazed killer.

"I don't understand. If you're on the right side of the law, then why the secrecy and the alias?"

"It's not as simple as being a big city cop. I'm a detective with the Counterterrorism Bureau of the NYPD."

And knowing there was no other way, Zak explained what he did. It was no surprise to him Margo didn't even know about NYPD's Counterterrorism Bureau. The Bureau had been created in 2002 after the terrorist attacks of 9/11. He was never surprised at the number of people who, like Margo, didn't realize the Bureau existed. When most people thought about counter surveillance, they thought about the CIA, the FBI, or the Office of Homeland Security. The NYPD was always open about the hundreds of men and women with the Counterterrorism Bureau, working in conjunction with national and international organizations, to make the world safer. Although well-known to the media and New Yorkers, it didn't necessarily translate into the average citizen paying attention to the agency. As long as people felt safe from terrorism in their own communities, they often didn't pay attention to what was going on elsewhere. He gathered there were only a minority of people in Baxley who spent any amount of time thinking about terrorism. Unfortunately, those people were more likely to see him as a terrorist than the man who protected them.

Zak revealed to Margo more than he had told anyone, other than fellow colleagues. He disclosed being recruited out of college, initially hired to work as a civilian in translations. Eventually, this grew to surveillance work, and a couple of years later he ended up being an NYPD member, rising to the rank of detective. It was a career involving undercover assignments. Demanding work, requiring him to lead a double life. Work where he had to go undercover as a supporter of extreme Islamic ideology, or what was more accurate, un-Islamic ideology. He despised the terrorists and their supporters; however, his job was to be amongst them. And to do it well and survive, he had to integrate into their world. He had no family ties, so disappearing for months at a time was relatively easy.

Without going into details on the particulars of his assignment in New York, he recounted to Margo how his team was making serious gains.

"We were looking to wrap up this six-month operation. I was looking forward to a short break, a chance to relax and maybe take a quick vacation. But then it all started to unravel when the terrorists found out they were under surveillance."

How the operation fell apart was not something he would divulge, and frankly, she didn't need to know. It had been over two years ago, just before Thanksgiving, when the covert operation had been detected by Al-Qaeda. The NYPD eventually discovered the nephew of a senior officer had given the terrorists information, leading to the exposure of the operation. The nephew had an expensive drug habit, and in exchange for drugs, he'd handed over stolen documents to Al-Qaeda operatives. While in custody, the nephew had died – an apparent overdose. His uncle, the senior official, had ended up under investigation for improperly storing protected documents, and ultimately resigned.

"When it all came apart, I was deep inside, working alongside the terrorists. They trusted me, but when they got a hold of the information, things started to unravel. Their paranoia set in and they weren't sure what side I was on. They held me captive as they tried to figure out whether or not I was one of them."

Three days of being held captive. Endless hours of being subjected to various methods of torture. He left the horrifying details out. He'd divulged very little to the NYPD psychologist about what he had endured, and certainly would never disclose the grisly details to the kind-hearted older lady sitting in front of him.

Miraculously, he had the stamina to survive the cruelty inflicted on him and continued to conceal his identity from the terrorists. By the third day, he was beginning to convince his captors, through his tortured body, that they were wrong about him.

"Eventually my captors started to believe that perhaps I was on their side, that maybe I wanted to destroy as many American lives as they did. While they were sorting out my fate, my colleagues were working on tracking me down."

He paused in an attempt to prevent the visual images of that horrific day from engulfing him. He sought to continue but he had to detach himself to get through it. Once he started to feel grounded, he carried on.

"Eventually, the NYPD tracked me down and a special tactical rescue team was sent in."

"Oh, Zak, that must have been terrifying. You must have been so relieved when they got you out of there."

"Two NYPD officers died during the rescue." He looked down when he said those words. He hated recounting what had happened, but once he started, he felt compelled to finish. "A firestorm of shots erupted during the rescue, ending with the deaths of five terrorists and two NYPD officers. Good men with families."

It also ended with Zak clinging to life, but he didn't tell her this. He didn't want her sympathy; besides he was the lucky one, or so he had been repeatedly told. A lucky man, shot in the chest near his heart. Nine hours of surgery, a lengthy hospital stay and released with a massive scar and memories that never faded.

Although his team blamed the senior officer's nephew for what happened, Zak's guilt for the deaths of the two officers who had died saving him had become unbearable. Although the torture haunted him, witnessing the two officers' deaths had caused most of his anguish. It was such a vivid memory, the details of which were his burden, his pain, and certainly nothing he would share with Margo.

Murder was a horrible thing to witness. The gruesome details were etched into his psyche. However, there was more than just the visual; there were the noises, the smells, the gurgling of blood pouring out of the officer's bodies, the panic-stricken voices of men struggling to expel their final words. Recovering from his own injuries, he would see their faces every time he closed his eyes. Afraid to sleep, he walked around in a near-zombie state from prolonged sleep deprivation.

He left out the part about visiting the gravesites of the deceased officers, and how he had nearly ended his own life. He had been in a dark, inescapable place, a place known as depression. Unable to attend either officers' funeral due to his own hospitalization, he'd decided he needed to visit the officers' graves. So, a couple of days after his release, he'd set out to do that. He wasn't sure what he'd expected to gain, perhaps some closure, perhaps some relief from the guilt he felt. Sure, he had a few friends, but he had no family. And therefore if he had died instead, he assumed, it wouldn't have been felt as deeply as the death of those officers.

The first grave he had visited nearly destroyed him. He'd broken down, collapsing on the ground, wishing it was him lying buried in the cold dirt. The visit had made him even more unstable. He'd waited a week before deciding to go to the second officer's grave and had never made it to the headstone. Entering the graveyard, he'd seen the officer's wife and two young daughters from a distance, grieving. The piercing wails coming from the youngest girl had crushed him.

He had totally isolated himself for weeks. He hadn't answered the phone, or responded to any text messages, and when Safia and Omeir had come to his apartment, he refused to answer. Safia, who could get into the most secure of places, had broken in. They'd taken him to the hospital, where he had stayed for two weeks, diagnosed with post-traumatic stress disorder, PTSD. He had been treated with a cocktail of medications; some worked, and some didn't. When he'd no longer been considered suicidal, he was released. Required by the NYPD to see a psychiatrist on an outpatient basis, he had complied for three months.

Although he was better, he still had episodes, as they were called. The NYPD had reassigned him to what they referred to as "light" duties, a temporary assignment until he was deemed fit enough to go back to chasing down terrorists. Zak had convinced the officials and medical professionals it would be best if he got out of New York while it was determined whether his cover was blown. It was initially unclear if he'd been shot by accident during the confusion of the NYPD raid, or intentionally by the terrorists. Six months later, the Bureau had concluded the shooting was accidental, citing his cover was still intact. However, Zak was not convinced. He refused to return to New York. The Bureau didn't push him. The work he and his teammates had been doing had been suspended. The terrorists themselves were laying low and regrouping after their own casualties.

Zak went off the grid, with only Safia, Omeir, and his commanding officer knowing where he was. Initially he planned to go to Boston, but realized he needed to get away from the noises of a big city, sounds that could trigger PTSD. He decided to go live quietly in the country with only a dog as a companion, and in effect, ended up in Baxley.

When he finished telling Margo the watered-downed version, which consisted of an undercover operation gone bad, she had tears in her eyes. Of course, she knew there was more to the story than what he told her, but she understood how affected he was with even the carefully edited version.

"My dear Zak, I can't imagine what you have been through." She reached out and touched his right hand, which was resting on the kitchen table, away from the gun.

He recognized the pity in her voice and hated it, but after pointing a gun at Margo it wouldn't be right to show his disdain. And he couldn't brush off what he had gone through, as that would be disingenuous. Instead, he said nothing, hoping she would now just leave.

"Zak, just tell me how I can help you."

Normally he would say there was nothing she could do, nothing anyone could do – but with Margo, there was something he needed from her.

"Forgive me for holding a gun to you, if you can?" he asked. "I would never intentionally hurt you."

"Of course, Zak. I know you wouldn't," she reassured him. "You're one of the good guys. Whenever you need something, no matter what it is and whether it's today or in the future, just know I'll do it."

"I just need you to keep what I said in confidence. The less people who know about me, the better. I don't want to bring trouble to anyone."

"But Zak, maybe it would be better if people knew. They'd understand you, they'd…"

"No, Margo." He cut her off, as he knew the people of Baxley would just want to know more. They wouldn't be satisfied knowing he was a police officer, they'd want details. Details, he couldn't give, or details he didn't want to give. "This may be asking a lot Margo, but trust me, this is what I need."

She read pleading in his troubled face. "Okay. If this is what you want, I'll keep quiet."

She had no idea how challenging this promise would later become.

Chapter Six

It was Friday afternoon, nearing the end of a long and boring workweek at the clinic. Lexie was disappointed. She hadn't seen or heard from Zak since their chat at the farmer's market. He had mentioned he would drop by the clinic. Perhaps she misread him. Maybe he wasn't interested. Just a couple of weeks ago she had no interest in seeing anyone. And now she was sulking because this guy, a guy she barely knew, hadn't dropped by.

As luck would have it, her last patient was Willow Defaux, the bird lady from the market last week. She presumed it would be a drawn-out appointment since the woman loved to talk. On the plus side, Lexie was in no hurry to leave work to go home, where she would be alone.

As soon as she walked into the examination room, Willow looked up in surprise. "Lexie? The lovely young lady from the market. You're the new doctor?" Before Lexie could answer, Willow continued, "Well, why didn't you say something last week?"

Again, there was no chance for Lexie to respond as Willow continued to chatter. "I was thrilled when Margo told me she could squeeze in one more patient before the weekend. I don't want to keep you long, but I just don't want to leave this matter for longer than necessary. The pain is unbearable."

"Take all the time you need. I don't have any place else to go."

"Well, I know it's not life threatening, but my eczema has been acting up. The over-the-counter cream I've been using just doesn't do a thing to stop the itching."

Lexie leaned over to Willow and had her pull up her pant legs.

"That's not looking too good. You definitely need a prescription for something stronger."

"Thanks, I so appreciate it. I haven't slept in days. It's worse at night."

As Lexie was busy making a notation in her patient's chart, Willow leaned toward her. "I hope you know a beautiful lady, and obviously a smart one like yourself, should not be alone on a Friday night. I know Baxley doesn't have a great pick of bachelors in comparison to the big cities, but there are a few nice men around."

"I've got a lot to do this weekend. Still have boxes I need to unpack." It was a lie; she had unpacked her belongings within the first week of her move. She found the conversation about her lack of a personal life both inappropriate and embarrassing.

"You did attract a fair share of male attention at the market last week." When Lexie shot her a warning look, Willow shrugged. "I couldn't help but notice, dear. That handsome Zak Tifour seemed particularly interested in you. Come to think of it, so did Tom Harring. Though I'd advise against encouraging Harring."

Lexie arched her brows. She was now intrigued.

"If you haven't yet heard, Tom Harring is like the Saltmarsh Sparrow when it comes to women."

"Pardon?" Lexie had no idea what Willow was talking about.

"The Saltmarsh Sparrow is an extremely promiscuous bird, with multiple mating partners. Zak... well, he's more of a noble species. He settled in the area a couple of years ago, owns his own house. You do know he bought the house from Margo? Paid cash for it, too." Willow let out a giggle. "I guess that was silly of me. You're a doctor, I would imagine you take care of your own financial security. Zak is a gem. He paid Margo exactly what the house was listed at. Didn't even try to negotiate. It's a nice enough property, but clearly he could have offered her ten grand less. She was desperate to sell after holding onto it for too long. She had hoped her daughter and son-in-law would come back to Baxley and live there. However, when it became apparent her girl was soaring like an eagle in the big city, Margo knew it was best to get some money out of it. And the amount she got surprised even her."

Willow certainly knew a lot about people in the area. So too did Amelia, but Amelia would not likely engage in gossip as easily as Willow. Lexie didn't normally entertain such hearsay, however, she wanted to know as much as she could about the man she couldn't stop thinking about. The fact Willow saw Tom Harring as a player and Zak as noble confirmed Lexie's intuition. She figured having Willow as her last patient of the day might provide her with the opportunity to ask a bit more about Zak, something she wouldn't do if others were around.

Hesitating for a brief moment, Lexie spoke, "Can I ask you something without you reading too much into it? I'm a bit curious and I don't know a lot of people in Baxley yet."

"Go on, dear. I'll answer as honestly as I can."

"What do you know about Zak Tifour and Cicily McQuay?"

"I'm not sure I'm following you."

"Well, it seems to me Cicily doesn't like Zak too much and I was just wondering if there was a reason for it. Did Zak do something?"

"No. The man didn't do anything beyond moving to Baxley, forcing Cicily to deal with him."

"What do you mean?"

"It's about Cicily's son."

"Sheriff McQuay?"

"No, her oldest son, Colton. He served in the military, was killed in Iraq about four years ago. Very tragic. The whole town mourned the loss. He was such a treasure. Made his momma very proud."

When Willow paused, something she rarely did, Lexie could see how Colton's death had affected her too. "So ever since his death in a foreign country, by people who Cicily naturally despises, the woman has had issues. But her issues aren't just focused on her son's killers, but on anyone who looks like they might have a connection to the Middle East. She blames an entire religion and ethnic group for her son's death. She even started up with Zak possibly being a terrorist. What would a terrorist be doing in a place like Baxley?" It was more of a statement than a question. "The grief Cicily endured sure did change her. You wouldn't know it being new to Baxley, but Cicily used to be a delightful woman, very community oriented. Then when Colton died, she went off the rails and never came back. Margo, who used to be tight with Cicily, has tried to talk to her, but Cicily's way too angry to listen. She's even starting to look like the Great Horned Owl with that permanent scowl on her face."

"So why would she link Zak with being a terrorist? It sounds so far-fetched, even for Cicily."

"When Zak first came to Baxley, he was a bit mysterious to people. Just paying cash for a home sent people into a tizzy. And then there were other peculiarities. He never spoke of his family he kept to himself, and he didn't seem interested in the local women – well, not enough to date any of them. Some of us just figured he came here to get away from some family issue, or perhaps a bad break-up. A few others, mostly influenced by Cicily, thought maybe he was on the run and hiding out in Baxley. She even had her son the sheriff do a check on him. Nothing turned up. As time went on and Zak remained in Baxley, the suspicions became less, as did the gossip. But not for Cicily. She continues to believe Zak's some sort of terrorist or criminal. She's less verbal about it these days, but she still makes her subtle innuendos about the man."

"Seems ridiculous to me. I've heard several patients talk about Zak. They seem quite fond of him. He's always been polite to me."

Willow smiled and nodded. "Perhaps he's just an exceedingly private person waiting around for the right one to open up to. Sort of like the Turtle Dove, waiting for a mate for a beautiful lifelong bonding."

It was another fifteen minutes of bird analogies before Lexie was anywhere near finishing up with Willow. Although she started to tire when the woman went full gear into her latest adventure of birding, she endured. After all, she had given her more insight into Zak than anyone else in town. Just as she was easing her out the door, Willow turned to her rather seriously. "Zak Tifour is like the Pionus Parrot, exotic and beautiful – exceptionally intelligent, and because they are independent, it can make them seem aloof. Incredibly special. If only I was younger."

The woman's comparisons of the different people in Baxley to various birds was hilarious and oddly accurate. When she made the last comment, Lexie almost choked to keep from laughing.

Chapter Seven

The danger of being hyper-vigilant was now back. Zak had been told to expect some minor setbacks and perhaps this was all it was. But what if Margo had made a sudden move, making him panic? What if he had lost his composure and pulled the trigger? Although she had forgiven him for terrifying her, Zak still had not gotten over what he had done.

He had intended to drop by the clinic last week with his creation of *Tajine d'haricot blanc,* a Moroccan lamb dish. That was before he'd aimed a gun at Margo's head. Now he wondered what good he could bring to Lexie's life. She was a woman grieving, trying to heal after her niece's death. He didn't doubt she could bring a world of good to his life, but what could he offer in return? Deception, lies, erratic mood swings? Although he would never intentionally harm her, he couldn't promise he wouldn't have a meltdown in the future. That was what PTSD was like. Some days were good, and other days... well, they were downright frightening.

He couldn't avoid Lexie forever. He had already made the decision to return to New York. One last assignment. But he didn't want to just disappear from the pretty doctor. He sensed she had some abandonment issues, likely connected with the death of her niece. Families either pulled together in times of sorrow or split apart. Hers appeared to be the latter. He didn't want to be another person bailing on her. As long as there was a positive outcome in New York, he would be back. He never thought he would like small town living, but it suited him. He had not felt at ease since the shooting, however, he was less anxious in Baxley. Other than Safia and Omeir, he had no one in New York. They had each other, whether it was just a friendship or the start of something else. Zak didn't belong in New York and he knew it.

As he was washing dishes, his phone rang, making him drop the cutlery. Making a mental note to change the ring tone to something less piercing and irritating, he glanced at the number. The call he could no longer avoid.

"*Assalamu alaikum.*" There was a slight crackle in Omeir's voice when he said the Arabic words meaning *peace be with you.*

"And upon you be peace," Zak responded calmly.

An awkward silence followed before Omeir spoke again. "So how's it going?"

Zak understood exactly what his friend was asking. He wanted to know if Zak was ready to return to the Bureau.

"I need a few days to take care of a few things around here, and then I'll be in New York." He was direct and confident when he spoke. It was deliberate. He not only needed to convince Omeir he was ready, he also needed to convince himself. What made Zak indispensable to the Bureau was his ability to be calm and confident as he manipulated situations. He generally avoided the manipulation with friends, but he could easily pull it off when he needed to.

"Is there anything you need?" Omeir asked.

"No, I'm good. I'll call you once I book my flight."

After the call ended, he took a moment to pray. He desperately needed for New York to be a success this time and to finally be able to move on. Returning to the city and the job that nearly destroyed him was a difficult decision for Zak; now he needed to see Lexie.

* * * *

"This is for the antiviral medication," Lexie said, as she scribbled on her prescription pad.

"Is there anything else I should do, Dr. Draden?"

"Well, make sure they get plenty of fluids, whether it be water, fruit smoothies, or even popsicles." The Samford twins, who were busy imitating a sword fight, temporarily halted at the mention of popsicles.

Although it was probably futile with these two, Lexie added, "And they should rest."

"I'll try," said an exhausted Tamara Samford.

Lexie had seen several patients this Monday morning, including five-year-olds Sarah and Samuel, who each had a bout of the flu. Tamara, the mother of the rambunctious twins, was at her wits end from two sick kids stuck indoors all weekend. Although Lexie prescribed medication and gave suggestions on reducing the duration of symptoms, she knew the mother needed help the most.

After Tamara hauled the duelling twins away, both Margo and Lexie were ready for a break. Thankfully, it was lunchtime and the next appointment was an hour away. Margo, in need of some fresh air, eagerly volunteered to go to Colton's to pick up lunch. Just as Margo was grabbing her coat, Zak walked thru the door.

Margo greeted him with a big smile. "Hi, Zak. Good to see you."

He smiled back, relieved by her sincere greeting. When she'd left his house last week, he believed he could trust Margo to keep his secret, but he knew sometimes people had second thoughts.

He could see she was struggling to put her winter coat on. "Let me help you." Zak pulled up on the back of the coat and eased it over Margo's shoulders.

"Thanks. If you're looking for the doctor, she's washing up. She'll be out front when she's done. I'm headed over to Colton's. Probably gone for at least half an hour."

Busted. Margo's declaration of how long she would be signalled that she knew he was there to see Lexie on a social basis. Zak hadn't spoken to Margo about Lexie, and although it was possible Lexie might have spoken to her, it was even more probable that someone in Baxley had seen him and Lexie having lunch at Colton's. It was a normal hazard of a small town to be the subject of gossip. Although Zak didn't like the prying eyes, he was a little more accustomed to it now.

He held open the door for her. "Thanks, Margo."

He wasn't just thanking her for giving him some privacy with Lexie; he was also thanking her for being so forgiving. The woman was a saint.

As he waited, he wandered around, taking in the décor. It wasn't cold and clinical looking like most doctor offices. It had a nice soothing appeal to it, almost like a spa with its neutral light and gray walls with teal-green accents. He doubted the place was like this before Lexie took over. Dr. Thornton seemed to be the kind of man who would have mismatched furniture and five-year-old golf magazines. It seemed to be organized in an orderly manner, which he knew was Margo's doing. Well, orderly except for the area off to the side. Toys were scattered all over there, and some furniture had even been tipped over. Some serious child play had gone on. He couldn't help but smile.

"You'll have to excuse the mess, we just had some rather boisterous little patients. I doubt there's any strain of the flu that could deter them from fun."

Hearing her voice, he turned around. "Let me guess, the Samford twins?"

"Guess they're legendary around here," she responded.

She avoided his gaze as she walked past him. Immediately, she busied herself with cleaning up the area, bending down to pick up the various toys. He couldn't tell if she was annoyed with him or simply focused on cleaning up the office.

To assist her, he grabbed a toy giraffe along with a weird squishy object and some blocks. With an armful of toys, he leaned toward her, attempting to make eye contact. With her hair falling over her eyes as she was gathering up the toys, Zak's efforts were futile. He was, however able to inhale her sweet scent, which he imagined to be a heavenly mist of jasmine combined with all that is right in the world.

"I brought you the lamb dish," he said. "It's an Algerian recipe called *Tajine d'haricot blanc*. It's lamb stew with white beans." Sensing she was either still pre-occupied or upset, he added, "Sorry it took me a while. I got busy with work." It wasn't a total lie, but there was certainly more to it.

Finally, Lexie looked up at Zak with piercing ink-blue eyes. It read as a friendly glance, or at least Zak interpreted it to be.

"Thanks. You didn't have to."

"But I wanted to." He wondered if it sounded pathetic, but quickly decided he didn't care.

"Well, I'm glad you did." Her voice softened as a smile brightened her face.

He had come to tell her he would be gone for a while, but now he wasn't sure what to say. They weren't dating so he didn't want to make a big deal out of it. But being too cavalier would be a mistake. She mattered to him, and he wanted her to know it without saying the words. Just the thought of her dating someone else punched at his heart. He had been so confident about many things in his life, but when it came to relationships, he floundered. Sure, he could flirt with women, but when it came to having a real relationship, he struggled. Years spent undercover, being someone he wasn't, had messed him up. But it wasn't right to just disappear. Providing all went well, it would probably only be for two weeks, but a lot could happen. He thought back to Tom Harring at the market. The man had been seriously checking out Lexie, and it bothered him more than it should.

"I'm going... to New York... for a while and..." he stuttered. He seldom was at a loss for words and he wasn't a stutterer but looking at her was making him nervous. It wasn't necessarily a bad nervous, but it prevented him from speaking coherently.

"And what?" she asked, her voice as soft as velvet.

"Umm, would you like to go out for dinner sometime? Before I go to New York?" he clarified.

When he stepped through the door minutes ago, he had no intention of asking her out. But somehow an image of Lexie laughing it up with Tom Harring, wedged its way into his head, making him jealous. Stupid and juvenile, but suddenly he didn't give a damn about playing it safe.

"Sure." Lexie's casual one-syllable response threw Zak off whatever feeble game he had.

"Umm, good. How about Saturday?"

"Saturday? Yes."

Again with the short response. A silly grin formed on his face, transforming him into a teenage boy who just got the girl from math class to come over and talk about logarithmic differentiation. Get it together, he told himself, as he erased the childish grin from his face.

She scribbled on a piece of paper and handed it to him. Again, her smooth hand touched his, making the smile appear once more.

"So here's the directions to my place and my phone number. Just let me know what time on Saturday."

He wanted to say something intelligent, or at least a complete sentence without stuttering, but the door to the clinic flew open. Sherriff McQuay came barging through with a teenage boy in tow. The teen's face contorted, and a low moan emerged from his mouth. The sheriff, ignoring the sounds coming from the boy, focused his attention on Lexie.

"Doc, I need you to take a look at Daniel," McQuay demanded. "He was out off-roading and had an accident. Think his arm might be broke. I'll see if I can track down one of his parents to let them know."

"Come on, Daniel. Let's take care of this." She gave Zak a quick smile before she led the teen to one of the examination rooms.

Before exiting out the main door, he heard Sheriff McQuay's fake cough – an obvious attempt to catch his attention. The guy was a bully and seemed to enjoy intimidating others. Zak had put up with the man simply because he didn't want problems.

"Yes, Sheriff?" He said as he turned around, not even bothering to control the annoyance in his voice.

"I'm surprised to find you here, Zak. You look mighty healthy to be seeing the doctor."

"Well, I guess that's what you call preventive medicine. You see the doctor to stay healthy."

"I'm all for healthy, Zak, eating well, exercising, living a good and honest life."

"I guess we both agree then. Good day, Sheriff." And with the final word, at least for now, Zak turned and left the clinic.

Upon examining Daniel's arm, Lexie determined it was sprained and not broken. She set it in a sling and prescribed an anti-inflammatory to take down the swelling. She was in no hurry to finish with him. It would take time for the sheriff to get a hold of Daniel's mother, and then more time for the woman to get over to the clinic. Conversing with Daniel was preferable to being around Sheriff McQuay in the waiting room.

Lexie wasn't blind to the visual daggers McQuay had given Zak upon discovering him alone with her. She knew he held opinions similar to his mother. She'd love to be one of those hot-tempered women who could easily wag her finger, putting men like Sheriff McQuay in their place. It infuriated her that he thought women actually needed him to rescue and protect them. Lexie had never been a damsel-in-distress type of girl when she was growing up, and certainly not now as a twenty-nine-year-old woman. She was smart, not just in a scholarly way, but also when it came to men. Sure, she didn't date a lot, but she was confident she could read most men well. She certainly didn't need him to lecture her about a man who was nothing but respectful toward her.

As she adjusted Daniel's arm in the sling to alleviate his pain, she brushed the annoying man from her mind. Most teenagers with pain were either verbally abusive or sullen, but not Daniel.

"Hey, Doc... It's okay I call you Doc?"

She nodded as she busied herself with tidying up the examination room.

"Have you ever been on an ATV?"

She cocked her head in his direction.

"You know, an all-terrain vehicle, a four-wheeler, a quad?"

"No, can't say I have."

"Oh, man... I mean, Doc. You really should. It's a blast. You can go anywhere with it: fields, ditches, up over hills. It's a rush. I can't wait to go out again."

She shot him a look, giving a quick glance at his sling.

"Well, I guess I'll have to wait a bit for this to heal. Hopefully I won't get grounded. Mom's probably going to freak out. I know I should have waited for Dad to go with me, but he's always working late."

It was obvious his regret was short-lived when a huge grin crossed his face once again. "Man, it was so cool, especially down by the creek. That beast can cross anything."

If this was her son, she wouldn't have been impressed with his short-lived insight into the dangers of what he had done, but his parents would likely educate him on it. She had to admit Daniel's enthusiasm was infectious, and also a pleasant distraction from having to deal with Sheriff McGrumpy.

With Daniel all attended to and an unnecessary tidying of the room completed, Lexie had stalled enough. She walked her patient back to the waiting room where Sheriff McQuay was leaning against the wall.

"Did you get a hold of my mom?" Daniel asked McQuay.

"You bet. She's on her way now."

"Did she sound upset?"

"Can't answer that, kid. You'll find out soon enough."

"I'm not supposed to go out alone," Daniel confessed. "It's so frigging boring around here. She can't really expect me to stay cooped up in the house until Dad comes home. He always says we'll go out, but we never do."

"Your mom's just concerned. Sometimes a person disapproves because they don't want to see someone get hurt." And to make his subliminal message abundantly clear, he moved his eyes over to Lexie. She gritted her teeth as her faced reddened, knowing exactly what the sheriff was doing. As she was thinking of something coy but diplomatic to say, Margo walked in the door. Lexie hurried over, helping with the bagged lunches and coffees in her assistant's hands. Intent on leaving her with the insufferable man, she gave Margo an apologetic look.

"I'm just going to finish up with the chart and have lunch in my office," Lexie said, by way of explanation. "Daniel, just let Margo know when your mother comes in. I'd like to explain your injury to her."

"Thanks, Doc, and you should try off-roading sometime. You'd love it."

"Maybe I will. A new adventure, something intriguing, sounds perfect." She smiled at the teenage boy, and without saying anything to Sheriff McQuay, she headed to the sanctuary of her office.

Eating her sandwich, she found herself thinking of her earlier visit from Zak. He was confident when he chatted with her at the market, but today he didn't seem so self-assured. A different side of him had come out and she liked it. He was awkward, perhaps a bit worried she would turn him down. His trepidation was appealing. She hated arrogant guys who assumed women would always say yes to them, like that sleazoid Tom Harring.

Although she was delighted Zak had finally made a move, she found herself bothered about his upcoming trip to New York. It wasn't permanent, but it also wasn't clear exactly how long he would be gone. He used the word 'awhile,' but what did that mean? A few days, a week, a month, or was it even longer? She had wanted to ask him more about the trip, but it wasn't appropriate to bombard a man she hardly knew. He didn't owe her any explanation, but still, she would have liked to know more. She hoped to find out more on her upcoming date.

It would be her first date since Hailie's death. Her last one was months ago, an accountant in Chicago. He was the cousin of one of her doctor colleagues. The date was fine, but there was no attraction and they had little in common. He hinted at a second outing, but she politely hinted how busy her schedule was. Thankfully, he read between the lines and backed off.

With Zak, there was definitely a strong physical attraction. But the man was more than a chiseled jawline, dark, sexy eyes, and a sturdy muscular build which she imagined held six-pack abs. He was interesting, well-traveled, and well-educated. He was intuitive about the world around him and had a sensitivity to people's feelings, including her own. He sensed when she was uncomfortable with certain personal topics and didn't push her to open up. He had rescued her during a blizzard, but never made her feel like she needed rescuing. He definitely oozed masculinity, but he was also extremely well-mannered. He seemed like the type of man who wouldn't hurry getting a woman into his bed. Sure, this was good, but a part of her liked the idea of getting into bed with him. He seemed complex, but not in a shred-your-heart kind of way – or at least she hoped not.

Chapter Eight

Previously, dating had been simple for Zak. Pick a nice restaurant, make a reservation, and enjoy the easy flow of conversation while having a good meal. Stick to safe topics: food, travel, leisure pursuits. Enjoyable, but ordinary. This time he didn't want ordinary, not with Lexie. He wanted to avoid messing it up, making the date just another forgettable outing. Although he enjoyed conversing with her, he knew the perils of just sitting around talking. Inevitably, conversation would lead to questions about his trip to New York. Questions he would have to avoid or lie about. It was best if she believed he was headed to New York to finish up some translation projects. Once the mission was done, and providing she was interested in a second date, he would cautiously open up to her.

Meaningful dating, that was his aim. Boy, could he use help on this. Why wasn't there some course on effective dating for the clueless? He was without any female relatives to call for advice. The only person he could think of who might be helpful was Safia. How odd was that? His female Muslim friend, who didn't really date, was the only person who would give him sound advice. He could count on Safia to be honest with him. She'd tell him if his ideas were lame. But he wouldn't go to her. He didn't want Safia or Omeir to know he was interested in someone. They needed to know he was fully committed and focused on the mission, and he was. A minor distraction in the way of a date with a beautiful woman was manageable. He was good at compartmentalizing, and besides, once he was in New York there would be no distractions.

He wanted to avoid the boring dinner date, where Lexie would politely stifle a yawn as she wished she was somewhere else. He couldn't bring her to his place and make dinner for her. Yes, he could cook a wonderful meal, but suggesting his place on a first date didn't seem right to him. It was too forward, something Mr. Smooth Tom

Harring would try if he ever got an opportunity. Damn, he hoped Lexie would never give the playboy an opportunity.

Zak wouldn't be taking her to any local place in town. Baxley didn't have any nice restaurants, and even if it did, he didn't need the whole town knowing. He didn't want her to be gossiped about, especially when he wouldn't be around to quell anything malicious. Most of the gossip would be relatively harmless he thought, but there was always Cicily and her son the sheriff. Undoubtedly, they would give Lexie grief about Zak – the Muslim stranger who shouldn't be trusted.

* * * *

For the fourth time in the last hour, Lexie looked up at the wall clock in her office. She couldn't wait for the workweek to end. She had plans for the weekend, definitely for Saturday. A date. An actual date with a decent, interesting man who made her pulse jump erratically.

She was anxious to get home so she could look through her closet and decide what to wear for Saturday. Shopping for stylish dresses in Baxley was not an option, it was not a town with clothing options beyond mom jeans and basic t-shirts. No sexy thongs or lacy lingerie, only flannel nightgowns and big cotton granny panties at Franny's Frocks on Main Street. She was hoping for a long-forgotten dress hanging in the back of her closet. A little black number that would make her feel like a glamourous movie star. Probably not, but hopefully she had something appropriate.

She knew she wasn't a stunning woman, but men had found her attractive in a girl-next-door way. But when Hailie died, she'd lost her confidence. Surely people could see the horrible and careless person she was. She hated the negative thoughts popping up in her head, but she couldn't shake them. Today, with nothing but time on her hands, she was over-thinking everything. Enough, she decided. She rose from her chair, ready to chat with the most optimistic person in Baxley.

"It's been a really slow day, hasn't it?" Lexie said to her receptionist, who looked almost as bored as she was.

"Yes, it's certainly slower than the norm. I guess Baxley has a town full of healthy people. Not a bad problem to have." Margo certainly had a way of putting things in perspective. "Oh, I forgot to tell you, Daniel called to thank you for treating him the other day. He appreciated you not lecturing him about the accident."

"I figured Daniel's parents, as well as Sherriff McQuay, would do enough scolding. Besides, I didn't want his first meeting with me to scare him. I want him to feel comfortable coming back if he needs to."

"He's a sweet kid, but like a lot of the kids around here, easily bored. The kids back in Chicago probably had a lot more to do?"

Thinking about her nephew Liam, she replied, "Certainly more activities available in a big city, but the kids still get into trouble. Probably more risky behavior than here. Unfortunately, loneliness is there even when you have skateboard parks and movie theaters."

"True, it's not always having something to do, it's having someone to do it with."

Margo's words rang true and without even thinking about it she blurted out, "So, Margo, got any plans for the weekend?"

It was only after she heard her question she realized how insensitive it might be. Margo was after all a widow, and Lexie wasn't quite sure how extensive her social circle was. And what if Margo shared what she was doing, only to ask her the same question. Lexie could talk about her weekend plans that didn't include Zak, but who wanted to hear about cleaning the oven and sorting the recycling? Maybe telling the truth wasn't so bad. Margo might inadvertently give her some insight into Zak. She knew from Amelia that Margo had some dealings with Zak. After all, she'd sold her home to the man.

"I've got my daughter and son-in-law coming over on Sunday for a visit. Nothing scheduled for Saturday, so I'll just stay out of the cold and read some tedious novel from my book club. Unfortunately, it was Willow Defaux's turn to pick the book. Who would have thought there actually was a novel out there from a bird's perspective?"

Lexie couldn't help but smile as she imagined the first-hand account of a sparrow describing the barn he was trapped in.

There was silence after Margo had spoken, so Lexie figured she wasn't going to ask about her plans. But just as Lexie was relaxing, Margo looked directly at her. "So, Dr. Draden, what are you doing this weekend?"

"I'm going out with Zak Tifour on Saturday." She didn't even pause, she just blurted it out. She wasn't sure if the silly grin planted on her face was making her feel stupid, or was it the way she didn't even try to hold back on blabbing about her personal life.

She caught Margo smiling back at her. Not with a silly grin like hers, but with a nice maternal smile. There was an awkward pause, or at least awkward for Lexie. Slowly, Margo got up from behind the reception desk and stood beside Lexie. The elderly woman looked at Lexie and winked. "Sounds like a nice way to spend a Saturday."

"Yes, I think so too," she said, her voice the most confident it had sounded since arriving in Baxley.

Chapter Nine

Glancing at his phone, Zak was relieved that he still had plenty of time. He had arranged to pick up Lexie mid-afternoon. He would take her for an early dinner and then head into Chicago. He'd contemplated a late dinner, but he didn't want it to look like he was trying to snare Lexie into an overnighter in the city. Snow was forecasted, and although his four-wheel drive handled well, he didn't want her to fret about being trapped in a blizzard with a man she barely knew. Being with Lexie in a quaint Chicago hotel was an image he more than enjoyed, but he would never take advantage of a woman's vulnerability. He shouldn't even be going out with her. He needed to keep a clear head for what lay ahead in New York, but somehow, he repeatedly told himself an evening with an attractive woman was not a big deal. Men all over America did this every day. Except they didn't lead a double life, lying about who they were. Sure, some lied, downplaying the number of sexual partners they had or exaggerating how much money they made, but they didn't live under a false name, hiding from the past. He felt bad for the deception. However, he had a plan, and once executed he would return to Baxley and live the truth.

He eased into his dark wool jacket. He was pleased the Armani suit still fit him, as he had beefed up a bit while in Baxley and was afraid it might be too snug. Doing something physical would sometimes lessen the PTSD symptoms. Zak chose lifting weights and running. He could do both in and around his home. He hated the power the PTSD had and attempted to control the damage by being in top physical shape.

He passed on the necktie, opting instead for a crisp, white, open-collared shirt. He'd never liked wearing a tie. When he'd lived in Paris he begun to dress without them. A French tailor once told him if you wear quality, a tie is only as necessary as a deep V-neck shirt or socks with sandals. In other words, not at all. Whether this was true didn't matter to Zak. After being tied up and tortured, he hated anything restrictive.

Along with saying no to the neckwear, he also decided to forgo a shave. He now had a two-day growth, the start of the beard he planned to maintain while undercover. He hoped the quality of his suit and its custom fit would prevent his date from focusing on his unshaven face, assuming he was too lazy to put in the effort.

Dating had become more difficult as he'd gotten older. The PTSD, the seclusion, and the messed up double life made him cautious. Sure he had dated, maybe not to the level of a professional athlete, but surely more than George, the local waste disposal officer who lived in his mom's basement. And though Zak might not have a lot of recent dating experience, he was smart enough to know what would constitute a disastrous time. He had never felt this way about a woman before and he didn't want this first date with Lexie to be the last. He wasn't sure if it was maturity changing the way he saw Lexie, or whether he had gone through so much ruin, it was now easy to recognize when something good stood before him.

As he was getting ready to slide into his Italian leather dress boots, Abby came trotting into the room. "Come here, girl."

He didn't need to call her since she had already decided to get the ear scratching she figured she deserved. Zak hated the idea of Abby being in a kennel while he went to New York. He'd give Omeir the name of the boarder in case things went sideways. Omeir wouldn't take her permanently, but he'd ensure she'd end up with a kind owner with a large yard. Zak hoped for the best, but he also had to plan for the worst.

Abby was frantically wagging her tail from the sheer pleasure of the ear scratching. Due to his own guilt, he gave her a few extra peanut butter biscuits. Like most dogs, she didn't like being alone for too long. She was a herding dog and was easily bored. Tomorrow, he would spend the day with her, taking her on a long run. It would be a feeble attempt to alleviate the guilt for leaving her tonight and for the next couple of weeks. After one more biscuit, Zak patted her on the head and headed out.

* * * *

Lexie could hear a vehicle puttering up the driveway. Her date was prompt, a trait she liked. She peaked at him through her living room window while he got out of the truck. She admired his broad shoulders and tall, muscular frame. As he approached the porch, she could tell he was at least a good six inches taller than her five-and-a-half-foot frame. She didn't stare for long, afraid he would see her ogling him through the window. Damn, it was difficult to look away. Unknowingly, he drew her in by the simple things, and right now it was the way he walked. He had great posture, moving with purpose and unabashed confidence. This stride was in contrast to the way he spoke when he had asked her out. Then, he had been all nervous, fumbling to find the right choice of words. But now there was no uncertainty.

The sound of the doorbell made her jump back. She wasn't quite sure why she was startled, as she was aware of his presence. Maybe she was flustered because she was too intensely aware, or maybe it was the horrible sound of the doorbell. It was an old-style chime with a sharp, annoying, screechy sound. She loved the old colonial home but the awful chime needed to go.

She took one last glance at herself in the entranceway mirror. She hoped the crimson-red shift dress with its lace sleeves would be appropriate for where they were going. She took a slow breath in and opened the heavy mahogany door. He stood before her with a magnetic smile.

He looked different. She had always seen him in worn jeans with some casual, yet form-fitting shirt. A nice, yet rugged look. Today, however, he was wearing a suit – an expensive and well-fitted dark suit. And although he was dressed sharply, what captivated her most was his face. Those thick dark lashes and the light stubble of facial hair. It was enough scruff, along with the tailored suit, to make him look like he had just come from a *GQ* photoshoot.

After a too-long stare, which she just couldn't help, she realized he was still outside on the front porch. The wind was blowing and he didn't have a winter coat on, just his suit jacket. Surely, he would feel the slicing cold air, but somehow he stood patiently with not the slightest hint of a shiver. Embarrassed by her long and not so innocent gaze, she stuttered a hello and stepped aside so he could enter the front hallway.

"I'll just get my coat and we can be on our way." She looked down at her heels, already feeling the cold penetrating her toes. "I'll carry these shoes and wear my boots. My feet freeze so easily." She kicked off the matching red velvet stilettos and shrank several inches.

"Good idea. I brought winter gear. Part of living in the country, I guess."

As she pulled on her boots, she caught him discretely glancing at her legs. The near mid-thigh dress was definitely the right choice.

"So do I get another clue as to where we're going?"

"Well, I thought we'd go for an early dinner in the countryside and then into Chicago. I got us tickets to an event I hope, that's okay with you?"

A surprise event? It sounded romantic, unless it was wrestling or a monster truck rally. Seeing how impeccably dressed he was, she doubted it would be. She loathed the idea of going into Chicago, but how could she tell him that? He seemed to have gone out of his way to do something nice for her. She couldn't remember the last time a man did that. So she answered the only way she could.

"Not much of a clue, but I'm looking forward to it."

They drove on the interstate for about forty-five minutes before turning down a paved road to the east. The winter roads were clear of the snow, which had fallen the previous day. The drifts of snow in the distant fields sparkled from the sunlight, providing additional warmth inside the heated vehicle. It was a scenic drive, distracting them both from the nervousness accompanying a first date. The conversation was slow to start, but ten minutes later they both eased up as they talked about New York, Chicago and their childhoods. He talked about places he had traveled, including Paris. He even spoke a few words in French for her.

"It sounds beautiful, Zak. What does it mean?"

"You look beautiful," he responded.

"Sounds like you said a lot more than just three words."

"I also made a comment about how your white artic boots make the outfit complete."

She laughed, one of many carefree giggles during the drive. Before she realized it, he had turned from the pavement onto a gravel road with large spruce trees lining both sides. The fallen snow from yesterday flocked the trees, plumping them into large mesmerizing clusters. It was picturesque, like a brochure for some glamourous ski resort, except with sprawling hills as opposed to alpine mountains. After about a half mile of towering spruce trees, an enormous house with a full-size wrap-around veranda came into view. A sign in front of the house identified the place as Spruce Haven Inn.

Before Lexie could ask, Zak quickly clarified, "This place also has a wonderful restaurant overlooking the countryside." Sensing her relief, he continued, "I discovered it by accident one day. Great food. They've got a fantastic chef, but to me the appeal is the setting. It's tranquil. Even when the winds are blowing or it's pouring rain, there's a quiet peacefulness to the place. I thought we would have dinner and then it's about forty-five minutes to where we need to go in Chicago."

She was embarrassed for thinking he was taking her here for any other reason than dinner. She hoped he didn't pick up on her initial crazy thought. Of course, it was presumptuous for a man to take a woman to a cozy little inn for sex on a first date, and certainly out of character for Zak. Logically she knew this, but still, she couldn't stop the provocative image of her and Zak in one of the Inn's suites, wrapped in nothing but a plush blanket, passionately kissing by a crackling fire. Although the idea of being with Zak in a quaint little room intrigued her, she was relieved to find out it was only going to be dinner, at least this time.

As she was changing into her shoes, he came around to the passenger door, opening it. He held out his hand, helping her to maneuver out of the vehicle. She appreciated the chivalrous gesture. It was a bit of a challenge getting down modestly in a short cocktail dress. She felt the warmth of his hand as he steadied her. She hurriedly pulled on her coat. He put a protective arm around her as he led her to the front door of the inn.

Looking up, she was awestruck by the beauty of the Victorian inn. There was such detail, from the corner turret to the paired cornice brackets on the wrap-around veranda. The entrance, with its double doors of deep blue and raspberry-red stained glass, was a work of art. The aroma of rosemary and basil filled her senses as she entered the expansive foyer. The floors, a dark cherry wood, led to a grand staircase rising to the second floor, where presumably the guestrooms were. Zak guided her to the right. They stood at the entranceway to the sprawling dining room. The ceiling height was at least twelve feet, trimmed with the beautiful cherry wood. A young attractive lady greeted Zak.

"Welcome back, Zak. Nice to see you again."

"Thanks, Katrina," he replied to the hostess.

The young woman's eyes lingered over his body a little too long, ignoring Lexie. Breaking her spell and wishing to move away from the ensuing awkwardness, Zak spoke. "I made reservations for five p.m. We're a tad bit early."

Nervously stroking her long, champagne-blonde hair, the woman forced a smile at Lexie. "Umm... yes. Just give me a second," she muttered. After fumbling with a pen in the reservation book, Katrina led them to a table in the back of the restaurant.

As Lexie walked between tables in front of Zak, she glanced around. She was in awe of the beautiful Victorian architecture and décor. Gleaming woodwork accentuated the room and large crystal chandeliers dangled from the high ornate ceilings. She was still taking in the ambience of the restaurant when they came upon the beautifully set table. Freshly cut cream-colored hydrangeas intertwined with silver brunia filled a crystal vase.

Zak pulled back her chair. Instead of immediately sitting, she looked out the window near their table and let out a soft gasp. She had never seen such a breathtaking winter sight. There was a veranda around the back of the Inn, equally matching the beauty of the front porch. Beyond the veranda was a truly heavenly view. Beautifully manicured hedges surrounded the property, with a large gazebo near a frozen pond. Further in the distance she saw the progression of rolling hills, framed by massive intertwining spruce and popular trees. Zak was right, the setting was tranquil, but what made the view majestic was the glistening snow blanketing the landscape wherever she looked. She felt as if she had just entered a real-life snow globe. Suddenly aware that Zak was waiting patiently with the chair pulled back, she sat.

Before Lexie could speak, Katrina handed them their menus and wished them, or more specifically Zak, an enjoyable meal. With obvious disappointment, she strolled away.

Lexie's eyes continued to be wide with wonder as she stared outside.

"It is magnificent, isn't it?" he said.

"Yes, it definitely is," she said as she slowly moved her gaze away from the outdoors to the delightful man who had brought her here. "I never knew such a place existed so close to Chicago. I've never heard of this place."

"It is a hidden gem, isn't it?" It was more of a statement than a question. "Every time I come here it looks different. The view totally changes with the seasons. Every season offers its own beauty, but winter is my favorite."

"Sounds like you're quite the regular here."

Zak figured she may have been referring to the hostess, Katrina. She was always a bit too friendly. Yes she was pretty, but he wasn't interested in someone that young. No, he definitely preferred a woman closer to his age, like the one in front of him.

"I've been here about a dozen times. I discovered the Inn when I took Abby out this way. I dropped in for lunch and now I try to get here at least once during each of the four seasons. The food is gourmet. Rivals some of the best restaurants in New York, but with a better view."

"I'm sure Abby must have liked it." Lexie tried to sound casual, but feared it might have sounded like jealousy.

Zak smiled from ear to ear and made a slight laugh. He had mentioned he had a dog but he never mentioned her name. "Well, Abby never got in the door." He paused for a bit, enjoying the tease. "Abby's my dog. I dropped her off at the kennel, ten miles east of here." Then wanting to ensure Lexie understood what type of man he was, he leaned closer. "I've always come here alone, except for tonight."

Those words, spoken in that husky voice, nearly undid her. She knew she was probably blushing. There was no way to stop it.

"Thanks for taking me here."

He wanted to reach out and touch her hand, which she had placed on the stem of the crystal water glass, but instead he reciprocated with a smile. Before he could say another word, a tall, slender waiter came to the table to take their drink orders. Lexie ordered a glass of Chablis with Zak ordering a simple club soda with lime.

When the waiter dropped off their drinks, he noticed her shoulders tensing. He didn't inquire, choosing not to embarrass her. After taking a couple of sips of his drink, he noticed she still hadn't touched hers. Finally, he motioned over to her wine glass, "Is it not what you ordered?"

"It is. It's just..." She hesitated, as if trying to find the right words. He sat patiently, having a general idea where she was headed, but curious on how she would broach the issue. Finally, she blurted out, "I should have asked if you drink. I had colleagues who didn't drink for religious reasons. I'm fine not drinking. I could have ordered club soda, too."

She was amazing, he thought. Unnecessary for her to not drink the wine sitting before her, but considerate she would second-guess having the glass just to make him more comfortable. He sensed she wanted to know more about him, but she didn't want to be offensive. He didn't owe her an explanation for the club soda, but he wanted her to know. There was so much he couldn't tell her about himself, but this he could.

"I don't drink. But I wouldn't really say it's because of religious reasons. I'm connected to both Islam and Christianity, but I don't consider myself Muslim or Christian. Raised by a Muslim father and a Roman Catholic mother, I studied both the Bible and Qur'an as an undergrad as well as in my graduate studies. I can't say I practice either fully, but I believe in God and can relate to the good in both religions. My parents followed most of the major doctrines of their faith, but they also respected each other's different beliefs. People usually assume I'm Muslim, and normally I let them. Saying anything causes all sorts of confusion. Besides, I have a connection to Islam and have a profound respect for my father's faith. My beliefs may seem complicated to people, but to me they're not." He wanted to say that his belief in God was the least complicated aspect of his life, but he didn't. He didn't want her to know how complicated his life really was.

Instead he said, "When it comes to religions, I've found it's the human element that's complicated. I've been around people who drink and people who don't. Neither bothers me, but for me, drinking is just not my thing. I used to have a couple of drinks at parties in college and even got stupidly drunk once. Not to the point where I streaked naked around campus, but enough to have regretted it in the morning."

He heard her slight giggle and her shoulders relaxed. He continued, "Drinking and getting drunk was part of the college ritual I guess. But when I totally stopped drinking, for some strange reason, I got judged more. People would make all sorts of strange assumptions. Maybe I was a recovering alcoholic, perhaps I had a wicked temper when drunk, maybe I was a control freak who couldn't relax, and of course the more common assumption, my religion prohibits it. People tend not to ask, and just assume. So it's actually nice to have you ask me, even in a hesitating and round-about way."

"I like how you see things, the way you can peel back the layers, and get to what's important," she said.

He smiled at her comment. He never really thought of it that way it was just how he was.

"Studying languages has a down side. It makes you end up saying a lot of words. But I want you to know me, not just what other people say about me. So please enjoy your wonderful glass of Chablis. And Lexie, always order what you want. You'll never have to change for me."

And with that she took her first sip.

He had a knack for putting her at ease. So much so that she talked about her family, how her father had died from a heart attack when she was in high school, and how her mother had worked hard to provide for her and her older sister, Claudia. Since she didn't have the sting of tears at the mere mention of Claudia's name, she continued on; mentioning she had a nephew who was now eighteen years old, and a niece who suffered from a rare disease, and who was now deceased. Although she didn't mention how Hailie had died, Zak like most people, presumed it was solely due to the progressive disease. She let him.

By the end of the main course he felt comfortable enough to talk about the Arabic, Kurdish, and other languages he was fluent in. At her urging, he spoke a few words in the various languages. She got him to teach her a few words and her horrible pronunciation made them both laugh.

Zak couldn't get over how beautiful she was. She had this understated elegance to her, and that short dress with the lace sleeves was downright sexy. It didn't hug her body, but he could tell she had some serious curves by the way it draped. The dress highlighted one of her best assets, her toned legs, aided no doubt by being an avid runner. He would have to be blind not to notice. Trying to be a gentleman, he only made brief, and what he hoped were discrete, glances at her legs. He focused on her beautiful face, easy to do since her smile was nothing short of inspiring. The look of wonder, which sparkled in her eyes when she first saw the beautiful scenery, is what his eyes did when he picked her up earlier today. He imagined he still had the look. She was brilliant in so many ways, including her quick-witted humor, but what struck him the most was how he could talk so freely with her.

"So what kind of dog is Abby?"

"She's a Komondor. Most people have never heard of the breed."

"The dog with dreadlocks?" asked Lexie.

"Yes, I should have named her Moppy Floppy. But I would sound ridiculous yelling her name."

"Awe, but if you said it in a different language, perhaps French, it would sound divine," she teased. "So are you taking her to New York?"

Zak felt a pang of guilt. "No, I'm going to drop her off on the way to O'Hare."

"I'll take her," Lexie blurted out.

"To the kennel?"

"No. I'll look after her while you're gone."

"That's kind of you, but she's a massive dog. She could easily destroy your house." It was an exaggeration as Abby was well-trained. He didn't want to bother her with personal matters, including his dog.

"Seriously, I don't mind. I was actually thinking of getting a cat, so it will be good practice for me. Besides, looking after her will give me something to do in the evening. I might have to forgo attending a few of the cultural activities in Baxley, but I'm sure the town won't shun me for missing the chili cook-off."

They both laughed.

Suddenly, Zak's face got serious. "I should only be in New York for a week or two, but sometimes business can take longer. I don't want to burden you with my dog." He purposely used the term business, as he hated to repeatedly lie to her.

"I offered because I want to. Honestly, it's kind of lonely living in the country and having another being around would help. A lot of dogs don't do well in kennels. They don't eat like they should and they don't get enough exercise. I like to get out for a run, so she'll get lots of exercise."

He was going to protest, but he struggled to form the words when he looked at those pleading blue eyes.

"Hey, I'm sure Abby is loyal to you. You're not worried she'll spill any secrets or talk about all your wild times in Baxley?"

"Yep, all sorts of wildness in Baxley," he said with a grin.

"You are planning on coming back from New York?"

The worry on her face tore at him. This time he did reach across the table, taking her hand.

"As soon as I can. I like Baxley, and lately I like it even more."

She blushed.

"So?"

"I'm sure Abby would love to stay with you. But if she gets to be too much, promise you'll take her to the kennel."

She nodded and her smile spread across her face.

They finished dessert, and while Zak was busy paying the bill, Lexie stepped outside to the back veranda to fully savor the beautiful winter paradise. She took a deep breath and tried to prepare herself for the trip to Chicago where her most recent memories were clouded with sorrow.

Sensing Lexie's growing stillness as they left the restaurant, Zak put on some easy listening type of music. They drove without speaking, watching the snow gently trickling onto the highway. The windshield wipers swept the large, thick snowflakes back and forth in an almost soothing rhythm.

After the third song, Lexie finally broke the silence. "I haven't been back to Chicago since I left for Baxley. Although I have fond memories of Chicago, my more recent ones revolve around Hailie's death. Just wanted you to know why I'm a little quiet."

He reached out for her hand, holding it. "If you want me to turn around and go back to Baxley, I will."

"Thanks, Zak, but Chicago owes me some good memories. Let's see if she delivers," she said, while enjoying his touch. They continued with their fingers intertwined for a few seconds longer before he pulled back, placing his hand on the steering wheel. The roads had started to get a bit slick. As he cautiously navigated the downtown streets of Chicago, she peered out the side window to the city where all her troubles began. She had gotten lost in her thoughts when she suddenly realized he had pulled up to a massive skyscraper. She recognized the landmark structure – the Civic Opera House.

"The opera?" she asked.

The excitement in her voice made Zak relax. The opera was certainly not for everyone.

"Yup, it's a night at the opera. Have you been?"

"No, but I always wanted to go. How about you?"

"Yes. I've gone to quite a few but never in Chicago. This is a first of sorts for me too."

"I'm afraid I don't know much about it. I hope I don't ruin it for you."

"Lexie, I can't imagine you ruining anything."

She looked up at him. He was incredible with words. Did he truly believe she wasn't capable of ruining anything?

As they stood in the Rice Grand Foyer, Lexie felt Zak's gaze on her. Sure, he quickly glanced around when they entered the historic building, and she could tell the ornate décor impressed him, but he never lost focus on her. And when she spoke, he looked at her as if they were standing in a barren field, as opposed to being inside the luxurious Chicago landmark. She liked it. She liked him. She liked the way he made her feel, as though nothing was as important as the moment they were in.

As he told her about Puccini's last opera *Turandot*, she realized how well-schooled he was. "How did you develop such an interest?"

"My mother. She took me to my first opera when I was about ten years old. I was an only child, so I spent a lot of time with my parents. They loved to immerse themselves in new experiences and usually took me along. Several months prior to my first opera experience, my father took my mom and me fishing at Van Cortlandt Lake in the Bronx. My father and I loved it, my mother, not so much. She tried to be a good sport about it, but she absolutely hated it. She hated not catching fish, but she hated catching them, too. She was such an independent woman, refusing to ask my dad to kill the fish for her, but she couldn't stomach doing it herself. She ended up releasing any fish she caught, claiming it was too small, which it wasn't. By the fourth trip, she opted out. It was just my father and me from then on. But Mom wanted to have an activity for just us, something she and I would do that didn't interest my father.

She found it. At first I wasn't crazy about opera. I was a fidgety child, so sitting for any length of time was difficult. But by the second season, I started to love the intensity, how immersive and powerful the stories are, and, of course, the beauty of the music, of the arias. We went every year until her death. I stopped going for a few years. Then one Christmas, when I was living abroad, I decided to go back. I guess I was afraid I would lose my connection with her if I didn't go back. And although it's intense and passionate, I also find it relaxing. It might not make sense, but to me the opera gives me the peaceful connection I need with my past – with my childhood."

The way he described his love for this art, had elements of opera itself. It had elements of tragedy but it was also a beautiful revelation, giving her another glimpse into this private man.

"I'm sorry. I didn't know your mother is no longer alive."

"Yes, both my parents were killed when I was just shy of my eighteenth birthday. They had gone out for a celebratory dinner for their anniversary. On the way home, their vehicle was T-boned. The other driver, a middle-aged woman, was impaired. She had mixed a fair amount of alcohol with a variety of prescription pills. That's another reason why I was never fond of drinking."

Lexie could feel the lump in her throat. "It must have been so hard on you. Did you have other family?"

"No, not really. My parents had little contact with their families after immigrating to the United States. Because I was almost eighteen, I was allowed to live in the family home on my own. My parents had a good circle of friends and neighbors who regularly dropped by to check on me. Brought me more casseroles than I could possibly eat, made sure I was going to school, and ensured I wasn't doing anything deplorable. Drugs, alcohol, girls," he clarified when she gave him a confused look. "They meant well but the pity and sorrow surrounding me was suffocating. I needed to go somewhere where I wasn't known as the teenage orphan. So I left New York to study abroad. I got in at *L'Institut d'études politiques de Paris*, commonly known as Sciences Po. Stayed for four full years before returning to New York for graduate studies. It was good to get away. Now I can look on all the wonderful memories I was fortunate to have with my parents, but at the time, the grief overwhelmed me. I was terrified if I stayed I wouldn't get past it."

"I can't imagine how difficult it must have been." As she said these words, Lexie realized this wasn't exactly true. She, too, had faced an all-consuming grief when Hailie died. She still had trouble recalling the good memories of Hailie, because the sorrow and regret drowned them out.

Sensing pity, which Zak despised even coming from Lexie's kind face, he quickly added, "They loved each other so much, and I guess there's some comfort that they died together. I think it would have been tremendously difficult had one died and the other was left to mourn."

It was in this moment that Lexie understood who this man was. He was a man who would rather hurt than to see the ones he loves suffer. He was on the cusp of adulthood when he was left to mourn, not just one parent, but both of them. Through a sorrow that would have been painfully intense, he was able to find solace in his parents being eternally together.

Lexie wanted to reach out, to touch him. To put her arms around him or even just to brush her hand against his face. She wanted to console him physically, but she didn't know how he would respond. She feared being too awkward or intimate with him. It was clear he hadn't revealed this in order to illicit sympathy; the man abhorred pity. So Lexie just stood there, hoping the warmth in her eyes would convey how she felt. Before she could transition the conversation, an announcement that the theater doors were opening came over the intercom. He reached for her hand and led her to their seats.

The opera was in Italian and although he wasn't fluent, Zak had some basic knowledge of the romantic language as well as having seen *Turandot* on a few previous occasions. Lexie didn't understand Italian but she was able to follow most of the opera without difficulty.

When the Tenor performed the aria, *Nessun dorma*, it was with such intensity, Lexie's eyes began to fill. Struggling, she became unable to supress the tears. Slowly, a few flowed down her cheek. A wave of embarrassment flushed over her as she attempted to shield her face from Zak. Before she was able to dab away the moisture, he put his arm around her. Reaching with his other hand, he gently touched her cheek, wiping away the tears. The gesture so heartfelt. A profound gratitude for this remarkable man swept over her. When she turned to thank him for his kindness, she couldn't help but stare. Although he smiled at her, his dark eyes contained such sorrow. The intensity of the music and the tragic story brought out her emotions, so she imagined it did with him, too.

The beauty of this particular opera had always touched him, but unbeknownst to his date, it was much more than that. It didn't surprise him when the underlying violence and the scene of torture struck too close for his comfort. He knew this when he purchased the tickets, but he also knew the beauty of the story and wanted to share it with Lexie.

He was relieved that she didn't notice him cringing during some of the scenes. *Turandot* had been performed so splendidly that her focus was on the stage until the very end. When the curtain closed and the clapping faded, she leaned toward his face and kissed him on the cheek.

"Thank you, Zak, for taking me to this. It was breathtakingly beautiful."

Those words could be used to describe her. But it wasn't enough. Her beauty was more than breathtaking, it reached into the depths of her. Places where a stranger couldn't see, and where he had thus far only been able to sample a taste. He was conversant with many languages and there were many ways to describe beauty, yet, when he looked at her, she transcended the words of the languages he knew. He'd have to study prose and poetry of an ancient civilization to do her beauty justice.

He needed the trip to New York to be over with. He craved spending more time with this remarkable woman. Although he could never relax, she made it easier for him to open up. It was probably never going to be easy for him to talk about his past, and he probably wouldn't tell her all the things he had gone through, but sharing his parents' death with her eased the burden that had settled so deep within him.

It was time to get her back to Baxley. He promised himself he would not take advantage of her. He'd known her vulnerabilities before tonight, and when she talked of her niece Hailie, he could sense how deep the hurt went. He just prayed he wouldn't end up hurting her more. She was good for him in so many ways, but he questioned if he could ever be the type of man who could give her what she deserved.

As they walked into the night, the snow continued to lightly fall. The visibility on the highways would still be good. He helped her to the passenger side of his truck since the shoes she was wearing, although extremely sexy, were useless for moving about. When he was a kid, he'd often wondered why women wore such ridiculous and useless footwear. However, when he got older and saw how they made a woman's leg look, he felt indebted to those shoe designers. They were geniuses.

After settling her into the passenger side, he opened the driver's side and started up the truck. The vehicle was lightly covered with snow, so he stepped out, brushing the fluffy white layer off. When he got back in, he noticed she was shivering. Leaning over, he gave her a big hug. It wasn't just some chivalrous gesture; it was also self-serving as he craved the intimacy with her. He didn't want to move away, but he had to get her home. Slowly releasing her from the embrace, he sat up and put the truck into gear.

Lexie loved the peacefulness of the evening. The opera had stirred up a lot of emotions for her but it also soothed the restlessness she had about going into Chicago. The headlights, illuminating the large snowflakes falling softly from the sky, added to the magical ambience of the evening. They continued to chat effortlessly on the way home. He explained some of the moments in the opera she hadn't quite pieced together. He listened to her novice questions on opera with such patience, making her feel like every question was a good one, which she highly doubted. It was definitely an evening she didn't want to end too soon and she was starting to think maybe it wouldn't have to.

Just a few hours ago, she'd nearly panicked when they pulled up to the Inn in the country, and now here she was thinking about inviting him to spend the night. The man was well-educated, raised by a strong, independent woman, and tonight he was heartfelt as he spoke of beauty and loss. Surely he was enlightened enough to not judge her if she made the first move.

But was she ready? She wanted him. Yes, she definitely wanted him, but she was afraid she wasn't good enough for him. He could definitely make her feel better about herself, but then morning would come and she would look in the mirror and see the ugliness of a woman who made a reckless decision.

When they pulled up to her house, he jumped out and walked to the passenger door, helping her maneuver to her house safely over the icy walkway. It was a bitterly cold night. If she didn't open her door quickly, any good night kiss on the front porch would be quick. She didn't want quick when there was a far better option.

Hurriedly, she unlocked the door, hopped inside, and motioned for him to join her in the warmth of the house. He gave her an apologetic look and for a moment, she was afraid he was going to leave, but a gust of frigid air made his hesitation come to an end. As soon as he had both feet inside the foyer, he closed the door behind him, preventing the heat between them from cooling down.

As though sensing her trepidation, Zak moved toward her and gave her a kiss on the lips. It was a sweet and almost chaste kiss, making her desire more. His kiss didn't match his gaze, which was dark and intense, as though he, too, wanted more. When he leaned back, Lexie moved toward him and returned the kiss, but hers was a passionate one, with lips parting. He eagerly reciprocated with his mouth fully accepting of her. The warmth of being inside her mouth overwhelmed him. He struggled to gain control, afraid of his darkness. A darkness that would unravel him and unwittingly destroy her. Slowly, he pulled back. He extended his hand to her, stroking the side of her face with his thumb.

"I don't want to, but I have to go," he whispered. "I'll be back tomorrow, if the offer still stands." Then to clarify, he added, "The offer to take care of Abby."

"Of course the offer still stands." She spoke the words with a subtle breathlessness, hoping he would realize she was talking about more than just dog sitting.

He grasped her hands, stroking them with his. "Call me when you want me to drop Abby off. Again, thanks for a wonderful evening." And with a gentle kiss to her cheek, he turned around, walking into the chilly night air.

Chapter Ten

What is wrong with me? Stupid idiot.

Zak had just left the home of a sexy and smart woman. A woman who was probably willing to sleep with him. And what did he do, but watch her standing in the doorway as he left her warm and inviting home. In the morning he would realize he had made the right decision, but right now his libido was overpowering his brain. The kiss had exhilarated him, but also terrified him. She was the type of woman he wouldn't want to let go of once he had her. And he so wanted to have her.

He considered turning around, barging through her doorway and ravishing her in his arms, but he just couldn't do that to her. So instead, he opened the truck window, wishing the blast of cold air would push his less than noble thoughts aside.

He'd agreed to leave Abby with her. He didn't want to say yes, but her pleading eyes made it hard to deny her, and when she spoke about dogs not doing well in kennels, it got the best of him. Abby would love being in a warm home with this compassionate woman. Hell, he would too.

Now he couldn't help but think about tomorrow. He knew he shouldn't, but he was eager to see her, even if it was just to drop Abby off. Maybe one last sight of her, before he put himself in harm's way, could help him. Maybe give him a boost of confidence. But it wasn't about his needs, and he had no right to leave her on the hook. He appreciated her trust in him, even if he didn't deserve it. She didn't interrogate him on details pertaining to New York. She likely knew something didn't sound right as she was smart, but she didn't seem to be overly concerned by it. And why, he thought? Because she trusted him. He hated himself for it.

By the time he got home, the cold air had lessened his arousal. He was glad to see Abby, and before he could even reach down to pet her, his phone buzzed with a text message. It was Lexie.

Thx for the nice evening. If you are not 2 busy, bring Abby by in the aft and stay for dinner. She had ended it with a smiley face.

Zak pushed his head back and closed his eyes. Then he did what he was sure to regret.

Sounds great, and uncharacteristic of him, he added a smiley face.

* * * *

Lexie wasn't sure what she was doing. Zak had turned down her advances last night, and now she was having him over for dinner. She was sexually frustrated with the way the evening ended, but she wasn't offended when he left her standing at the doorway. She knew she wasn't the only one aching to be touched. She saw the desire in his eyes after the heated kiss. There was just something holding him back, but she had no idea what it was. Perhaps she would have been successful if she had persisted, but she didn't want to push herself on him. Whatever was holding him back was something he needed to figure out.

She wasn't a Martha Stewart kind of woman, and in fact, her culinary skills sucked. She had invited Zak over for dinner though, and she had to make a decent meal especially after he had gone through the trouble of making the delicious lamb stew, or what he'd called *Tajine d'haricot blanc* in that sexy French voice. She loved it when he spoke different languages. It was so exotic and sensual to her ears, even though he could be reciting a speech from a medical convention and she wouldn't know it.

She opted for a simple, yet tasty chicken dish for dinner. Since she wasn't going to see him for a couple of weeks, she wanted to spend time with Zak as opposed to fluttering around in the kitchen. Besides, she needed to ensure Abby adapted to the new environment. Yesterday, when she'd volunteered to dog sit, it sounded like a great idea. But thinking about it now, she wasn't so sure. She remembered the story of this surgical nurse back in Chicago who had gotten a Rottweiler puppy who'd eaten anything leather, including the woman's sofa. Okay, maybe that was an exaggeration, but the dog had done some major damage. Luckily, she had a chenille fabric on her sofa.

But what if Abby didn't like her? She had no experience with dogs. Her mother and sister were cat people and she was always so busy, she didn't even have time for goldfish. If things got too harried with Abby, she could take her to the kennel like Zak had suggested. However, she didn't want to disappoint Zak; she sensed Abby meant a lot to him.

Within half an hour, Abby and her wonderful master would walk through the door. She didn't have time to run out and get dog treats. Without a food bribe, the dog would have to come to its own conclusion about her. As she was stuffing the chicken breasts with creamed spinach and herbs, she wondered what Zak would do if Abby growled at her. Would it be game over, not only for dog sitting, but for seeing him again?

After tossing a variety of vegetables into a bowl of romaine lettuce, she decided to head upstairs to do a little work on her appearance. It wouldn't make a difference to her canine guest, but she hoped her human guest would appreciate the effort. Adding a few springy curls to her glossy sable hair, she refreshed her face with some light make up. She didn't want to look like she put a lot of time into her appearance but she certainly wanted a boost to her carefree style. She changed into her favorite and moderately snug low-rise jeans and tossed on a flowy, periwinkle blouse. A light blush-colored lipstick completed the look.

She had just come down the stairs from her bedroom when she heard the shrill sound of the doorbell. She took a deep breath, and closed her eyes for a quick moment before opening the door. Zak still hadn't shaved and the sexy stubble on his face was making her hunger for something other than chicken dinner. He leaned in, giving her a quick kiss on the cheek. The intoxicating scent of his cologne lingered. It was an outdoorsy fragrance: a subtle hint of sandalwood and, what she could only think to describe as smouldering man. Recovering, from what she hoped was a discreet inhale of Zak, she noticed his beautiful animal. She anticipated a matted, long-haired dog, but instead the dog had short curly hair the color of oatmeal. It stood obediently at his side with curious eyes.

He rubbed the dog's head in a way that commanded the animal to relax, although it was Zak who appeared most nervous.

Slowly moving her open hand toward Abby, she allowed the dog to sniff her. She had once made the mistake of moving too quickly to pet a Dachshund, and nearly got her hand bit off by the startled animal. She had at least learned something about canines from the experience. Abby gracefully positioned herself into Lexie's hand, and before she was conscious of it, she was petting the animal, feeling her woolly texture. She was amazed at Abby's quiet and gentle demeanor. As she stepped back from Abby, Lexie noticed flowers and a thin box in Zak's hand.

"The box is only meant to be opened after I leave, so no peeking." He smiled as he handed her the small bouquet of grocery store flowers and the plain wrapped box.

She wanted to object because she was curious, but instead she graciously agreed, then took his coat and placed it on the antique coat rack by the door. He was wearing a light blue sweater which hugged his muscular chest, and worn jeans that hung perfectly on his hips. Prior to his arrival, she had vowed to restrain herself around him. She now regretted the decision.

Abby moved in tandem with Zak into the center of the house when Lexie led them into the living area. The two-story home had a good-sized living area with solid wood beams across the ceiling. It was tastefully decorated in mainly dark hues with some ivory-colored accents, which allowed the room to be cozy without coming across as gloomy. There was an overstuffed chenille sofa in solid deep blue and a comfy armchair in a black and ivory Victorian print. There were wooden accent tables here and there, some original and a few excellent reproductions. It had a relaxing and a homey feel to it, but it didn't put him at ease. He stood awkwardly rigid in the middle of the room.

"I'm just going to get these flowers in some water. I'll be right back." She gave Zak a sweet smile, hoping the tension in his body would dissolve.

Noticing the soft pillows of the sofa, Zak chose the high back armchair to sit in. Abby sat obediently next to him, and after a few moments, she decided to lie down. From a decent vantage point, he was able to glance around the room into the dining room and hallway. Eventually he fixed his eyes on the imposing stone fireplace in the center of the living room, wondering if the thick, dark-wood mantel was original work.

"Can I get you anything to drink? I have club soda," Lexie shouted from the kitchen.

"No, thanks, I'm good," he stiffly responded.

Lexie returned to the living room and placed a bowl of water for Abby by the fireplace. The dog she was afraid would growl at her, was in a relaxed lying-down position. At least the dog seemed to like it here. It was obvious there was tension in the room and Lexie wasn't sure why. Did Zak not want to be here?

* * * *

I shouldn't be here. I should have said no. Damn it, I'm such a jerk.

Zak kept doubting, worried he would mess up this woman's life. She was so gracious, and the way Abby had relaxed so quickly in this new environment surprised him. He had hardly spoken and this, which was now their second date, was becoming awkward. He needed to get some fresh air before an anxiety attack took hold of him. He remembered he had left Abby's pillow and food in his truck, so he told Lexie he was just going to run out and get them. She offered to help him, but he needed some time to himself to clear his head, or take off. He wasn't sure which.

He took his time once he got outside. He did some simple breathing exercises and told himself to stop being an ass.

You can do it. Inhale, exhale, repeat. It'll be fine.

He grabbed the dog bedding and kibble and headed back into the house. To further calm himself, he spent the next fifteen minutes talking about the amount of food to give Abby, how often to feed her, and what kind of routine she normally had. He warned Lexie about the wolves in the area. It was best not to go for a run unless it was daylight, he told her. He wasn't just worried for Abby; he couldn't stand the thought of something happening to Lexie, either, although he was certain Abby would protect her.

"One last thing, if something happens to her, take her to Dr. Carden in Baxley. She's been there before."

Lexie chuckled, and he realized he was telling a first-rate surgeon what to do in an emergency.

"Seriously, Zak, don't worry. Abby will be fine."

"I know." And he did know that Abby would be fine in Lexie's hands. But focusing on mundane details regarding his dog helped to relax him. Now that the anxiety had subsided, he was able to focus on his surroundings.

"I've only ever seen a glimpse of this place when I would drive by. I've wondered what the inside was like." He cocked his head upward, looking at the ornate ceiling. "It's quite remarkable."

"Well, it took some work. There was a bit of a rodent issue when I first moved in. Thank God it was mice and not rats. Not that I like the idea of scampering mice, but I don't think I could even sleep in a home that had one rat, let alone a dozen of them. I found the space overwhelming when I first moved in, but with the right large pieces of furniture, it started to fill in. I'm still in need of some smaller pieces, but it's coming along."

"I'm not an expert on home décor, but I think it suits you."

"And how's that?"

"Well, it's elegant, beautiful, and warm." As soon as he said it, he realized how cheesy he sounded.

"That's pretty smooth," she said with a laugh.

Well, at least she hadn't groaned repulsively.

"The guy I'm renting from might put it on the market. If he does, I'm considering making an offer. It's twice the size of my old city condo, but it'll probably cost less money. I'm a bit hesitant. I don't know a thing about old houses. I'm sure it requires updated electrical and plumbing, but I really have no clue as to the extent of any other work or the cost."

"I'm not saying I'm an expert but I do know a few things about old homes. I even did some of my own renovations. I can take a look and give you an opinion, if you want."

"Wow, a man of many languages, a man who can cook, and now a fix-it man. What can't you do, Zak Tifour?" she teased.

Maintain a relationship with a woman. Of course, he didn't vocalize it. Instead he blurted out, "I can't sing."

"Probably because you haven't tried," she said with a laugh. "Come on, I'll show you the rest of the place and you can let me know what you think."

He got up and followed Lexie. He liked the idea of her purchasing the house. It would mean she would be staying in Baxley. Going from room to room, he commented on what she would probably need to have done, and even volunteered to do some of the minor work for her.

There was some hesitation before she led him up the wooden stairway to where he assumed the bedrooms were.

"Providing the price is right, I think this would be a great house to buy. It's really solid, and the work will cost a bit, but it's probably a good investment," he said, as he reached the top of the stairs.

"Good, I really like the idea of living in an historic home. I just don't want it to become a money pit."

After showing him the two small guest bedrooms with sparse furniture, she led him to the master. It was again beautifully decorated, but it wasn't subtle like the downstairs. A queen-size bed with a dark-leather upholstered headboard was the focal point, or at least that is what Zak chose to focus on. Several large faux fur pillows lay at the head, making it luxurious as well as primal. He imagined the bedding felt as comfortable as it looked. A sparkling chandelier, with a sheer black shade provided dim yet sensual illumination over her bed. The room was as sexy as the woman who slept there. There was something both forbidden and dangerous about being in her bedroom with the curtains pulled closed. A less responsible man might have blamed the erotic décor, but he knew it was his own wicked thoughts directing him. His arousal began way before he stepped into the room.

Oblivious to Zak's internal thoughts, Lexie stepped ahead, intent on leading him into the ensuite. She was still talking about the particulars of the house, but he was no longer listening. He was lost in his own mind, thinking carnal thoughts. She had no idea what being in this room next to her was doing to him. He couldn't bear it any longer. After taking only one giant step, his chest was up against her back. She let out a startled gasp, but didn't move away.

"I'm going to do what I should have done last night," he whispered into her ear.

Spinning her around, he pressed her against the bedroom door, shutting it behind them. He reached for the nearby wall switch, turning the lights off. The darkness was matched equally by the intensity in the air. Bringing his mouth to hers, he kissed her hard, pressing his body against hers. She let out a light and pleasing whimper as he felt the heat of her mouth welcoming him. She tasted as good as she looked.

Interlocking his hands with hers, he pushed them up over her head as he moved his lips down her neck, his body aching with desire. She let out an encouraging moan. He knew what he wanted, and he wasn't going to let reason interfere this time. They fumbled in the dark as they disrobed and fell onto her bed.

The intensity of their lovemaking rivaled that of a passionate opera, minus the tragedy. The giving and taking continued until they were both completely satisfied and exhausted. Afterward, he nuzzled her neck, soaking in her heat. He could hear her breathe as she went into a light sleep. He fought the urge to sleep, wanting to remain conscious, feeling her smooth skin against his body. He couldn't imagine ever getting enough of her.

He wouldn't allow this to be one-night stand. He'd had casual sexual encounters in his life, most of them occurring when he was new to the NYPD, but as time went on, he began to want more. But relationships didn't come easy, especially when working undercover. Few women wanted to date a man whose long erratic hours made him unreliable and whose secrets made him deceptive. And frankly, for many years he found relationships to be too much of a bother. Now that he was older, and he had the maturity to try and make it work, the PTSD became the obstacle. And although he'd had sex with a few women in the last couple of years, this was different. Previous encounters left him physically satisfied but emotionally numb. With Lexie, he felt a vastness of emotions, including a sense of belonging. And he didn't want any of it to end, so he remained awake with her beautiful face against his heart.

An hour later she awoke, and instinctively leaned toward the end table, switching on the small table lamp. She turned to him and kissed him lightly on the lips. As she pulled back, she tilted her head so she could focus on his dark brown eyes. She smiled. But what began as a tender moment between lovers, turned to uncertainty when she noticed the massive scar on his chest.

It was a nasty scar. It wasn't hideous, or at least he didn't think it was, but the last time a woman saw it she had been repulsed. Of course, the woman never said anything, but he could tell by her look. Since then, he tried to stay in the dark during intimate moments, putting a t-shirt on before daylight came. And now here he was, fully exposed and vulnerable. A vulnerability so raw, it made him question whether he could prevent the gaping wounds of truth from seeping out.

But she didn't seem horrified by his obvious imperfections, and what she did actually shocked him. Instead of pulling away or asking him about it, she took her hand to the scar and touched it lightly. She then placed her lips on his chest and kissed the wound. It undid him to a depth he had never known before. He quickly closed his eyes, holding on to the sensation for as long as he could.

There was no use in lying about it. She had likely operated on many gunshot wounds. She had a right to an explanation, and she also had a right to the truth, but he just wasn't ready for both.

As she laid in his arms he broke the silence. "I was shot when I lived in New York." It was indeed the truth. "Some punk kid was robbing this convenience store in the Bronx, and I tried to stop him." And what a mammoth lie that was. "Unfortunately, I didn't see the gun. It's one of those mistakes you don't make twice, like frying bacon without a shirt on."

She disregarded his ill attempt at humor. "How bad was the damage?"

She was a surgeon. She could likely tell how serious it was by the size and angle of the scar tissue.

"I can't remember all the technical terms you doctors use, but it wasn't good. Multiple chambers were affected, as the bullet extensively damaged both bone and tissue. I was laid up in the hospital for months."

He didn't mention how he could have been released weeks earlier if it weren't for the psychological damage, which didn't heal like his pulverized flesh did.

She once again put her lips to his scar. When she lifted her head to look at him, he could see the moisture building in her eyes.

"You're lucky to be alive."

"Yeah, I know," he whispered.

"Well, I hope you aren't going to any convenience stores in New York on this trip?" She said it with a sweet smile, which didn't lessen the concern in her eyes.

"No, I can do without the pack of gum," he tried to joke.

When the concern stayed on her face, he reached out and pushed the stray strand of hair back from her eyes. Leaning in, he gave her a most appreciative kiss. A heartfelt thank you for simply being Lexie.

* * * *

Due to the bedroom escapades, dinner ended up being a little later than what Lexie had planned. It wasn't spectacular, but it was edible. Besides, the quality of the meal was certainly not going to be the highlight of the day.

"Do you find it a bit chilly in here?" she asked as she handed him the last of the dishes to dry. The large house tended to cool down as soon as the sun set.

"I can light a fire if you want." He was hoping she would say yes. He preferred the crackling of a wood fire as opposed to turning up the thermostat.

"That would be great."

As he stacked the wood in the large stone fireplace, she dragged a faux fur throw and tossed some large cushions on the floor near the hearth. He was pleased she was as eager to cozy up under a luxurious blanket as he was. Once the kindling was in place, he lit a scrunched-up piece of paper and the fire took.

"Pretty good with starting a fire," she remarked.

"I've learned a few things living out in the country," he said as he sat down on the pillows beside her.

"You aren't pickling vegetables and making jams?" she asked, teasingly.

"Not yet, but I do make my own candles," he replied.

She gave him a serious look that made him bust out laughing.

"Had you believing, didn't I?"

"Sort of," she admitted.

He leaned in and gave her an apologetic kiss. "I'll stick to building fires on cold evenings," he said.

She smiled at him as she curled into his chest. He began running his hands through her hair. Feeling the heat, not only from the fire, but also from being so close to her, he couldn't help but touch her. He gave her another sweet kiss and soon the sweet kisses turned passionate. Encouraging him, she ran her hands up under his sweater, stroking his chest before lifting the sweater off. Soon he found her straddled on top of him. Her intense eyes signaling she was ready for him to make love to her again. Happy to comply with her wishes, he began peppering kisses down her neck. His movements weren't urgent like last time, where clothes were almost torn. This time it was slow and gentle, bringing back memories of the tenderness they shared at the opera. It was definitely passionate but also settling, like coming home after a long trip. Afterward, they stayed wrapped in each other, silently watching the last log burn before heading upstairs to sleep.

* * * *

It was dark when Zak awoke at six. He wouldn't have time to wait for the sun to come up. It was time to head home, shower quickly, and get to the airport. He glanced down at Lexie's leg on top of him and regretted having to move it. He enjoyed exploring her body and marveled at her magnificently toned legs. He laid still, enjoying her touch for a few more minutes. Finally, he stirred, trying to be gentle with her. The movement woke her from her blissful slumber. He kissed her gently on the lips.

"Hey, beautiful," he whispered, "I've got to go."

"Zak?"

"Yeah?"

"When you get to New York, hurry."

"Hurry?" he asked, confused.

"Hurry so you can get back here."

He smiled. He figured she meant her bed, not the town of Baxley.

And then, in what he sincerely meant, and would later realize was a mistake, he kissed her passionately and said, "I'll be back before you know it."

As soon as he left, he knew what he had to do. She had his phone number and soon enough she would try to reach him. He knew how powerful the temptation to respond would be, so he did the only thing he could do. He shut the phone off and left it at home. He felt like an S.O.B., but if he wanted to get back to her, he needed to have his head in the game. He couldn't do that if he didn't let her go. He had told her enough lies. Any further conversations had to be truthful. Conversations that would have to wait until he got back.

PART TWO

Chapter Eleven

It was exactly how Zak remembered – hectic, loud, and overwhelming. At one time, he welcomed the sounds: the conversations in foreign languages, the enthusiastic voices of reunited lovers, and even the squeals of enthusiastic children on vacation. Now the airport and the noises emitted from the various travellers grated on him. He had gotten used to the quiet sounds of rural Illinois and now he was back in the middle of chaos. The airport reminding him of the potential mayhem to come.

At least a familiar face would greet him. Omeir had insisted on picking him up at the airport. Zak hated being back in New York, but meeting up with his old friend would help to distract him. He needed to be distracted from who he had just left, as well as from the shame and guilt of what he had done. What kind of man takes a beautiful and trusting woman to bed, only to disappear on her?

Looking around, he spotted Omeir by the baggage carousel. With a wide grin, Omeir waved frantically, even though it was clear Zak had seen him. Omeir, like all those who worked in the Counterterrorism Bureau, took his job seriously, but unlike many of the men Zak worked with, had an incredible quirky sense of humor. In fact, he was probably one of the funniest guys Zak had ever met. He was like the kid who was the practical joker in class. Even when you didn't want to laugh, he always ended up doing something which just couldn't help but make you bust a smile. He had an innate ability to be serious when called for, but he also knew when comic relief was necessary.

As soon as he was within reach of the man, he was engulfed in a hug. "*Salaam*," they quickly greeted each other. When Zak pulled back,

Omeir quickly looked him over. "You look great." Inside he felt like shit, but with the best sleep he had in a long time, he knew he probably looked decent.

"How are you doing, buddy?" Omeir tried to make it sound casual, but ever since the shooting, it was no secret Zak wasn't always doing as well as he pretended. He knew what his friend was truly asking him.

"No need to worry. If I couldn't handle it, I wouldn't be here."

It was a lie, but one Zak was hoping Omeir would believe. He wasn't fine, and he figured he might never be fine, but this was perhaps as good as it would get. He did however have the confidence to believe he would be able to get through this assignment, which he had every intention would be his last.

As they were walking out of the airport to Omeir's parked car, Zak turned to him, "What's the plan for today?"

"Thought we would meet Safia at Fazaris for lunch and then afterward we have a quick meeting with Lieutenant Pratt and the rest of the team." Fazaris was an intimate eatery, serving Middle Eastern Cuisine. Zak was quite fond of it and had enjoyed many meals there. If there was a positive side to being back in New York, it was having lunch at Fazaris.

"How's Safia?" he inquired.

Omeir's face turned into a big grin. "Madly in love with me, that's how she is."

Zak chuckled. "Does she know about this mad love she has for you?"

"Well, maybe only subconsciously thus far, but any day it will come to the surface."

They both laughed.

Lunch at Fazaris didn't disappoint. It was exactly what Zak had remembered. The restaurant was filled with comforting smells – cloves, nutmeg, and a subtle hint of saffron. After catching up with Safia and having a delicious meal, the conversation turned to the two new guys assigned to their team.

Omeir and Safia had been working with Nate Larner, one of the new members, for about two months now. Nate was the youngest member at twenty-six years old. He didn't belong to the Counterterrorism Bureau or any part of the NYPD, but was hired as a consultant from Homeland Security. He was an expert in bioweaponry, which made him essential to the assignment. Nate authored most of the documents Omeir and Safia had delivered to Zak. According to Omeir, Nate came off a little too self-assured and borderline offensive at times, but he was knowledgeable.

"Sure, Nate sometimes blurts words out without thinking," said Safia, "but all you guys have that combination of arrogance and testosterone that makes you unbearable. But I wouldn't want to work with anyone else."

"So who's the other guy?" Zak asked.

"I don't know a lot about Detective Traversini," Omeir responded. "He's around our age, maybe a couple years younger. He's rumored to have been some Special Ops guy in the Marines before he joined the NYPD. Apparently, he had a bad reputation for being a hell raiser, but also an excellent reputation for getting the job done."

"I heard he goes by the nickname of Scorp, short for Scorpion," added Safia.

"Do you want to find out more?" Omeir asked.

He shook his head no. Zak knew what he meant. He would hack into Detective Traversini's life: social media, bank accounts, tax returns, even on-line dating, and whatever else there was out there that Omeir could get into. It was illegal and risky, even for him, but his friend would do it if Zak wanted him to. And although Zak was leery of new team members, he wasn't going to have Omeir risk his job just to find out Scorp lied on some ridiculous dating site about liking puppies and poetry. Zak would wait until he met Nate and Scorp and then assess how much he could trust them. He could usually read people well. Hopefully, he was still at the top of his game when it came to such things. He knew that with a nickname like Scorp, the man would certainly be interesting.

After each covert assignment, the location for the team would change. There was always the risk of someone noticing something unusual going on, and the longer a team stayed in one place, the greater the risk would be. This time they would meet and set up their operation out of an old, well-fortified building in an industrial area of Brooklyn. Zak and Omeir had travelled together in Omeir's Fiat to the restaurant to meet Safia. When Safia offered Zak a ride with her to the meeting, he jumped at the chance. He was starting to feel claustrophobic in the small car and welcomed riding along in Safia's spacious SUV.

The drive from the restaurant to the industrial area took about forty minutes, and he was thankful he was no longer cramped. Zak was cognizant of his sour mood, and had grown exhausted by Omeir's constant chatter. It was not a negative reflection on Omeir, as he normally enjoyed his uplifting banter. His darkened mood wasn't lifting. Being alone would be best, but that wasn't possible, so he hoped riding with Safia would at least not escalate his irritability.

Ten minutes into the ride Zak finally spoke, "Thanks for offering the ride."

"No problem. I figured you'd want to stretch out."

"Sorry about the mood. It's not you guys. It's this place. I can handle it, it's just that I don't like being in the city." He felt compelled to try to explain the obvious to her.

"It's okay, Zak. We know."

The silence returned for a few more minutes. When they came to a crawl on the congested roadway, Safia spoke, "Baxley seems like a nice quiet place. You seem comfortable there."

"Comfortable?" he questioned. It seemed an odd word to describe his new life.

"Well, at peace." She saw the puzzled look he gave her, so she clarified, "You seem more like you... less troubled."

There was a reluctance to admit to any amount of contentment, since Zak wasn't sure he would be able to hang on to it. "Yeah, it was a good choice for me, but I can't say I can totally relax there. I don't think what we know, and what we've experienced, can let any one of us relax totally." It was certainly true for him.

"Yeah, you're probably right. Omeir thinks if this assignment goes as planned, then it will be different for all of us. Maybe you'll stay in New York." She quickly glanced over to see his reaction. When she couldn't gage him, she continued, "Omeir misses having a guy friend around. He's actually been bugging me to go fishing with him. Says he needs a new fishing buddy since you left. Can you imagine my father's face if I told him I was going fishing with one of the guys from work?" It was a given that her overprotective father would be upset with his daughter socializing with a fellow officer.

He smiled at Safia. "Probably wouldn't go over so well," he responded. It wasn't the image of her irate father that had Zak smiling, it was Omeir. He knew Omeir could care less about fishing. He hated it when Zak dragged him along. He hated everything about fishing: the getting up early, the sitting patiently for hours, and of course the sparseness of conversation. No, the only reason Omeir wanted Safia to go fishing with him was to spend time with her. His grin disappeared as he went back to what Safia had said about him remaining in New York. He thought it best to be honest.

"I'm done with New York after this assignment." There was darkness in his eyes. "I'm going back to Baxley when it's all done."

She heard him, but didn't respond. Instead, she changed the subject.

"So where did you leave Abby? Is she at a kennel here in New York?" There was no way for Safia to have known that her attempt to transition to a lighter topic would fall flat.

"She's with a friend in Baxley," he muttered as he turned and looked out the passenger window.

Safia looked over at Zak. It was common knowledge that Zak was hiding out in Baxley and wasn't into making friends with the locals. He stayed staring out the window, but he caught her knowing smile in the window's reflection. She had figured out that *friend* meant a woman who was more important to Zak than he was ready to admit.

It was critical to keep Lexie out of his head until he was done with the assignment. It was not only practical and safe to avoid thinking of her, it was necessary. But the conversation with Safia about Abby had pushed his thoughts to Lexie. And that was a problem. It was a problem for many reasons, and right now he was overwhelmed with guilt. A useless emotion that wasn't helping him with why he had come to New York. He was at least relieved Safia hadn't pushed him on any details on the "friend" who was taking care of Abby. He liked that about Safia, as she knew when to leave matters alone.

When Safia pulled into a parking spot, Omeir was already exiting his vehicle. They utilized the biometric fingerprint lock to get into the metal door of the building. Two NYPD members in civilian clothing greeted them and let them into another locked door. They walked down a long concrete corridor to an unlocked door and into a large warehouse space. There was a guy seated on a metal chair in front of a large steel table. He was bent over a laptop, obviously pre-occupied enough not to notice he was no longer alone. He was a slightly built man with a pale complexion, not quite as pasty as one of the characters from those popular vampire movies, but it was clear he spent most of his time indoors. Clearly, he was no ex-Marine. Must be the bioterrorism expert, Nate Larner.

As Zak neared, the guy finally looked up from his laptop. He was just a kid. He could easily pass for a junior in college as opposed to one of America's top experts in biological agents. He was certainly not what he had imagined from Omeir's earlier comments. The guy didn't fit the bill of an arrogant, cocky man, but Zak knew appearances could be deceiving. Nate was older than he looked, but the guy still had to be some kind of genius to have already obtained the credentials he had.

Omeir did the formal introductions. "Nate, this is Detective Zak Ahmadi."

Nate reached out his hand and shook Zak's. "So you're the guy who's going to need me?"

"Not sure what you mean," Zak responded.

"You know, the guy with the brawn, who needs my brain to get this done."

Zak's gaze narrowed on him. He now understood what Omeir had meant by arrogant. The kid actually thought Zak was just muscle and didn't have a brain to match. Irritated, he moved toward Nate. He wasn't sure what he was going to do but he wanted his physical presence to consume the guy's space. Zak wasn't in the best of moods to start with, and he wasn't going to let some ignorant little schmuck talk down to him. Before he could respond by words or further action, Safia interrupted, ushering a clueless Nate to safety. They were out of earshot, so Zak couldn't hear them, but he could see that Safia had Nate's full attention. The kid was now sheepishly nodding his head in agreement with her.

Omeir leaned toward his riled-up colleague. "Told you so, buddy. Kind of a jerk, with no people skills, but he is knowledgeable, and we need him. He looks like he has tiny bird bones in his body, so even a slight push on him might make him crack like Tweety Bird. Better to forget his stupidity. He'll learn you're almost as brilliant as me."

Omeir's words made the tension leave Zak's body as he let out a laugh. His friend had the ability to take him from anger to laughter in a few seconds. He so missed that.

Upon hearing Zak's laughter, Safia led Nate back to the table. Just as they reached the group, Nate looked toward the doorway beyond Zak and Omeir. Nate was no poker player. His eyes grew round, and his mouth opened as disbelief washed over his face.

Instinctively, Omeir and Zak turned around. An enormous figure was walking toward them. Zak himself was a large man with a strong presence, but this man took up the entire doorway. This guy definitely fit the image of an ex-Marine with a nickname of Scorp. Upon seeing the size of the man, Zak was truly thankful the guy was on their side. He would hate to go up against this herculean force.

When the man finally reached the table, his features came into focus in the light. He had on a T-shirt, which hugged his massive frame, and cargo pants, with heavy boots you wouldn't want to come your way.

He was covered in graphic ink, full-sleeve tattoos shooting down his arms with the bloodied fangs of a viper wrapped around his neck. His face appeared worn, a probable combination of adverse circumstances and years spent in unforgiving elements. He was certainly the most physically intimidating man Zak had ever encountered, and he had encountered many in his line of work.

"Hope I'm not late. Traffic problems," the man said. His voice was deep, which didn't surprise any of them. He appeared to be speaking to Zak and Omeir, his gaze focused on them. Slowly, he angled his tree trunk of a neck over toward Nate, and then to Safia. Reaching out to her, he flashed a wide grin. "Hey, I'm Scorp."

Safia shook his enormous hand, introducing herself and then Nate. Even while shaking Nate's hand, he kept his focus on Safia. Finally breaking from Safia, Scorp moved over to Zak and Omeir for further introductions. It was a slow saunter, full of confidence as well as arrogance. Zak notice Omeir's annoyance. The man was being far too intense with Safia. Once the introductions were over, Scorp grabbed a metal chair, turned it around and sat down with his hands resting against the metal back. Zak seriously thought the chair would give way to the man's massive body, but somehow it didn't.

"This all of us?" Scorp asked.

"Yup, just waiting for Lieutenant Pratt," Zak responded.

Lieutenant Bryant Pratt was the lead on this assignment. His job was to brief the team and ensure the task went as smoothly as possible. Pratt knew Zak's history. He had been around during his last assignment – the assignment that ended disastrously. Lieutenant Pratt was a no-nonsense type of man, who had worked his way up the ranks of the NYPD. He had been a first responder during 9/11 and he took his job seriously. He didn't have any tolerance for those who weren't devoted to the job, and ensured any man or woman who had other commitments which didn't coincide with his strong work ethic were reassigned from the Bureau.

Pratt didn't have much of a sense of humor, but he was smart enough to tolerate Omeir's antics, providing they released tension when needed. He had been a bona fide ass to Safia when she was first under his command. He reckoned Safia, a second-generation cop, hadn't earned her place within the Bureau and had been given special treatment due to her father, who was a high-ranking member of the NYPD. Fortunately, for all their sakes, Pratt was a smart man. Soon he realized what most hard-core members discerned about the attractive police detective – she was indispensable. Safia worked twice as hard as most of the other members and she was remarkable when it came to her specialties, which included her physical prowess. One of Zak's best memories with the NYPD was the day Safia finally earned Pratt's respect. Pratt had teamed Safia with this cocky male officer during self-defence training. The man had been twice Safia's size, with an ego that matched the size of his biceps. Pratt had figured he would get Safia run off the Bureau, returning to regular patrol or even resigning. But Safia had ended up pummelling her opponent in no time. Witnessing Pratt's rather stoic face turning to shock had been priceless. Pratt had finally seen Safia for who she truly was, and what she could contribute to the police force. Safia never had any further problems with her boss.

Pratt always treated Zak with respect. When he was diagnosed with PTSD, he was actually surprised with how supportive Pratt was. Although Pratt wasn't the emotional type, he ensured there was ample support for Zak, whether it was time off, professional help, or financial assistance. He hadn't heard from Pratt in a long time, and he knew why. Pratt had Safia and Omeir checking in on him. It wasn't Pratt's style to beleaguer Zak with phone calls. The lieutenant understood a broken man just wanting to be left alone. He was aware Pratt was the major force in getting him back in the field. He didn't like it, but he understood it.

The wait for Pratt became increasingly awkward. Zak had nothing to say to Nate. He wasn't into faking nice with someone who, only a few minutes ago, he'd felt like smacking. Normally he would use the waiting time to practice his skills of charm and deception on the new guy, but he was now too moody to do so. Omeir was just as irritable, quietly fuming about Scorp cozying up to Safia. Due to the chat with Safia, Nate had grasped the importance of silence and once again focused on his laptop.

Only Safia and Scorp seemed to be interacting, which made Omeir even more jealous. Zak was thinking about heading outside for some fresh air, when Pratt finally walked in.

The lieutenant was a rather stout man nearing fifty. He had bulging biceps, which contradicted his enlarged and soft mid-section. His job entailed sitting behind a desk, and it was starting to show.

"Got stuck on the expressway," Pratt said. It was a statement and not an apology. "I trust you took the time to introduce yourselves." He gave Scorp a questionable look when he noticed him leaning a little too close to Safia. Scorp either didn't notice or didn't care. "So let me go over what it is you will be doing." It was typical of Pratt to get to the point.

He started by briefing the team on what Nate would be doing. Essentially, Nate would be behind the scenes, working out of the warehouse, providing expert advice to Zak on biological agents. He acknowledged reading the background information on the microorganism Nate had theoretically created, as well as the information about the contacts who were looking to buy this formula. Zak wasn't crazy about Nate, but he was there to get the job done. He would brush aside his ego, his anger, and once he got some sleep, even his disdain for the guy. Nate was the whiz kid when it came to biological weapons. Zak wouldn't hesitate to contact him for additional information or clarification on the subject matter.

Safia's role was to get Omeir in and out of various designated areas so he could set up the necessary surveillance equipment. Once the equipment was in place, they would go back to the warehouse to monitor the activities alongside Nate and Pratt.

Zak's role was what he did best. He would be the point man. He would arrange the sale of the formula pertaining to the microorganism to the contacts, who were brokers for Al-Qaeda, the actual buyers. The contacts were familiar with him from the last assignment, and the intelligence the NYPD received indicated they trusted Zak since he passed their test last time. The test, of course, had been the torture he'd endured. It was a test which had irrevocably damaged Zak, but the contacts thankfully appeared unaware of this. Defining Scorp's role was next, and Zak and the other team members were curious as to where the big guy fit in.

Pratt focused on Zak as he spoke. "Because you were beat up and shot last time, the contacts know that you're going to be more cautious this time."

Pratt's use of *beat up* annoyed Zak. He hadn't been beat up, roughed up, or knocked around. He'd been bloody well tortured. He chose not to voice his irritation. He wasn't sure if Pratt was trying to avoid advertising what happened to him to the new team members, or if he was actually minimizing what occurred.

Pratt continued, "So it makes sense you would have a bodyguard with you, and that's where Scorp here comes in."

He felt the anger rising, and this time, Zak couldn't contain it. Abruptly, he stood up from the table, closing in on Pratt. "I'm not going in with a babysitter. I take care of myself," he shouted.

Omeir and Safia exchanged glances with each other. Zak had a reputation of being calm and following orders. The outburst was uncharacteristic and concerning. Scorp, however, didn't appeared bothered by Zak's opposition, and Nate looked like he could care less about big boy problems.

Although they were only a foot apart, Pratt took another step toward Zak. The physical gap between superior and subordinate was mere inches. Zak towered over the lieutenant by several inches, but Pratt would not be intimidated. He glared back at Zak, his eyes stone cold, his body unwavering.

"Shut it down, Zak. I know better than anyone you can handle yourself. This isn't about your capabilities and I'm not going to have it become about your ego." He was sharp and unapologetic. "It's about reasonable expectations from the contacts. The enemy expects your motivation is money. They must believe you are doing this because you hate Americans but love the American dollar. They won't buy you taking another chance going in alone this time. They want this enough to trust you, but they aren't stupid. They'll track you. If they see you're not protected, they'll think you're either insane or planning to entrap them."

Pratt continued to glare at Zak for a few more seconds before backing away from him. Once he was on the other side of the table, he added, "Scorp won't be your only bodyguard. There will be three other plainclothes officers accompanying you when you meet the contacts, but Scorp's the only one who will be living with you until this is done."

Zak knew Pratt was right. He hated the idea, but it made sense. He also hated the idea of bringing in the other officers. The larger the team, the greater the risk of information being leaked, like last time.

* * * *

After they had knocked off for the day, Omeir suggested Zak hang out with him, but he declined. He was eager to officially start the assignment, and that meant checking in to a posh Manhattan hotel with his 'bodyguard' Scorp. The hotel was on Fifth Avenue, overlooking Central Park. It cost the NYPD over five thousand dollars a night for the two-bedroom suite. No expenses were spared. Zak needed to be convincing in his role as a greedy and affluent ally to terrorists.

The hotel suite was just over thirteen hundred square feet, ample room for two men. Scorp was either a bright enough guy to pick up on Zak's mood or wanted time to himself; either way, he gave Zak space. They hardly spoke to each other throughout the evening except for agreeing to get up early to go to the hotel's swanky health club. For the amount the Bureau was paying for the suite, they figured they might as well utilize the hotel's amenities as much as possible.

The first couple of days were uneventful. Scorp wanted to go to the health club to relieve tension as much as Zak. Working out helped to dispel some of the moodiness developing not only in Zak, but also in Scorp. He had no idea what Scorp's deal was, and frankly he didn't care. As long as the man could do the job, that was all that mattered. Well, that and not setting off Omeir.

Zak was used to the serene country sounds in Baxley. It was an adjustment to hear the wailing sirens in New York. He kept busy to not only block out the city noises, but also so he didn't end up thinking about Lexie. If he wasn't pumping weights or running, he was going over more documents from Nate. Scorp spent his spare time watching the sports channel and just chilling quietly, staying out of Zak's way. He could tell by the third day Scorp was getting a bit antsy, and they were both glad for the weekend to have ended. On Monday they would meet with the rest of the team, hoping the contacts would get in touch with them soon.

Chapter Twelve

A strange feeling came over Lexie the morning Zak left for New York. Something was off, but she didn't know what. When he stayed the night, she felt the longing he had for her, a starving thirst that went beyond just the physical craving he showed her when he took her body. But when morning came, a sadness crept into him. Sure, they were going to be apart for a couple of weeks, but that wasn't the root of his sadness. It was something else that caused the painful angst to consume him. He reminded her of the Zak she met during the blizzard, hidden by a mask. A man who was there when she needed him, but who was afraid of getting too close. And his words contradicted what she saw. His words were soothing, telling her he would be back soon, but his eyes told a different story. That morning she saw fear.

She wanted to deny what she saw. And she did momentarily, telling herself she was reading too much into it. Maybe it was her own doubts, a fear of allowing this man to get too close to her that was messing up her mind.

She then remembered the present he gave her. The wrapped gift he made her promise not to open until after he left. She went to the antique hutch in the dining room where she had placed it. It was wrapped in plain brown paper, the kind used at the post office. She ripped apart the paper, exposing a slim cardboard box with a lid. She lifted the flimsy lid off the box. Realizing what it was, she smiled, letting go of the doubt she had felt earlier. In her hand was a disc of opera arias Zak had downloaded for her. A handwritten note explained the different arias and marked which ones were his favorites. He also included a short personal note:

Thanks for sharing my love of opera with me. I hope you enjoy this gift and I look forward to sharing more upon my return.
Zak

Without having to recall any previous gifts, Lexie undoubtedly knew this simple disc of music was the most heartfelt she had ever received. She couldn't wait to hear from Zak. She wanted to let him know how much she loved it, how much it touched her. She had already commenced listening to the exquisite music and was eager to talk to him about it. Talking to him would settle her. His voice would sooth her, putting her fears to rest. She waited for the call, the call that never came.

* * * *

On Monday, Lexie was stricken with worry, convinced he hadn't called because something horrible had happened – a car accident, a mugging in Central Park, or even another shooting during a convenience store robbery. All these scenarios, and a few others, consuming space in her head. By Tuesday, the worry remained, but annoyance was starting to move in. By Wednesday, anger had taken the reins. She could no longer hide her bad mood and finally Margo confronted her during the lunch break.

"I know I said I wouldn't pry and I certainly meant it, Dr. Draden, but we both know something's bothering you. If you need to go home to Chicago for a while, it's not a problem. I can arrange for another doctor from Lands Crossing to cover."

"No, I don't need to go to Chicago," Lexie snapped. Seeing the hurt come across Margo's face, she let out a deep sigh. "It's Zak."

"Zak?"

"Yes, I'm annoyed with him." It wasn't all annoyance, there was also sadness and fear, but being irritated was the only emotion she was willing to admit to.

"Oh, I'm sorry," Margo said with trepidation.

"We had a great time on Saturday, so great, he came over on Sunday, as well." Not wanting to spill Zak staying over on Sunday night, she tried to leave out the intimately private details while still trying to convey what she was annoyed about. "He told me prior to our date he would be going to New York for work."

"For work?" Margo inquired. She wanted to see if Lexie knew more about what work Zak was actually involved in.

"Yes, some major corporation was hiring him for translations."

"So he's in New York after telling you he was going?" Margo was trying to follow along, but she was still confused on what had gotten Lexie upset.

"I left a voice message, and also texted him. He hasn't responded," she said.

Lexie had actually ended up leaving several messages, filling up his voice mail, and was now unable to leave any more. She didn't tell Margo this; it was embarrassing to admit. She felt like a stalker leaving message after message. "I'm taking care of his dog. What if there was an emergency with Abby?" She hadn't expected Margo to answer, she just wanted reassurance that she wasn't overreacting.

Margo was also now worried, but didn't want to show it. She had promised Zak she would keep his secret. "Did he tell you where he was staying in New York and when he would be back?"

"No, I don't know where or with whom he's staying." She could no longer hide the bitterness in her voice. "He said he would be back in a week or two."

Margo was trying to figure it out in her head. She guessed Zak had returned to the NYPD, an undercover operation. The fact he said he gave Lexie a particular timeframe was a strong indicator he would be back soon, although not likely soon enough for Lexie. Margo hoped it was something mundane that lured him back to New York and nothing dangerous. Being in possession of a personal cell phone was probably against some undercover police policy. She didn't want Lexie to worry, but she promised her loyalty to Zak. Besides, even if she told Lexie the truth, it would likely result in Lexie being even more concerned. Once Zak got back to Baxley, she figured he would tell Lexie, and if he didn't, then she would ensure he did. She didn't want to get involved in her boss' life, even though she liked Lexie. It was certainly easier with old Dr. Thornton.

"Maybe he lost his phone with your number in it," Margo quipped.

"It's possible, but he could always call me at work," Lexie refuted.

"Yes, but guys, they don't always get it. They get busy and figure they'll make it up to the girl when they get back." Margo realized she sounded flippant, which wasn't her intent. She quickly added, "I'm not just saying this to make you feel better, but I really think Zak's a nice guy. I don't think he's purposely being a jerk."

Lexie was now feeling awkward with the discussion, and to an extent, even foolish. She only had one real date with Zak, maybe two if she counted Sunday. She had been so far removed from dating, she wasn't even sure if cooking dinner and having sex counted as a date. Although she felt a connection beyond just a night of passion, she might have been overthinking this whole thing. She used to have good instincts, but after her mistake with Hailie, she'd started to doubt herself.

"Maybe you're right." As Lexie said the words, she smiled slightly in an effort to convince Margo it wasn't a big deal to her anymore. She doubted she convinced the elderly woman, but she needed to get back to work. Discussing the subject further wasn't going to change things.

Chapter Thirteen

Zak was relieved when the contact, Nadir Girgis, finally called near the end of the week. He was used to waiting and he tended to be a patient man, but since this was to be his last mission, he was eager to get going. Girgis had suggested he meet with Zak on Wednesday next week. Zak made him aware he would have a security detail with him. There was no objection from Girgis, which reinforced Pratt's belief it was actually an expectation. Zak was aiming for the assignment to be completed on Wednesday and the required paperwork and debriefing wrapped up by Friday. He figured he could catch a late Friday flight to Chicago and be in Baxley for the weekend. Lexie would likely be furious with him, but he was intent on doing what it took to regain her trust, a trust he hoped he could restore.

Zak and Scorp met with the rest of the team later in the day to finalize some further details. The news of a meeting on Wednesday seemed to help ease the tension with the team. As was routine when they were about to head into a dangerous mission, Omeir and Safia had planned to go to the Mosque for prayers. Nate was heading back to Washington for the weekend and would return on Sunday night. If things changed, he would be readily available and would be brought back immediately.

Discreetly, Omeir leaned over to Zak and whispered, "Do you want to go for prayers? Maybe grab some dinner afterward?"

"Sure, I'll see if Scorp can meet me later."

Apparently, their whispered conversation was not discreet enough because Scorp uttered, "I'll go to the mosque, too."

Omeir and Zak looked at each other. It never occurred to them that Scorp would go to a mosque. Worshiping God, whether it be in a church, synagogue, or mosque, just didn't seem to fit Scorp. Sure, it wasn't a fair assumption for Zak to make, but he had to admit he just didn't see Scorp as bowing down to praise God. It was too humbling for a man with an ego that barely fit into a room.

Zak knew it wasn't right to feel apprehensive toward anyone for wanting to pray. He himself wasn't a devout Muslim, like Safia and Omeir. But he was a respectful man, well-versed in the Qur'an and Islamic customs. And he didn't go to the mosque to appease his Muslim friends. Although he believed his prayers went unanswered, he did believe in God's mercy. Praying centered him. It helped to calm the storm that so often brewed inside of him.

Omeir and Safia never asked why he went. It didn't matter. And it wasn't only Zak they had asked in the past. Often, they had non-Muslim colleagues who would go for prayers with them. They would have invited even Nate. And now that Nate hadn't said anything else stupid to Zak, he likely would have welcomed him, too. But Scorp? His motives were suspect. Zak didn't like to judge him like this, but he couldn't help it.

Scorp was rather obvious in his admiration of Safia, and Zak wasn't exactly sure how she felt about him. Her private life was her business, and if she was somehow interested in Scorp, then Zak should just let her figure it out. The problem was that Scorp came across as a player. And even though they were not blood related, Safia was family to Zak, and noticeably more to Omeir. He didn't have any issues with Scorp, but he wasn't so naïve as to trust him explicitly when it came to Safia. He had never mixed work with relationships, and was growing annoyed with how he was now drawn into all this drama. The focus should be on the mission, not his colleagues' egos and fantasies.

While Omeir and Zak were looking at each other and deciding how best to respond, Safia had already turned to Scorp. "Great! Omeir and I will meet you and Zak there at seven this evening." Turning to Omeir and Zak, she added, "We'll go to the one in Queens."

The mosque she referred to was held in the basement of an old Anglican Church hall. A place which did not separate the women with a physical barrier from the men. Safia had long ago decided she would not be segregated, as she labeled it, and had been attending this mosque in

Queens for some time now. She worked with men all day long and she was adamant she would pray along with them, too. She didn't object to the custom of men praying side by side with men on one side and the women on the other side, but loathed the idea of separation via a physical barrier.

After she made the decision for them all, Safia turned away from the guys to collect her gear. As she was walking away, Scorp grinned. He didn't even have the decency to hide his amusement. It was no surprise when Omeir made up a bogus excuse to talk privately about the surveillance equipment with Zak. Once they were alone, he let loose.

"There is no way that jerk is coming for prayers. He's only going to ogle Safia and probably check out all the other women as well."

Zak had never seen Omeir so livid and for a second, he thought Omeir was even going to cuss. "I don't know what motive Scorp has, or if he even has a motive, but Safia is welcoming him. You've always extended an open invite to prayers."

"Yes, an open invite, but this guy's a jerk."

Zak was feeling torn. He was leery of Scorp's true motivation, but he didn't like the idea of turning anyone away from prayers. He recalled his father's words: *God welcomes everyone to worship and give thanks.* Scorp was a team member and had actually become a decent roommate over the last few days. He respected Zak's sullen mood, his need for privacy. It was one thing to suggest Scorp didn't have to come, but to tell him he wasn't welcome didn't sit right with Zak. Besides, Safia wanted him to join them. Group cohesiveness was essential and the mounting tension between Omeir and Scorp was getting in the way.

"Look, I'll talk to Scorp on the way over and make it painfully clear what the expectations are. If he isn't interested in abiding, I'll text you and let you know we won't be coming." It was only a short-term solution. Somehow, Scorp's interest in Safia had to be curtailed for all their sakes, and more importantly for the sake of the mission.

Omeir scowled and shook his head at Zak's suggestion.

Screw this. Zak wasn't going to get into a showdown with Omeir and he wasn't going to be the one to tell Scorp he wasn't welcome, just because he didn't look like the type of guy who prayed. It was wrong. Yeah, a lot had changed in a few years. He wasn't the optimistic guy he used to be. There was an edge to him, a bitterness. But he still knew he had no right to tell a man he couldn't pray. Omeir was a frigging NYPD detective, a big enough man to handle his own problems, so if he wanted to banish Scorp, then he better be prepared to do it himself, and to also face the wrath of Safia. Zak had offered to talk to Scorp on the way to the Mosque. If Omeir didn't want the assistance, then he could deal with Scorp himself.

"Okay, Omeir, go tell him."

"You want me to tell him?"

"Uh, yes. You're the one that doesn't want him to come."

After a few moments, it appeared Omeir realized he couldn't win this battle, or at least not without looking like an ass in front of Safia.

"Fine, Zak, but if you show up with him and he looks at any woman in an inappropriate manner, I'm going to lose it on him, and I don't care how big of a guy he is."

At least he relented. "Trust me, Omeir, I'm good at reading people. If he's not going for the right reason, he won't be walking in the door."

Omeir mumbled something indiscernible and hurried off to find Safia.

As if amused by it all, Scorp was grinning when Zak finally returned.

"Are we ready to go, roomie?" Scorp asked.

"Yup. So you ever been to a mosque? Do you know anything about Islam?"

"Nope, but I know you'll fill me in." And again, he grinned, which made Zak even more concerned.

It would take at least thirty minutes to get to the mosque. Zak decided it was best to be forthright, no need driving there just to turn around.

"Look, anyone is welcome to attend prayers. We just ask you to be there for the right reasons. We don't care what religion you follow or don't follow, we just want you to show respect. So I gotta ask this,

Scorp, do you have any issues with this? I get it if it's not your thing. You don't have to go for my sake. I can pray back at the hotel." For a second, he thought Scorp was going to opt out, but then he heard him clearing his throat.

"I know I come off as an ass, because frankly I am, but I am not a stupid man, Zak. I know better than to mess with a man's religion, and now the same goes for a man's woman. I don't know what, if anything is going on between Safia and Omeir. Frankly, I think it might be all in Omeir's mind, but I'm done messing with him. He's part of our team, and I don't need him to think twice about saving my ass if it comes down to it. Like you probably guessed, I'm not a deeply religious man, but I've been through a lot of shit in my life. I've been in many dire situations that I should not have survived. But here I am. I don't know if it was luck or some Divinity pulling me through. Regardless, I decided quite a few years ago I wasn't going to disrespect any man's religion. So to answer the question you're really aiming to ask: no, you don't need to worry about me scoping out Safia or any other woman at the mosque. I'm going there to pray."

Zak was stunned, surprised not only by his candor, but because this was the most he had spoken since they'd met. Most of the talk between them had been short conversations about trivial matters. Brief conversations about working out, getting something to eat, or football banter since he was a Giants fan and Scorp, a Jets fan. The man knew all along what Zak and Omeir had been thinking, and although he seemed to enjoy toying with them, he apparently had decided to put Zak's mind at ease and not cause any more friction. At least Zak hoped this was the case.

* * * *

True to his word, Scorp behaved like a perfect gentleman at prayers. In fact, he appeared quite focused during the ritual and it made Zak wonder what a man like Scorp would pray for. Zak prayed for the usual: he prayed for healing; for the nightmares to end; to be able to feel whole.

He prayed for forgiveness for the violence he'd had a hand in, and for the men who had died because of him. He prayed that the assignment he was embarking on wouldn't end in any more casualties. The men they were dealing with were vile, but to inflict violence on others even if necessary, was still something that compelled him to seek God's forgiveness. Lastly, he prayed to be able to return to Baxley, and for healing for Lexie. He had seen in her eyes how the loss of her niece affected her. He tried not to think of Lexie, though at times this was difficult. When he was inside a mosque, he would never deny the truth.

After prayers, the four of them went out for dinner. Zak could tell Omeir was still irked about Scorp hanging out with them, but the big man was definitely staying in line. He immediately sat next to Zak, leaving the space beside Safia in the narrow booth free for Omeir. It would have been more comfortable had Scorp sat next to Safia instead of the two biggest men being shoulder to shoulder, but Zak resigned himself to the uncomfortable seating arrangements. A few times, he discreetly nudged Scorp to give him a bit more room, but Scorp wasn't budging. He sensed it was his humorous way of saying, *I've given enough for one day and you're not getting even an inch more.*

Fair enough, thought Zak. He had come through like he had promised.

As soon as they got back to the suite, Scorp ordered a few beers from room service and settled in to watch a hockey game in the shared and spacious living quarters. Zak joined him for the first two periods of the game, before deciding to knock off for the night. Scorp scoffed at him for bailing on the tied game, but Zak just couldn't keep his eyes open any longer.

* * * *

The fear, the confusion, and then the panic, it was real. The graphic images shot out, and they, too, seemed real. Zak was in a large swampy pool of water that reached up to his waist. The water was weighted, an inexplicably dense liquid substance. It wasn't a current pushing against him, but its effect was the same, restricting the movement in his legs. Slowly, he swooshed forward in the water. At first, it was quiet but then a chirping sound began. It sounded like crickets off in the distance. The chirping faded, replaced by labored thrashing sounds coming from the sediment-filled waters. It got louder and louder. He tried looking around, but because of the fog-like darkness, he was not able to see the source of the noise. He tilted his head downward, away from the sky and to the water in front of him. It was people, lifeless human bodies, floating past him. They moved gradually, like swimmers drifting leisurely on their backs, and then the flow picked up speed, becoming faster and faster. There were more and more bodies, to the point where it was moot to count their numbers. The water began to change colors, no longer a murky grey color but a light pinkish hue. The color darkened until it was a crimson-red. He was confused for a moment, before he understood. It was blood. Human blood, bleeding into the water.

When he finally awoke, he was confused. Time, place, what was happening, it was all a blur. His heart raced and he gasped for air, too focused on the blood in his nightmare to realize his body's reaction. The room was dark, disorienting him as to where he was. His brain tried to convey to him what had happened, what was happening, but it couldn't process fast enough.

He saw the shadowy figure moving, but it was too dark in the room to make sense of it all. His survival instinct kicked into high gear and he bounded out of the bed, ramming toward the figure. As he hit his target with his right shoulder, he heard the loud thundering voice.

"What the hell?"

The bellowed words kicked his brain into high gear. He recognized Scorp's voice. As the fog lifted from his cerebral matter, he remembered that he was in a luxury hotel in New York, as opposed to being trapped in a blood-ridden swamp with decomposing bodies. The large figure he'd just smashed with his shoulder was his colleague. He was still emotionally charged, but because Scorp was not coming back toward him, he didn't have the inclination to take another run at him. It was lucky he didn't, it was doubtful Scorp would allow another hit to occur without retaliation.

"What the hell are you doing in my room?" Confusion and anger filling Zak's voice.

"There was noise. I came to check it out," Scorp barked back.

Zak took a few breaths. A sense of foolishness began to flow through him as he realized he had been thrashing around from his nightmare, and by Scorp's response, it must have been quite a thrashing.

Trying to downplay what had happened, Zak muttered, "Just a bit of a nightmare. Sorry, man, but at least I know you got my back."

Although Zak hadn't talked about his PTSD diagnosis with him, Scorp knew about it. When a guy as legendary as Zak Ahmadi gets sidelined, cops talk. Scorp figured it was best to downplay what happened. He had confidence in Zak's abilities, but he understood how easily an episode could shake his perception of his own mental health.

"You know, you shouldn't have ordered spicy food at dinner. I'm fortunate because when I eat spicy food, I just get dreams of spicy women. And I was just in the middle of a good one when you started thumping around." It was Scorp's attempt to lighten the mood as well as get Zak back on track. "Oh, by the way, thanks for messing that up."

"I'm sure you'll survive. And next time, I'll ensure I order something bland and boring, so I don't hurt you."

"It'll take more than just that feeble tackle to hurt me. You learn that girly move from the Giants?"

He wasn't sure how much force it would take to hurt Scorp and it wasn't something he wanted to find out. But he did appreciate Scorp's mocking banter to lessen the tension.

Chapter Fourteen

The following days were uneventful. Zak didn't sleep great, but at least there were no further nightmares. He spent most of the time memorizing the documents Nate had given him. He made a few calls to Nate to clarify some matters and surprisingly, Nate was cordial to him. He mentioned this to Scorp who just grinned, making him wonder if Scorp had had a one-sided discussion with Nate about his pompous attitude. A Scorp-initiated chat would have been a lot more intense, and a hell of a lot less diplomatic than the one Safia had with Nate.

They all got together on Monday at the fortified industrial site. It was a long day of more scenarios to go over and contingency planning. Zak was used to the tedious and time-consuming work of going over detail after detail. It was something he was trained to do and had become second nature to him. He had the patience to sit for hours reviewing every angle and facet.

When Zak finally took a break from his own intense focus, he glanced around at his colleagues. They seemed as equally engaged, with the exception of the big guy. Scorp was antsy. He was slowly moving his bull neck up and down, in an effort to keep awake and to prevent the thick muscles from seizing up. It was easy to pick up on Scorp's boredom and Zak knew the inattention would soon be mistaken by the others as a *don't give a damn* attitude. But Zak knew different. Scorp was an action guy and too much inaction didn't sit well with him. He wasn't an academic like Nate; he was a doer and not a planner.

After Nate had finished droning on about the molecular make-up of the respiratory droplets, Zak finally got Pratt's attention. "I think we should call it a day, Lieutenant."

"Yup, no use overthinking. We've got a good solid plan. Time to get out of this stuffy place and blow off some steam," Scorp eagerly added.

Pratt ran his hand over his bald head while he looked around at his team. "Yeah, maybe you guys should go have some fun before Wednesday but do it as a group and in a safe place."

Before they left, Pratt took Zak aside and told him to make sure the team didn't get carried away. Pratt wasn't actually meaning the team, he clearly meant one particular guy. The lieutenant wouldn't be worried about Nate; he looked like the type who wouldn't even have an overdue library book. Omeir and Safia didn't consume alcohol, and Zak... well Zak didn't drink either and wasn't one who would get into bar fights. Scorp, on the other hand, was known to get into trouble, especially if he went on a bender. The last thing anyone needed was for this assignment to be derailed.

It was Scorp's suggestion that the team go to this sports bar only a short drive away. It was in the basement of an old historic building near Brooklyn College. Omeir and Safia weren't too keen on the idea but Scorp had convinced Safia to go, at least for a bite to eat. And once Safia was going, so was Omeir. Nate didn't object at all, probably relieved it wasn't some biker bar. Zak wasn't one for bars, but decided to go along with the idea. It was Monday, and therefore likely a quiet night. A few college kids wandering in to have a quick beer before heading off to study. The risk of exposing their cover would be relatively low. They were undercover police officers with the Counterterrorism Bureau, and the last thing they needed was to run into someone who would jeopardize their cover. Being they were in America's largest urban center, it wasn't likely, but it was still something Zak considered.

There was only a smattering of vehicles parked outside when they arrived. Inside, small television screens adorned the walls, with the focal point being a huge big screen above the bar. The servers were dressed in jeans and fitted t-shirts with the name of the bar on them. Probably college students trying to make a few bucks toward tuition. At least they weren't wearing skimpy clothing that would have set Safia into a tirade.

Zak motioned for the group to move to the back of the bar, to a large U-shaped booth in the corner. Once they were seated, a waitress came by and handed out menus. She smiled at Zak, before turning to the others, speaking about the featured beers on tap.

"I'll have a ginger-ale," said Safia.

"Make it two," Omeir quickly added.

Scorp looked at Zak and Nate, "Beers?"

Nate readily nodded.

"Club soda, please," Zak said, addressing the server.

The young woman looked a little disappointed; she was probably used to ringing up copious amounts of alcohol, and now she had a table of mainly teetotalers. A New York Rangers hockey game on the large screen consumed Scorp's attention while they waited for their drinks. While Nate and Safia were discussing the menu, Omeir was chatting with Zak about the hotel he was staying at. He lived in a cramped one-bedroom apartment in Brooklyn, less than half the size of the hotel suite they were staying in. Omeir would love to have been staying there, so Zak tried to downplay the luxuriousness of the hotel.

When the drinks arrived, Scorp insisted on paying, leaving a generous tip. It would ensure continued great service as well as some flirting coming his way. Drinking and women were definitely Scorp's vices, but Zak let it go. The guy had settled down quite a bit, besides, how much trouble could he get into in a place like this? He had also been going out of his way to make nice with Omeir. The skepticism was still there, but at least Omeir wasn't seething anymore.

Although they likely looked like an odd group, their evening out was similar to any other group of office workers getting together after a long day at work. But instead of working toward increasing sales of stationary products, they spent the day going over plans to take down terrorists. While they were enjoying their drinks and bar bites, a group of boisterous college students came pouring into the bar. Zak counted ten, equally men and women. It was obvious they were ready to party as they rolled into the bar in an obviously jovial mood.

Zak figured it was probably time to head out. He was about to wrap up the gathering when Scorp caught the waitress' attention and ordered another round of drinks for the team. Placing some money on the table, Scorp headed for the restroom. A few minutes later, Zak noticed him stop to talk to one of the college girls from the group. She was a pretty redhead, scantily dressed in a tight, mid-thigh, pleated black skirt with thigh-high boots and a low-cut V-neck sweater. She was obviously dressed to attract the male species. Even Omeir took a quick peek, careful to ensure Safia didn't notice. College Red appeared quite enamored with Scorp, swaying her head and laughing at whatever he was telling her. Zak redirected his focus to the large screen, checking on the hockey score. When he turned back toward Scorp and Red, he saw Scorp pointing to the group. The big guy was inviting College Red to join them. He gave Scorp a warning look, unsure if his colleague noticed.

It was a relief when Scorp returned to the table alone. Zak didn't want any complications. He had a hunch Safia would be irked if the scantily dressed one joined them. She didn't want to be around the guys if their focus was on picking up women, and frankly, neither did Zak. Safia at least could take off, but he promised Pratt he would keep an eye on Scorp.

When the second round of drinks arrived at their table, Scorp grabbed his beer and went over to College Red and her female co-eds. Zak continued to engage in conversation with the others while keeping tabs on the big guy. When Scorp downed his second beer, he ordered yet another drink for himself as well as for the girl. Zak could see him leaning in to talk to the clearly smitten college student. Either she was seriously into Scorp or he was hilarious, as she kept tilting her head back and laughing. Zak doubted Scorp was that funny, so it was definitely the serious flirting and the drinking that made her laugh so heartily. Scorp was getting a little touchy with the girl and again she continued to encourage this. Zak looked over at Safia, who had gone from slightly annoyed with Scorp to all-out disgusted by his salacious behavior. Zak wasn't sure if Safia's scowl was because she was interested in Scorp, or if it was simply her disapproval of a man treating a woman as a purely sexual object. He hoped for the latter as he figured Scorp wasn't a relationship type of guy, and Safia didn't need the trouble a man like him could bring her.

By the second period of the hockey game, Scorp was back at the table. As soon as he sat down, Safia got up and headed to the back of the bar. Zak wasn't sure if it was nature calling or if Safia was avoiding Scorp's smug face. As Zak took a sip of his club soda, he kept an eye on Safia making her way to the restroom at the back. Prior to getting to her intended destination, he noticed one of the college boys cornering her. From where Zak was sitting, it was clearly an attempt by this guy to hit on Safia. The guy had this annoying grin, the kind that oozed of unbridled confidence, as he placed his arm across the narrow aisle and onto a chair. It was a jerk-move intended to block Safia from moving past him. Unfortunately, Zak wasn't the only one to notice the situation, and his view was interrupted when Omeir stood up. Zak swiftly caught his arm before he could slide out of the booth. His attempt to pull him back down was met with resistance.

"We're not here to start a brawl with a bunch of college kids," Zak warned him.

Omeir ignored him, continuing to glare at the jerk hitting on Safia.

"Sit," Zak demanded.

Omeir turned, and narrowed his eyes, surprising Zak with a never before seen defiance.

Scorp elbowed Zak. "The kid over there needs manners." Turning to Omeir, he light-heartedly cautioned, "Just don't demolish him."

Zak was now irked having to battle both of these guys. "She can handle herself," he said. "If it looks like she's having problems, we'll help, but let's just wait before doing something stupid. We can't jeopardize the assignment."

Scorp grinned at Zak, the smug, irritating grin he wanted to slap off his face. Turning to Omeir, he motioned to the back, "Go rescue her and if any other guy in here is stupid enough to stop you, then take them down too. Zak and I got you covered, but you won't need us."

Zak couldn't believe what he just heard. Scorp's recklessness was unbelievable, and Omeir, what the hell was he thinking? When did he get all testosterone charged? Omeir was rational. He was logical. He didn't take stupid risks. But here he was, doing something stupid, all because he felt compelled to rescue a woman who was in no danger, a woman who could take down most of the men in this bar, including Omeir and perhaps even Zak himself. Before he could stop him, Omeir was marching over to Safia. Zak got up to follow, but Scorp quickly grabbed his elbow.

"He needs to be her hero. Trust me, it will be okay."

Zak glared at Scorp, challenging him in a way he had never done to a fellow colleague. He was still a little tender in his shoulder from where he rammed into Scorp the other night. That was by accident. A real physical battle with him would hurt, maybe even cause some serious injury, but he was so annoyed he started not to care. Scorp again grinned at him, which only infuriated Zak even more.

"What the hell, Scorp?"

"Shh."

Condescending asshole. Who shushes another adult?

Scorp leaned toward Zak, shifted his eyes to the right and whispered, "Hey, look."

Frustrated, Zak looked over at Omeir and Safia. Omeir was face to face with the college boy who was now holding up his hands and backing away. It looked like he muttered some apology to both Safia and Omeir before sheepishly heading back to his group.

"See? It all turned out," Scorp boasted.

It took self-restraint for Zak not to reach out and pummel the smug grin off the man's face.

When Omeir and Safia came back to the table, it was obvious Omeir was pleased with himself. He leaned over to Safia and spoke a few words, indiscernible to the others. Whatever they were, they made her laugh for the first time since their arrival. After they finished up their sodas, Omeir whispered to Zak, "Safia and I are headed out. We need to go over a few more details for the assignment. She suggested we head over to a coffee shop, so we don't bother the rest of you guys unwinding."

Some unwinding. Being in this stupid bar with Scorp was just making him wind up tighter. He simply nodded at Omeir, deciding he was better off not speaking his mind, since he would likely just explode. On the way out, Omeir stopped to say goodbye to Scorp, now ordering tequila shots for him and Nate. Shaking his head, Zak vowed this would be the last time he babysat this asinine group.

Nate and Scorp continued to drink and chat up the college girls, Scorp with Red and Nate with a leggy brunette. The college boys with whom they had arrived, didn't seem to care that two of the girls were off flirting with Scorp and Nate. It seemed odd to Zak. They weren't drunk enough to try and mess with Scorp, but they didn't even look bothered by the situation. Maybe college guys had changed from what he remembered.

Nate was starting to show signs of intoxication, but Scorp looked rather sober for a man who'd consumed several beers and shooters. Nate had staggered off with the statuesque brunette to a corner booth. Zak felt out of place, like a priest who ended up booking a hotel amongst horny teenagers on spring break. He wanted to get out of there, but he had to ensure these two came with him.

He continued to sit by himself, pretending to watch the televised hockey game. Admittedly, what he was doing was watching his colleagues, so he could protect their dumb asses even though they didn't deserve it. After a half an hour of Zak sitting alone and festering, Scorp brought over a blonde college student who was wearing a short skirt with leggings. Her loose-fitting top revealed her ample bosom every time she leaned forward, which was rather often. Her name was Bree and she was all too pleased to meet Zak. He exchanged pleasantries with her but wasn't interested in any real conversation. When the conversation stalled, Scorp took Zak aside, suggesting they invite Bree and College Red to their hotel suite. When Zak grunted a firm no, Scorp actually tried to rationalize that bringing the girls would make their cover look more authentic. Zak doubted this, but it didn't matter, Bree and Red were definitely not coming back with them. There was only one woman he was interested in and she was miles away.

After telling Scorp for the third time the women weren't coming along, Zak had finally had enough of him and his recklessness. "We're going now," he barked to Scorp. The girls, who were within earshot, giggling, scattered away.

Scorp initially glared at Zak. As Zak was getting battle ready, Scorp released a grin. "Yeah, you're right. I'll just grab Sparky from the lust of his life." True to his word, the big guy went and gathered Nate, who had killed plenty of brain cells with too much drink. Thankfully, the pompous genius had plenty left.

"Hey, buddy, you're driving," Scorp said, as he tossed the keys to Zak.

When they got to their hotel suite in Manhattan, Zak was still fuming. He was pissed at Scorp and Scorp was going to know it.

"Don't you ever pull that shit again. We both know Omeir should have kept his ass in the booth. Those college kids could have started a fight. Yes, we can take them, Scorp, but what the hell would it accomplish? We are here for a reason. It may be a game to you, but it's not to me. People's lives are at stake."

"Hey, man, I had it covered."

"You had nothing covered. You're such a jerk."

"Perhaps I am, but I did have it covered. You're not the only one who knows how to set things up." Scorp again grinned. Zak wondered if all his grins were smug-bastard ones.

Slowly, the smirk faded and Scorp's tone became serious. "Look, it was obvious Omeir was pissed at me about Safia, and rightfully so. I'm not going to lie and say she's not my type, because she is. She's hot and fiercely independent. Basically she's every smart man's dream. But she deserves more than a guy like me has to offer. She actually deserves someone decent, like Omeir. I admit, I messed it up with Omeir and Safia when I first met them. I wanted to make it right. Omeir was lacking confidence. He thinks a guy like me can just swoop in and take a woman like Safia. He's probably been pining after her forever. I might seem like a Neanderthal, but I know about what confidence can achieve. I don't want to go in on Wednesday with any one of us lacking an iota of confidence. So I paid college boy to hit on Safia and to back away when Omeir came to the rescue. And Nate? All that kid needs is to feel like part of the team. His arrogance is just a mechanism to deal with all the bullying he probably received as a kid. So he was my drinking buddy tonight. He's kind of fun once he gets on a roll." Scorp paused, ensuring he was paying attention. "And you, my friend? Well, I didn't think I needed to do anything to enhance your game. You're one of the best. You're a legend. I know it and you know it. But, Zak, don't think you're the only guy with smarts around here. I know how to play to win, too."

Zak was totally caught off guard. He was guilty of seeing Scorp as just some muscle head and didn't give him credit for his leadership skills. Sort of what Nate had done to him when they'd first met. Tonight, he'd actually brought the team closer together. It was a calculated strategy to achieve team cohesiveness, and it was Scorp who had planned and executed it.

"So flirting with the redhead was to annoy Safia, making her realize what a gentleman Omeir is in comparison to you?"

"Nope, I just wanted to get laid. That was definitely one hundred percent authentic Scorp. No game there."

Zak shook his head and laughed, which got Scorp to chuckle too. Once they stopped, Zak inquired, "The girl who liked Nate, you paid her?"

A quick flash of anger came across Scorp's face. He paused, as if processing his anger. "I never have and never will pay a woman to pretend to like me or anyone else." Then easing up, he smiled. "I was just as surprised as you were the hot brunette took a shine to Sparky. But I guess some girls get turned on by the bookish-nerd persona. Maybe I should get a pair of black-rimmed glasses to up my game."

He sensed he'd struck a nerve with Scorp with the comment he made about paying the coed to like Nate. He hadn't meant to offend him, and he honestly didn't fully grasp Scorp's anger about it. But he was seeing a different side of Scorp, and because Zak had experienced such rash judgements from strangers himself, he knew an apology was warranted. He was thinking of the best way to phrase an apology when Scorp interrupted his thoughts.

"So I'm guessing she's quite special?"

Zak heard him but gave no response, hoping to deter Scorp. It didn't.

"She must be. You were adamant with not having anything to do with little blonde dimples tonight. A guy doesn't normally turn down a hot woman unless he already has someone special waiting for him."

"Yeah," Zak muttered. "She's special, and I hope she'll wait for me."

* * * *

Nate hurried out of the room. It was the second time he had done so this morning. This time, Lieutenant Pratt gave Zak a puzzled look. He was just about to shrug his shoulders when Scorp let out a chuckle. Scorp didn't even try to hide his amusement over Nate's hangover from their boss. It was easy for Scorp to have an open chuckle. Pratt didn't expect Scorp to keep the team in line. No, it was Zak who Pratt relied on to keep such things from happening.

Thankfully, Nate returned to the group almost as fast as he'd left it and remained healthy enough to participate in the final plan. Pratt would normally be fuming about Nate's condition, except his focus was on Omeir and Scorp. What they were doing was amazing. Maybe not to Zak, or anyone else that had gone to the bar last night, but Pratt was clearly impressed. For the first time, Omeir and Scorp were acting like allies instead of adversaries.

Pratt was willing to overlook Nate's visits to the porcelain god, only because last night's outing led to a solid truce between Omeir and Scorp. Zak knew Pratt was crediting him with the new alliance and he decided not to say anything. Scorp wasn't one who wanted any credit, and it was best for all of them if Pratt didn't know the details. Scorp and Zak differed greatly when it came to women and booze, but they were quite similar when it came to work. They recognized the importance of a solid team in getting the job done.

They wrapped up early and before Omeir departed for the day, Zak took him aside privately. "I need a favor."

"Sure, anything."

"I don't want you to ever doubt that you and Safia are like family to me. When I went to Baxley, I wasn't in any condition to be a decent friend to anyone, including you guys. I regret it. Tomorrow everything will go well, but you know I'm a detail person, and I didn't get a chance to… well, I didn't have time to take care of all my personal details before I left Baxley. I need you to…" He stumbled for the words. He handed an envelope over to Omeir. "Just deliver this to Dr. Draden in Baxley, if necessary, okay?"

Normally, Omeir would make some joke to ease the moment, but he didn't. He didn't know what was in the envelope or who Dr. Draden was, but he knew exactly what Zak meant when he said *if necessary*.

Chapter Fifteen

The meeting with Nadir Girgis was set for early evening on Wednesday in an abandoned train station. The morning commenced with a slow and steady drizzle, eventually turning to a drenching sleet by evening. Ice had formed on the streets as the temperature took a drastic dip. For the average office worker, it was a day to contemplate calling in sick, but to Zak and his fellow workers, sick days didn't exist. A job needed to be done and he was ready. When he entered the old train station there was no reprieve from the cold. The air was almost as frosty and damp inside the run-down building as it was on the streets outside.

Along with Scorp, three other NYPD undercover officers marched in with him, their faces expressionless against their solid physiques. It was a diverse group. There was Scorp, another Caucasian guy, an African-American guy, and a Persian man. Zak had only been in the building for a moment, when he saw Nadir Girgis and his men approaching through the lighted corridor. Girgis had shown up with five men, which meant they were outmanned. It didn't alarm Zak, he had prepared for this scenario. If things got ugly, it wouldn't be hand to hand combat, but a firestorm of weapons being discharged. It was always better to have fast and accurate shooters than superior numbers. He was confident in the sharpshooters he had in his group, but he was painfully aware of the multitude of variables that could go wrong.

Girgis' group was as diverse as Zak's, which wasn't surprising. Those who collaborated with terrorists were opportunists. Some may have been homegrown terrorists with deranged beliefs, but they were more likely to be callous criminals, whose sole motivation was the handsome fee they were paid. They were soulless, not caring about the lives they would destroy.

"Never thought we would meet, but it's an interesting world, isn't it?"

Girgis' comment was a reference to the widely held belief that Zak had been killed. Once word had leaked out that he was still alive, Girgis had set about tracking him down. Thanks to an undercover FBI agent, whom Girgis believed was a terrorist sympathizer, Zak was revealed to be alive and eager to do business.

"It certainly is, and I trust once we are done, the interest will go away."

The formula for the biological agent he would sell to Girgis theoretically would cause enough havoc on American soil making further deals with Zak unnecessary. The blueprint for the super-bug Girgis was purchasing would be handed over to scientists who planned to create a deadly virus. The plan was for Girgis to leave with the bogus formula. Omeir would track Girgis, who they hoped would lead them to the scientists. The scientists were believed to be somewhere on the East Coast, and possibly even in New York. Once the scientists were located, the Counterterrorism Bureau, in conjunction with agents from the CIA and Homeland Security, would move in and arrest them, along with Girgis.

Zak's information was prepared under Nate's leadership. It was a decent fake formula for a deadly virus. It should be enough to fool Girgis and his people so that they would take it to the scientists. It was essential the Bureau discover who the scientists were. Arresting only Girgis would not solve the bigger picture. It would only be a matter of time before Al-Qaeda, ISIS, or another terrorist organization would hire another contact who might end up making a deal for a working virus formula which the scientists could actually generate.

The Bureau was confident in Nate's counterfeit formula. The scientists would eventually realize it wouldn't work, but the goal was to find out who and where the scientists were, and to arrest them before they made the realization. As long as things went well today, the probability of Girgis inadvertently leading them to the scientists was high. There were no guarantees that once Girgis and the scientists were arrested, that there wouldn't be others recruited by terrorists. However, the level of experience available to create a deadly virus was limited. It would likely take a long time for the terrorists to again recruit the expertise needed.

"So, my friend, let's go for a walk and discuss the details." Before Zak could respond, Girgis added, "Just you and me. Our associates can stay here."

Although it was a scenario that the team had gone over, he didn't like Girgis' proposal and neither did Scorp, who discreetly glanced at Zak, warning him to abort. Zak knew the risks with Girgis and how the terrorist's middle-man wanted to proceed. It could be a set-up to eliminate Scorp and the undercover officers, or it could be a set-up to eliminate Zak. He had the option of walking away from the encounter. He could tell Girgis he wasn't willing to go forward but doing so could cause Girgis to be more suspicious. He could probably spin it where he was the one who was suspicious, accuse Girgis of being an informant, and therefore justifying shutting down the meeting. It was a viable option, but Zak didn't like the idea of scrapping the whole assignment, which had taken months to set up. Besides, he didn't want to put his life on hold, sticking around New York until they were able to re-group. He would go ahead, but this time he would ensure the men working with him would be able to walk away. He wasn't going to be responsible for Scorp's death, or the other men. It happened to him before and he vowed it would never happen again.

"I'll go, providing all our men walk out of here now."

"So, you don't trust me? Or you think you can handle me alone?" Girgis looked at Zak for a response.

"It's both. And if you are as smart as me, you're thinking the same. There is no trust in this business." It was certainly true.

"But you are my brother in this, no?"

"I'm as much your brother as you are mine."

Girgis' response was a knowing laugh, and then he nodded.

"Fine, we'll send these men on their way."

"Not so fast, Girgis. I don't want any more bullet holes, so no weapons."

Girgis nodded and motioned for one of his men to frisk Zak. Then Scorp moved over to Girgis and thoroughly frisked him. Scorp gave Zak one last glance, a cautionary look with a wordless plea of *don't*. He ignored it and nodded for his men to move on out.

Zak and Girgis waited a couple of minutes as they watched their team of men leave in opposite directions. Once they were all a safe distance away, they began to walk. Zak wasn't concerned about going outside. Omeir had ensured surveillance extended visually and audibly around the building. The NYPD didn't place any agents outside the building, as they would have been detected, but there were visual aids in the distant areas to capture anything unusual.

They had only taken a few steps outside when Girgis appeared to have lost his footing on an icy patch. Stretching out his hand near a wooden beam, Zak assumed Girgis was reaching out to regain his balance. Touching the beam, Girgis' body straightened out. In a fast and sweeping motion, Girgis moved into Zak. Noticing something shiny coming toward his face, he tried to duck. It was too late. Feeling the cold metal slicing into him, his body went limp.

Chapter Sixteen

Lexie had waited, trying to be patient and rational. It didn't work. The hurt, the anger, grew in intensity. It was now past the two-week mark, and still no word from Zak. The last time she had felt such a wide range of emotions was when Hailie died. Her death had brought an onslaught of overwhelming grief, coupled with shame and guilt. This time she refused to let the shame and guilt of an intimate relationship, with who she was starting to believe was the wrong man, define who she was. Although a part of her was clinging to the hope he would come back with a reasonable explanation, she needed to face the fact that he had lied to her. She had no idea what the lie was, or why he lied. Perhaps she might never know. She loathed pining for the man, but she couldn't just turn it off like some valve. She needed a diversion. She decided it was time to immerse herself in her new life. Admittedly, she had only dabbled in small town living so far. Now she needed to plunge into it.

She wasn't exactly sure what plunging into Baxley life meant. She was certain she wouldn't be throwing herself into a new romantic relationship anytime soon. She wasn't ready to trust again. There must be more to Baxley than the historical society. Some other avenue to meet people and busy herself. And if there wasn't, then maybe she could find a group of like-minded women and create a social club. With the right attitude, today could be the start of her new life in Baxley.

To commensurate her aspiringly bold approach, she decided to stride into Colton's. She had stopped going to Colton's to get her morning coffee because she couldn't stomach the way Cicily looked at her, like she was some pathetic fool. It was no secret Lexie was looking after Abby. This alone led to all sorts of rumors about her and Zak. But today, she wasn't going to let small town gossip and Cicily's pettiness get in the way of her craving for a latte. She would handle Cicily, and any other person foolish enough to take on the new, unapologetic Lexie. She had done nothing wrong. She didn't have to account for her mistakes in love.

"Morning, Dr. Lexie." Just the sound of Cicily's nasally voice irked her.

"Morning, Cicily. I'll have a non-fat vanilla latte to go." She looked Cicily in the eye, nearly daring her to say something inappropriate.

"Certainly. Would you like anything else? I made some blueberry rhubarb muffins this morning."

Lexie noticed the sweetness in Cicily's voice. She had encountered this before. The gentle undertones seeping out, making Lexie open up. Then the woman would strike, ambushing her with malicious words. Cicily was just getting ready. Soon she would throw in some zinger about Zak.

She wondered why Cicily was staring at her with a plastered-on grin, and then realized she hadn't responded to the woman. "No muffins, but I've changed my mind. I'll have two lattes." She figured she might as well get one for Margo who had been nothing but kind to her. Although Lexie had curtailed her sour mood, she still wasn't her usual self at the clinic.

When Lexie went to hand over payment for the lattes, Cicily shook her head. "These are on me."

Confusion swept Lexie. Cicily showing a token act of generosity toward her? Was she trying to apologize for the way she'd reacted in the past, or did she pity her for being used by Zak? Was it a way of saying, *sorry for the heartbreak, but I told you so?*

Cicily's unforeseen pleasantness was throwing Lexie off. Finally, Lexie snapped out of what her southern grandmother would describe as rudeness; after all, Cicily was giving her complimentary beverages. She briskly thanked Cicily and turned to leave. When she heard Cicily clearing her throat to speak, she braced herself for the zinger.

"It's good to see you, Dr. Lexie," Cicily said with novel sincerity in her voice.

Lexie was now feeling foolish, and without turning around to show the shame on her face, she let out a barely audible whisper of thanks.

She was still feeling sheepish by the time she walked in the doors of the clinic. She still didn't trust Cicily, but maybe it was time for Lexie to let it go. It was also time to start making some friends in Baxley. The only friend she had made since she moved to Baxley had been Zak, which hadn't turned out so well. She was on friendly terms with Amelia and Margo, but she didn't have any friends to confide in. She wouldn't confide everything, especially not what happened the night Hailie died, but at least she could have some semblance of a social life.

She walked into the clinic with the lattes and set one down on the receptionist's desk where Margo was busy sorting files. She caught Margo's look of surprise when she saw the latte with Colton's logo on the cup.

"Thanks, Dr. Draden."

"They're complimentary from Cicily."

"Oh-oh…" said Margo.

When Margo stammered, it made Lexie feel good. It confirmed her thoughts about Cicily weren't unreasonable. Margo was also surprised by the uncharacteristically kind gesture from the owner of Colton's.

"Margo, can I ask you something about the women in Baxley?" Lexie asked hesitantly.

"Sure, dear."

"I don't mean this to sound offensive. I was just wondering, what do the women do for fun?" She cleared her throat, before going on, "I like Baxley and the people here. It's just I don't know anyone well. I don't do much except go to work, and then home. Are there any social clubs?"

"Well, there is the Historical Society as you know, and there's a quilting bee…" Sensing her lack of enthusiasm, Margo added, "I guess you probably want something more suitable for your age group."

Lexie nodded.

"Well, I'm not sure, Dr. Draden. Why don't you come to our weekly book club? It meets every Thursday night. There's a few women around your age attending. Maybe they can be of more assistance than me." Sensing Lexie's skepticism, she added, "We all bring wine to drink so it's quite fun. It would be a good way to meet more people."

"Where's it held?" She had to at least try.

"We take turns hosting. We're gathering at Kristina McQuay's this week."

"Any relation to Cicily or Sheriff McQuay?" Lexie inquired cautiously.

"She's the daughter-in-law of Cicily and the wife of the sheriff."

"I don't know if it's such a good idea." It was one thing entering Colton's once again, but to go to the home of Sheriff McQuay, the unbearable man who treated her like an idiot just because she was friendly to Zak, was quite another.

"If you're worried about Emmett being around, don't. He always hightails it when the ladies come over. You'll like Kristina. She's…" Margo paused to find the right word, finally settling on: "…spirited. Yes, Kristina's a spirited woman. Even though she's quite a bit different than you, I think you'll like her."

Lexie had no idea what Margo meant. She was still unsure about going, but anything was better than spending another evening at home. "Well, I'll try it, but you must promise me something."

Margo dreaded making a promise. The last one she made was to Zak, the one that caused her nothing but grief. "Well, if I can," she said cautiously.

"Please call me Lexie when we're not at work. You truly have been a wonderful friend to me."

She quietly sighed with relief. "That I can do."

Chapter Seventeen

Zak didn't know if he was dreaming. He was used to vivid dreams, or rather nightmares, but this was somehow different. He couldn't explain how it was different. He couldn't actually explain much of anything. But he had an awareness that his eyes were open. He wasn't seeing clearly. Everything was blurry, like looking through a windshield in a downpour. Slowly, a familiar face came into focus. It was Omeir, although he found it strange his friend was looking down on him. Excitement was all over Omeir's face and he said something, but Zak wasn't sure if it was to him or not. The words seemed mumbled, even though they were spoken loudly. He disappeared, leaving Zak to question that maybe it was a dream. But boy, did it feel real.

Omeir's face came back and this time there was another face with him – a woman. Zak didn't recognize the person, but she smiled at him as she spoke. The words he still could not decipher. Maybe it was a dream, or perhaps some sort of hallucination. The woman leaned toward him and touched him. He felt her hand on his arm.

Warmth. I can't be dreaming. She must be real.

Omeir was still muttering something but he was talking too fast for Zak to catch the words. The woman looked over at Omeir as if trying to slow him down. Finally, he understood why their faces were above him. The woman and Omeir were standing, while he was lying down. He was lying in a bed, but it wasn't his bed. He looked around and saw dull-colored walls. A lifeless, institutionalized shade of pastel green, which could be found in an old airport, a school, or… *a hospital.* He was in a hospital. But why?

Slowly the woman spoke again, and this time he was able to process the words. "Mr. Ahmadi, my name's Janet. I'm your primary nurse. You're at Kings County Hospital in Brooklyn. I'm going to go get the attending physician to come see you and provide an update."

Seeing the confusion on Zak's face, Omeir moved closer toward him after the nurse left. "You're going to be okay. The worst is over."

The worst is over? What does that mean? His mind was clouded, and it hurt as he tried to make sense of it all. He continued to stare at Omeir, who was desperate to reassure him he was fine, but Zak was too confused to understand. He struggled to keep his eyes open, and just when he was giving in to sleep, he heard an unfamiliar man's voice. Fighting the urge to sleep, he opened his weighted eyelids. He couldn't understand why it was taking so much energy to focus. God, how he wanted to close his eyes, but he was determined to find out what was going on, and the only way to do it was to stay awake.

"I'm Dr. Biasi, the attending physician." The man's voice was even and calm.

The doctor likely dealt with clueless patients every day. People who woke up unaware of what was going on. The man spoke a few more words but they didn't register with Zak. The soothing monotone voice of the doctor, along with the physician's kind but tired eyes, only made it harder for Zak to focus and not drift off.

"You're probably quite groggy. Don't worry, it's normal as we have you on some serious medication."

Aw, it's the medication causing the heaviness in the eyelids. So that's good, right?

Before he could relax and return to a REM state, the doctor continued, "Your injuries were quite extensive, and we had to induce you into a coma."

Coma? What the hell?

He tried to remember, but nothing was coming to him. Zak tried to form the word *coma*, but it came out garbled. The doctor gave him a weird look, and then continued with the medical update.

"You will likely feel disoriented for the next few days, but your vital signs are good so far. You'll stay in intensive care for at least the next forty-eight hours. Once it looks like you have stabilized, we'll move you to a regular unit here in the hospital."

Intensive care?

Again, Zak tried to figure out what was going on, but he couldn't quite grasp it. He looked to Omeir, who kept smiling at him, although his eyes betrayed his fear. As the doctor's voice carried on, Zak tried to concentrate on the syllables coming from the man's mouth. It was a patchwork of sounds. Knowing he had missed several words, he hoped they weren't as important as the ones he did hear.

"The best thing you can do for now, Mr. Ahmadi, is to rest. We will continue with pain medication, however, now that you are out of the coma, we will be reducing the medication. I'll come back later to see how you're doing." The doctor gave a quick smile before departing. Omeir trailed behind the doctor, leaving Zak alone.

He had so many questions, but he didn't have the strength to speak. The word *coma* kept bouncing around in his mind, until his body, too weary, surrendered to sleep.

* * * *

It was several hours before Zak awoke again. His eyes fluttered opened, still weighted. He closed them briefly, before reopening them. With the fluttering no longer happening, he looked around. The same ugly green walls confronted him. And if that wasn't enough to signify where he was, the subtle antiseptic cleaners, so familiar in hospitals, whiffed through the air.

So, it's not a dream, I'm actually lying in a hospital.

Slowly, but with less effort than before, he was able to recall key words spoken to him, the words *induced coma* and *intensive care* punching him. Now, with no one else in the room, the words seemed to be more potent, more alarming. The confusion was still there, but he was able to recall a few things. He remembered the abandoned train station. He remembered meeting with Nadir Girgis, but not what came after. Frustration fueled him.

Damn, there's more. Just think. What did I see? Who did I see?

Then a memory came to him. *Omeir! He was at my bedside when I awoke before.*

The concern in Omeir's face came flooding back at him. Omeir would do anything for him, including making jokes in an effort to ease tension, a forced calmness in the midst of chaos. But he wasn't joking. *Was the situation so bad even Omeir couldn't mask the gravity with humor?*

He felt the panic rising. Pushing his muscles to move his limbs, first his feet and toes, and then moving his hands, wiggling his fingers. He relaxed his tense shoulders, sinking fully back against the pillow. Thank God, he wasn't paralyzed. But the tension quickly returned as a new tide of panic set in.

What the hell?

Looking down toward his chest, covered with a blue hospital blanket, he saw the plastic tubing. It emerged from his blanketed chest and appeared to be draining fluid. Attached to an intravenous pole, there were several other wires and tubes flowing in and around his body, commanding his attention. Just a few seconds ago, he feared paralysis. Focused on being able to move his limbs, he hadn't even noticed the tubes jetting out around him.

He cautiously peaked under the thin blanket to his chest. He saw the scar tissue from the old bullet wound, relieved to see no new wounds to his chest. There were unexplained marks and severe bruising, but at least no holes. He closed his eyes, offering a prayer of thanks.

When he opened his eyes again, he noticed something odd in his peripheral vision. It was something protruding from the right side of his neck. It looked like a large lumpy patch. At first, he wondered if he had been shot in the neck. He couldn't remember any sound of gunshots, but he couldn't remember much. Bits of memory came to him rather sporadically. It took concentration, but he was able to pull up a memory of walking alone with Nadir. But there was nothing after that. Frustrated, he began to peel back the patch on his neck.

Omeir rushed into the room screaming. "Zak, don't!"

His friend had a look of horror so intense it made Zak jump, causing pain as well as fear to radiate through his body. He could hear his heart pounding. His pulse was erratic as sweat began to bead on his forehead. He shook his head in an attempt to regain some control. It didn't work. He desperately needed to know what was going on.

"Tell me," he began shouting at Omeir. "Was I shot in the neck?"

When Omeir shook his head, it didn't register.

"Was I shot?" Zak bellowed, his voice a mix of fear and panic.

"No, you weren't shot."

"Then what the hell is this?" he demanded. He still had his hand on the bandage, although he was no longer trying to remove it.

"You were stabbed."

"Stabbed," he repeated. The confusion and panic had returned.

"Buddy, you're going to be okay." Omeir said, as he slowly moved closer, stopping when he was within arm's length. "Just don't mess with the bandage. I'll track down the doctor. He'll explain everything."

Irritated, he wasn't going to wait patiently for the doctor to show up. Zak wanted answers now. He tried to sit up, but he was too weak and fell back down on the bed. He gave Omeir an icy glare, warning him not to help, even though it was clear he needed assistance.

He obeyed and stood frozen, awaiting Zak's next move.

"Tell me." Zak was no longer asking but demanding.

Reading the fear in Zak's eyes, Omeir tried to remain calm, but his voice betrayed him as it crackled, "I told you. You were stabbed, but you're okay. Just lie back and relax. I'll get a nurse."

Zak reached up and grabbed at Omeir's arm, but he was too weak to hold on. "Omeir, I need to know," he pleaded.

Omeir saw the exhaustion and helplessness of this strong man, a man who would do anything for his friends, a man who gave up the comfort of living peacefully to protect others. He had been instructed by the surgeon not to discuss details with Zak, especially if Zak didn't remember any. They had protocols, ways of dealing with traumatic situations. Omeir intended to follow the doctor's orders, but now Zak was pleading. He had seen concern, uncertainty and even anger in Zak's eyes before. But it was the fear, the intensity of the fear that he had only seen once before, that made him relent.

"You were stabbed in the neck by Nadir. It was bad. You lost a lot of blood and it took its toll on your heart." Omeir paused, before he continued, "You went into cardiac arrest. Scorp got to you first and did CPR until the paramedics got there. They used the defibrillator and got your heart going again. When you got here, you went straight into surgery." Omeir's eyes started to fill. Zak grabbed his friend's arm, pleading with his eyes for him to go on.

Omeir's voice was unsteady as he continued, "Your heart stopped again in surgery and you flatlined." He could no longer contain himself and a tear rolled down his face. "We thought we lost you, but thank God, *Alhamdulillah,* the doctors got you back." There was such trauma to your body, they had to induce a coma. They weren't sure if you would come out of it, and if you did, what would be the extent of the damage."

Zak stared at Omeir, trying to soak in what he had just heard. He had been clinically dead and brought back to life. Then deep panic struck him as he thought of something worse than dying.

"Our guys? Did all our guys get out?"

"Yes, you were the only one wounded."

The tension in Zak's shoulders eased as he sank back into the bed. The sense of relief was only momentary; he wasn't yet done with Omeir.

"Nadir?" he asked. He needed to know what happened to the man who tried to kill him.

"He's in custody."

"Did we get any information from him?"

"That I don't know. He was taken by the FBI, we're waiting to hear what Intel they have."

Before they could talk anymore, a doctor entered the room. It was the chief surgeon, the man who had operated on Zak. Omeir confessed immediately that he had disobeyed instructions, and the patient now knew he had been stabbed. The doctor was clearly annoyed with Omeir; he not only gave him an icy stare, but also mumbled some inaudible cuss words his way. The doctor settled down and spoke to Zak. Using medical terminology, he explained what happened and what they did to save Zak's life. The prognosis was still uncertain but being able to formulate speech was a good sign. If things went well, he might get released within the week.

Zak's head was spinning with all he had learned. Almost three weeks had gone by since the meeting with Nadir and the subsequent stabbing. He always figured being shot was potentially more lethal than being stabbed, but as he found out, this was not always the case.

He should have been appreciative he was alive, but he didn't feel it. In fact, he started not to feel much at all, and within a few hours, he became devoid of all emotion, except anger. The anger was building in him and he was afraid its power would strike like lightning during a storm, reaching out and taking hold of whatever was in its path. He was hoping it was the medication causing this. It would be an easy fix, he would cease the medication and the rage would vanish. He'd rather live with the physical pain and discomfort than to feel a burning rage he couldn't contain.

Omeir called the rest of the team and one by one they came trickling in to see him. The Intensive Care Unit only allowed one visitor at a time. Zak didn't want them there at all. Naturally, they were all worried about him, but he didn't want to see anyone. The anger was taking control over any logical thoughts. Omeir tried to make him laugh, but Zak wasn't in the mood to even pretend to find humor in what he was saying.

Safia, who was always so strong, actually broke down in tears when she saw Zak. He mustered the energy to verbalize words of comfort to her. He wasn't sincere in what he said, but he doubted Safia could tell. His sole intent was to get her to stop. When he told her he needed to rest, she left the room. He knew no one would argue with the patient sleeping, even though he was too wired to do so. He wanted to be left alone and for the anger to go away. He could at least control whether or not he had visitors. But with the anger he seemed to have no control, and it scared him.

A few hours after Safia had left, Lieutenant Pratt popped in, reassuring him the department would provide whatever support he needed. He was angry at Pratt, although he tried to mask his resentment during the brief visit. Pratt was after all, the person who persisted in getting him back to New York. He knew logically Pratt was not to blame for what happened, but he couldn't help how he felt. He only needed to fake yawn once for the lieutenant to get the hint and leave his side. Nate was back in DC but had sent a message for Pratt to pass on. Zak listened and pretended he cared.

It was near nine in the evening when Scorp came by. Totally fed up with the intrusion of visitors, he was the one person Zak wanted to see. Scorp looked horrible, the lids of his bloodshot eyes cringing as he struggled to recover from a brutal bender. Although he wasn't drunk when he showed up, Zak could smell the alcohol oozing from his pores. An older nurse came by as he walked into Zak's room.

"Visiting hours are long over," she abruptly told him.

Zak knew the staff had some flexibility. He figured the nurse took one look at Scorp and decided her patient didn't need the stress this savage-looking man might cause. He wondered where this nurse, and her protective nature, was earlier in the day when his parade of colleagues fluttered in and out.

Even though Zak was done and exhausted with well-wishers, he couldn't let Scorp leave without talking to him. He understood all too well why Scorp was there, and it was imperative they talk. Manipulating the nurse with a smile, Zak asked ever so sweetly if he could have this one last visitor. After giving Scorp an icy glare, signalling she wasn't going to tolerate any misbehavior, she walked away, giving them privacy.

"You look worse than I feel," he said to Scorp.

"I just wanted to come by and…" The words caught in Scorp's throat. He was about to try again when Zak shook his head.

"Don't, Scorp. I've been there. I know it sucks but it's how I wanted it. If you guys hadn't left, I'd probably be at your funerals, and believe me, that's a worse feeling than what happencd to me."

"I screwed up. I should have had your back."

"You followed orders, that's your job and you did it." Zak's voice was starting to crackle a bit, but he had to go on. "Don't let this mess with you. Don't go finding solace in a bottle. It soon becomes a dark hole you can't get out of. I know we got off to a shaky start when we first met but I didn't know you. You're not a dick, you're a decent man, who like the rest of us has a shit job. And Scorp, you do the job well, so don't go second-guessing yourself."

Zak could see Scorp wasn't ready to let it all go, but at least he didn't continue to apologize.

"So, what's next for you?"

It was clear to him what Scorp was asking, but he wasn't sure himself, so he just stuck to what he knew. "They say within the week I might be out of here. I'll leave New York."

"Back to Baxley?"

"I hope so."

It was the truth. Zak wanted to go back to Baxley, but the waves of anger consuming him would make a return to the life he had in Baxley impossible. He hoped it was only a side effect of the medication, subsiding as the dosage decreased, gone completely by the time he got released. But right now, with uncontrollable rage fueling him, he knew he could not be around anyone, especially not Lexie.

Chapter Eighteen

It was book club night at Kristina's and as anticipated, Sheriff McQuay was not at home. Lexie had gone out of her way to drive past the sheriff's office, just to make sure. She was already nerve-racked going to the sheriff's home and meeting his wife, and certainly didn't want any further judgement from Baxley's number one lawman.

When she pulled up to the large two-story home on a quiet cul-de-sac, she noticed several vehicles nearby and felt relieved she was not the first to arrive. A pretty blonde lady in tight jeans and a low-cut t-shirt made of thin fabric answered the door.

"Hi, you must be Lexie. I'm Kristina."

Lexie was going to extend her hand when Kristina reached forward, giving her a hug. "So glad you could make it. It's great to have another young person in the group. Hopefully we won't be stuck reading some ancient boring book, like *Sense and Sensibility*."

Lexie loved the classics, including Jane Austen's nineteenth-century romantic fiction, but she figured it was best not to mention it. "I appreciate being invited into the book club." It was a safe, though somewhat formal response. She was happy not to be sitting home alone like a crazy, bored cat lady, especially since she didn't even own a cat.

Kristina threw her head back, letting out a giggle. "It's a lot of fun since I convinced the ladies to switch from coffee to wine at our gatherings. Oh, just so you know, I've talked Emmett into giving anyone a ride home if they need one."

Lexie had a difficult time picturing Sheriff McQuay being pleased to be the designated driver for the tipsy, loquacious book club ladies. She would stick to a small glass of wine, ensuring she didn't need his services.

Kristina led Lexie into the large open living room, and to her pleasant surprise, she had previously met most of the ladies. There was

Willow, the chatty bird-infatuated lady; Bernice, the cranky competitive quilter; Doreen, the pleasant woman who worked at Colton's; and of course, Margo. Closer to her age was Tamara, the mother of the rambunctious twins whom Lexie had treated a few weeks ago; and one other lady Lexie was not familiar with. Kristina quickly introduced her as Megan. Megan, Lexie found out, was the mother of Emily, the teenager who worked part-time at Colton's. Realizing she was the last to arrive, Lexie apologized for holding up the group.

"Don't worry," Kristina said with another wine-induced giggle. "We don't start discussing the book until we all have a bit of wine. It makes it a little more interesting."

Bernice just rolled her eyes, and Margo simply smiled at Lexie. Now Lexie got what Margo meant by the word 'spirited' as it pertained to the sheriff's alcohol-enhanced, bubbly spouse.

An hour into the gathering, Lexie was relaxed enough to be having a good time. The ladies, including Bernice, were friendly to her and no one brought up Zak's name. The discussion centered on the book Willow had chosen. It was from the perspective of a snowy owl living in the wilds of Alaska. Although Lexie didn't have anything to add, as she hadn't read the book, the conversation was quite entertaining. After wrapping up with the adventures of Edmon the owl, they turned to Kristina to give an overview of the book she had suggested as the next read. Not surprisingly, Kristina had a fondness for erotic romance. Kristina listened to other women's recommendations, but as the host, the final say was hers. *Stranger in the Fog* won out in the end and Lexie imagined it was more erotica than story. It wasn't likely a book she would ever pick up on her own, but perhaps some steamy sex, albeit fictional, would do her some good. Besides, the book club ladies were fun, and she could certainly use a little fun in her life. Now, if only she could get through a night without thinking about Zak.

Chapter Nineteen

"So, switching to another type of pain killer is futile?"

Zak got just a nod.

"How about lessening the dosage?" he asked.

This time, he didn't get a simple non-verbal response. Instead, the doctor gave a droning lecture on how pain will make it harder for his body to heal. Besides, the doctor informed him, a lower dosage wouldn't make a difference as it pertained to his levels of anxiety and anger. These were not side effects of the medication. He tried not to show panic, but it must have come through and the doctor offered to prescribe Valium.

"No, it won't be necessary. Hospitals always make me a little anxious. I'll be fine once I get released."

It was a lie, but he didn't want the damn Valium. Fear radiated through him as he realized there was no other explanation for the anxiety and anger raging through his veins. The truth could no longer be denied. He was back in full-blown PTSD mode.

He always knew it would never fully go away, but he had been doing better, actually much better until he ended up in the hospital again. He should be thankful for being back from the brink of death, but he had moments where he yearned for the numbness of being in a coma. He wasn't sure if he would be able to survive this round of trauma. He'd barely survived after the shooting, and now to go through it again was unimaginable to him.

He had a new mission now: to deceive those closest to him. He had to conceal the storm raging within. Their concern, pity, and misguided advice wouldn't help him. No one had the power to alleviate his suffering.

As it wasn't an option to turn his visitors away without raising their suspicions, he went along with the open house atmosphere going on in his room. He graciously thanked Omeir and Safia for coming by. He outright lied to Safia and laughed whole heartedly at Omeir's jokes. When the guilt refused to be quashed, he told himself he wasn't totally deceiving; he *was* better. His physical injuries were healing, better than anticipated according to the doctor. Thanks to his convincing, easygoing demeanor, his friends had no idea that he was emotionally sliding backward and sliding fast. He had fooled his colleagues as well as the hospital staff. The charade continued for days, and just when he was close to being released, he had a meltdown of nuclear proportions.

It was a basic conversation, initiated by one of the nurses, which led to his unraveling. The nurse normally worked in pediatrics but was reassigned to his recovery unit due to a staff shortage. She was explaining to Zak how he needed to attend to his neck wound after he got released. He was having difficulties concentrating on what she was saying, a common PTSD symptom during times of stress. He was also exhausted; memories of the shooting from years ago had begun to resurface in both his sleep and his waking hours. The nurse, who was accustomed to dealing with children, made the mistake of talking down to Zak in order to get him to understand. Being treated like a defiant toddler, even though he may have inadvertently been acting like one, made him rage inside. He ended up hastily telling the nurse to just leave him written instructions. The nurse, who was frustrated as well, agreed and promptly left.

Five minutes later, a physician, whom he had not met before, came into his room and said he had reviewed Zak's chart. Because he had a documented history of PTSD, including severe depression, a psychiatric consult was required prior to any release. Upon hearing this, Zak became unglued. He told the doctor unequivocally he didn't need to see a shrink. The doctor tried to persuade him, and when it was clear it wasn't working, he informed Zak he had no choice if he wanted to be discharged.

Feeling trapped by a situation he could not control, Zak directed a firestorm of anger toward the doctor. He began with a colorful verbal tirade about how he would just walk out of the hospital and they couldn't do a damn thing about it. He was determined to distance himself from the hospital and their meddling staff. No way would he talk to some hospital shrink about feelings, the past, or anything else. This doctor was useless and so was any pill-pushing shrink he would refer Zak to. They couldn't heal him, at least not the part of him that needed healing. The doctor and the hospital served no purpose other than to confine him, and he couldn't bear to be confined. He needed to get away to eliminate the pressure pulling tight around his chest. So, he rose from the hospital bed to escape, to breathe, and to save himself.

Unfortunately, the doctor wasn't going to allow it. Instead of getting out of the way when he leapt from the bed, the doctor made the mistake of grabbing Zak's arm. He still had an IV and his abrupt movement had nearly caused it to be ripped from his limb. Focused on getting the hell out of the room, Zak didn't feel his skin tug. He was unaware the doctor's physical interference was to prevent the IV from popping out. His mind had travelled back to the day the shooting had occurred, to a moment of helplessness surrounded by the raining blood of his colleagues. When the doctor grabbed his arm to ease him back to the bed, Zak simply reacted to his own stimulus. He landed a blow, cold-cocking the doctor flat on the floor, and was still in survival mode when three security guards came rushing in to subdue him. It took them a while, but eventually they were able to pin him down to the floor. By now his IV had fully ripped out. Three enormous men pinning him to the cold hard floor, finally forced his brain to register the pain. He stopped struggling, allowing the men to ease him off the floor in a controlled wristlock. The ordeal was witnessed by several of the nurses on the unit, and although most had dealt with unruly patients before, the intensity of Zak's anger frightened them.

From there things moved fast. The hospital administrator was informed of the incident. She was given limited information on the patient, but plenty of descriptive details on what Zak had done. She called the police, looking to lay assault charges against Zak for what he had done to the doctor. Confusion initially ensued. When the NYPD ran the name of the assailant, they discovered it was one of their own who had caused the violent mayhem. A call was made to the chief of the Counterterrorism Bureau, who contacted Lieutenant Pratt. Within a short span of time, Pratt arrived at the hospital, along with Omeir, Safia, and Scorp.

After being briefed by the head of hospital security, Pratt forced a meeting with the hospital administrator. Fortunately, the attending physician had no serious injuries, but he was rightfully pissed. Upon reviewing Zak's file, the hospital administrator agreed they were dealing with a man who had suffered inconceivable trauma and not a violent criminal. The hospital administrator was ready to back away from laying charges; however, the victimized doctor wasn't ready to let it go. Once Pratt informed Zak's colleagues of the doctor's stance, they jumped in with ways to solve the matter. Pratt winced when Scorp volunteered to have a discussion with the doctor. Pratt recognized Scorp had skills beyond his sheer muscle power but feared just the sight of him would result in the doctor lodging a complaint of police intimidation. Omeir had wanted to hack into the doctor's life in order to obtain leverage, an idea Pratt shut down right away. Safia simply smiled sweetly at all three men and said, "I'll take care of it."

Though they all envisaged, or rather fantasized, how she might have done it, not one of them asked Safia. The hospital administrator asked to meet with Pratt once again; the doctor would not be pursuing the matter. When Pratt returned from the second meeting with the hospital administrator, he told his team he was going to talk to Zak, warning them that after he did, Zak might not want to see any of them.

* * * *

The anger had been such an overriding emotion earlier but dissipated quickly after the assault. In a way, the outburst had acted like a release valve, and now Zak was deflated. The fear was still there, but it was more subdued. It was now shame that overtook him. The hospital security team had placed him in a small room that resembled a vacant storage area. There he sat, awaiting his fate with both his wrists and ankles restrained by cold metal.

He was sitting in a chair with his head bowed down when Pratt walked in. Upon hearing footsteps, he looked up.

"How's the doctor?"

"He's got a big shiner, which will die down in a week or so, but no other injuries."

"Shit, Lieutenant, I'm so sorry. I don't know what happened to me. I guess I was just eager to leave and…"

He was having difficulty explaining and before he could gather his thoughts, Pratt interrupted him.

"Zak, we both know what happened." It was clear he was referring to the PTSD.

"I'll be okay, I just need to relax. Get out of New York, and I promise I won't cause any more problems for the Bureau."

"It's not the Bureau I'm concerned about. I'm concerned about you."

"Yeah, I messed up big time. I'll apologize to the doctor. I've already apologized to the security staff."

"It's not that simple, Zak. They were looking at assault charges."

Zak's heart was racing. He'd hit the doctor hard, and the doctor had every right to be pissed at him. But assault charges? How quickly he unraveled and lost control alarmed him. Letting the gravity of what he had done soak in, he realized that if he was alarmed, then the doctor would have been downright terrified. Why wouldn't there be charges? He'd hit an innocent man who was trying to help him. He had no defense, and frankly, he couldn't imagine trying to fight the charge.

"So, what happens now?" His voice cracked.

"The doctor has been convinced not to press charges. The hospital administration, given your circumstances, isn't going to pursue the matter either."

Given your circumstances. The words echoed in his head. Circumstances meant so many things: his position with the NYPD, his near-fatal physical trauma, and of course, the big circumstance that Pratt really meant, the one that would never go away – PTSD.

He muttered a feeble yet sincere, "Thanks, Lieutenant."

"Well, it's not me who deserves thanks. It's Safia on this one. The doctor wasn't budging when I talked to him, but she got him to change his mind." Pratt sighed heavily and continued, "Although there's not going to be any assault charges, the hospital still has an obligation to the safety of its staff. The NYPD has an obligation to you, to make sure you're okay."

Zak knew where Pratt was heading with the spiel. "I'm being admitted to the psych ward?"

"It's for thirty days. They'll do an assessment, get you stabilized."

* * * *

Zak had been down this road before two and a half years ago, just after the shooting. It was a different hospital, but essentially it would be the same. They would look at medicating him. He wasn't opposed to medications in general. It worked for some people, and for a while it even worked for him. The sleep meds had gotten him through the nights, and the anti-anxiety meds had helped with the panic attacks. But the longer he'd been on them, the more he'd lost himself, becoming a shell of the person he was. Much to the psychiatrist's objections, he'd discontinued the meds once he had been discharged.

He remembered how horrible it had been back then, especially the first couple of days without anything to numb the pain. The flashbacks, the nightmares, a mind constantly at war with itself. He hadn't been able to take it anymore. To escape the constant reminders of the violence, he'd left the city where it all happened. With no destination in mind, he'd gone to the airport and bought whatever cheap flight was available. It happened to be Chicago. When he'd gotten to Chicago, he'd rented a car and driven west. While driving around the countryside, the idea of finding a secluded area had entered his mind. He could wander into a densely bushed area, put his service pistol to his temple and pull the trigger. But he couldn't get rid of the image of some poor soul finding the gruesome scene of his head blown apart. He was exhausted with living, but he kept thinking what right did he have to splatter his brain so someone else would have to deal with his blood? To put someone else into the hell he was trying to escape from? And he'd continued to drive.

How he'd ended up in small town Baxley, as opposed to anywhere else, he later came to believe was fate. He'd driven around the town until he'd found some sense of peace, tempering his suicidal urges. He'd found it unusual for the drive to have calmed him, but he hadn't dwelled on it. He'd just felt relieved to have the hopelessness subside.

Departing the quiet streets of Baxley, he'd headed out into the surrounding rural area. Rolling hills of fertile fields, interlaced with patches of trees and shrubs, stretched for miles. Crossing a small bridge over a flowing stream, he'd seen a stretch of towering eastern pines. When he'd gotten near the majestic trees, he'd noticed a gravel entranceway. A few branches had fallen down, likely due to a recent storm. With no vehicle tracks, he'd figured the road would lead to an abandoned shed or barn. Intrigued by the privacy of the property, and wanting a secluded place to pray, he'd driven down the narrow roadway. He'd been surprised to find a small wood-paneled house with a large front porch. At the bottom of the porch, a weathered 'for sale' sign had stood. There had been a certain unexpected charm to the place, and before he could second-guess himself, he'd dialed the number on the sign. A woman named Margo with the gentlest voice had answered. Elated that someone had called about the house, she'd told him she was on her way. When a flicker of doubt had entered his mind, he'd pushed it away, agreeing to wait for her.

He remembered how the silver-haired woman had talked so fondly of Baxley. As if knowing what his tormented soul needed, she'd told him it was the type of place where "one could heal and be whole again." Some people would say it was all a coincidence, but to Zak it was more.

Some men lose their faith when darkness comes, but for Zak, faith was all he had left, so he held on even tighter. Now he hoped the faith which had led him to Baxley would help him again as he prepared to transfer to the psychiatric unit.

He sat waiting for the staff to escort him to the mental health wing of the hospital. It would be at least half an hour before the paperwork was processed for his admittance. He was embarrassed about the whole ordeal. He had set a black mark upon the NYPD with his actions. Having to deal with Pratt was hard enough; he couldn't bear dealing with Omeir or Scorp right now. He didn't want to see Safia, but he felt obligated to thank her in person. If it wasn't for her, he would have been a cop with an assault charge pending.

By the time she came into the room, the security staff had agreed to remove the handcuffs and leg irons from Zak's limbs. The last time Safia had seen him so broken, she had been full of tears, but this time she was the resilient woman he had always admired. She walked into the tiny room, moved a chair next to him, and sat down.

"Thanks for talking to the doctor. You know I really don't deserve a friend like you." His voice crackled as he spoke.

"Come on, Zak, you don't deserve to be tied up in some legal battle. You've gone through enough. Besides, the charges would've eventually been dismissed."

"Yeah, maybe, but I totally lost it on the poor guy."

"Trust me, the man's going to be okay. But how about you?"

"I don't know if I'm going to get through it this time." It was honest and terrifying.

"So what will help?"

"I really don't know."

"Think of your life as one of our assignments. What are the options? What can you control, and what do you have no control over? Break it into components. It's what you do. It's what you're good at."

"But that's the problem, I don't have control anymore." It hurt just to admit the truth, to have worked so hard to battle, just to realize he had been defeated.

"Zakariya, that's not true. You have control over getting out of here, of staying in New York or going to Baxley. Sure, some aspects you don't have control over. Our assignments are like that, too. That's why we have faith, why we go to prayers as a team."

"I may not have any control over getting out of here. It's up to the doctors when they release me. I'm a mess."

"Will it help to be here, or is it better for you to leave?"

"I can't heal here, that I know."

"Well, then convince them you're stable. It doesn't matter if you don't think you are. It only matters what they think. Okay, so after you're released, what's next? Omeir and I are here for you. You can stay in New York. Do you want that?"

When he didn't respond, Safia continued, "Well, I'm not sure what options there are, but I know you have at least one more. So what about it? Is going back to Baxley better for you?"

"It used to be, but I don't know."

"Stay in New York then."

"No, it can't be New York." His voice had an air of certainty to it.

"Yeah, I figured that. You have a partial plan already. You focus on getting discharged, convincing the doctors to release you. And then you head back to Baxley."

"So, my by-the-book colleague, and the most honest person I know is advising me to deceive the psychiatrist into believing I'm stable, even when I'm not?"

"Zak, I know you're exhausted. I would be too. I know you can and will heal, but you need to do what works for you. If it means using your skills of deception to get out of here, then do it. Don't think of deception in a negative way. It's a gift, a gift that has saved lives. Now use it to save yours."

Chapter Twenty

As Lexie started to get out more, she became more relaxed with her new community and at ease with the people she was meeting. Monday evenings, she spent with the Historical Society and Thursday night was book club. The weekends were still difficult, and she knew she contributed to it. She couldn't help but drive by Zak's place, hoping he had returned. With each uneventful visit, her heart sank a little more. At least she had Abby. Abby was more than just a foot warmer at the end of her bed. The dog appeared to sense when she was stressed. She would come trotting over, gently nudging her nose against Lexie's thigh to get her attention. It was as if Abby had some canine calming abilities.

It was the third book club meeting she had gone to, this one being hosted at Megan's home. Kristina was the last to arrive and apologized for holding up the group. Emmett had insisted on giving her a ride over to Megan's, even though it was only a fifteen minute walk from their home.

"Sorry for running late. Being married to the sheriff isn't so easy. He's a little protective of me walking alone in the dark. I don't know what he's worried about. The only thing that's happened this year was the lame graffiti on the water tower."

Lexie doubted the sheriff worried about his wife getting mugged. He was more likely just trying to prevent the embarrassment of having Kristina staggering home from wine night, as she liked to call it. Lexie liked Kristina. She had come to realize that getting a little sloshed was her way of coping with Emmett's sullen moods.

They were still reading Kristina's choice of *Stranger in the Fog*, which was by far the most erotic book Lexie had ever read. Bernice could not contain her love for this spicy novel, which by now was more amusing than disturbing. Willow, who constantly had birds on her mind, was making comparisons of various passages in the book to the mating habits of particular birds. This made Kristina, who was now a little tipsy, giggle. Margo, who realized what was happening and fearful Willow's feelings might get hurt, distracted her with questions about spring gardening. Lexie too, was starting to get the giggles, as Kristina's girlish snickering kept seeping out and was becoming contagious.

"Hey, Lexie and Kristina, I think Megan needs a hand in the kitchen," Tamara said, both beckoning and saving them.

As soon as they got into the kitchen, Tamara, who was previously unruffled, broke into uncontrollable laughter. Lexie and Kristina doubled over with a mixture of laughter and outright howling. Megan joined in, laughing so hard she was actually snorting. Tears were rolling down their faces at the images of an emperor penguin swaggering in the fog, looking for a mate. Kristina began to mime the enormous penguin waddling back and forth, oh so desperate to connect with a mate. It was oddly hilarious, and it was the first time since Zak's departure that Lexie had sincerely laughed. She wasn't just smiling to make others feel comfortable, she was actually enjoying herself.

Once they returned to a civilized state, Kristina spoke, "You ladies are so much fun. We should go to the bar on Saturday for some real fun."

"The Black Dog?" asked a puzzled Megan. The Black Dog was the only bar in Baxley. It was a small establishment where the elderly men in Baxley went to watch sports and get away from their wives. It was rare to find anyone under the age of sixty there.

"Hell, no, that place is for old men. Besides, I'm the sheriff's wife. I can't go to the bar in Baxley. Every person there will be talking to Emmett about what his wife said or did. No, I'm talking about going into Lands Crossing and going to a real country bar."

"I'm in," said Megan.

"Well, why not?" piped in Tamara. "I just need to make sure I can get a sitter for the twins."

"I've got that covered. Emily's available," said Megan, volunteering her daughter.

Lexie felt the heat of their eyes as they waited for another eager affirmative response. She wanted to come up with an excuse. She wasn't the bar type. Sure, she had the occasional glass of wine or an all too expensive cocktail at a quiet, high-end lounge when she'd been in Chicago, but she had never gone to a honky-tonk saloon. She didn't actually like country music, finding it both twangy and depressing. Her sister Claudia used to tell her she was just listening to the wrong type of country music.

"Well, girl, are you in?" asked an impatient Kristina.

Finally, she squeaked out, "Yeah, I'll go."

Chapter Twenty-One

The first couple of days were the toughest for Zak as the nightmares were back. He despised swallowing the medication, but he did; he couldn't risk hurting anyone again. Without the meds he wouldn't be able to sleep, and there was always a strong correlation between exhaustion and drastic mood swings. The assault on the doctor, although unsettling, made him work hard to control his emotions and avoid further confrontations.

He knew what it was like when a team member got hurt or even worse, like when your colleagues were killed. It made a person angry, even vengeful. He had assailed upon their team member, the attending physician. He fully expected the nurses and other healthcare workers to treat him poorly. Surprisingly, they didn't. Even the cranky burnt-out ones were professional in their conduct, and some were downright kind. He discerned they were likely taking pity on him, cognizant he was an NYPD member who had previously been shot in the line of duty and now had been stabbed. He hated pity, but at least they didn't overtly show it.

He had undergone one session with a psychiatrist. It had lasted approximately thirty minutes and had more to do with adjusting his medication than any type of counselling. He hated the medication, but he hated having to open up to a stranger even more. He wasn't ready to disclose to his best friend Omeir, let alone some shrink he had never met. He did implement new relaxation techniques and he wasn't sure if it was the medication finally kicking in, or if it was the exercises, but by the third day he was definitely more settled.

Omeir was the first to visit him in the psych ward. He had been there last time when Zak's world fell apart, so at least he knew what to expect and didn't bombard him with questions. While they were debating the best Middle-Eastern eatery in the Bronx, Omeir remembered the envelope Zak had given him.

"Here, take this back. I was so relieved I didn't need to do anything with it."

The day after coming out of the coma, Zak asked Omeir where the envelope was. He was extremely relieved to find out Omeir had kept it and it hadn't found its way to Lexie. He never intended to hurt her, but he knew he had. He still planned to go back to Baxley, but he couldn't go back to her. After assaulting a doctor, a man who was trying to help him, it terrified him to know what he was capable of. He needed to stay away from Lexie. Until the incident with the doctor, he never thought himself capable of physically hurting an innocent person, but now he knew different. He wasn't the man she thought he was.

Safia was right. He needed to look at his options. He contemplated not returning to Baxley, but where would he go? He was welcomed to crash at Omeir's place but sleeping on a lumpy sofa at his buddy's cramped, one-bedroom apartment wouldn't help with his PTSD symptoms, and it wouldn't take long for his moodiness to end up ruining the best friendship he had. Going back to his country home near Baxley was his best option. He would avoid the town of Baxley and go into Lands Crossing for groceries and whatever other essentials he would need.

Lexie would eventually find out he had returned, and he would have to deal with her somehow. Maybe by now, she was so angry, she wouldn't care to see him again. Although it saddened him, disliking or even hating him might make it easier for her. He was prepared to sell the house in Baxley if it ended up causing more problems for Lexie, but for now he had no place else to go. He liked Baxley but, with the exception of Lexie, he wasn't connected to anyone there. Several people had been nice to him: Kristina, Emily, and there were the elderly residents he helped with tech gadgets. And of course, there was sweet Margo. The woman had saved his life when he'd first arrived in Baxley, even though she probably had no idea she had. He gathered most of the people in town would be indifferent to him leaving, and there would be a few, like

Cicily McQuay and her sheriff son, who would be thrilled if he was gone for good.

Zak realized he had zoned out when he saw Omeir with a blank stare.

"Sorry, these damn meds make me a bit spacey. What did you say?"

"Just admiring what an honest guy you are."

"How's that?"

"Making sure your bill to this Dr. Draden was paid up."

He now realized what Omeir was doing. He was digging for information, curious about the contents of the envelope. He didn't honestly think Zak would ask him to hand deliver payment on an outstanding medical bill. He knew Dr. Draden was Baxley's new physician; he had been the one who did the background check on her, but that's all he knew. As a hacker, Omeir was constantly able to access private information, and not knowing what he held in his hands was killing him.

"Abby's staying with Dr. Draden, so that's what it's about." It was partly true and hopefully enough information to slow down the gears in Omeir's head.

Scorp dropped by later in the day. He looked much better than when he'd seen him a few days before, after an obvious night of binge drinking. When he entered the ward, the nurses were initially wary of him. The way Scorp presented, with his massive frame and abundance of grisly tattoos, drew unwanted attention and worry. When they discovered he was there to see Zak, they eased up, realizing he was probably an undercover NYPD member, as opposed to trouble. His intimidating nature was an asset on the job, but Zak sensed the big guy hated the fear in women's eyes when he walked into a room. The man would probably love to blend in, but when you're six-foot-five with a thunderous presence, it's not possible. Thankfully, the man had plenty of charm. And once he flashed a dimpled smile, his larger than life charisma shone through. In no time, he was being treated like a big adorable puppy, and Zak couldn't help but notice how women love puppies.

Although Zak was messed up, he could still read people. He could see Scorp still felt a sense of responsibility for the stabbing, but at least he seemed not to be in such a dark place about it. Maybe the connection with the team was helping Scorp in some way. According to Omeir, he was fitting in. The testosterone-charged issue with Omeir was a thing of the past, and Zak could tell he wasn't hitting the booze, or at least not lately. His eyes were clear, his clothes neat and not rumpled, and there wasn't even the faintest odor of alcohol on him. But maybe it wasn't the comradery with Safia and Omeir, but the distraction of various women that was helping him along. Regardless, Zak was just relieved Scorp seemed to be doing better.

"I brought your duffle bag with your stuff from the hotel suite," Scorp said. "It's with the unit nurse, the one with the sexy curves."

"Guess they have to make sure I don't try to hang myself with a belt." He meant it as a joke and was glad it was Scorp he had said it to. Omeir and Safia might not see the humor.

"A man should never complain about a hot nurse going through his pants. She'll probably redo my shitty folding job. Not so bad of a deal, is it?"

Zak forced a grin. "Thanks, Scorp."

It was obvious Scorp felt uncomfortable and didn't know what else to say. Zak had been through this with colleagues before who were afraid they would say the wrong thing. A couple of days ago every spoken word might have been wrong, but now the rage was gone, or at least dormant. Scorp had his own demons. Zak didn't know what they were, he just knew the man had tried to chase them away with alcohol. His binge drinking didn't just happen after Zak was stabbed, it had been going on for some time. At one time Zak wondered about medicating himself with alcohol, maybe he would be able to cope better. But alcohol worsened PTSD symptoms, intensifying the negative emotions, making him more volatile.

Zak felt comfortable enough with Scorp now to be straightforward with him on most matters. Not comfortable enough to reveal his fears, but at least he could trust Scorp, like he trusted Omeir and Safia.

"So, I'm looking at only being here for another three or four weeks tops. The anger's gone, which is probably due to the severity of losing it as well as the meds they've got me on."

"That's good," he said. "I heard it took three guys to restrain you when you went all crazy."

Zak read the regret on Scorp's face as soon as he said the word crazy. It wasn't the best term to use when talking to a guy sitting in a psychiatric ward.

"Sorry man, I didn't mean…"

"To say crazy?" Zak finished the sentence for him. "It's okay. It was crazy what I did. It was also stupid and regrettable too. I appreciate you guys all coming to the hospital with Pratt, trying to bail my stupid ass out of an assault charge I really did deserve."

"Look Zak, I'm not saying the doctor deserved what happened. He didn't. But you didn't deserve an assault charge either. Omeir filled me in on your career with the NYPD. You've gone through more shit than most guys. I thought I had quite a few guardian angels saving my sorry skin, but man, you must have a whole team of them. You need to stop beating yourself up for shit you can't control. You basically told me something similar the other day when I showed up to see you with vodka oozing from my eyes, so now I'm telling you. Don't let the knockout punch of the doctor define who you are. If you think I'm even close to being in the decent category, like you told me the other day, then you're damn near a saint. You came back to this shit job and this even shittier assignment, risking your life to save others. So, don't ever put yourself in the same category as some punk criminal who goes around assaulting people."

Zak understood Scorp was serious, but he couldn't help but smile at how blunt the man was. Slowly the smile left his face and the seriousness came back. "I'm all medicated now. I hate the meds, but I know I need them to balance me out. What I don't know, Scorp, is what will happen when I stop taking them."

"Can't you just keep taking them?"

"I probably can, but I won't. Everyone is different. Some guys will stay on them, but me, it makes me not me, if that makes any sense."

Scorp gave him a look that told him he understood. Zak imagined the alcohol did the same to Scorp.

"So what's your plan?"

"The same as last time – stop the meds as soon as I get discharged."

"But won't the hospital give you some support, some follow up to make sure you're doing okay?"

"Yeah, they do, but I'm not sticking around. I can't stay in the city. I'm going back to Baxley."

"Is that a good idea?"

Zak shrugged. Maybe it wasn't a good idea, but it was better than his other options.

Chapter Twenty-Two

It was no surprise when Tamara declared herself the designated driver for their girls' night out. As a single parent with no family nearby, Tamara was accustomed to being solely responsible for her twins, which meant ensuring she was fully sober 24/7.

Lexie was the only one who lived outside of Baxley, so Tamara had picked up Megan and Kristina and then swung around to get her. It took about thirty minutes to get to the Stompin Loft in Lands Crossing. When they walked in, a live band was already playing. It was a banjo-inspired tune about some woman cheated on by her man. How cliché, thought Lexie. Kristina, who was wearing a denim micro-miniskirt with red cowboy boots, swayed to the music. She, too, looked like a cliché.

Lexie took in her surroundings. It was what she imagined a country bar in a rural town would look like. The place had old wooden floors with a dance area in the center, and the band off to the side. There was a large rectangular bar with a rugged butcher-block top facing both the dance floor to one side and a couple of pool tables on the other. True to its name, the Stompin Loft had an open second floor overlooking the dance area. There were bar stools and a wooden ledge circling around the upstairs railing. This area was currently vacant but would fill up later, an ideal spot for those interested in checking out the dance floor below. It had a meat-market type of vibe, which made Lexie regret her decision to come out tonight. Brooding alone in her house was depressing, but now standing here, she wished she were home.

A scattering of people stood around the bar, with most of the patrons seated in either booths or tables near the far walls. Kristina led the group over to a vacant table with bar stools. It was still rather early, and there were only a few couples dancing to the music. Kristina was singing along to a song the band was playing. She seemed to be in her element. When the waitress came by, Kristina was eager to order a round of tequila shots. Thankfully, Megan talked her into starting with a shared pitcher of beer. Preferring a nice Chablis, or even a Cosmopolitan, Lexie went along with the cold hops. It was a beer and whiskey kind of establishment and ordering anything else would just be disappointing. The service was fast, with beer and Tamara's club soda arriving within minutes.

"To having a great time!" Kristina said loudly as she raised her glass. The other ladies smiled politely and clinked glasses.

Besides being loud, Kristina was also quite funny and had some wonderful stories to tell about growing up in Baxley. The more swigs of beer she took, the funnier, as well as more boisterous, she became. About an hour later, when the second pitcher of beer arrived, Kristina began to talk about the five years she spent away from Baxley, when Emmett had enlisted in the Army. Her storytelling was still hilarious, but there was warmth when she mentioned her life with Emmett away from the town she'd grown up in. It was the first time Lexie recalled hearing Kristina talk lovingly of her husband.

When a line dance began, Kristina dragged a reluctant Tamara to the dance floor. Megan and Lexie were somewhat relieved to sit this one out and remain holding down the table. Abandoning it now would only result in having to go up to the loft, as vacant tables were now getting scarce. They both wanted to avoid the overtly testosterone-filled second floor.

Lexie enjoyed conversing with Megan. She was a kindred spirit in so many ways, including that she regretted going along with Kristina's idea to come to the Stompin Loft. Lexie got the feeling that Megan's focus was on raising her teenage daughter and not on meeting some guy in a bar. She cringed every time Kristina pointed out some guy for her. From what Lexie could see, Megan had done a great job raising her daughter, a compassionate yet level-headed teen. Lexie had seen her fair share of troubled adolescents, including her nephew Liam. She knew that some kids had poor parenting and got into drugs and crime due to poor role models, but there were tons of kids with great parents who just drifted. Although her sister Claudia had become pre-occupied with

Hailie's needs, she did love Liam and tried her best. He was just one of those kids that drifted, and hopefully now he was through the worst of it.

The line dance ended, and Kristina had returned to the table alone.

"Where's Tamara?" asked Megan.

"She's dancing. Some cowboy came by, wanting to dance with her," replied Kristina.

Megan and Lexie scanned the dance floor for Tamara. Lexie wasn't sure if Megan wanted to see if the guy was some hottie, but Lexie's motive was to ensure Tamara was safe. She was aware of the risks of meeting men in bars, and what could happen if you didn't have someone looking out for you. She had treated rape victims who had been roofied by handsome strangers. She wasn't paranoid, but she was cautious. She caught sight of Tamara and the stranger who was leading her around the dance floor in a two-step. Tamara seemed to be enjoying herself. She figured Tamara to be a woman with good instincts, but Lexie also knew some men weren't what they seemed.

Without Lexie realizing it, Megan went off to dance, leaving her with Kristina. She figured within moments Kristina would be out dancing as well, leaving her alone. Sure enough, a slender man approached Kristina, asking her to dance. He was courteous with nothing peculiar in his demeanor, however she politely declined.

"If you wanted to dance, you should have gone. I'm okay sitting here by myself," Lexie told her. She didn't want to be sitting alone like some loser, but she didn't want Kristina to feel obligated to sit with her.

"I don't abandon my friend, especially when she's not having a good time."

"Hey, I'm having fun," Lexie protested. Clearly it was a lie, but she wasn't going to admit it and ruin the evening out. "It's good to be out. I like hanging out with you guys," she said, trying to be convincing.

"Well, if that's true Lexie, why aren't you dancing?"

"I haven't been asked."

"If you didn't have a scowl on your face, I'm sure the men would be lined up to ask you. But right now, you're intimidating them."

"I'm not," she protested.

"Look, Lexie, I'm not trying to get under your skin. I just sense you'd rather be somewhere else. And to tell you the truth, so would I."

"Really, like where?" Lexie had difficulty believing this. It was Kristina's idea to come here and she seemed so pumped when they walked through the door.

"Truthfully, I'd rather be at home, curled up on the couch with Emmett watching a movie, or even some dumb ballgame."

"Oh, is Emmett working tonight?"

"No, he'd just rather be alone than with me."

Kristina's face looked so glum, it was actually heartbreaking. She reached over to her new friend's hand and gave it a squeeze. "I'm sorry."

"Me, too." Kristina quivered. She took a big swig of beer. "You know, he wasn't always so grumpy. We actually had fun, lots of fun. He changed when Colton died. His mom should never have guilted him into returning. He liked being in the Army, away from Baxley. But the obligation to his mother, and Colton's death changed him. He wasn't the easy-going man I met and married. He became serious, way too serious. And I became just another obligation to him."

"Does he know how you feel?"

"I tried telling him, but he just keeps reminding me he needs to be a better son, his mother only has him left. As far as I'm concerned, he's a great son. He gave up what he loved for her. What he isn't great at anymore is being a husband, and when I say it, I feel lousy. I feel selfish." She choked up again.

"Kristina, don't. You're not selfish for wanting your husband to enjoy his life and wishing for the life you used to have."

"Thanks for saying that. I hate not being able to reach him anymore." In an attempt to ease her pain, she took another large gulp of beer.

Not knowing what else to say, Lexie remained silent. She wasn't one to pry into the personal affairs of others, and she certainly wasn't one to give relationship advice. She had never had a long-term relationship, and the man she'd hoped might change that had vanished on her.

"So, Lex, what's your story?" Kristina asked, breaking the silence.

"Me? I don't have a story." Of course, it was a lie, but avoidance was her plan since her story made her too sad for words.

"I know Zak Tifour was crazy about you, and I heard you're looking after his dog. So where is Mr. Handsome?"

"I wish I knew."

"You don't know?" she yelled, a little too loud.

"He told me he had to go to New York for business. It was only supposed to be for two weeks and now it's almost six weeks later. I have no idea if he's still somewhere in New York, or someplace else."

"No word at all?"

"Nope, nothing. Don't even know where he was staying. For all I know he could be married with a wife in New York." Lexie hadn't intended to sound bitter, but feeling the buzz from the beer, she couldn't help it.

"He's not married," Kristina said, her words beginning to slur.

"How do you know he's not? You hear about guys doing this all the time, a wife here, a girlfriend there. Maybe he's even got some kids." The more she spoke, the angrier she got.

Kristina grabbed Lexie's hand to get her attention. "Listen, I flirted with Zak. I'm not proud of it and it didn't mean anything, it's just that I was looking for some attention, to be noticed. I know I shouldn't disrespect Emmett that way…"

Before she rambled on even more in her partial drunken state, Lexie pulled her hand away, giving her a heated glare.

"No, no, Lexie, what I'm saying is Zak was nice to me. He was polite and humored me, but he didn't want me. He wasn't interested. He's not that kind of guy. And after he had eyes on you, he actually tried to avoid me. He's no two-timing cheat."

"But then why haven't I heard from him?"

"I don't know, but I believe he has every intention of coming back if he said he would."

Then, noticing Tamara and Megan kicking up a storm on the dance floor, they did the only thing they could think to do and ordered tequila shots.

Chapter Twenty-Three

The extended hospital stay gave Zak an appreciation for what medical professionals have to deal with. The ward contained a wide range of patients, with a variety of issues. Some were cooperative, even appreciative, but many were ornery and disorderly. Then there was the downright dangerous group. He had demonstrated that he fit into this latter category and had tried his best to move into the appreciative group. But it wasn't always the patients who were difficult. Their families were often rude or abusive to the healthcare workers. Zak wondered how often this had happened to Lexie when she worked in Chicago. How many times patients and their families were demanding or threatening toward her. He shuddered to think of her being physically assaulted, like he had done to the doctor.

He still struggled, but he was able to maintain control on the surface. Those observing him were not aware of what was truly going on inside him, he was after all a great manipulator. The medication he reluctantly complied with, helped to slow things down. It was like he was paddling a canoe near a deadly waterfall. It took all his strength to prevent going over. With determination, he stayed away from the sharply plunging edge. But he couldn't do it forever. Eventually he would tire and plummet into the raging waters. Getting to Baxley was the only hope he had. Going home wasn't necessarily a rescue but staying here was certain doom. So every day he swallowed the damn pills and bore the unbearable. There would be no slip ups, no missteps this time.

As expected, thirty days later, Zak was ready to be discharged. He had completed his in-patient portion of treatment, with a scheduled appointment for follow-up group therapy to start within the week. Continued treatment and medication compliance were the goals the professionals had set for him, goals he had no intention of following.

Because of patient confidentiality, Pratt received few details from the hospital. The lieutenant was informed that Zak no longer required hospitalization, and that he was no longer an undue risk to himself or others. Because his physical injuries prevented a return to duty, Zak had no obligation to disclose further details to his employer. A further assessment would occur prior to returning to work, but he knew he had at least four months before this would occur. He knew he would not be returning, but he wasn't up to discussing it. Pratt had been good to him, but he didn't kid himself about where Pratt's loyalties were. Zak was an asset to the Counterterrorism Bureau, and like all assets, he held value. Neither Pratt, nor the Bureau, were likely to let him slip away permanently, but that was their issue, and right now he had to take care of himself.

* * * *

Although the psychiatrist recommended he remain in New York, Zak was free to return to Baxley. When as a courtesy, he told Pratt he'd be leaving New York, he figured the lieutenant would try to convince him to hold off. But he didn't. The man was letting him leave without a discussion. Not that a nice chit chat with the boss would change things, but Pratt's reaction, or rather lack of reaction, was odd and even unsettling to him. But a few hours later when Scorp waltzed into his hospital room, the picture came together. Pratt had a game plan, one which royally pissed Zak off.

"Really, a public relations course, and you're the guy they're sending?" he yelled as he stood, violating Scorp's personal space.

Scorp didn't flinch, as he gazed emotionlessly back at Zak.

"And just by coincidence, you're on the same flight as me? Come on, I'm not an idiot."

Again, Scorp didn't say anything, allowing him to rant. At least the man respected him enough not to deny the obvious. Good thing, as Zak was near the edge and another incident in the hospital would seal his fate for more than just a few additional weeks.

"I came to New York on my own. I can damn well leave this city on my own. What does Pratt think I'm going to do? Have a meltdown or go into some verbal tirade while in the air? I was good enough to drag here and take a knife to the neck, but now I need someone to hold my hand on a plane?"

"I won't be holding your hairy hand," Scorp said, breaking his silence. "You're not my type." The humor didn't work. Zak wasn't ready to be diffused.

"If I see you anywhere near the airport tomorrow, I'll cancel my flight."

"Look, Zak, Pratt's not going to give up on this. If you cancel the flight, he'll just wait until you rebook. And if it's not me, he'll send someone else. Once you get to Baxley, he'll let you be. He knows you're probably going to stop the meds as soon as you walk out of this hospital. He's concerned, and rightfully so. Altitude, confined spaces, screaming toddlers – planes are full of triggers."

Zak wasn't just stubborn. He was scared. Scorp was right about triggers.

"Don't do it for Pratt. Do it for me. Even if you don't get on that flight, I still have to go to Chicago for that stupid course."

"You know, you suck at this?"

"At what?"

"Trying to manipulate me."

"I know I'm going to suck at the PR course, but I'm not manipulating you. I hate flying. I need a distraction, and surprisingly those sexy flight attendants aren't distracting enough."

"So, Mr. Tough Guy, you're afraid of flying?" Zak hadn't meant to sound like some bully teasing his buddy, but that's exactly how it came out.

"Hey, let's not use the word afraid. I just hate flying."

"Yeah, me, too," Zak's voice had settled down. "I thought about driving, but figured I'd be too drowsy. And the bus... well, there are more weird sounds and people, than on a plane. At least with my ears popping, sounds get muted in the air."

"For me it's noises and the jerking movements. On my flight out of Iraq, I had to be subdued when I damn near opened up the emergency exit when we hit turbulence. I thought I was under attack when a large metal box came crashing down from the overhead bin. I'm still not crazy about loud noises. Cars backfiring unsettle me. I frigging hate fireworks. I head out of the city on July Fourth and New Year's Eve. So if you really think I'm going to be all in your face to make sure you're not going to freak on the plane, you're wrong. I'm more likely to be the one coming unglued, and you the one running interference. It's certainly not what Pratt envisioned when he orchestrated this, but I wasn't going to tell him I'm beyond terrified of flying. Yeah, I said it, I'm afraid."

It was the first time Scorp ever talked about being in the Marines. Zak still wasn't sure if Scorp truly was terrified of flying, or if he was just trying to make him feel better, but he understood him well enough by now to know he, too, was haunted by the past, just in a different way.

After listening to Scorp, Zak realized he was stuck with the situation. He still didn't like it, but he knew from his outburst how unstable he was. He needed to work harder on staying calm, and at least Scorp would be a buffer in dealing with travel annoyances and triggers.

* * * *

They got to the airport early the next day with plenty of time to check in and grab a coffee. Zak noticed Scorp glancing at the various airport cocktail lounges as they walked past. It was obvious that he would rather be sitting bar-side with a beer in his hand than with the steaming liquid in the paper cup he was holding. Perhaps Scorp was telling the truth about his fear of flying. Zak didn't know what it was like to wrestle with sobriety, but he knew what it was like to want so badly that you couldn't think of anything else.

Giving up the notion of downing a drink, Scorp followed Zak over to the east side terminal. Zak took a seat across from the departure gate, away from the congestion of passengers. Dropping his duffle bag next to Zak, Scorp headed over to the attractive customer service agent standing at the gate. The woman was likely Scorp's way of distracting himself from what he really wanted. He seemed to have two responses in dealing with stress: one was binge drinking and the other was women. Zak could tell by his wolfish grin he was flirting with her. Resisting the booze, he had kicked it up a notch with this pretty blonde. Clearly, she didn't mind, as the woman let out a laugh before saying something and nodding. Scorp said a few more words, and from where Zak sat, it looked like he gave her a wink before walking away. The man was so physically intimidating, yet he had an almost magical charm switch when it came to women.

Scorp plopped down in a chair across from Zak and motioned over to the woman he was just chatting with. "The flight isn't full, so she might be able to get us bumped up to first class."

"First class? I like the sound of that," he admitted.

Zak was hoping not to sit next to Scorp on the plane. Two large men shoulder to shoulder would be highly uncomfortable, and likely not even feasible. However, if they were bumped to first class, with the more expansive and wider seats, it would be fine.

"How'd you do that?" He was curious what Scorp would admit to.

"Well, I do have skills and sometimes I even use them for good."

It made Zak chuckle. He was still feeling lousy, but the meds he took yesterday were at least keeping him glued together. Besides, Scorp was rather amusing. They sat several minutes without speaking, finishing their coffees.

"You done?" Scorp asked, motioning toward the paper cup.

He handed Scorp the empty cup and went back to perusing his library of music on his phone. After tossing the cups in a nearby trash can, Scorp sat back down. His eyes scanned over the small group of passengers that congregated nearby.

"This is certainly a first," Scorp said.

"What's that?"

"Not being the number-one concern."

Zak looked up from his phone and noticed the heated glares coming his way.

"Guess the beard doesn't help," he said, and then went back to his phone.

"Does it ever piss you off?"

"You do know that Pratt's paying you to keep me level-headed."

"Yeah. I guess that was a dumb question."

"How about you? Is it pissing you off?" Zak asked.

"Yeah."

"Good."

"You want a guy who's terrified of flying to be pissed off?"

"Not so pissed that you're going to cause a scene but pissed enough that you care. You'd be amazed at how many people think it's okay to do what that jerk over in the corner is doing. Staring me down, thinking I'm going to blow up the plane and getting ready to tackle me."

"So it does piss you off?"

"Yup. Not much I can do about it. I travel with my badge. It lessens the hassles with security, but it's not like I can flash it around to every Islamophobe walking through the airport. I try to ignore it. It's worse for Omeir. He was born in Iraq, so he gets a lot more hassle than I normally do. He refuses to use his badge. He says he doesn't want to forget what it's like for the average Muslim in America."

"Should we start speaking in Arabic and really freak out that asshole over there?"

Zak laughed. "It's your ass Pratt is going to kick if I don't get on the flight. Besides, I heard you speak Arabic. It's embarrassingly bad."

"Good point. Not about my great language skills, but about Pratt. I like working in counterterrorism, and I get the feeling that Pratt isn't a man you want to piss off."

"You got that right."

They went back to the silence. A few minutes later an announcement came over the airport intercom: "Attention, Mr. Marion Traversini please report to terminal five C. Marion Traversini to terminal Five C."

With a scowl on his face, Scorp stood up and headed back to the customer service rep. Zak knew the big man as Detective Traversini and Scorp, but Marion? He would have never guessed.

"Marion?" Zak asked with amusement when Scorp returned.

With a low warning growl, Scorp glared at him. When Zak's grin didn't disappear, Scorp began to speak. "My biological mother named me Marion Eliot Traversini. Prior to my first day of school, I decided I would only respond to Eliot. Went by Eliot or Traversini for years. Even forgot what Marion sounded like. But it resurfaced thanks to this other jarhead in the Marines. He was a real dick, even a thief. While rifling through my stuff, he found my papers, papers that had Marion on them. He kept going on about what a sissy name it was, how my parents must have wanted a girl, a bunch of juvenile shit. He finally said something I couldn't let go of. I was pretty drunk, though I would have done the same thing sober. That night, I earned the name Scorp, which is short for Scorpion. Scorpions can cause unbearable pain to their victims. Like a Scorpion, I didn't go looking for trouble, but when it came at me, I wasn't going to back away. He got stung good that night." A wide grin flashed over his face. It stayed for a few moments, before the scowl returned. He then leaned into Zak's space, his voice becoming even lower. "Continue to call me Scorp. I have tolerated Eliot, but never will you or anyone else, except for an unknowing sexy blonde airline agent call me Marion. Got it?"

Zak smiled because he just couldn't get Marion out of his mind. "Got it, Scorp. So did the sexy blonde get us into first class?"

"Yup, she certainly did."

* * * *

Thankfully, the flight to Chicago was rather smooth. Zak was exhausted, but unable to sleep. He ended up listening to some music in an effort to relax. It didn't do the job, but at least he kept it together. Scorp, who seemed genuinely on edge during take-off, fell into a deep slumber mid-flight, complete with a low, whistling snore.

When they got to Chicago, Zak figured he would part ways with Scorp and take a costly taxi to Baxley. He still had a heavy amount of medication working its way out of his system. He wouldn't take his own truck, which he had left at the airport. Eventually, he would get one of those car delivery services to haul his truck out to Baxley. But as soon as they got off the plane, Scorp offered to drive him home. Scorp had a rental car courtesy of the NYPD and had told him it was no big deal to drive him out to Baxley. It was too early for him to check into the Chicago hotel near the training course, so why not kill a few hours? Zak didn't buy it. Pratt's plan was for Scorp to escort him to his doorstep. It still annoyed him, but he didn't fight it. Scorp had been a decent travelling companion. Taking the offered ride would prevent him from ending up with some chatty cab driver. Besides, he'd get Scorp to stop at a grocery store on the way.

When they got to the small country grocery mart just outside Lands Crossing, they both went inside. Zak bought enough groceries to last for a couple of weeks and Scorp bought a bottle of cheap vodka, signifying an end to his sobriety. Scorp's purchase worried Zak, but he didn't say anything. He had enough of his own problems, which he wasn't prepared to deal with, so he had no intention of calling Scorp out on his poor choices.

PART THREE

Chapter Twenty-Four

Cawhhh, Cawhhh, Cawhhh...

The awful caw sound had gotten louder. More of the annoying bastards had gathered. They were likely perched on the nearby shed or high up in the trees, surrounding the house. Spring was supposed to be peaceful, like the sounds of sweet robins chirping in the distance, or a gentle breeze making the branches whistle in the distance. No, as luck would have it, Zak had these awful crows kicking up a fuss. Preposterous as it may have sounded, he felt their irritating sound was deliberately taunting him. He longed for quiet, for stillness, for the way it was before he'd left. Most of all, he wanted the world he found himself imprisoned in to stop pounding like a hurricane hitting the shore.

Zak had been back for four days now. He was on edge, declining into a tumultuous wreck. When he was in New York, the medication had eased his anxieties, but now the medication was seeping out of his system, leaving him to cope on his own. He was sensitive to noise, to the daylight streaming in the windows, and even to his own erratic breathing. The horrible nightmares were back, and they were intensely vivid. At times, it was hard to recognize reality. Sleep was a rare occurrence. He had a few fleeting moments when he was able to turn off his mind and fall into a slumber, but those moments terrified him, made him afraid of the chaos his demons would unleash into the dark corners of his unconscious mind.

Right now, it was those hideous crows making him come unglued. It began as a slow, burning anger within him, eventually developing into a rage. He actually contemplated going outside and shooting the damn birds. But he didn't want to give in to raving lunacy, shooting birds with a pistol, and more importantly, he didn't want to draw attention to his return.

Life couldn't go on like this, but he was too lost in a storm of misery and depression to figure out a solution other than to wait it out, hoping the withdrawals from the prescription medication he'd abruptly stopped would cease. Once they were gone, perhaps his irritability would ease up.

Omeir had called earlier in the morning, and a couple hours later, Safia had called. He had spoken briefly, telling them he was doing better, which of course was a lie. If he didn't lie, they would land on his doorstep, which was the last thing he wanted. He didn't like being around himself, so he certainly wasn't up to having visitors, no matter how much their friendship meant.

Getting up from the uncomfortable wooden kitchen chair he had spent too many hours sitting on, he went to the front window. He couldn't see the screechy birds, but damn it, they were there, cowards lurking in the shadows.

Seeing the empty driveway, his brain kicked into gear. Someone would be pulling into the yard soon. He had arranged to have his truck delivered from the airport. Quickly, he decided to have it hauled to the rear of the property, behind the shed, where it would be hidden. He couldn't avoid people forever, including Lexie, but he wasn't fit to have people hovering around him.

He had lost about fifteen pounds, mainly muscle, because he hadn't worked out since the stabbing. He hadn't shaved, and now had a full-grown beard hiding his facial features. He looked and felt like he had been tortured. To him that's what PTSD felt like when it was full blown, like being tortured. And even when your captors took a break, it was only a matter of time before they would creep back and inflict more excruciating pain. At times, he could tolerate it, and at other times, like right now, he wanted to die so the hurting would end. He hated admitting the suicidal feelings, and perhaps that was a good thing. There was still a force within him begging to survive.

He heard the slow crunch of gravel. Peering outside, he recognized his truck along with an accompanying vehicle to pick up the driver. He went outside to meet the two men and to direct them on where to park his truck. While he was busy talking to the driver, a third car had come onto the property. He had finished paying the men, and was heading back to the house, when he heard the deep, husky bark. He knew right away it was Abby, and with Abby, would be Lexie.

* * * *

It had been almost a week since she had driven to Zak's place. She was expecting her current little excursion onto his well-treed property to be like all the others – uneventful. It was the usual routine for her and Abby. She'd drive onto the property, park her vehicle near the front door, and with Abby by her side, she would walk around the house looking for any sign he had returned. After concluding nothing had changed, other than the odd broken branch from a storm, she would coax Abby back into her vehicle and drive off. Today she was prepared for more of the same. Today wasn't the same.

The first thing that caught her attention was the vehicle driving past her as she eased along the gravel path toward the house. She saw the two men in the silver-colored truck and turned her head toward the side window to make out the words painted on the side. She just got the last two words: Vehicle Delivery. As she turned her head back toward the driveway, she realized her distraction had almost led to a near hit with a sycamore tree. She quickly slammed on her brakes, making the gravel on the driveway crunch louder than normal. It was then she noticed him. She did a double take to ensure it wasn't just her imagination. Zak was outside and headed toward the house. He had a thick beard and looked thinner from the distance, but there was no mistaking him. Abby had readily recognized her master as well. The dog let out a deep bark, almost like a howl, something Lexie had never heard before.

A few weeks ago, Lexie wasn't sure what kind of reaction she would have should she see Zak again. She even imagined the possibility she would never see him again. She was angry with him, and although there were other emotions, anger had been the overriding one. It was different now, with him only a few yards away. It wasn't some theoretical scenario of what she would do or say. It was real.

She quickly stepped on the gas, pulling the vehicle into the driveway by the house. Shoving the door open, she ran toward him. As soon as she was near him, she thrust herself into his chest. Abby, who had escaped out of the open vehicle door, also shot toward Zak, pouncing on both of them with her massive paws.

He embraced her, or Lexie thought he did. Then something unexpected happened. She felt him pushing her back. At first, she thought it was to get a better look at her, to see the woman he yearned for. Connecting with his dark eyes, she realized that wasn't it. There was no warmth in the way he looked at her. His eyes seemed lifeless at first, and when he spoke, the words were stone cold.

"I can't do this," he told her. Simple words, but they confused her. She searched his face for some clarity, for understanding. It wasn't coming to her. Instead, she saw something else. She saw the large scar on his neck. Right away, she recognized what it was. She had dealt with the outcome of violence before. Individuals who had gotten in the way of someone's rage. Leaning forward, she lifted her hand to touch the scar.

"Don't," he yelled. There was urgency in his voice, a pleading panic. Lifting his jacket collar to hide the injury, he took a step back.

"Zak, I don't understand."

The confusion was there, but so was her desire to ensure the deep wound on his neck was cared for. Although a scar had formed over it, it looked bad. Something horrible had happened to him.

"What happened? Who did this to you?" The words poured out of her. She needed answers.

He shook his head. He would not have this conversation. When she refused to back away, he blazed into her eyes and spoke those crushing words. "I'm sorry, but I'm not the man you thought I was. Please, for your sake, go."

She stood speechless, cemented in the gravel beneath her feet. *He didn't mean it. Just give him a moment, and he'll explain.*

"Now! You need to go now!"

His voice, so explosive it startled her. Without realizing it, tears started streaming down her face. Abby, who had been at Zak's side, trotted over to her. It was as if Abby sensed she needed to be comforted against his harsh words.

She stepped back, afraid to hear his thunderous voice if she didn't move away. She was about to turn and walk away when he looked at his dog, and then back at her.

"Take Abby with you."

She shook her head. The dog was his. She had grown to love the furry companion, but Abby did not belong to her.

"Please," he said, in a barely audible voice.

Lexie was at a loss for words. He was undeniably harsh, as he demanded she leave, yet he softened as he pled with her to take Abby. She heard the anger, but she saw the fragility. She turned and walked back to her vehicle. When she opened the door, Abby jumped in. She pulled out of the driveway, tears staining her face. It wasn't only Zak's rejection that hurt; it was the confusion of what he said. If he wasn't the kind of man she thought he was, then what kind was he?

* * * *

It was inevitable Zak would encounter Lexie. But why today? Today, when he had been taunted by crows and sunk in misery. Returning to Baxley, he dreaded the thought of seeing her. He knew it would be heart-rending to see her and not be able to have her. But he also knew he had to deal with the situation. A situation he so haphazardly caused by inserting himself into her life. He'd had a plan. A plan on how he would talk to Lexie. Not a detailed plan, but a way of apologizing, a way of explaining. A way of letting her know how special she was, and how messed up he was. He'd wait for when his anxiety had lessened, for a day better than today. He'd meet with her, sit her down, and tell her what had happened. He would tell her who he was, about the PTSD, and the unpredictable person he had become. It wouldn't be easy for him to do this, and perhaps she had already written him off as being some jerk, but he would at least try and explain.

What happened earlier was *not* the plan. It wasn't even close to the plan. He wasn't ready to see her yet. It was too raw. *He* was too raw. The guilt and shame for lying and then leaving crushed him, but that wasn't the worst. The worst was her tears, the sorrow in her eyes, and the fear. He'd made her afraid of him. She should be afraid of him. He had always been dangerous and capable of violence, but it had been contained, aimed at those who provoked. Now he was unpredictable. He hadn't planned on yelling, but he'd had to. She needed to go. It wasn't her fault that she hadn't. He'd sent mixed messages.

When she ran to him and embraced him, he'd briefly allowed himself to soak in her warmth and goodness. He should have stopped her from embracing him, but he'd wanted to return to a place where he felt safe. But what was safe for him offered only danger to her. He couldn't explain who he was, who he had become, not with the air constricting his chest. He'd closed his eyes when she pressed against him, taking in all that was her, knowing he had to push her away. But he'd wanted that moment, a moment of utter joy, even though it was selfish of him.

He hated himself for pushing her away, but he would hate himself even more if he lost control when Lexie was nearby, like he did with Scorp in the hotel suite, or when the doctor had tried to prevent him from ripping out his IV. He had endured a lot of pain during his life. Seeing her reaction when he'd pushed her away was certainly at the top of his pain experience. He figured she would have had an adverse reaction to seeing him. He had braced himself for her wrath, even a dramatic slap across the face, as he deserved. What he wasn't prepared for was the way her confusion had turned to hurt. He was so broken already, but the hurt he caused her made him shatter.

Abby, his beloved dog had been there, torn between him and Lexie. An extremely intuitive animal, Abby had sensed how damaged he was. But the dog had forged a bond with Lexie. It didn't surprise him. Any intelligent being would likely cling to her, embrace her warmth. Zak needed for Lexie to be okay, and because he didn't have this capability, he'd begged her to take Abby. She would offer her comfort, something he couldn't.

He longed for the numbness he had experienced when he was in the hospital. The numbness the medications gave him. Had he not flushed them, he would have certainly swallowed a few now. He had nothing at his disposal to numb the pain, other than what was lethal. Afraid to enter his house, he stayed outside on the front porch, allowing the cold air, which had come with the evening darkness, to penetrate his body. He remained slumped on the porch for the next two hours. When he could no longer bear the cold, he wandered inside, sitting in darkness.

Chapter Twenty-Five

Lexie didn't need an alarm. She had been awake for hours, lying in bed thinking, letting the hurt, frustration, and anger build. She mulled over her encounter with Zak for hours. She had so many questions, and no answers. Why was he pushing her away? Did she only imagine him holding her when she had run to him? What had happened to him? Who had stabbed him? The last one kept circling around in her mind. He said he was not the man she thought he was. Was he involved in something sinister? Was he some sort of criminal? What if there was some truth to what Cicily and Emmett believed? She hated herself for thinking this, but she had to admit she just didn't know the man she had encountered yesterday.

After applying a little extra concealer to the dark circles under her eyes, she got dressed and headed off to work. She wanted to avoid Margo, the woman had become rather adept in reading her ill moods. She figured if she was running late, the patients would be there already, and she could jump right into work, and thus side-step Margo. Parking her vehicle a couple of blocks from the clinic, she sat for forty minutes before showing up late.

Three patients were already in the waiting area when Lexie hurried through the door. She could feel their stares as she walked past them.

"You okay?" Margo asked.

"Yeah, just slept late. I'd better get started."

She dove right into work, forgoing her usual cup of java. By late morning she was caught up, the waiting room vacant. She had contemplated talking to Margo about Zak. She still thought it inappropriate to bring her personal problems to work, but today it was apparent something was going on with her. Perhaps the patients wouldn't pick up on it, but Margo was different. She saw Margo more than anyone else in Baxley. Besides, Margo was good at figuring people out. Nobody in town seemed to know much about Zak, other than some cursory information, but Margo had sold him his property. Perhaps she knew a bit more than the others. She knew she was grasping, but she was desperate.

"Do you have a moment, Margo?" Her voice had a quiet urgency to it.

"Certainly, dear."

Lexie stood, uncertain how to begin.

"What is it?" Margo asked, unclear about why her boss seemed so hesitant.

"He's back," Lexie blurted out. She didn't have to say Zak's name, Margo knew.

"That's great!"

Lexie's eyes started to fill with tears because Zak's return hadn't been great, it had been heart-wrenching.

"Lexie, what's wrong? Did you talk to him?"

"Yes, I talked to him… but he didn't talk to me."

"What do you mean he didn't talk to you?"

"Well, he said a few words…" She trailed off, and then looked down at her feet.

Margo reached for Lexie's hands to get her attention. "What did he say, dear?"

"He said something about him not being the man I thought he was, and then told me to leave."

"Leave?"

"Yes, he wanted me gone. Out of his sight right away." Although Lexie might have been confused about Zak, she clearly understood the meaning of *leave now*.

"Doesn't sound like Zak."

"I didn't think so either, but that's exactly what he said. He looked so horrible."

"Horrible?"

"He's thinner. He has this… scraggly beard, dark circles… under his eyes, like he's sleep deprived and…" she stuttered for a moment before blurting out, "He has this deep scar on his neck. He's been stabbed."

"Stabbed?"

"Yes, he didn't say it, but I saw it and I recognized it as a deep penetration, probably affecting the carotid artery. A life-threatening infliction…" She rambled on as if describing an injury to a consulting physician.

"Did you ask what happened?"

"Of course I did." She regretted the annoyance in her voice, but it was an instinctive response. "He wouldn't answer. He just wanted me gone."

"I'm so sorry, Lexie."

"I'm worried, Margo. He isn't the Zak I know. He's… well, he's detached, and when I tried to find out why, he became angry." She looked down, and then looked back up as she recalled more about Zak. "Did you know he was shot a few years ago?"

Margo shook her head. She knew only what Zak chose to tell her. Being shot had never come up in conversation.

"And now he's been stabbed. What kind of life is he leading?" Her body trembled, but she continued. "He even told Abby to go with me. That dog meant so much to him and he just gave her away."

Margo was worried. She didn't want to panic in front of Lexie.

"Maybe just give him some time, and then try and talk to him again." It was a feeble attempt to console Lexie, but she didn't have any really good advice for the doctor.

Lexie just nodded. She didn't know what to say. She doubted time would make Zak open up to her and it was possible the man she thought she knew was forever gone.

****

Lying on the sofa in misery, the knock on the front door interrupted his vegetative state. It was an intrusive succession of three thuds. He wasn't expecting anyone, and he certainly didn't want to see anyone.

No, please don't let it be Lexie at the door.

He shuddered at the thought of having a repeat of yesterday. The pain from the unexpected encounter was still so fresh, the memory of her tear-filled eyes. He couldn't go through it again. He would remain on the sofa, careful not to make any sounds revealing his presence.

The knocking occurred again, getting louder and louder.

He would stay the course, continuing to ignore it. Lexie, or whoever, would go away; at least he hoped they would.

Now he could hear the crunch of loose gravel as the person stepped off the porch and began to walk around the side of the house. The sound of light footsteps stopped outside the kitchen window. Then he heard the disturber jumping, trying to peak through the elevated window. He had the curtains closed, so their jumping was futile.

He listened, hoping to hear the footsteps move away from the house, signaling their defeat. But it didn't happen. The disturber had moved to the backdoor, banging obnoxiously. Go away, he wanted to scream, but dared not.

The banging stopped. He waited to hear the footsteps move away, but instead he heard a familiar voice. "Zak, I know you're in there. Come to this door, now."

He didn't answer, he didn't move. There was a long silent pause, but still no sound of her departing as he had hoped for.

The voice started again and this time there was no mistaking the anger in it, "Damn it Zak. Don't think I won't smash this window and let myself in."

He muttered under his breath, "Damn you." Leaving the sofa, he plodded down the narrow hallway and opened the back door.

Margo gasped when she saw him, his eyes so lifeless, his shoulders slumped, his face so full of despair. He was wearing dark grey sweat pants and an old, faded-print t-shirt, which had at one time been form-fitting but was now a size too big. He was exhausted with deep creases around his eyes and facial hair sprouting wildly, making him look older than his actual years. Although Lexie had painted Margo a sorrowful description of Zak, seeing him like this shocked her, making her even more worried. She had seen those vacant eyes once before. Seeing him today reminded her of that time. She hadn't known anything about him then, but she'd sensed he was deeply troubled. Now, at least she knew the source of his troubles. It was his career, a duty to protect others, his commitment to put himself in harm's way for a safer world. He'd spent years undercover, inside a darkened world full of evil, and it was clear it had taken a toll on him.

He didn't want to let Margo into his home to see him like this, but she was so persistent, and he realized she wasn't going to go away. There was a moment of relief when he heard her voice, knowing it wasn't Lexie's. It didn't take long for the relief to be replaced with irritation, an irritation he tried to contain. He'd always had a soft spot for Margo, but he didn't want to see anyone, including her. He gave her time to look at his face, to soak in what he now was, and the needed time to calm himself before he spoke.

"You shouldn't be here."

"Well, then, tell me where I should be?"

Her sharp tone startled him. Before he could respond, she stepped closer, invading his space. "Perhaps I should be at the clinic with my boss, a decent woman who has no idea what is going on, and who is heartbroken."

"I didn't mean to..."

Before he could finish, Margo slammed him with more words. "No, you didn't, but you did, Zak. It's time to tell her. To stop her from guessing about where you've been and who you are. You at least owe her that."

He didn't respond. Instead he looked away in shame from her steely gaze.

"Zak, you owe her the truth."

"You're right," his voice elevated. "But, Margo, it's easier for her to see me as some selfish jerk who treated her badly. Telling her the truth, she'll pity me or worse, believe she can help."

"Damn you, Zak, you have no right to decide what Lexie is going to feel or do. That's up to her."

He bit down on his lower lip and began pacing around the back entranceway.

Softening her speech, Margo stepped further inside his home. "What's wrong with help? You need it. Lexie can help you, and there's a whole lot of other people who can, too. You've dedicated your life to helping others. Now let us be there for you."

He stopped pacing, looking into Margo's hazel eyes with all the creases the years had brought her. "But that's the problem. I can't be helped."

"That's ridiculous. You're a good man whose darkness is from what others have done to you. It's not your darkness to own. You're not meant to be shut off from others. You weren't when I first met you and you're not now. Lexie's strong. She can handle it. You just need to let her in to your world."

"My world is violence and chaos. I won't let her in. I can't destroy her. The only thing I can do is to let her go on with her life, without me in it. I appreciate everything you've done, Margo, not only by coming out here, but also for keeping my secret. I know I should never have put you in that position. You're right. I owe Lexie the truth, not so she will rescue me, but so she can move on. I'll do it in my own way and in my own time."

She seemed to ignore his words, though she didn't try to convince him further.

He sighed, hoping she would leave on her own. But she didn't. He didn't want this woman's meddling. He let her into his home out of a combination of defeat and obligation. But now it was time for her to go.

"I'm done. It's not a conversation I want to continue." He gave her an icy glare, not to intimidate her but because he was serious.

She turned to go, taking a couple steps toward the back door. When she was within reach of the door, she spun around. "I'm not leaving yet."

"What do you mean, you're not leaving?" he asked incredulously.

"Oh, I'll go, Zak, just not yet."

"Margo, please, I don't want to discuss this anymore."

"Good, because I don't want to either. Just give me your gun, and I'll be gone."

"My gun? Are you insane?"

She stood firm, staring into his face.

"I'm not giving you or anyone my gun." His jaw clenched, as he became desperate to quell his anger.

"Well, then I'll just stay." She brushed past him, went into the kitchen and sat down by the table.

He remained standing, towering over her petite frame.

"Look, Margo, I get what you're trying to do, but you need to go."

"Just give me the gun, and I'll go!" She wasn't budging from her position.

"I can't give some civilian a firearm, and besides, I might need it for protection." He was now trying to reason with her. It was exhausting him, but he didn't want his rage to unleash on this woman. A woman who was always so kind to him. A woman who had been crucial in saving his life when he first arrived in Baxley.

"Zak, I'm not keeping the gun. I'm just holding on to it until you're better. And if you need protection, take back your dog."

"I can't."

She stood up, tilting her head to ensure he was paying attention to her words yet to be spoken, and not simply dismissing her. "Oh, you can, and you will give me the gun. If you refuse, I'll get Sheriff McQuay to come get it. After all, you did hold a gun to my head, and I'm sure the sheriff's not going to let that sort of thing happen in his peaceful town."

"I didn't mean to harm you." His voice was tinged with regret.

"I know that. I know you would never hurt me. You are one of the good guys. I'm not worried about you hurting anyone in this town. I'm worried about you hurting yourself. So until you start believing in yourself, I'll have the gun."

She wasn't letting it go. She probably would get Sheriff McQuay involved if he didn't relent. She was right to worry about him hurting himself, as he'd recently had suicidal thoughts. He had prayed the thoughts would vanish and they did, but he was still afraid they would return.

Reluctantly, he retrieved the Glock. He showed her it was empty and when it wasn't enough to satisfy her, he handed it to her. She dropped the weapon in her purse, and true to her word, she left.

* * * *

Lexie suspected something was bothering Margo when she returned from lunch. Margo said she was going to Colton's, but she came back empty handed. Maybe she had eaten at the café. She certainly had taken a long enough lunch break to do so, but she seemed off, as though preoccupied by something.

The clinic was now abuzz and before Lexie could talk to Margo, she had escorted two patients into examining rooms for Lexie to attend to. The afternoon continued to be busy, including a visit from Cicily who had a routine exam scheduled. This was the first time she had been to the clinic since Lexie had taken over as the town's physician. Although Cicily had been civil to her the last few times she had gone into Colton's, she couldn't help but be guarded around her.

While in the examining room, Cicily was cordial. Lexie was relieved. It had been an exhausting day and she had no energy for any of Cicily's antics. It was a relatively quick appointment, at least by Baxley standards. She seemed as eager to get back to work as Lexie was to see the next patient. Her blood pressure was borderline high, so Lexie gave her some suggestions on how to lower it and told her to book a follow-up appointment through Margo.

Lexie had been in the second examining room with another patient when there was a loud, intrusive knock at the door. Figuring it was Margo, she opened the door to see a flustered Cicily standing there.

"I need to talk to you." It wasn't a question. It was clearly a demand.

Irritated by Cicily's tone, which bordered on rudeness, Lexie replied, "Just have a seat in the waiting room, and I'll see you once I finish up here."

"Emmett's on his way."

Why was the sheriff on his way to the clinic? she thought. Then a wave of panic came pounding over her. Was it Zak? Did something happen with him? Was he in trouble with the law? Telling her patient there was an emergency, Lexie quickly stepped out of the examination room and into the corridor. Grabbing Cicily by the arm, she led her to the privacy of her office.

"Cicily, what happened?" her voice sounding frantic.

"It's about the gun."

"Gun? What are you talking about?"

"The gun in your office."

"Someone's got a gun?" Lexie was now visualizing a crazed gunman in the waiting room.

"Yes, the weapon in Margo's desk." Cicily spoke as though this was all making sense to Lexie.

"A gun? What would a gun be doing in Margo's desk?"

"Well, that's what I'm wondering. I went to book my next appointment and Margo wasn't at the receptionist desk, so I just reached in the top drawer to get a pen to leave her a note. Then I saw the handgun."

"Are you sure?" asked Lexie, incredulously.

"Of course I'm sure. I know what a gun looks like," Cicily shouted, clearly annoyed by the question.

The idea of a weapon at the clinic infuriated Lexie. She had seen the damage firearms could do. There was certainly no need for Margo to bring a gun to work. And what was Margo doing with a gun in Baxley? She didn't seem to be the type who went around carrying a pistol anywhere, let alone in a small sleepy town. There must be some mistake, even though Cicily sounded so sure.

Abruptly, she left her office, while Cicily trailed behind her. Margo was back at her desk, putting away the day's files. She had expected to see the last patient walk by, but instead it was Lexie and Cicily approaching. There was no mistaking the concerned look on Lexie's face and the sour scowl on Cicily's. Before anyone could speak, Sheriff

McQuay barged through the door like a cobra ready to strike its prey. In this case, the prey being a sixty-year-old woman.

Seeing the sheriff in clear crisis mode made Margo's thoughts race. *Had something happened to Zak? Was Emmett here to give some bad news?* She knew Zak was distraught. *But please God, don't let anything happen to that poor man.*

Before she could continue with her thoughts, Cicily barked, "There Emmett, in the top drawer."

The top drawer. Margo now understood what was going on.

Margo stepped aside, allowing Emmett access to her desk.

Lexie let out a loud gasp when the drawer opened. "What the hell? Why is there a gun in my clinic?"

"Lexie, let me deal with this." It wasn't a request so much as it was an order from the sheriff.

"Do you have a permit for this gun?" Emmett asked Margo. Moments passed with no answer. "Do you have a permit?" he asked again.

Margo shook her head.

"Margo, is it your gun?" Again this question had to be repeated twice before Margo shook her head no.

The sheriff moved closer to Margo before asking the question Margo was hoping to avoid.

"So whose gun is it?"

She hesitated once again and then meekly muttered, "It's Zak's."

Margo's voice was so low only Lexie heard it. She let out a gasp. For a brief moment, Lexie's shocked reaction took the attention off of Margo.

"Say that again?" Emmett demanded.

"It belongs to Zak Tifour."

"I knew it," barked Cicily. "That man's a threat to us all."

"Settle down. Let me finish," Emmett snapped impatiently at his mother.

Cicily had no intention of letting her son finish. She had made up her mind about Zak the day he'd walked into her diner. "And you,

Margo, you provided him with a home. Are you involved in this, too?" And not waiting for an answer, Cicily continued her barrage of accusations, ranging from Zak being a terrorist to Margo being, as Cicily worded it, *in cahoots* with a terrorist organization.

It was all absurd. If the accusations coming from Cicily weren't so preposterous and downright cruel, Margo might have stayed in a state of shame for bringing a gun into her employer's place of business. But the bigotry-fueled assumptions angered and enraged her. Enraged at Cicily and Emmett for their biases, for not even trying to understand, or listen to her. Then her anger spilled over to Lexie for not defending Zak against Cicily's ridiculous remarks. How could Lexie believe Cicily? And if she didn't believe Cicily, then why wasn't she speaking up? Finally, she'd had enough with them all.

"What the hell is wrong with you people?" she yelled. "Cicily, I used to think it was grief making you so bitter, but now I don't know, maybe you were always this narrow-minded. And Emmett, you're no better than your mother; in fact, you're even worse. That uniform you wear, it's supposed to represent justice. But you apply your own brand of justice. You've treated Zak with almost the same amount of contempt as your mother does. We all know why. It's time you shake that big chip off your shoulder. You've been nothing but a bully since you returned to Baxley."

It was now Lexie's turn to get chastised. Margo turned to her, her eyes glowing and her hands shaking. "I thought you would at least defend the man, but instead you remained silent. I know he hurt you. He was wrong, and he regrets it. But if you stepped out of your own hurt and anger, you'd realize he's hurting, too. He's essentially alone, lost in the shadows."

Turning away from Lexie, she went back to facing Cicily and Emmett.

"Colton was a hero, there's no doubt about it. You loved him, the town loved him. I loved that kid, too, but not all heroes look like Colton. Zak's just as much of a hero as Colton was, and if this community doesn't help him, we'll have another hero to mourn."

They were looking at her not only shocked but confused. They had never seen Margo react like this. She was all fired up, but it wasn't making sense to them.

The confusion in their faces finally registered with Margo. And before she could stop herself, she blurted out the secret she vowed to keep. "The man's an undercover detective with the NYPD. He's gone through a lot. He's been shot, and most recently, he was stabbed. It's a miracle he's alive. Right now he's sitting in his house all alone, cut off from this community." Her voice was bitter as she continued. "This community boasts about being neighborly. I guess that's true until the neighbor doesn't share your particular faith or ethnic background, when the new guy doesn't fit your image of who should belong."

Margo was on a roll, and the woman wasn't in a mood to hear from any of the group gathered in front of her. No, she had been silent long enough.

"He has PTSD," she said, as she scowled at them. "He's in bad shape right now. This gun you're freaking over, well, I'm holding it for him until he's better. And no, Cicily, he's not some crazed lunatic you need to be afraid of. He's a kind and gentle man who is struggling with depression." She shifted her gaze back over to Lexie. "I'm sorry I didn't tell you about the gun, but I was going to take it home. It was never my intent to keep it here. I just didn't have time to take it home after I saw him today. If you want to fire me, then just do it. And Sheriff, if you want to arrest me for having a gun without a permit, fine, do it. But just don't call yourself neighborly when you treated Zak like some pariah, judging him without even trying to know him."

They were all speechless, and after a few awkward moments, the sheriff finally said, "No, I'm not going to arrest you, but you need to hand it over."

Margo motioned toward the desk where the gun was sitting, and walked out the door, leaving them all to hear the pounding footsteps from the woman who normally walked softly.

Chapter Twenty-Six

Lexie drove right past Colton's without even glancing sideways. Coffee wasn't a priority today, and besides, she didn't want to deal with Cicily after yesterday's debacle at the clinic. Lexie was on a mission and that mission entailed getting to the clinic before Margo did. That is, if Margo decided to show up.

When she got to the clinic, it was locked. She unlocked the door and went inside to wait. Ten minutes later, a sense of relief washed over her as she saw Margo enter.

"Morning, Margo." She spoke calmly, afraid her presence at the clinic might startle her receptionist, who was used to an empty office in the early hours.

"Umm, morning, Dr. Draden." She sounded surprised, but thankfully didn't jump out of her skin.

"Let's talk about yesterday."

Margo simply nodded and followed Lexie to the waiting room. They sat down across from one another. Lexie was about to break the silence, when Margo spoke.

"It's okay, Dr. Draden. I understand. I did it to myself, not telling you the whole story and then bringing the gun to the clinic. I'm at the age when most people retire. I'll grab my belongings and be gone."

Lexie reached across and placed her hand on Margo. "Please, hear me out."

Margo nodded and settled back into her chair.

"You're right. You should not have brought a gun into the clinic, but you did so with good intentions, and more importantly, to try and save someone. When I had a chance to reflect on what you did, I realized it was a selfless act, and although I certainly wish you had told me, I understand your loyalty to Zak. So, unless you want to quit, I'm not letting you go. You really do run this place and this clinic is yours, too. You're much more than an employee. You're passionate about your job, and now I know how loyal you are about those you care about. I can't fire a woman I admire."

With tears in her eyes, Margo nodded. She didn't have to tell Lexie she wasn't going to quit the clinic. They both knew if she wasn't being fired, she wasn't leaving.

"I rely on you not only as a receptionist, but as a friend. And as a friend, I need your advice."

Margo understood Lexie wanted advice pertaining to Zak. She waited for her boss to continue.

"I want to help him, but I just don't know how, or if I can."

"I don't know how either, but I believe you can, and perhaps all of us can in some small way." Margo was always the optimist and Lexie needed to hear those words, even if she wasn't yet convinced of them.

Margo took Lexie's hand and asked what seemed to be an odd question. "When you were in med school did you ever just want to quit? A moment when you thought this is all too much. Where you contemplated forgoing the idea of being a doctor."

"Yes, I can recall several times. Being a medical student can be brutal. It takes up a lot of your time and the course work is difficult, with never-ending hours of reading, studying, and memorizing." Although she answered, she was lost on the relevance of this question.

"Well, why didn't you just quit?"

Lexie didn't have to think about it as she knew why she endured those years. "Because I truly wanted to be a doctor. I wanted to help people heal."

"Contributing to Zak's healing won't be easy either, but it will be worth it. It will be worth it for you, Lexie, and worth it for all of us. Zak's part of this community. I know he may not have *felt* he was part of the community, because not everyone treated him that way. But he chose to come back here, which means on some level he wants to belong in Baxley. We need to make him feel welcome."

"I agree, but where do we start when he doesn't even want me, or anyone else around."

"We start with Abby."

"Abby?"

"Yes, you need to return Abby to Zak. Even in his despair, he won't neglect Abby. He'll have to get out of bed in the morning. He'll need to fill her food bowl, let her out into the yard, and maybe even take her for a run like he used to. A dog isn't just some animal co-existing with humans. A dog is a companion who gives unconditional love. Zak isn't feeling worthy of anyone's love, but he won't be able to stop Abby from doing so."

"You're right." For the first time, Lexie had hope. "Abby's not any dog either. She sensed when I was miserable, and she comforted me. I know it sounds strange, but it's exactly what she did. Zak needs her more than I do. I now know why he wanted me to keep her. He wanted her to comfort me because he didn't think he would be able to. I don't know if he'll take her back, but I guess I have to try."

Lexie leapt off the chair and gave Margo a big hug. "I always knew this clinic couldn't function without you, but now I know this town can't function without you, either."

Chapter Twenty-Seven

Not that Zak wanted to be, but he was right. Answering the phone call would only be a temporary distraction, with him lying about how his life was getting back to normal. A normal life, an absurd notion, and if it wasn't so painful, he would have laughed.

When Omeir's name popped up on his phone, he thought of not taking the call, but quickly reconsidered Omeir's lighthearted humor might be the distraction he needed. He was desperate for some diversion to prevent going over his last conversation with Lexie. He had been haunted for years by the violence he had seen, and now he was haunted by the hurt he had caused her. The torment kept piling on.

Omeir was his usual upbeat self and rambled about some charity event he volunteered to help Safia with. Zak tuned out for a while; he wasn't in the mood for happy tales. When tuning out no longer worked, he briskly changed topics and asked how Scorp was doing. It surprised him to hear they had planned to go fishing on their day off. Perhaps Omeir didn't hate fishing as much as he'd thought, or maybe he just wanted a buddy to hang out with. People who had bad first impressions would sometimes end up being friends, and this is exactly what had happened between these two. How time seemed to have changed the lives of Omeir and Scorp, and probably for almost everyone except him.

As he was getting ready to end the call, Omeir tossed him a zinger. Apparently, Omeir and Safia were instructed by Pratt to assist the Chicago Police Department with some technological aspect of this mundane operation next month. He said they would drive out to see him. They were booked to fly out early Saturday, though they weren't needed in Chicago till Monday. Pratt told them the airfare was cheaper this way. Omeir was a genius when it came to hacking into any communication or computer system, but when it came to figuring out what Pratt was up to, he was simply clueless. Zak wasn't surprised Pratt would send his former colleagues to check up on him periodically. He didn't want visitors, but he decided not to argue about it at this time. If he wasn't up to seeing them next month, he would think of some excuse, but for now, best to pretend normal.

Zak was still dumbfounded with how Margo had gotten him to hand over his gun. She may have been a tiny elderly lady, but she was definitely fearless, and her tenacity astonished him. He had undoubtedly been in rough shape when she'd dropped by. He had contemplated physically removing her if she hadn't left on her own, but he'd known even when she'd angered him, he wouldn't.

Shortly after she left, his emotions had settled, and he'd began to think maybe he wasn't a danger to Lexie. Margo had certainly pushed his buttons with her demands. And what had he done, but cave? But what if he was having a nightmare and Lexie was lying next to him? If he was startled and confused when he awoke from the nightmare? Or what if Lexie startled him some other way? He wasn't confident he would be able to handle the situation.

After mulling it over, he concluded he made the right choice in turning the pretty doctor away. Maybe one day he would be better, but it could be a long time away and Lexie would have moved on. He didn't like the thought of Lexie with someone else, but she deserved to be happy and to be safe, neither of which he could guarantee.

* * * *

Lexie had studied PTSD in med school and had treated patients in Chicago for physical symptoms associated with the disorder. Sometimes a person would show up in the emergency room, thinking they were having a heart attack when in fact it was a panic attack as a result of reliving some horrible event.

It was a slow afternoon at work, so she went online researching PTSD, hoping she could help Zak, or at the very least, not make things worse for him. She remembered when he'd told her about his parents' death, and how he'd changed the topic when he'd detected her feeling bad for him. She'd noticed how he had flinched when he sensed her edging too close to pity. Even though she longed to soothe him by wrapping her arms around him, she knew it wasn't that simple. It would take time and patience, small steps.

She wasn't small, but Abby was the first step. Lexie had to return his beloved dog. She had seen the effects of startling Zak the other day, and for both their sakes, she didn't want to go through it again. She dialed the only number she had. There was no answer, but at least the phone was in service. Nervously, she left a voice message, informing him she was coming by at six this evening to drop off Abby. Thirty minutes later she received a text message from Zak.

Will be home. Need to talk to you.

It was terse, but at least it was a response.

* * * *

When he saw it was Lexie calling, he decided not to answer it, but checking his messages, he realized he had to talk to her. He was exhausted avoiding her, avoiding the truth. She deserved so much more, but all he could offer her was a promise to stay out of her life. He wasn't sure about taking Abby back. Sure, the dog helped him, but he was worried about Lexie. He saw how the dog was torn regarding her loyalties to him and her need to comfort Lexie. Finally, he decided Abby should stay with Lexie. She was better equipped to take care of the dog. He was a mess, unable to even care for himself.

He looked horrible and he felt awful, though he wasn't as bad as a few days ago. The severe depression, resulting from abruptly ceasing the medication, was slowly disappearing. He wasn't where he was before he left Baxley, but at least the suicidal feelings had dissipated. He still wasn't taking care of himself and he knew his appearance had shocked Lexie. The last thing he wanted was to worry her further. Hauling himself into the shower, he stood under the icy water, attempting to rouse himself from his misery. It didn't work, but at least he smelled better.

It was six o'clock sharp when he heard the muted hum of a vehicle slowly pulling into the driveway. He heard the car door close and wandered out to the porch where he was instantly mauled by an enthusiastic Abby. His beloved canine didn't have the capacity to hide her emotions or to hold onto the past. Zak envied her for being able to live so fully in the present. Reaching down to her oatmeal-colored coat, he stroked her behind the ears.

He hated the range of emotions which came with PTSD. It was an ongoing struggle to push them away. Kneeling down, he put his arms around Abby's neck. He fought back the tears. Giving way to his emotions made him more unstable, but this moment was harder than he thought it would be. He missed Abby. He took a moment to compose himself before slowly getting up. Lexie had hauled Abby's pillow from her vehicle and was now standing before him.

He had just seen her two days ago, but now that his mind was less cloudy, he was able to focus more clearly on her. She was dressed casually in dark jeans and a navy coat. Her long sable hair flowed freely around her. The cold air reddened her cheeks, and her eyes softened as they connected with him. She was radiant, and it ached knowing he couldn't hold her. Her mere presence stirred him, making him unsure if he would break.

He realized she had been just as shocked to see him the other day as he was to see her. He wasn't the only one who had an emotional reaction; she'd gone from elation to despair, and he guessed, anger as well. Today, as she stood in front of him, she was poised like she would be before going into surgery. She kept her distance. There was no leaping to embrace him, but she did softly smile at him when he stood up from Abby to greet her. He stepped aside and motioned for her to enter his home. He led her into the kitchen area, sitting down at the table, relieved it would provide a barrier between them.

He began to speak. "I don't even know where to start. I could spend hours apologizing and it wouldn't be enough." Seeing into her soulful eyes gutted him, so he shifted his sight down to the table. "Not contacting you after I left was wrong. I realize it now. I just knew how I felt about you, and I couldn't let those feelings interfere with what I needed to do in New York." Looking at the scratched-up table wasn't helping, so he raised his gaze to her. "I had every intention of returning to Baxley within a couple of weeks like I told you, but in my line of work, things don't always go as planned."

He wanted to say the right words, to communicate clearly his thoughts, so he paused. But then it occurred to him that she didn't even blink when he used the phrase "in my line of work." She knew what the words meant.

"So what did Margo tell you?" he asked.

"Don't think she betrayed you Zak. She would have kept your confidence if it hadn't been for Cicily and Sheriff McQuay discovering the gun."

His jaw clenched. "Gun?" he asked nervously.

She nodded and briefly told him what Margo had done.

He stood up and began pacing. "I never wanted Margo involved in this mess. I'm an idiot to have caved in to her." Realizing he was starting to get worked up, he sat back down, clasping his hands together on the table. "I'm sure she would have taken the gun home and locked it up. She's not a careless woman. Look, I'll do whatever to make it right for her."

Lexie heard the profound regret and worry in Zak's voice. "I was furious with Margo when I found out she had a gun at the clinic. But once I learned why, I realized I should be grateful."

"Grateful?"

"Yes, I was grateful she did what she could to help you. I was grateful she told off Cicily and Emmett, and to a degree myself as well. And I was grateful to know the truth. I would have preferred you telling me, but at least I found out."

He was curious about Margo telling off Cicily and Emmett, but he didn't want to stray from his apology.

"I'm sorry I messed up. I planned to tell you I was with NYPD's Counterterrorism Bureau as soon as I returned to Baxley, but after I got stabbed things just fell apart for me. When I saw you two days ago, you were entitled to an explanation, but I was afraid…" He trailed off as he tried to find the words to tell her he was concerned he would hurt her, and not just emotionally, but one day physically.

How do you say that to someone you care about without sounding like some sort of monster? He hated who he had become.

"What are you afraid of, Zak? Did you think I wouldn't be there for you because you have a dangerous job? Because you have physical and emotional scars? Or is it because you have post-traumatic stress and you're scared of hurting me?"

Her directness hit hard, but she was right. He was afraid, actually terrified. He was afraid of her rejection of him, but mostly he was terrified if she didn't reject him, of getting too close, and then one day hurting her.

He felt the lump in his throat when he finally responded. "I'm afraid of a lot of things, most of which I can handle, except hurting you. I know I've already hurt you, but I'm talking about a different level of hurt. The kind where you end up afraid of me, the kind where you are scared to death of me, where you end up hating me and I end up hating myself for what I have done."

"What do you think you're going to do to me, Zak? You're not the kind of man who would ever physically hurt a woman or harm an innocent person."

He diverted from her face, looking down at the kitchen floor as he spoke, "I thought so, too, but I know different now. I've done it. I attacked a doctor in New York who was trying to help me. I knocked him down. I left bruises on him."

Silence filled the air. She was shocked and unfortunately her face betrayed her. Even with the shame blanketing him, Zak had to tell her the whole story. She needed to know who he had become so she would understand the threat he posed. This way she could move on.

"My colleague convinced the doctor not to press assault charges, although he had every right to do so. I was admitted to the psychiatric ward for further assessment and stabilization, which basically meant pumping me with heavy duty medications to calm me. In a way the medication worked. I was finally able to sleep, and eventually the rage and anger diminished. But the medication, it makes me numb. I can't live like that. When I got discharged from the hospital, I stopped taking it. Lexie, this is the second time I've been through this. The last time was when I got shot. It wasn't a corner-store robbery. I was shot during an undercover operation. It was a bad situation where two officers got pumped with bullet holes and died."

It was eerie to talk about them. He had to work hard to not see their bodies lying there, smell the stench of their deaths, hear the sounds of blood rushing out of their mangled torsos. He kept it together as he continued to push the images out of his mind, focusing instead on the cream-colored swirl from the kitchen floor tile.

"They were good men who risked their lives to rescue me." His voice trembled as he spoke those words. He paused to collect himself, raised his head and looked into her eyes. "I'm broken. I'm sure you're a great doctor, but this isn't something you can heal or cure. This is who I am now."

"Zak, there's lots of different kinds of medication and therapies; you should look at the options."

"Lexie, I know, and I have looked at options. I'll probably try some other non-medicated options again. I want to hope, and some days I do, and it gets me through another day. But there are no assurances. I might be fine for a while, maybe even a few months, but then some trigger will happen. I'll have moments of peacefulness where I even start to believe the worst is over. I start to see myself as who I used to be, but before too long someone or something startles me, and I end up back to that horrible day when those men were killed. It happens so easily, collapsing my world. Assaulting the doctor in New York terrified me, but most of all it terrified the doctor who was just doing his job. I don't want to hurt anyone anymore. The more I keep to myself the better off everyone will be."

"No, it's not true. You won't be better off. I won't be better off."

"Don't you understand? I can hurt you, really hurt you. And when I do, I'll be even worse off than now. I can't live with that. I want nothing more than to be with you, to have you in my life, but I can't. It's not my reality." He took a deep sigh, "Please keep Abby. I can't be there for you, but she can and that's all I can give you."

Lexie was quiet for a while, making Zak think she was going to walk away with the dog. Finally, she leaned toward him and placed her hands on top of his. He allowed her as it was soothing to feel her touch.

"Zak, Abby is going to stay in this house with you. It's all you can accept at this time from me. So that is what I am going to give you. I'm going to walk out that door tonight, but I'm coming back and I'll keep returning. It won't be to have any further conversations like this one. You said what you needed to say, and I heard you. When I come back it will be to drop off groceries; take Abby for a run; and plant some spring flowers outside your porch. I might even bake some cookies for you. Now don't hold me to the last one. I truly suck at baking, so they'll probably be cookies from Colton's. But what I won't do is give up on you. I promise I'll be careful not to startle you. I'll let you know when I'm coming over. If you aren't up to seeing me, don't let me inside the house. But I will be here, whether it means just dropping off food on the porch or tending to the yard." Her voice became just above a whisper. She wanted him to have to lean in to hear her next words. "Zak, I won't spend my time trying to convince you I'm not afraid of you, because I know you don't want to hear it. But you need to stop trying to convince me that I should just forget about you. I don't want to hear it, and more importantly I won't forget about you."

She didn't wait for him to respond. The conversation was over. She stood up, gave Abby a pat on the head, and walked out.

* * * *

When he told her about the assault, he could tell it shocked her. He was sure the disclosure would be enough for her to stay away from him. Instead, she absorbed what he had said and then surprised him when she came back with her own plan. And it didn't feel like pity, it came across as determination.

He wasn't sure what to do with her determination, or, in fact, what to do with her. Maybe with time she would draw back when she saw that kind-hearted gestures wouldn't change who he had become. Sure, he appreciated her offer to help. He appreciated everything about her, but it wasn't going to make things different for them. He thought maybe it was her way of easing out of what had started between them, maybe she couldn't just pull back from him without a fight. Maybe she needed to do this to realize he was a lost cause. Regardless, he would stop pushing her away, at least for now. He liked the idea of her being around, even though he feared how hard it would be when she finally realized she needed to move on.

* * * *

It floored her when Zak told her he had assaulted a doctor, so much so that she didn't ask any questions. Once the shock subsided, she should have questioned him, but she wanted him to know she believed in him. Although he carried out this violent act, it wasn't who he was.

She wasn't afraid of him, even though he warned her to be. Margo had inadvertently tested the waters when she got Zak to hand over his gun. Her petite elderly receptionist was no physical match for Zak. He could have easily hauled her out of his house. But instead, he'd let her inside and listened to her. And when she'd demanded his gun, he'd complied. It was apparent Zak was still the warm, considerate man who had taken her to the opera only a few months ago. Yes, with his level of PTSD, she had to be careful. He required psychological help and what she offered as a physician and as a woman wouldn't be enough. She had contacts in Chicago who could assist him. But right now, he wasn't ready for the specialists she could access. He required time to find his way back and she needed to be patient and show him she wasn't going to run off scared. She had told him she'd left Chicago and her family when her niece had died, and she hated for him to think she would take off on him. She hadn't run away from her problems in Chicago. She had done what she did to protect those she loved.

Chapter Twenty-Eight

The rain had started. Lexie could hear it pinging on the kitchen window. According to the forecast, it would continue all night. The last time it had rained like this was a couple of weeks ago. She remembered it being so gloomy, how it left her in a sad, nostalgic mood. But today, the rain seemed cleansing to her. The downpour signifying an optimistic sense of renewal.

Living in Baxley had made her patient, and hopefully patience would come to Zak, allowing him to weather the storm brewing inside him. In Chicago, everything was fast paced, the never-ending streams of traffic, responses with life and death implications in the hospital she worked at, and even day-to-day errands were hurried. Baxley was a stark contrast to this. There was no rush-hour traffic; the work at the clinic was more than manageable; and the simplicity of life could be enjoyed.

At first, the slow pace had irritated her. She'd go into the grocery store to pick up a few items and have to wait while the salesclerk chatted with the customer in front of her about the high school fund raiser, the new parking bylaw, or even worse, the weather. *So it called for yet more snow? Did people need to have a full conversation about snow?* She'd just wanted to shout at the salesclerk to take the customer's damn money, but of course she hadn't. She'd just waited with a fake smile on her face. But gradually, she'd begun to enjoy the slower pace. She'd found herself engaging in easy flowing chit-chat with the teller at the bank, the grocery store clerk, and the gas station attendant at Grizzlies Gas-bar. Soon she wasn't even having to pretend to be patient. It was just the way it was. It became normal, and she liked it. She had changed.

For the first time, her move to Baxley felt right to her. The move had been done rather hastily, and had it not been for Dr. Thornton selling his clinic, she would not have chosen the sleepy little town. The people she had recently become close to had allowed her to focus on something other than her own misery. Yes, she'd lost her beautiful niece and her relationship with her sister, but she'd begun to accept it. She didn't like it, but what could she do? She wasn't able to change the past. And she wasn't the only one who had suffered.

She was surrounded by people who had their own grief issues. Cicily had lost a beloved son. Her anguish had left her crazed with anger, and a bitterness so strong it was destroying her. Emmett had lost his older brother and in a way, he was also mourning a life he used to have, a life he'd felt obligated to give up to help ease his mother's grief, which itself was an impossible task. Kristina was confused and in agony over slowly losing the love and attention of her husband. Then there was Zak, a man who had endured so much. He had lost both parents when he was on the edge of entering adulthood. He was haunted by the violent death of his colleagues. He had been physically tortured, enduring unimaginable pain. He had been shot and, after the wound had healed, stabbed. He had nearly died on two occasions. As a surgeon, she knew his survival went beyond just great medical care. It was a bona fide miracle. He was treated badly because he didn't look like what people thought an American should look like. But he was an American, and even if he wasn't, why should it matter? A child cannot select the place of their birth, or the circumstances they are born into. Zak was more patriotic than those who judged him. He didn't just say he loved his country; he risked his life for it. He was a hero who deserved respect.

All this pain she now saw in Baxley made her realize that although she had problems, it wasn't healthy for her to just fixate on them. She needed to be of use to those in the community, and especially to Zak. It was time to live in the present and not the past.

****

She pulled up to Willow's place a few minutes late for book club. She had thought of calling Zak to see if it was okay for her to drop by. But it was too soon to see him. He would need time to absorb the conversation they'd had yesterday.

She genuinely liked the book club ladies, but tonight she was hesitant to gather. She was cognizant of how quickly gossip spread in the small community. By now, the ladies would have heard Zak was back in Baxley. She was afraid what their reaction might be. PTSD sufferers tended to get a bad reputation. With a lot of misinformation on the disorder, she worried that some of the ladies would have preconceived notions of Zak.

As she climbed up the painted wooden steps of the front porch, she could hear the boisterous chatter of the women inside. *Please let this evening pass quickly.* She rang the doorbell. It was a soft, pleasant chime. She wished she could find a similar one to replace the wretched sound she was subjected to.

Willow opened the door, welcoming her. Lexie had imagined Willow's home would be cluttered with knickknacks, such as bird figurines and pictures, but it wasn't. It actually looked like something out of a designer magazine, with its whitewashed wooden floors, and walls painted a light blue, ironically named robin's egg. The beautiful white credenza at the front entrance held a couple of books along with a large coral ornament, and a frosted-globe lamp. There were no bird pictures, but instead, stylish black-and-white photos of different lake views. It was tasteful and had a relaxing feel to it.

As Willow led her into the living area, she could hear the humming voices of the other ladies. Walking into the room, she noticed the large gathering of women. They were already sipping wine, and she noticed some of the glasses were near empty. She was a bit tardy, but she certainly wasn't that late. She was about to inquire if there had been a time change to the gathering, when Kristina leapt off the sofa to give her a hug. Kristina, who had decided to give up the short skirts and the excessive liquor after their night at the Stompin Loft, was wearing a pair of light grey, slim capris and a flowing silk blouse in periwinkle blue. She blended so elegantly with Willow's home décor. Kristina's transformation was remarkable, but she still maintained her exuberance for life, which Lexie so loved about her. After a few cordial greetings, Willow motioned for Lexie to sit down in the empty armchair. As Willow seemed impatient to get started, Lexie reached into her handbag, pulling out her book. When she looked up, she saw that they were all staring at her.

It was Willow who spoke. "Lexie, I asked the ladies to get here early, so we could talk about Zak Tifour's return. Zak Ahmadi, I mean."

Lexie could feel her temper coming to the surface. *What right did these women have to talk about Zak behind his back, and to do so in an obviously planned and calculated way?* She was starting to get up, when Margo gently tapped her on the arm. "You'll want to hear this."

Lexie let out an audible sigh, and she reluctantly remained seated.

"We know as a community we haven't always treated Zak well. We want to do better."

Hearing those words come from Willow shocked Lexie. It was not what she had anticipated. She shifted herself back in the chair as Willow continued.

"We want to be there for Zak. We want to be the community this young man deserves. So, with Margo's help, I gathered all these ladies tonight to see who was willing to assist. I didn't want to discuss it with you here, just in case someone wasn't willing, making it all rather awkward. But there was no need to convince anyone. Everyone feels the same way. We're all committed to making our town Zak's home. Now, let us tell you what we've come up with."

* * * *

Zak opened the door, and immediately Abby ran, chasing squirrels she would probably never catch. He admired how uninhibited she was; she ran around in circles, simply enjoying the crisp spring air. Although Zak had tried to get Lexie to keep her, he undoubtedly benefited from having the stately animal with him.

Being startled concerned Zak. There were so many things that could alarm him. A car backfiring, turning on the television to find out the volume was at a maximum level, or driving near train tracks and hearing a sudden train whistle. What he didn't worry about was Abby startling him. She was finely tuned into his moods. If anything, she would alert him to any perceived threat, preventing him from being caught off guard. While the squirrels were keeping Abby occupied, Zak knew an off leash run on the backroads would be more beneficial, but he wasn't up to it, so the freedom of playing in the backyard would have to suffice. He sat on the back steps with a coffee and watched Abbey continue to run back and forth, full of boundless energy. As he sipped his coffee, he glanced around the yard, noticing all the work that needed to be done. A particularly nasty winter storm had occurred while he had been away, resulting in smashed tree branches all down the driveway and in the backyard. The front steps needed some painting from regular usage, and the lawn needed to be aerated. He felt guilty for his lack of motivation. Maybe he would make a list of all the outstanding chores and look at accomplishing at least one task a day.

He was getting overwhelmed just thinking about all the chores. When he got overwhelmed, he was at risk of having a panic attack. He tried to shut down his mind, focusing only on Abby, who had given up on the squirrels and was now leisurely exploring, sniffing the base of the various trees in the yard. He sat there for about an hour more before heading back inside. Abby had enjoyed the fresh air. He decided her contentment would be the completed task of the day.

He was restless and bored but lacked the energy to do anything. He tried watching television, but as usual, it unnerved him when he flicked through the channels and saw any sort of violence. Eventually, he just lay down on the sofa, letting the fatigue take over.

He awoke drowning in panic and fear. He could feel his heart pumping faster and faster, like it was struggling to get out of the walls formed by his skin. At first, he thought he was having heart failure, his body giving in to all the physical trauma he had endured. His breathing was fast and erratic, and he could hear his own gasps for air. When he closed his eyes in an effort to focus on what was happening, the bloody images came to him. A thick, ruby-colored liquid, pooling and drenching everywhere, like a scene in a horror movie where the director doesn't yell cut, and instead the camera pans in closer. It wasn't his heart giving out. He was reliving the officers' deaths in graphic detail.

His chest felt crushed, like there was a metal beam laying on top of him. His adrenaline was able to propel him. He ran out of the house into the crisp air, trying to breathe, gasping frantically. Fortunately, Abby had been able to follow him, narrowly missing the door as it shut behind her. Sitting down on the back stairs, Zak tried to get his breathing under control. Eventually, his mind recalled the relaxation techniques and the visualizations, which helped to calm him. Reaching out, stroking Abby's head, he concentrated on his breathing, taking small lungfuls in, and releasing them in slow rhythm. His heart rate slowly returned to normal. It had been a bad one.

He was still wound up when Lexie texted him a couple of hours later. She was going to drop by with some groceries later in the day. She offered to pick up anything he might need, but he wasn't going to use her as his errand girl, even though he was thinking he should get some decaf coffee. The strongly caffeinated bold only intensified his jumpiness. He had thought about telling her not to bother showing up, but he just couldn't. He ached to see her soulful indigo eyes and generous smile. Besides, he had agreed that he wouldn't roadblock her. It was dangerous and wrong to see her, but he'd had such a horrible day. The thought of closing his eyes at the end of the day and not having a vivid memory of her bothered him. Maybe a moment with her could chase away the horrible memories that overtook him earlier.

At a prompt six o'clock, Abby alerted Zak to noise in the distance. A few seconds later, Zak heard the sound of a vehicle approaching the house. He glanced out the window to confirm it was Lexie. He was shocked to see she was trying to manage four large cloth bags of groceries. He hurried over to help her.

"Lexie, this is too much. You don't need to grocery shop for me." He tried to quell the irritation from his voice, unsure if he was able to mask it.

"I just picked up a few vegetables and some decaf coffee, in case you didn't have any. The rest is from George Sims, the owner of the grocery mart."

"I didn't call the store for anything."

"Zak, the people in Baxley care about you, and this is how they show it."

"But Lexie, I can't take advantage of these people. I can well afford groceries. I'm not a charity case," he grumbled.

"George is simply saying thanks for what you have done. For what you have done as a police officer, and also for helping him personally. He told me about how you helped him with a glitch he had in his computerized inventory system. How you essentially saved him a few hundred dollars. He's just paying you back."

"So I guess the whole town knows I lied to them, that I'm not Zak Tifour."

Lexie could see the shame in his face. "Well, it is a small town. They know you're not Mr. Tifour, and they know you worked undercover for the NYPD, although neither Margo nor I mentioned the Counterterrorism Bureau. We didn't feel it was our place to give details. Just so you know, the people of Baxley don't see it as a lie. They actually see you as a hero, which is what you are, Mr. Ahmadi."

He loved the way she made his last name sound, but the use of the word *hero* bothered him.

"Please don't say that. I'm not a hero."

Realizing it was best to leave this conversation, she looked down at the groceries. "Let's get these bags inside. There's some frozen cherry yogurt melting away in there."

He allowed her to come inside, even though the place was a mess. Without commenting, she cleared the dirty dishes from the table so she could set the bags down. She began to hand him the groceries to put away. When the task was completed, she gave him a smile. He wasn't ready to let that smile disappear.

"Want a bowl of yogurt?" he offered.

"Can't say no to frozen yogurt."

Conversation was sparse as they ate. Silence didn't bother him, he was used to a solitary life. He was just happy to have this moment of peace with her. Of enjoying her company without worrying about the past or the future.

"So I'll come by tomorrow after work to take Abby for a run. If you're up to it, you can join us."

"Lexie, you don't have to. She's been running in the yard a lot, so she's getting her exercise."

She patted her stomach. "Did you not notice how much yogurt I ate? The run's not so much for Abby, as it is for me."

He smiled in defeat, a defeat he didn't mind; he was looking forward to seeing her tomorrow. Just the *idea* of seeing her lifted his spirits. It was only last week when he had nothing to look forward to, so today gave him something. He tried to tell himself it wasn't hope, but rather anticipation. Anticipation he would see her again. He knew from the nightmare and panic attack earlier in the day, he wasn't getting better. He longed for Lexie to be his forever, but it meant trusting in the future. The attack reminded him the future wasn't looking good. But focusing on the present was bearable. And only because he was with Lexie.

* * * *

Lexie couldn't help but get her hopes up; Zak had smiled today. It was a genuine smile, not a forced one to make her feel at ease or to express gratitude. It was a smile you'd see on a child's face, totally uninhibited, a brief moment of pure joy. She didn't want nostalgia to get in the way of reality, but she thought he looked better. His hair was still long and unruly, yet it retained its beautiful lustre. His eyes had a sparkle to them when he talked with her at the kitchen table. Although the yogurt they shared was mouth-wateringly delicious, she sensed it wasn't the food which momentarily enlivened him. He did object when she mentioned him being a hero, and as soon as she said the word, she regretted it. She saw how he despised being called it. But it was fitting for a man who demonstrated what commitment and sacrifice meant.

She had to be patient with him, but she wanted to believe that being invited to share yogurt was a big first step. Talking to her, sharing with her made him vulnerable, but it was his vulnerability that also made him strong. He wasn't shutting himself away from her, and although he still didn't say much, just letting her sit with him was promising.

Chapter Twenty-Nine

It had now become routine for Lexie to drop by several times a week. Often, she would take Abby for a run. She stopped asking Zak to join them. He didn't need a guilt trip. Working out would be good for him, but she understood he just wasn't able to do it yet.

Cicily had baked some baklava especially for Zak. She was also working on perfecting a recipe for *kunafeh*, which Lexie found out was like a Middle Eastern version of cheesecake. It was Cicily's way of apologizing for her behavior. She didn't say the words. She could certainly be an infuriatingly stubborn woman, but her attitude had changed, and slowly she was working on changing how she behaved.

Others were there for Zak like they promised Lexie they would be. Willow had donated a hummingbird feeder for his yard. Initially, he seemed bothered by the gift and Lexie was afraid he was shutting down, going back into a world where no one else was allowed to enter. But that wasn't it. It was simply a case of annoying crows, and once he found out that the feeder didn't attract crows, he smiled, equal parts appreciation and relief. There were casseroles made by various ladies, and Bernice had knitted a sweater for him. It was an odd sweater, something for one of those ugly sweater parties, but when Lexie dropped it off, he seemed not only amused, but touched by the gesture.

Some days Zak wasn't up to seeing Lexie, but for the most part he invited her in for coffee or to sample some dessert or casserole he had been given. Conversation was still rather sparse, but to Lexie it didn't matter. Just being with him made her happier than she had been in a long time.

There were challenges, and one of the biggest arrived three weeks after the town began its mission to support Zak's recovery. Sheriff Emmett McQuay had volunteered to come over on the weekend to do some yard work for him. Kristina told Lexie her husband was feeling like a heel for the way he'd treated Zak. He wanted to make amends. As had become the norm, Lexie was the one they would approach. Until now, it wasn't an issue, as the townsfolk would just drop off food and hurry off. No one stayed for more than a few minutes of small talk with Zak. Lexie was the only one who had been invited inside the house. Now she had to approach Zak about Emmett coming by for a full day.

She was sitting in his kitchen, enjoying the ginger cookies Margo had sent over. Zak had an insatiable sweet tooth. He leaned across the table, grabbing cookie number five.

She cleared her throat, "I got a call from Emmett yesterday."

"What did the sheriff want?" There was a cold gruffness to his voice.

"Well…" She hesitated, trying to find the right words. He had just taken another bite, this time from cookie number six. As he crunched away, she knew she had a few moments before he would again ask what the sheriff wanted.

"Well, he kind of volunteered to come by on Saturday."

"Why?" he grumbled, between bites.

"He wants to help with some of the outside work."

He dropped his half-eaten cookie on the platter. "No," he said abruptly.

It was the arching of her eyebrows that made him elaborate.

"It's one thing for the ladies to fatten me up with their baking and to knit me a funky kind of sweater, but I don't need that man getting into my business. I'll get around to the yard work."

"Zak, he's just wanting to help out a neighbor. It's what people do around here."

"Come on, Lexie, you don't really believe that?"

"Actually, I do. Yes, I know how he treated you. He angered me too, but he's changed. Kristina swears he's not the same bitter person anymore. I believe her. It's an opportunity to help him. To forgive him for all his stupidity toward you."

"I don't need him seeing me like this. Tossing pity my way."

"I get the sense he needs this, so if anything, you would be pitying him."

"Well, I don't pity people." He was still argumentative, but she felt some give.

"So don't pity him, just let him apologize, and his way of apologizing is by action. You know he's not a man who would talk about feelings, and I would think you would be glad." She smiled as she clearly made her point.

He gave her another irritated look. He knew he was softening and he had to force it.

"Come on, Zak, just give him an opportunity."

No, don't bat those pretty eyelashes.

"I'll even come over and make sandwiches for you guys. I'll bring cookies."

No batted lashes, but a cookie bribe. That was almost as bad.

"Chocolate chip oatmeal?" he asked. He was losing the battle, but at least he was going to negotiate.

"I'll make them myself."

"Fine," he half grumbled. There was so much he wanted to give her and couldn't. So if he had to be civil to Sheriff Emmett for a day, he would do it for her.

Chapter Thirty

Walking up the creaky porch steps, Lexie heard the violins and cellos from inside. She stood by the door knowing once she knocked, the peaceful serenity of the harmonic rhythm would cease. Her life was nowhere near ideal, but it was getting better. Being with Zak provided her with needed comfort. He was slowly opening up to her, and one day she would open up to him. Today wouldn't be the day. Today would be a day to help others. To help Zak, and in a way, Emmett as well. She arrived early, wanting to be there when Emmett showed up. She would be a buffer in case the sheriff said anything to anger Zak. She doubted he would, since he seemed to have taken Margo's scolding and shaming to heart.

Just as she was ready to knock on the door, she heard Abby's bark and, as she predicted, the music ceased. When the door opened, Abby rushed to her. She bent down, giving the dog a good ear scratching.

When she stood up, Zak had a wide smile. "Hey, how come she gets greeted first?"

Stepping inside, she leaned up and softly kissed him on the cheek. Although it was far from the passionate kiss she wanted to give him, it was the first time her lips had touched him since he'd returned. It was bold of her but being around him lately was making her feel bold. Whether he was ready to admit it or not, a relationship had developed between them. It wasn't an easily defined relationship, but it was obvious they were more than just friends.

He reciprocated by pulling her into an embrace. *Did he have any idea what being pressed against his body did to her?* She was hoping he would kiss her, but instead he pulled back. Her mind raced to the last time, when he'd rejected her, when he'd told her to leave. Terror ran through her as she thought back to that moment, afraid she had been too bold.

"Now, that's much better than an ear scratching," he teased.

She smiled with relief, but that moment of fear was a clear reminder not to push for more than he could give.

"Is that coffee I smell?" she asked, a clear diversion from the intimacy she craved.

"Yup. Thought I might have to lure you with coffee to get you inside the house, but I'm guessing it may not have been necessary."

"Well, maybe not necessary, but certainly appreciated." As she was walking toward the kitchen, she turned around to him. "What were you listening to?"

"It's a Tchaikovsky piece. Did you like it?"

"Absolutely. I could listen to it forever. It's so beautiful. It reminded me of when you took me to the opera. Did you know I could hear the music in my head even after we had left? It felt like it was never going to end"

"I'm sorry I had to turn it off."

Lexie knew he was trying to convey more than just turning off the beautiful classical piece. Before she could say anything, Abby let out a soft bark. Lexie turned toward the front window. A large black truck towing a trailer bed pulled into the driveway.

"Guess it's time to get to work." She forced a smile.

Lexie walked with Zak to the front door to greet Emmett and Kristina. She was pleased Kristina had agreed to give up a leisurely Saturday to hang out with her. Although she was different than Kristina in most ways, she loved the ease with which they could talk about almost any topic. Kristina was generous in her friendship, and along with Margo, was one of the few locals who had always believed Zak was a good man.

Almost immediately, Zak and Emmett went to work outside. It was the first time since Zak's return that Lexie had seen him do any physical work. It was another in a series of small steps he had taken in the last couple of weeks. While the guys busied themselves outside, Lexie and Kristina went inside.

"Thanks for coming over."

"No problem. So what's the plan?" Kristina asked.

"I thought I would clean up the place. Scrub the kitchen and bathroom, some dusting, that sort of thing."

"Zak won't mind?"

"Well, I'm not sure, but I'll find out."

"Count me in. I'll take the bathroom."

"Kristina, I can't ask you to do that."

"You didn't. I want to."

Lexie laughed. "No one wants to clean a man's bathroom."

"True, but I'm an expert. I'm married to McMessy, so I'm sure I can handle Zak's bathroom. Besides, that's what friends do. They help each other."

"Okay, but I owe you for this."

"You already paid up big time with those fashion tips. If it wasn't for you I would be scrubbing the toilet in Daisy Duke shorts."

"Well, the way Emmett's been acting, I bet he wouldn't mind seeing you in those," Lexie teased.

"Maybe I shouldn't have been so hasty in getting rid of them," she said with a giggle. "Seriously, I'm glad we're here today. I didn't know if Zak would accept help from Emmett, but he's truly changed. He regrets how he treated Zak."

"I know, I can see it too," acknowledged Lexie.

"Knowing what Zak has gone through has made Emmett more grateful. He's finally grateful for being able to have a place like Baxley to live and work in. A quiet community where he doesn't have to worry about violence taking over. The other night he even thanked me for putting up with his McGrouchiness. So what about you? How's things with Zak?"

"Better. He's still cautious and although we've been spending a lot of time together, he's still not ready to let me into his world. I'm okay with it because I know he'll get there. It's just going to take some time. Hanging around with Emmett is good for him. He needs guy friends. He has some police friends coming next week. I'm hoping their visit will help him, too."

"If you need anything, just let me know."

"Thanks. Just having friends makes the difference, and a friend who cleans a man's bathroom, that's epic friendship."

They both giggled.

* * * *

Working alongside Emmett surprised Zak. The sheriff certainly wasn't the same hard-nosed bigot he had dealt with prior to going to New York. As soon as he got out of his truck, he came over, shook Zak's hand, and said, "Welcome back."

The equipment Emmett had trailered over made the work easier. He made sure to mention it was kindly on loan from an elderly gentleman farmer named Oscar Griffin. Zak had shown Oscar how to set up and utilize internet banking.

Lexie was right. Emmett wasn't much of a talker. He was certainly a doer and got right to work, taking few breaks. He wasn't one for small talk; he worked hard and spoke when he had something to say. In some ways he reminded him of Scorp, although Scorp seemed haunted by the past where Emmett seemed full of regret.

He was shocked to see Kristina looking… Well, the only word he could think of was modest. She was still an attractive woman, and in some ways even more so. There was a subtleness to her. She wasn't flashing her sexuality with those tight shirts he had seen her wear to the town administration office. And best of all, she didn't try to flirt with him. Zak had ended their harmless flirtation when he had met Lexie. He was relieved that Kristina wasn't eyeing him like she used to. It was one thing to do so before he met Lexie, but now it would be wrong. Lexie and he weren't really a couple, but they were more than just friends. PTSD was the obstacle to a relationship he wished he could have. He hated how it had taken over his life. He reminded himself to take it one day at a time. Just to have held Lexie, even for the briefest of moments, qualified the day as good. Hanging out doing yard work with Emmett helped. It felt good to do something physical.

He appreciated Emmett not prying into his life, and most specifically the details of his work with the NYPD. He could probably trust Emmett with some of the basic information regarding what he did in counterterrorism, but he didn't like talking about it. He didn't like talking about terrorists. The terrorists he dealt with were thugs, criminals, and gang members of a different degree. They wanted the world to believe their acts were justified by their religion. But Zak understood Islam well. He grew up with Islam and his close friends were Muslim. He studied and read the Qur'an. He knew the truth, the beauty of the faith, the understanding and forgiveness of God. It angered him how peace-loving Muslims were expected to apologize for the deeds of terrorists and how they were targeted with hate crimes. Sure he was exasperated by it, but he learned a long time ago that anger didn't solve the problem. What solved the problem was what he was doing today. Getting to know the people in his community and letting them get to know him.

By late afternoon, the place was looking decent. The sun had gone into the clouds. With all the heavy lifting he had done, the now chilly air was a welcome relief. He helped Emmett load up the equipment while Kristina wandered out of the house, ready to leave. After they drove away, he went into the house to thank Lexie, not only for the sandwiches and cookies she served, but for convincing him to let Emmett help. A lot had been accomplished in one day.

As he walked through the back hallway, he noticed the cleanliness of the ceramic floor tiles. His outerwear was neatly hanging on wall hooks, his footwear tucked underneath. The house smelled of a soothing blend of lavender and citrus. The place looked different but in a good way. The way he used to keep his home. Well, except for the particular girly fragrance, which admittedly he liked.

He found Lexie in the kitchen bent over the dishwasher, loading it with the lunch plates. He was slightly annoyed, but mostly embarrassed. Lexie and Kristina had not only made lunch, but they'd thoroughly scrubbed his home. The annoyance dissipated quickly when she turned around and smiled at him. Her dark glossy hair pulled back into a ponytail with small wisps of hair falling near her cheeks. He was amazed with how she could look so downright sexy when she had obviously been cleaning for hours. But she was more than just physically beautiful. She was smart and funny, a brilliant surgeon who was now a small-town doctor. Her capabilities went far beyond the day-to-day ills she dealt with in Baxley, yet she humbly served the people of this close-knit community.

The truth soared into him. He was in love with her. In love with this wonderful, caring soul who was doing so much to help him out of his darkness. He wasn't healed. Having someone in his life, even someone as extraordinary as Lexie, wouldn't heal him. But seeing her every couple of days, like he had the last few weeks, was making living more bearable.

He moved closer to her and kissed her on the cheek, quickly stepping back.

"Thanks, but you shouldn't have cleaned my place. I would have got around to it." He saw a flash of hurt in her eyes, so he added with a grin, "If you keep this up, liberated women everywhere will be cursing you."

"It wasn't all my doing. Kristina helped. As far as disappointing liberated women, they'll understand once they find out you're going to make me dinner tomorrow night. And normally I'd demand a foot rub after a day like today, but I'm grimy and need go home and take a shower."

As she was walking to grab her keys from the kitchen table, he reached out and touched her elbow. The simple touch resulted in undeniable heat, making him desire more.

"There's a shower here, apparently a very clean shower," he said as he stepped closer. Positioning his lips just inches from her ear, he murmured, "Join me."

He hadn't set out to be this bold this morning, but the intensity of standing so close to her made him irrational. He could tell by the look on her face he had shocked her. Now embarrassed, he looked away, thinking she was not prepared for this. Hell, he wasn't either.

Just as he was going to apologize for his actions, she mouthed, "yes."

The one-word response undid him.

He took her hand, leading her to the bathroom, afraid if he didn't move now one of them might change their minds.

When they got to the shower, he switched on the water while Lexie pulled off her t-shirt, revealing a red lace bra. Zak moved closer and leaned down to gently kiss her on the neck. He moved up to her earlobe and gave her a teasing nibble. She let out a quiet moan and leaned back against the wall. Slowly, he moved back down her neck, down her front, toward her breasts. Undoing the top of her jeans, he hooked his fingers in the loops and lowered them. She stood wearing only her bra and panties. He paused, admiring the gorgeous woman in front of him. The woman he always needed.

"You don't know what you do to me," he growled next to her ear.

"I'm more than willing to find out," she responded in a raspy voice.

He grinned. Quickly removing his clothes, he watched as she unhooked her bra and stepped out of her matching lace panties. The sight of her naked body caused more to stir in him than his already obvious physical arousal. She undid her tied up hair, shaking it loose as she hopped into the steamy water.

He froze, as his mind worked to catch up to his body. His analytical reasoning was a strength, but right now it was a curse to have. He didn't want to think about all the reasons he shouldn't be doing this, he wanted only to have her.

As if she understood his hesitancy, she held out her hand to him.

He couldn't deny her, and even if he tried, his body wouldn't allow it now. He stepped into the shower and took in all she had to offer him. He loved feeling her, steamy and wet against his skin. Exploring every glorious inch of her, tasting her as she moaned, allowing her to awaken him. It was incredible to feel this good in such a darkened world.

After the shower, he led her to his bed. He gently made love to her, allowing himself the sweet sensation of being inside her. Savoring every precious moment: her passionate groans as he slid into her, the sensations radiating though her body as she began to climax, her fiery release of pleasure, followed by his own wave of ecstasy. It was more than sex; it was a sacred promise of tomorrow. Afterward, she softly kissed his lips and nuzzled into him, her dampened hair providing relief to his heated body. He wrapped his arms around her, feeling her soft breaths on his chest. Satisfied yet exhausted, he shut his eyes, willing the world to fade. Several minutes passed. The world stood defiant, immune to his needs.

He swept her hair aside and placed a sweet kiss on her forehead. Reluctantly, he eased her away from him. Slowly he sat up, feeling his overworked muscles as he swung his feet to the floor. Stirring from his movement, she opened her eyes.

"Stay," she muttered, as she tried gently pulling him back.

He resisted. "I can't," he said. "I sometimes get horrible nightmares and…" He struggled to find the words without alarming her.

How could he explain the demons? There wasn't a physical body to them, but it didn't matter; there was a moment that crept into his consciousness where they were real. He tried to battle the demons, but in order to do so, he risked becoming one himself. He sat at the edge of the bed, trying to figure out a way to tell the woman he wanted as his forever, that he couldn't be the man she wanted, the man she deserved.

"It's okay, Zak," she said, as she stroked his back.

"No, it's not okay." He turned around to face her. "I want nothing more than to stay with you in this bed, to fall asleep with you in my arms, but I can't. I'm sorry." He was starting to be the king of apologies. He didn't hate apologizing, but he hated how it sounded. The words so small, so feeble. Why wasn't there a stronger, clearer way to express the painful regret he longed to convey?

As he looked into those mesmerizing blue eyes of hers, she reached out and held his face. "Zak, never say you're sorry for having PTSD. If you had heart disease, cancer, or diabetes would you feel the need to apologize?" She didn't wait for him to answer. "No, of course not. You didn't ask for this, and you don't deserve to have it. No one does. But you do have it, and you can't change it. What you can do is get professional help. It's not for my sake. I want to be with you. I'm happy when I'm around you, and whatever parameters there must be, I'm good with. But your shame and guilt for events you had no control over is eating away at you. It's something you haven't been able to deal with and something I can't help you with. So, for your sake, stop being stubborn, defeatist, or whatever it is that's holding you back from getting help."

"I've been down that road and it didn't work out for me. The doctors just want to give me drugs, just numb me. I don't want to live like I am, but I can't live the way they want me to either."

"Okay, so no meds then. I know a therapist in Chicago who runs a group program. It's mainly soldiers and first responders. It might help to talk to other men and women who have had similar experiences. You could try it out and if you're not comfortable with it, then I'll leave the issue alone."

She was right. He had to keep trying. He had been prescribed various medications. They didn't work, other than to numb him or to make him even more messed up. Eventually, he refused to look at any pharmaceutical options. He went through a series of one-on-one sessions with a psychiatrist, but he never stuck it out long enough for any group therapy. There were other officers in the NYPD with PTSD, but it was still a culture where they didn't talk about it. There was a lot of denial and even stigma attached to having this disorder. And if Zak hadn't fully fallen apart, he would have continued with the denial. But the PTSD had become so severe, so apparent.

Lexie walked away from Zak. He was thinking she was just going to walk out the door, having given up trying to convince him. Instead, she walked toward the kitchen and returned with a piece of paper she had scrawled on. It was the name and number of the therapist she had spoken about.

She gently placed it in his hand. "I'll be here whether you decide to use this or not. I only hope you use it; you deserve peace. There's so much I want to give you, and I believe so much I can give you, but I can't give you peace. I'm not naïve. I know it won't go away, but it can get better."

She leaned up to him, kissing him lightly on the lips. "Just think about it. I'll see you tomorrow."

* * * *

Zak was outside on the porch stretching when she pulled up. She sat in her vehicle a little longer than she probably should have, imagining his muscles flexing underneath his winter track pants and jacket. When he looked up and caught her eye, he grinned as her face flushed.

Busted, but worth it.

She slowly got out of her vehicle and stood before the porch, looking up at him. His hair was still unruly as it peaked out of his wool beanie, but he had trimmed the ratty beard.

"Thought I would join you and Abby for a run. I hope I don't slow you down; I'm afraid I'm not in peak condition."

Was he kidding? He was in great condition. She had felt his great condition in the shower yesterday.

"My jogging is probably just a brisk walk for you, Mr. Ahmadi."

Lexie insisted on him setting the pace. He set a moderate one and she figured it wasn't because he was out of shape, but so she would be able to converse with him as they ran. She was an avid and decent runner, but Zak was a machine when it came to fitness. She was glad he didn't go hard-core with the running, not only for her sake but also his. He had suffered life threatening injuries only a few months back. The doctor in her worried about him.

"I never did ask you what aria was your favorite." He was referring to the disc of opera music he had given her.

"I liked several of them, but my favorite was definitely *Un bel di vedremo.*" She was hoping she didn't botch up the Italian words from *Madame Butterfly.*

"Well, then, I'll have to ensure I take you to see it performed live."

She was struggling to keep up, so she simply smiled and nodded. It was satisfying to know he was thinking of the future, a future with her in it.

"Omeir and Safia, my friends from New York are visiting this weekend. I thought I would do a simple dinner at my place. I'd love for you to come over."

"I'd love to meet them." She huffed out the words and took a few moments before continuing. "Have them come over to my house and I'll cook supper, so you can spend time visiting with them."

Noticing her huffing, he slowed his pace. "Hey, I asked you first. Besides, I'm the better cook," he said lightheartedly.

"Maybe I spent the last few months taking cooking lessons."

"Did you?"

"No," she said and puffed out a giggle. "But I'm great at researching, and I can find a great recipe online," she added before losing her breath entirely.

He slowed down some more. "You do know, the fire department in Baxley is not well equipped."

She gave him a playful smirk, sprinting ahead of him. He let her, knowing she couldn't maintain the increased pace. When she slowed down, he was quickly back at her side.

"Hey, that's not fair, you know I have heart issues slowing me down." It was meant as a teasing remark, but he could see the worry in her face. "I'm just kidding, I'm fine. But seriously, you've done enough for me, I can't have you cooking for my guests."

"I honestly don't mind, and from what you mentioned about Safia, she might feel more comfortable at my place than yours." She took a few panted breaths in and out. "If Safia wants, she can stay overnight at my place while Omeir goes back to yours. That way they don't have to drive to Chicago in the dark. Just the other day, I treated this man with whiplash. He ditched his car to avoid a herd of white tailed deer."

"She's her own person, but Safia still cares about not disappointing her father. Of course, he isn't happy about her coming out here with Omeir. He would probably be livid if she stayed with Omeir at my place." He purposely gave her a slight bump with his elbow. "Why do you always have to make sense?"

She smiled. "I don't know. Maybe because I'm brilliant," she joked.

"That you are. Smarter than me, Dr. Lexie, but remember I'm faster. See you," he said as he shot off and sprinted the final few hundred yards.

Once she got back to the house, he invited her to shower. Oh... how she loved those showers, his muscular body next to hers under the soothing hot water, the steamy sex that continued in his bedroom. It was certainly the best way to start a Sunday morning.

After getting dressed, he went to the kitchen to make breakfast. While Lexie was still in his room, straightening out the comforter on his bed, she could smell the omelet cooking in the kitchen along with the aroma of freshly brewed coffee. She was still amazed with how things were between them. Only a few weeks ago, he had pushed her away, leaving her so dejected.

She sauntered into the kitchen where he was just flipping the omelet onto a plate. She grabbed two mugs from the cupboard, filling them both with freshly brewed java. He smiled at her and they both sat down to eat. There was a nice quietness to this. They had spent the morning talking while they were out running, and now the peacefulness of a lazy Sunday morning had taken hold. She loved finding out more about him, but she was also content just being with him.

Finally, he disrupted the silence. "Can you shut down the clinic early one day to come with me to Chicago? Not this Thursday, but maybe the following one?" he clarified.

"Sure, I'll get Margo to reschedule any appointments I have. So what's up in Chicago?" she asked, wondering if he had tickets for the opera.

"I've made an appointment to meet with the therapist and he recommended you come along." He looked down at his empty plate. "I know it's my issue, but he says it's important to initially meet with any intimate partners."

Lexie reached over and took his hand in hers. He looked up to meet her eyes.

"I'll definitely be there. I've told you I'll help any way I can, and I meant it."

A giggle escaped her mouth. "So intimate partners? Well, I hope we don't have to pick anyone else up on the way."

He pulled her hand to his lips and kissed her hand gently. "Just in case you haven't figured me out, you don't have to ever worry. There's no one else, Lexie, and there won't be."

* * * *

Safia and Omeir were to arrive at his place anytime. Just a few weeks ago, he would have dreaded their visit but now he was eager to see his good friends and introduce them to Lexie. Admittedly, Lexie's home was better suited for entertaining than his small bungalow, but she shouldn't be the one having to entertain his friends. She was persistent, making him cave. After all, she might be right; Safia might prefer dinner at Lexie's home to his.

Zak had to admit he wasn't sure where Safia stood with going to a male colleague's home on a social basis. Back in New York, with thousands of restaurants and coffee shops, there was no need to have Safia over to his place. In fact, he could only recall about a half-dozen times when Omeir had been over to his apartment, and then it was only for a few minutes on the way to some eatery. But Baxley was a big contrast to New York. He assumed she would be fine with being at his home in Baxley. He was like a brother to her and she'd been at his little bungalow home with Omeir just a couple of months ago. But that really wasn't a social call. She might not be comfortable hanging out at his place.

Safia was an outspoken and independent woman, yet she was also a Muslim woman with a father who disapproved of some of her choices. She'd stood up to her father on a number of issues, including her decision to join the NYPD. But maybe this was different. Damn, how could he not know this? He vowed to be a better friend.

Lexie was clear in her instructions that he was not to come over until late afternoon. She told him she needed to get prepared and didn't need a distraction. He liked being her distraction. She wasn't the most skilled in the kitchen, but he knew she had exaggerated the amount of required prep time. Her motive was obvious. She knew spending time with his old friends would be good for him. It was another thing he loved about Lexie; she knew what he needed even when he didn't.

Abby made a deep bark, signalling Zak's guests had arrived. It was a beautiful spring day, so they went outside to the small wooden patio table Emmett had found in the back of Zak's shed last week. As the three of them sat watching Abby chase robins, they chatted away. They talked about work; it was inevitable. There were some solid leads from Homeland Security on the biochemical scientists they had been trying to track down. They had obtained the scientists' identities and were closing in on them. It was encouraging news, as the failure to capture them bothered him. He knew the guilt would overwhelm him if the scientists were able to obtain a legitimate formula, unleashing an airborne illness on innocent people.

He asked about Nate. Nate no longer irked him, and although they likely would never be close, the little pompous genius, their nickname for him, wasn't all that bad. He had expressed concern about Zak's well-being and had even called him since his return to Baxley. It wasn't the best day when he called, but it certainly wasn't Zak's worst either. On the worst days, Zak ignored phone calls, no matter who they were from. Sure, Nate's call was filled with awkward pauses, but at least he was decent enough to care.

Surprisingly, Scorp was the one who called most often, even more so than Omeir and Safia. He wondered if Scorp needed the routine of checking in for Zak's benefit, or was it a way for him to keep on track with his own sobriety. He sensed Scorp's drinking had slowed down, but with him, you couldn't always tell for sure.

The discussion inevitably turned to him and how he was doing. He was honest with them. He told them how horrible it had been for him at first. How unglued he had been and then he told them about the petite elderly lady named Margo, and how she'd basically rescued him from himself. He spoke about how Lexie had stood by him, how the community of Baxley had rallied to help him, and about this once-cranky sheriff who was now his friend. But when he talked of Lexie, they smiled, knowing smiles. They had been friends for several years, since they had all been recruits, without the weight of danger pushing down on them. And here he was, years later with all the darkness of the world encompassed in his soul, yet when he spoke of Lexie a fiery flame radiated from within. They knew their friend had found his forever.

* * * *

Lexie was nervous. In a way it was like meeting one's in-laws for the first time. She wanted to make a good first impression, and although she had worked with several Muslim doctors, she had never socialized with any Muslims beyond the occasional hospital charitable event. She knew the basics about no pork, and no alcohol, but was surprised to find out about other dietary restrictions such as marshmallows, which contain gelatin from pork.

She recalled her panic. "Zak, what if I made something with marshmallows?"

"I thought you could cook? And here I found out we were all going to sit down to a meal of s'mores."

"Seriously, what if I made some Ambrosia fruit salad with marshmallows so tiny they didn't notice?"

"Were you planning a dish of tiny marshmallows?"

"Well, no, but what if I did?"

"If you did, and they ate it without knowing it, it would be fine. Devout Muslims, like devout Christians and Jews, are believers in the goodness of God. They don't judge you for not knowing about their beliefs and practices. As a child of God, they see you for your true intentions. It's what's in your heart and you have the purest heart. I see it and they will, too."

His words touched her and although she was still nervous, she knew she would be fine with Zak by her side.

* * * *

The doorbell rang with a soft chime. She was thankful she had finally replaced it. Her hands shook ever so slightly when she reached to open the door. Zak immediately stepped toward her, embracing her with a sweet kiss on her cheek.

"Hey, beautiful," he whispered into her ear before stepping back.

"Lexie, these are my good friends, Safia and Omeir."

Omeir was a lean man with a compact yet muscular build. He was a few inches shorter than Zak, and had beautiful thick dark hair, with a well-trimmed beard. He was not as handsome as her Zak, but he was a good-looking man.

"Nice to meet you," he said. He appeared about to speak again but Safia stepped up and extended her hand.

"Thank you, Lexie for inviting us over." Safia had brought a peace lily plant as a gift and handed it over.

"Thank you. It's beautiful."

It wasn't just the white fan-shaped blooms on the plant that were beautiful. The woman who handed it to Lexie was, as well. She had long dark brown hair, held back in a loose ponytail. She wore only a trace of makeup, which accentuated her natural beauty. She was exotic-looking and could easily have been a fashion model, except where most models are tall and too slender, she was probably just a couple inches over five feet, with a lean, muscular build.

Lexie invited them inside, leading her guests back to the covered veranda where she had a pitcher of iced tea and lemon water waiting.

"Please sit," she said when they reached the wicker chairs. She wanted to kick herself for being so formal and uptight, but she was desperate for them to like her.

Sensing her nervousness, Zak reached for her hand. He looked over at Safia and Omeir. "Did I ever tell you guys how Lexie and I met?"

"Wasn't it at the local coffee shop?" Omeir responded.

Lexie looked at Zak, and he gave her a knowing smile. An intimate, sweet memory they shared. His smile made her relax.

"Well, not quite," Lexie said. "I met Zak when he came after me with an ax."

He saw the fear in Safia's face. Normally, he would have been hurt that his friend honestly thought he had gone ballistic, chasing down the town's doctor with an ax, but he loved that he and Lexie had this unique story, one that one day he hoped to tell their grandchildren.

"I hardly chased you," he said, feigning offense. "I dropped the ax."

"But not the *balaclava*," she reminded him.

"True."

Omeir began to laugh. "Geez, Zak, I always thought you were the one with the smooth moves. Maybe there's hope for a guy like me."

Zak couldn't help but notice the quick glance Safia gave Omeir. Before it became awkward, he explained the snowstorm, providing context to his bizarre first encounter with Lexie.

Omeir loved stories and was a great storyteller himself. He kept the laughter going with tales about when they had been young, clueless recruits. When Lexie had first met them at the door, she'd certainly seen why Omeir was crazy about Safia, but after listening to his stories, she understood he had his own unique appeal. He was wildly entertaining and had such enthusiasm, no matter the topic. They were both good for Zak, and now that she had relaxed, she enjoyed their company as well. There was a lightness to him when he was around them, a lightness she had previously caught a glimpse of but today was even more evident. She loved sitting out on the veranda, hearing wonderful anecdotes of the man she had fallen in love with.

With all the fun and laughter, she had forgotten about getting dinner. When Omeir asked her about her family, she excused herself. Turning on the oven provided a much-needed excuse to avoid the sensitive issue of her family. Zak immediately rose to assist, but Safia insisted he chat with Omeir while she went.

The salmon was already seasoned, and the assorted vegetables cleaned and cut. She simply had to pop them into the oven. Because

Safia was fascinated with her historical house, Lexie offered to show her around. While they were wandering into the various rooms they chatted about antiques. Lexie showed Safia the guestroom, telling her she was welcome to stay.

"Thanks Lexie. I'll talk to Omeir, but I'm sure he'll like the idea of spending more time with Zak."

"This visit is good for him," Lexie stated.

"We miss Zak and when he decided to come back here, Omeir didn't like it. I thought differently, and seeing him here today just reinforces this is where he belongs."

"I'm glad he came back," Lexie said, stating the obvious.

"He looks so much healthier than he did in New York. He reminds me of the Zak I had first met. I know he's not the same, and he won't be the same, but he's better. You made the difference, Lexie. You make him want to get better. Omeir and I can't thank you enough. You're perfect for him."

Those last words stung. She wasn't perfect, not even close. It brought back what Claudia used to call her: the perfect sister. However, she'd let Claudia down, and she just prayed she wouldn't let Zak down. She wouldn't do anything to purposely hurt him, but she wondered how he would feel about her, how his friends would feel about her if they knew the truth. How she had left a sick young child to die alone. She tried to shake her thoughts. Safia was obviously being kind and therefore she forced a polite smile. She quickly started talking about the eighteenth-century wainscoting on the stairwell.

* * * *

Although Zak and Omeir had offered to do the clean up after dinner, Lexie had insisted her guests just relax while she tidied up in the kitchen. Zak might not get another chance to visit with his friends for a while. She wanted him to be able to savor this time with them. She had only just met them, but she could tell the three of them had a strong bond. She was wiping down the countertops when Zak walked into the kitchen.

"What are you doing in here? I banned you from helping out."

"Not here to help," he said with a wide grin. He moved toward her, backing her up against the counter. Wrapping his arms around her waist, he leaned in, gently planting kisses along her neck. He moved back slowly, keeping his eyes locked on hers. "Just wanted to thank you. It was a great dinner."

"It's not as good as your cooking, but I enjoyed doing it."

"And I enjoy thanking you."

She laughed at his comment. She certainly liked the way he showed gratitude. "It's great to have a hot man with a gorgeous smile standing in my kitchen, but you really should go entertain Omeir and Safia. I'll make some coffee and join you in a few minutes."

"Nope, not going to do it. I like the scenery in here better." He smiled as he looked at her. "Besides, Omeir likes to entertain Safia all on his own." He gave her another kiss, this time on the lips, and with an intensity that made them both wish they could be alone.

Chapter Thirty-One

People believe in warning signs when it comes to tornados. Funnel clouds off in the distance, a hot thickness in the air, visible signs letting you know to take cover. But the truth is nature's deadliest destructive forces can sometimes occur without warning. And that is exactly what happened to Zak.

Omeir and Safia had left a couple of days before and Zak was scheduled to meet with the therapist in Chicago the following day. He had been sleeping relatively well for the last few nights and was feeling like his old self. He had spent a nice evening with Lexie over at her house, helping her move some boxes to the attic. He had even contemplated staying overnight but figured he should discuss this with the therapist first. He wasn't just hoping for a normal life. He was starting to live it.

Then mayhem hit. It certainly wasn't Abby's fault. She was doing what she normally did, running around in the surrounding fields before he got ready to take her for a run. He was in the bedroom changing into his running gear when he heard the commotion. He instantly knew it was some wild animal, whether it was a coywolf or an actual wolf he couldn't tell, but he could tell his dog was getting the worst of it. Abby's excruciating yelps echoed. Running out into the yard, he repeatedly called her name. Her only response was the continuing yelps off in the distance. Grabbing a large 2x4 board from the yard, he ran in the direction of the snarls and piercing shrieks.

When he got there, he could see it was a coywolf. He yelled and threw the 2x4 in the animal's direction. Realizing he was unarmed, he regretted throwing the old piece of lumber. Thankfully, his angry thunderous voice spooked the wild animal and it ran off. Locating Abby by her gut-wrenching wails, he ran to her. His visual senses overwhelmed the auditory when he saw the blood gushing out of his dog, pooling beneath her. It was everywhere; on the wild grass beside Abby, on her back legs, dripping down her neck, and matting her contrasting vanilla-colored fur. She was a mess.

As his body trembled, he searched his mind for what he should do. He couldn't leave her there. The stench of the blood was thick in the air and he was starting to gag. Time was running out. He had to react quickly, or he would end up paralyzed by panic. He briefly closed his eyes, reached down and lifted her into his arms. The discomfort of not only the attack but of her master picking her up, made her yelp even more. He tried to use words to soothe her, but they were really to soothe him.

* * * *

Lexie had finished with Oscar Morrison, who had come in to see her about his arthritis. She was making notes in Oscar's file when her phone vibrated on her desk. She normally didn't pick up her smartphone during office hours, but noticing it was Zak, she reached to answer.

"Hello, Mr. Ahmadi," she seductively cooed.

"You got to get here now!" He was uncharacteristically demanding, but more concerning was the panic in his voice.

"What's wrong?"

"She's been attacked. It's bad. I don't know what to do."

"Who?" she asked, trying to remain calm so she could understand what was going on.

"Abby," he yelled impatiently.

"Get her over to the vet. I'll meet you there."

"Lexie, I can't! There's so much blood."

She realized then that it wasn't just Abby who had been attacked and in need; Zak had been, too. His injuries weren't physical, but they were just as severe.

"You need to carefully listen. It's important. Can you do that, Zak?"

The gasps in his breath were loud. "Yeah," he responded.

"I'm on my way. But until I get there, you need to take care of her. Now get a clean towel and wrap it tightly around the wound. Put pressure on the worst of the wounds with the towel and your hands." She looked around her office, grabbing some needles, antibiotics, bandages, and whatever else she might need, and tossed them into a bag. As she hurried out the door, she told Margo she had a medical emergency, promising to call her later to explain. Keeping Zak on the phone, she continued to instruct him.

When she finally got to Zak's house, she ran to the front door. It was locked.

Quickly, she ran to the back door. Thank God it was open. She yelled to Zak, and he yelled back from the kitchen area. She saw the trail of blood and followed it. He was sitting on the kitchen floor with a whimpering Abby on his lap. He looked up at Lexie. The intensity of the fear in his eyes shocked her, but she didn't waste time thinking about him. Her primary patient was Abby. She would deal with Zak after the crisis was over.

She saw Zak's bloodied hands clenching Abby. Immediately, she crouched down, forcing his hands from the blood-soaked kitchen towel covering the poor dog. He remained transfixed on the blood-soaked cloth. She had to tell him twice to move her medical bag closer to her before he did. As soon as the bag was next to her, he went back to staring at the bloodied towel.

"Zak," she yelled. He had to stop looking at the blood. "I need you to focus on me and what I'm telling you to do. If we do this together, she's going to be all right."

Lexie wasn't sure at this point if Abby was, in fact, going to be all right, but she needed him to be able to function. Slowly, Zak nodded.

He did as Lexie had instructed him to do, holding the bloodied animal. Lexie injected the sedative, causing Abby to be lethargic but still conscious. The wounds on her backside were deep, but at least the wound by her neck was superficial.

Lexie cleaned up the wounds, and with Zak's help they stitched her up. Lexie wasn't used to suturing on a kitchen floor and had never treated a non-human patient. She had taken care of the emergency with the medications she kept on-hand at the clinic, but a veterinarian would definitely have the expertise when it came to the right ongoing medication Abby would need. She would also need to pick up a cone to prevent Abby from chewing on the bandage. These were manageable details now that the crisis was over. What was important was that she was able to save Abby thanks to Zak being able to keep it together.

She heard the creaking of the back screen door as she was cleaning up the blood in the kitchen. She figured Zak was just getting some fresh air and decided to give him some time while she finished disinfecting the floors. Abby was now sleeping on her pillow, which was what doctors liked to see – a quiet and recuperating patient. Carrying the garbage of blood-soaked towels, she made her way outside to the trash. She couldn't see Zak in the backyard, so she wandered to the front of the house.

There he was. Sitting on the front porch steps with his head bent. He didn't look up, and when she got closer, she saw his hands, clenching and unclenching.

"It's cleaned up. We can go back inside."

He didn't respond.

"Abby's sleeping in the back hallway. It's good for her to rest. She's going to be fine. The wounds didn't involve any organs." She had hoped the update on Abby's condition would reassure him.

It didn't. She crouched down and sat beside him. She took his shaking hand in hers. He didn't resist, which she interpreted as a good sign, until he moved his head and looked at her. She saw the tears filling in his eyes.

She squeezed his hand and tried to reassure him once again. "Zak, she's going to be fine."

"But I'm not," he replied.

Chapter Thirty-Two

I just couldn't deal with it all. The visual sight of the blood flowing from Abby's body, the smell of blood permeating the air, and the fear in her eyes. It all came back. I needed to get her to the house. I was afraid she would die. Die in the field where the animal had attacked her. She deserved to know I tried, that I tried to get her to safety. That I tried to save her life.

So I carried her limp mangled body to the house. I wanted to put her in the truck and drive her into Baxley, but I knew I couldn't get behind the wheel. I couldn't stop shaking. I couldn't remember where the keys for the truck were, and at that moment, I couldn't even remember where I had parked the truck. Was it in front of the house? Behind the shed? I didn't know. I couldn't think. The panic had set in and it was getting worse.

As I was figuring out what to do, I saw my phone on the table. I hit the last number I dialed, hoping it would be Lexie's. I don't remember exactly what I said to her, but I remember her telling me she was on her way. She told me to put pressure on the wounds. I knew how to do this. I had done this before, so I just did it. And I waited and waited. It seemed way too long. It probably wasn't since Lexie loves Abby as much as I do. I'm sure she just dropped everything and rushed over, but when you're waiting and hoping, it seems like no one's coming.

When she got there, things got blurry for me. I can't remember everything, but I do remember the blood-soaked towel. It was imprinted on my mind, and I couldn't shake it. I still can't shake it.

I had trouble focusing on anything else. Lexie kept repeating we had to help Abby. I guess I must have snapped out of the sort of trance I had been in. I'm not sure exactly what I did, but Lexie told me I did okay, and that Abby would be okay. But after it was over, I knew I was *the one who wouldn't be okay. The reality smacked me hard when I realized, if it wasn't for Lexie, Abby would have died.*

I would have been the reason why she died, just like I was the reason why those officers in New York died.

Zak had finished telling the therapist what had happened the day before. Yesterday's episode was a bad one. He hadn't wanted to go to the appointment and figured he would reschedule. Opening a wound so raw to a complete stranger seemed unsurmountable. But Lexie had been adamant that he go. She shut down the clinic early and arranged for Margo to watch Abby. He didn't want to be difficult so he yielded to her wishes.

People often say it helps to talk about it, but after Zak had spilled to the therapist, he didn't really feel any different. It wasn't a surprise as he had been down this road before and there were no miracles then, so why would there be now?

The therapist told him it would take time, and although he wouldn't be the same as before the traumatic events, it was possible he would get better. He recommended Zak meet with some of the other men and women who had PTSD and join this support group. He also gave Zak a homework assignment that involved both Lexie and Abby. Zak prided himself on being a man of his word, so when he agreed, he knew he would have to at least try the therapist's suggestion.

"So how did it go?" Lexie asked him, as they drove back to Baxley.

"We talked," is all he said. He didn't want to get her hopes up.

When they got to the house, Margo updated them on Abby and left. Lexie went to check on her, while Zak poured himself a glass of water. He didn't want to be detached, but it hurt too damn much to feel and she did that to him. She made him feel. It had been mostly good, actually great, but then yesterday it had all fallen apart.

She came into the kitchen, speaking about Abby, "She's good Zak. She's moving well on those back legs, better than I thought she would. Don't get me wrong. She's not going to go running in the fields anytime soon but she's doing remarkably well."

"Lexie, we need to talk," he said.

She sat down across from him at the kitchen table.

"I'm going to try. I'll go back to the therapist, I'll join the support group," he said.

"That's great, Zak."

"But I need you to promise me that if it's not working, you won't put your life on hold for me."

"It'll get better. It's just going to take some time," she said, trying to reassure him.

He leaned forward, brushing his hand gently over her face. "I know you would do anything for me. I've seen you do it and I love you for it. But I can't ruin your life for mine. I want to get better and I hope I do, but if I can't then I need you to be strong enough to accept that."

"We can talk about that if the time comes."

He knew what she was doing. She was avoiding making a promise to walk away from him.

"I don't want my issues to change you. To damage you somehow. You're perfect the way you are, and I don't want that to change. So I really do need you to promise me that if needed, you'll walk away."

"Damn you, Zak," she yelled. "You don't know me. I'm not perfect."

Unaware of what he had done to trigger such a reaction in her, he tried to soothe her with more words. She didn't bother to listen. Instead, she grabbed her car keys and stormed off.

Chapter Thirty-Three

Lexie knew she should not have gotten behind the wheel, but she needed to get out of there. Thankfully, she didn't have to drive too far to get to her place. As soon as she walked in the door, she let her tears spill down her face. She had wanted to be the strong one for him, and here she was the one coming unglued. He didn't need her emotional baggage, but she didn't think she could live with secrets anymore, at least not from him. Her phone was buzzing. It was him. She had to talk to him, but she couldn't do it yet. She had to let her tears run their course. She plopped down on the sofa, letting the anguish that had never left her pour out.

Minutes later, she heard a vehicle pull up. She knew it was him, and Abby's bark confirmed it.

"Lexie, are you okay?" he called through the door.

She wiped her face with the back of her hand as she rose to open the door.

He took her into his arms without hesitation. "I'm sorry, I didn't mean to sound so harsh," he said. "I want to get better. The psychologist even gave me an assignment. It involves both you and Abby and although it might sound odd, I think we should give it a try."

She pulled back from him abruptly, allowing him to see her bleary eyes. "I didn't run off because you want to protect me. I ran off because you called me perfect."

"I'm not following you."

"My niece Hailie died because of me. Because I messed up. If I had been perfect, it would never have happened." She began to quiver.

"What are you talking about?"

When she didn't answer, he reached for her hand. She thought she was all cried out, but the tears began to form again. Zak continued to hold her hand, even though she made a feeble attempt to remove her hand from his.

After wiping her eyes, she finally spoke. "When my sister found out her daughter had Alexander's disease, she figured it was one of those treatable conditions, where Hailie would just take medication and she would be fine. When she found out that wasn't the case, she was devastated. But then she became hopeful a cure would be found, or somehow Hailie would be an exception to the disease. She was in denial, but denial got her through the day, so I eventually stopped sharing information on the disease. It was wrong of me as a doctor, but it was my sister and my niece and I couldn't bear to see their pain."

She felt the lump in her throat but was intent on continuing. "My nephew Liam was old enough to see the truth, but after a while even I didn't talk to him like an adult. We all wanted to believe a miracle would happen, and in doing so, Liam's fears for Hailie's future, and even his own, were discarded. None of us intended for this to happen, but Hailie became the focus. Claudia was so exhausted taking care of Hailie, she didn't see how isolated Liam was becoming from his family. He had just gotten used to his parent's divorce and here he was facing what the adults around him were denying, that one day he would lose his sister. He probably could have gotten through the death of his sister with proper support, but he also lost his mother along the way. Claudia had no time for Liam. She was disconnected from him. She had no idea what was going on in his life. None of us did. I suggested she get assistance with Hailie, even some occasional respite, but she refused to do so. Finally, I convinced her to go with some friends to the lake for the weekend. I'm sure she figured I would be able to handle Hailie's care. I was the expert in taking care of critically injured people, of being calm and more than competent should any emergency occur."

She was determined to force the words out, afraid if she stopped, she'd end up with them trapped inside her. When Zak began to speak, she waved him off. He had to know all the bad she had done.

"So Claudia dropped both Hailie and Liam off at my place. Liam had wanted to go to the movies with some friends. He needed a break from all the heartache of having a sick sister and a distraught family twenty-four, seven, so I said sure. It was only a short time after he had left when I got a call from the trauma center. There had been a major gang shooting and they needed me to come in. They were short ER doctors to start with, and with the shooting, they were in dire need. I told my colleague I was looking after my niece, that I couldn't come in. But she pleaded with me to find a neighbor or someone who could take care of Hailie. I phoned my neighbor, a nurse practitioner. She wasn't home. I phoned my mother, but she didn't pick up. I didn't want to, but I was desperate, so I got a hold of Liam. He understood what his sister's needs were and he reluctantly agreed to come back. As soon as Liam got back, I reported to the hospital. What I didn't know was that Liam had slipped into the depths of drug addiction. He got a call from one of his friends a couple hours after I had left. His friend had scored some crystal meth, and Liam agreed to meet him a block away. Liam swears he was only gone for five minutes and hadn't ingested any drugs. He said he was planning to take them when I got back. I don't know if I believed him, but it really doesn't matter. When Liam returned to my home, Hailie was on the floor and not breathing. She'd had a seizure. She was getting them more and more frequently as the disease progressed. Liam called 911 and he got a hold of me at the hospital. I was just out of surgery. I raced back to my apartment. The ambulance attendants were already there." She began gasping and tears trickled down her face. "It was too late," she blurted out. "Hailie was gone."

Zak brushed his thumb over her wet cheek. "I'm so sorry. But listen, Lexie, it's not your fault. I can't imagine what it's like to lose a child, but Claudia's wrong to be blaming you. Even Liam isn't to blame. He messed up big time, but he didn't intend for his sister to die. It must be awful for him too, to have his mother condemning him for his sister's death."

"Claudia doesn't condemn Liam. She doesn't know about him being there that night. I never told her. I didn't want Claudia to blame Liam. It was my fault. I was the one who was to take care of Hailie. I was the adult. I begged Liam not to tell his mother about him leaving

Hailie alone. I feared Claudia's reaction. I didn't want the already fragile mother-son relationship to be destroyed. It was bad enough Liam was already feeling isolated from his mother. And I couldn't allow her grief to push him further away. Liam's a good kid. He loved his sister and never wanted any harm to come to her. So I told Claudia that I called Liam and left him a voice message to get back to my place. I told her I assumed he would check his messages. I lied, telling Claudia I made a judgement call to leave Hailie for a few moments until Liam got back. All he would have to say was he turned his ringer off at the movies and as soon as he checked his voice mail, he came back. He couldn't say the words, but when I said them for him, he didn't dispute them.

"Maybe Claudia should know the truth."

"God, no," she protested. "I couldn't do that to Liam. I'm the one responsible. It was my choice to call him, my decision to leave and go to the hospital.

"Lexie, you had no way of knowing Liam wouldn't be there, and no way of knowing Hailie would die." He tried to reason with her.

"But I was the adult, I should never have left. I should never had gone to the hospital. I promised Claudia I would be there for Hailie and I wasn't." She sobbed and her body shook. In between her sobs she blurted out, "She died alone. She died afraid."

Seeing her so broken tore at him. "You had good intentions. You're a surgeon. A surgeon who was called to save lives. That's what was in your heart."

She gulped for air and then spoke again. "She wasn't the only one who died because of me."

She took a deep breath. "When I went to the hospital, I was scheduled for surgery. The patient was a gang member. A seventeen-year-old kid, shot by a rival gang. I removed the bullet puncturing his lung, thus preventing further internal damage. I saved his life. After I got the call about Hailie, I forgot all about the surgery. Even though I wasn't ready, I went back to work a couple of weeks later. I needed a diversion. Even though I failed Hailie, I could at least do some good. In some warped way, I was trying to salvage my soul."

She saw the pained look he gave her, and she wondered if she was triggering his PTSD symptoms by dragging him through her story. But she wanted to get it all out. Maybe it was selfish of her, but she couldn't retreat now. She had to finish. She took a deep breath, exhaled and continued.

"When I got back to work, the nurses I usually worked with avoided me. I figured it was due to my niece's death. People often have difficulties dealing with someone when they have suffered a loss. I honestly thought that was it. Then this student doctor said he was sorry about what happened with the gang banger. At first, I didn't know what he was talking about since I had saved the gang member's life. When I asked him what he meant, he clammed up. I kept on him until he finally told me. The guy I saved went back for vengeance. He went on a rampage the following week. His intended target was the leader of this rival gang, except he missed the target. Instead, he shot and killed this six-year-old girl. The girl was riding her bike down the street with her older brother. It should never have had happened. Six-year-old kids shouldn't be killed playing in their own neighborhood." She clenched her hands and fought back tears. "The night I left Hailie to die, the night I spent saving this criminal's life, resulted in another child's death. A poor innocent child. And maybe that death wasn't my fault, but it was like the universe was acknowledging what a horrible human being I am."

This time he ignored her waving him off and took her into his arms. "Lexie, that's not how it works. When you saved his life, you didn't become responsible for what he did. You were just doing your job. You're not to blame for the circumstances of either child's death."

The grief had never left Lexie, but lately she was able to focus on Zak's recovery and not just on her own sorrow. But tonight, when she finally told Zak the truth, she felt as raw and exposed as the day Hailie had died.

* * * *

She woke up in her bedroom wearing her clothes from the night before. Looking around, her heart sank as she realized Zak was not next to her. She had held the secret of Hailie's death for so long, and although she knew one day she would share it with Zak, this wasn't how she had planned to tell him. She'd had a total meltdown. When she'd unraveled, he had been there to comfort her. He'd held her as she wept, repeatedly telling her it wasn't her fault. He'd been compassionate, understanding, and oh so wonderful. But today was a new day. He had done the knight-in-shining-armor thing, but she wasn't sure if he could love a woman as flawed as her. He was working on his own recovery, and now realized she wasn't as strong and put together as she appeared.

With her head throbbing, she got up and walked downstairs. Neither Zak nor Abby were around. She put on her shoes and pulled the door open. Immediately, Abby came rushing up to her, nudging her hand. She crouched down, feebly petting the dog, trying not to get emotional. When she stood back up, she noticed Zak sitting at the far side of the veranda. She felt her body sway, as if she was going to crumble. He got up and hurried over to her. When he reached to hold her, she stepped back.

She didn't want him to see any more tears. He didn't need the guilt.

"Lexie, it's going to be okay." His voice was calm and reassuring.

Her voice quivered, "But Zak, you don't know that…" He'd told her yesterday he wasn't sure if he would get better, so how could he know she would get over her grief, her guilt?

"Yesterday, I learned so much from you. About you and about me. I was so lost in my own fear and grief, I didn't even recognize you were carrying such a burden yourself. I'm going to be here for you. What you did the night Hailie died was because of the work you do. You're a doctor, a superbly skilled surgeon. You did your job, what you were trained and called to do. You're not to blame when things go wrong."

She shook her head.

"You're incredible, but you're also stubborn," he said, trying to be gentle. He reached out and held her face. "Listen to me. It's true. You're not to blame. Just like when people were telling me I wasn't to blame for my colleagues' deaths." Now that she was listening, he needed her to understand. He moved his hands away from her face but stayed firmly in front of her. "We were doing our jobs. Jobs requiring us to save people. Saving people isn't easy, but not saving them is worse. It's tragic, its heart-wrenching, but what it's not, is our fault. We're not perfect, we're not meant to be. Decisions need to be made, it's what we do. Unfortunately, our decisions left a mark on us. But we can't let it destroy us. Your niece Hailie, my colleagues Tyler and Brian. And that six-year-old girl…"

"Cassie. Her name was Cassie," she squeaked out.

"Cassie," he repeated. "They died and we can't change it, no matter how much we punish ourselves. But we can honor them."

"Honor, how?"

"We honor their lives with our lives. With getting past the darkness, by allowing the beauty in the world to touch us, by putting a stop to sabotaging our own lives. By letting *us* happen. Living in loneliness, in misery, in disgust of ourselves for not being perfect isn't the way. We need to find a way to forgive ourselves. I'm not saying all the guilt and regret goes away. It's a process, but at least I'm now ready for that process. I was blocking myself from healing. I didn't realize it, but my guilt was the obstacle. I don't want you to make the same mistake, too. I want you to see yourself the way I see you, the way your patients and the people in Baxley see you."

He took both of her hands and held them in his. He saw the fear and trepidation in her indigo eyes. "Lexie, I'm going to be there for you. I'll be by your side while you discover how loving, kind, and beautiful you are." She finally looked up into his face, a face filled with hope. "I'm going to the support group and I'll keep seeing the therapist. I need to do it for them, for the ones we couldn't save, and for us. You made me realize that I can have you in my life, and more importantly, you made me realize how much I love you."

Epilogue

Strolling over to Lexie, Zak wrapped his arm around her shoulder and pressed his lips next to her ear. "So this is what Kristina calls a small gathering? I bet there's at least a hundred people here."

"And probably a few more coming later," she replied.

He would probably always dislike crowds, but at least he was familiar with most of the people. Kristina, in all her exuberance, had decided to host what she told Lexie would be a nice little engagement party. It was being held on Cicily McQuay's property, which consisted of an acre-sized backyard. Cicily had never apologized to Zak, but this grand party and her collaboration in organizing it with her daughter-in-law, was her way of showing it. And showing it, she did. She had insisted on catering the event herself, and as soon as she announced she would be doing so, an outpouring of volunteers offered to assist. After fretting all morning about the delivery of a heart-shaped ice sculpture, Cicily was standing by the dessert table, laughing with Omeir. She had an odd, snorty laugh, but to Lexie and Zak it was an endearing sound to finally hear.

Baxley was used to town gatherings, but this was different. Large and festive, and even a little ostentatious thanks to Cicily, it was the most culturally diverse the town had ever experienced. Not surprising once people started to mingle, they discovered more to talk about than the weather or football. The men of Baxley were more eager to converse with Safia, than they were to sample Cicily's famous pecan pie, an apparent first. Safia seemed amused, surrounded by three elderly men hanging on her every word. Omeir regularly glanced at Safia, and when he noticed the elderly men dispersing and the younger men moving in, he headed over to her. Although she didn't need a rescue, Safia seemed to appreciate the gesture. Zak's friends from the PTSD support group were milling about, warmly greeted by the townsfolk. Everyone was fitting in well, that is until the man with the serpent tattoo showed up.

The guarded looks, the whispers, they began as soon as he was spotted crossing into the grassy yard. Zak immediately shot over.

"Hey, Scorp, glad you made it." He gave his friend a manly bear hug. He knew Scorp would hate the hug, but it was the best way to get the concerned onlookers to go back to chatting with each other, reassuring them the big man was not here to wreak mayhem. "So how was the flight?" Zak asked.

"I hate flying," Scorp grumbled.

"Did you at least get upgraded?"

The scowl disappeared, giving way to a big dimpled grin. "Yup, sure did."

Zak introduced Scorp to several people, and within minutes, the single women of Baxley descended upon them. There was an unusual charm about Scorp, something Zak and Omeir didn't fully understand, but something women found downright appealing. He was brawny, confident, and drawn to danger. Sensible women should have loathed his bold, womanizing ways, but they didn't. Instead, they were captivated by him. There was an aura of mystery to the guy. He was like a puzzle. A puzzle women wanted to solve. He gave them just enough pieces to intrigue them, but never enough to see the full picture. Even his own work colleagues didn't have all the pieces to the puzzle. But that was Scorp.

Leaving Scorp to entertain his many new admirers, Zak returned to Lexie's side. She was standing with her mother, Janice. He could tell by the serious look on Lexie's face they were talking about Claudia.

"Have you seen Margo?" Janice asked Zak. "I promised I would help her pour the champagne."

"She's over by the ice sculpture," he replied.

Janice kissed her daughter on the cheek and then gave Zak a big hug. "Thanks for making my girl so happy."

He smiled at her as she headed over to Margo.

"Talking about your sister?" he asked Lexie.

"That obvious?" she said.

He nodded. "I'm sorry Claudia and Liam didn't come."

She had invited them, but wasn't surprised by Claudia's absence. "Liam called to congratulate us. He wants to visit me once the semester is done."

"I'd love to meet him."

"He's going to Alcoholics Anonymous meetings. He went to a few Crystal Meth Anonymous meetings but he prefers AA. He says the AA guys have more sobriety time than the crystal meth addicts. He's got a sponsor."

"That's great."

"He wants to tell Claudia."

He was pleased to hear it. He knew how secrets could destroy relationships. "How do you feel about that?"

"I'm scared, Zak. I don't know how Claudia's going to react. I don't know if Liam is strong enough."

"There's a lot of guilt with living a lie. Perhaps he needs to do this so he can move on."

"Yeah, you might be right."

"You know I'm dying to marry you, but if you want to postpone, I'm okay with that. I know how much it means for you to have your sister in your wedding party."

She and Zak had moved in together a month ago, and every day he woke up next to her was a cherished moment, healing the broken pieces of his life. If she needed time for her family to heal, he would bestow on her a long engagement.

She smiled and gave him a kiss on the cheek. "Thanks, but I'm not giving up getting married at Spruce Haven Inn. The only reason we got that date was due to a cancellation." She loved the idea of a winter wedding at the inn he had taken her to on their first date. This time she would make it up the stairs to the beautiful hotel suite with the man she loved.

"You sure?"

"Absolutely. I'm certain about my future with you. I'm not certain about my future with my sister. I hope we can reconcile, but that depends on Claudia. I'd love to have her in my bridal party, but I'm not going to put our lives on hold. I can't wait to marry you."

He gave her a kiss on the mouth, a passionate kiss that neither of them cared was being watched by their abundance of family and friends.

Her life wasn't perfect. She wasn't perfect, and that was okay by her. What she had was real, and that was better than perfect. Zak's love for her was real. Her connection with the townsfolk was real. Zak was opening up more. She knew he still struggled but he was committed. He ate healthy, exercised, and had developed his support system. She woke up every morning with Zak at her side. It was something she had hoped for but was surprised when it happened so quickly. His fear of waking up startled from a nightmare was real. The homework assignment the therapist gave him after his first session provided the solution to a two-bedroom relationship. Oddly, the answer had been in front of them all along in the form of a large woolly mess known as Abby.

Abby no longer slept on her pillow by the back door. She now slept at the foot of the bed. A new king-size bed. Abby wasn't just a pampered pet sleeping on an expensive comfy mattress. She was at work. She had a new job, and that job was to alert Zak to his nightmares. To sense the restlessness that came from the nightmares and to move toward her master, gently nudging him awake. It worked, and Zak had no doubt if he started thrashing about, Abby would instinctively protect Lexie. The nightmares still occurred, but they were less frequent and less intense. The only thing increasing in intensity these days was his love for Lexie. He didn't kid himself that the past was behind him, but the present is where he decided to live. The future would have its challenges, but for the first time since he was a young child, it held promise. And a future with Lexie held all the promise he needed.

THE END